FORTUNE'S
HERO

FORTUNE'S HERO

JENNA BENNETT

Entangled Publishing, LLC
2614 South Timberline Road
Suite 109
Fort Collins, CO 80525
Visit our website at www.entangledpublishing.com.

Edited by Liz Pelletier
Cover design by Heather Howland

Ebook ISBN   978-1-62061-078-7
Print ISBN   978-1-62061-077-0

Manufactured in the United States of America

First Edition November 2012

To Wilfred Bereswill, for planting the seed, and to Heather Graham for watering it.

CHAPTER ONE

Quinn Conlan was bleeding to death.

Slowly, steadily, one drop at a time. One big-ass drop. He could feel the mechanism at his wrist working, opening and closing the artery to let the blood ebb and flow. At this rate, he calculated, it would take him about an hour to bleed out.

Down on the floor, a few of the drops turned into a trickle, and he watched as it made its slow way to the big drain in the middle of the room. And down it went, soon to be followed by others. Many others.

He put his head back and closed his eyes.

It wasn't a bad way to go. It wouldn't be quick, but it was mostly painless. A slight burn in his wrist every time the mechanism opened to let another few minutes of his life hit the floor. But compared to the other things that had been done to him in this room, it was nothing. The med tech had made sure of that. They weren't trying to hurt him. Not this time. By now, they must have realized that pain wouldn't make him talk. Been there, done that. Kept his mouth shut. So they'd decided to let him sit here instead, perfectly still, perfectly conscious, perfectly unable to move, as he watched his life drain away, drop by drop by drop. An hour from now, when his limbs were weak and darkness started to descend over his eyes, they'd expect him to call for help. That he'd start babbling, and tell them what they wanted to know.

Fat chance.

They'd brought him within a hairsbreadth of death before and revived him each time. Always their choice, never his. And this time would be no different. He wouldn't call for help, and they'd wait until it was almost too late to save him—almost, but not quite—and then they'd bring him back. Again.

Damn Rhenians. Never satisfied.

Quinn never thought there'd come a day when he'd welcome death. Always figured he'd fight to the bitter end. Beat death, or die trying. But when it came down to it, it hadn't taken long. Just a few months in the prison camp on Marica-3, and weekly sessions with the camp's medical team—the best in the galaxy, both when it came to bringing a prisoner to death's door and to making sure he didn't walk through it—and here he was, ready and willing to die.

Hell, scratch ready and willing. Try eager. He'd die now, this hour, this very *minute*, if he could cheat them out of being able to revive him again. If he could will himself stone dead right now, he'd do it.

A sound at the door brought his head up. The exsanguination must be happening more quickly than he thought, because it was already a little harder to move, and a little more difficult to make his eyes focus.

"Good afternoon, Captain Conlan."

A woman. They'd sent him a fucking woman.

And not just any woman. He recognized this one. She'd been at his earlier sessions, standing in the background taking notes while the doctor injected him with something that made him feel like he was being boiled alive. She'd watched out of those cool, green eyes as he writhed in pain and screamed until his voice was gone. Writing on her goddamn clipboard. With not a flicker of emotion on that perfect alabaster face.

Ice bitch.

Quinn wet his lips and cajoled his rusty vocal chords into cooperating. "Come to watch the big finish, sweetheart?"

Her eyes flicked to his, the clear green of glacier ice under brows the shape of bird wings. "It doesn't have to end this way."

Her voice was lovely, as cool and clear as those eyes. And as devoid of emotion. If he'd had the strength, Quinn would have laughed. As it was, all he could manage was a smile, and a weak one at that. "Sure it does."

She monitored the progress of the blood flow from his wrist between glances at his face. "You could tell them what they want to know."

Them. Like she wasn't part of the same unholy alliance.

Quinn shook his head. "Sorry, sweetheart. Not gonna happen."

One of those exquisite eyebrows raised. "You would rather take the whereabouts of the rebels to the grave with you? I'm not so sure they would return the favor. Are you certain you aren't sacrificing yourself for nothing?"

It would be almost laughable if he wasn't twenty minutes from bleeding to death.

"I think we both know that ain't gonna happen, sweetheart. Ten minutes from now, just when I think it might be too late to revive me, someone's gonna run in here and pump me full of synthetic blood. And next week I'll be back in this room with high and mighty

Doctor Sterling and his toys again. We both know it, so let's just stop pretending."

He looked away. Down to the floor in time to see another sizable trickle of blood head down the drain.

For a second, nothing happened. Then he heard her heels click on the floor, a quick, angry rhythm. At the door, she turned for a final salvo. "You think you're so smart, Captain Conlan. But we're smarter. You'll see."

The door opened and shut with a slam.

"Yeah, yeah," Quinn said, and closed his eyes again to wait for the darkness. With any luck, he'd be unconscious for a day or two before he woke up and realized he was back in hell. Again.

· · ·

He was the luckiest son of a bitch in the universe. He had everything he'd ever wanted. The Good Fortune, *the ship of his dreams; a solid little freighter with power boosters that let her outrun any but the most powerful of Rhenish destroyers. The best crew any captain could ask for. Excitement and adventure on every run. More money than he'd dared dream of when he first set himself up in the galactic smuggling trade six years ago.*

And Josie. The most beautiful woman in the world, here in his bed.

She was smiling up at him, dark eyes shining and those perfect lips swollen from his kisses. Her legs were wrapped around his waist, he was buried to the hilt inside her, trying with everything that was in him to hold on, to take her with him when he went over the edge, and she knew it, knew he was teetering on the brink and reveling in the power she had over him…and then he exploded, and felt her body arch up to meet his as her laughter trickled over his heated skin. And darkness descended, and he floated in utter bliss, safe in the cocoon of Josie's arms.

• • •

Quinn rose up to the surface of consciousness and forced his gluey eyes open. Blinking at the too-bright light, he realized he must have overslept. His mouth felt awful, full of cotton—had he been on a bender last night? That'd explain the pounding in his temples, and the way he could hardly lift his head from the pillow…

And then reality slammed back into focus as he recognized the five-by-seven cell he was in and remembered that he'd died a few days ago—again—and had been revived, again.

He'd been right. They'd waited until he was almost sure it was too late, and then they'd rushed into the room and unhooked the damned contraption on his wrist and filled him up with synthetic blood. They'd left him alone after that to recover. Here in this little room that had been his home since he was taken off the *Fortune*. This cell and the big laboratory with the tile floor had been his whole world since he arrived on this barren, inhospitable moon on the outer edge of the galaxy.

That was a while ago now. Months, maybe a year.

Or maybe not. It felt like an eternity, but maybe it had only been a few weeks.

There was just no way to know. No window to the outside, and the lights were always on. No way of telling day from night. They'd work on him until there was no life left, trying to break him, and then they'd let him recover until they could do it again. Sometimes he was pretty sure he'd slept for what must have been days.

Quinn shifted on the thin cot, wincing as the still tender scars on his back stretched uncomfortably. Those were from a couple sessions ago. There'd been the fingernails, and the burns, and the beatings and whippings, and then the injections. Plus some other things he'd rather not think about along the way.

The last thing they'd tried was the exsanguination. Now they'd probably go back to the thumbscrews again. And he didn't feel too awful at the moment, so that probably meant it would be soon. They always seemed to know when he'd recovered enough that they could come back for more.

No sooner had the thought crossed his mind than he heard the vacuum seal on the outer door hiss. It was almost as if he'd conjured it. For an insane moment he wondered whether they could read his thoughts, whether they'd implanted him with some sort of device during one of the many times he'd been temporarily dead—and then he realized the unlikelihood of such a thing. The Rhenians weren't that sophisticated; just look at the torture methods they favored. It was good old-fashioned thuggery, with whips and chains and brass knuckles. And besides, if they could read his mind, they'd stop trying to force the information out of him.

But just in case, maybe he'd better not think about anything important.

Carefully sitting up on the edge of the cot, he waited for the hiss of the inner door to follow the outer. After a moment it did, and two people stepped through. The door slid back in place, leaving them all sealed inside the small chamber.

Quinn dismissed the first of his visitors—one of the prison guards—after the first brief glance and felt his eyes narrow and bile rise in his throat at the sight of the second.

It was her. Doctor Sterling's assistant. The ice bitch His Highness kept around to take notes and to check how Quinn was holding up under the torture. To determine how much life was left in him and how much further they could go before he ran out.

This was the first time he'd had the opportunity for a good look at her when he wasn't in the process of dying or his brain wasn't fogged by pain, and he took his time, looking her up and down.

By Rhenish standards she was beautiful. By Quinn's standards…

Hell, maybe she was beautiful there, too. But not in the way Josie had been beautiful, with her flashing dark eyes and flowing black hair and red lips. Josie had been heat and passion personified. Love and laughter and life. The perfect temptation.

Until she sent him and his entire crew up the river.

But this woman…if she'd ever come apart in a man's arms, it hadn't been in recent history.

Not that she was old. Younger than Quinn, at a guess. Maybe thirty, maybe just above or below.

What she was was stone. A statue carved in marble, pale and perfect and devoid of life. Her face was stunning, but there was no warmth in it. Her hair would probably be lovely if left to its own devices, but it was scraped back from her face with ruthless determination and braided into a tight flaxen rope coiled at her nape in the Rhenish style. She was tall, at least half a foot taller than the tiny Josie, close to Quinn's own height, and she had none of Josie's warm, inviting curves. Her posture was ramrod straight, as if she had an imploder lance stuffed up her ass, and the tilt of her head was arrogant, balanced on top of that long, slender neck. Long legs, a little too skinny. Narrow hips. Not much of a waist. Not much in the way of breasts, either. Nothing for a man to enjoy. The shapeless gray sack she had on under the white lab coat did nothing for her complexion or her figure, and on her feet were the ugliest pair of lace-up shoes Quinn had ever laid eyes on.

Oh, yeah, she was Rhenian, all right. Tight-assed, militant, and frigid.

And perhaps not entirely made of stone, because he could swear he saw a blush stain those high cheekbones. His low opinion must have shown in his eyes.

He grinned wolfishly. "What's the matter, sweetheart? Been a while since you had a man?"

Something shifted in her eyes, but that was all he had time to see before the guard's fist connected with his chin and knocked him back against the wall. The impact of his head against the concrete had him seeing stars.

The guard let out a string of invective in guttural Rhenish. Between the knock on the head and a disinclination to languages, Quinn understood less than half.

He understood enough, though. He'd insulted the lady, and the guard took offense.

Interesting.

Observing through half-closed eyes, as he pretended to be more hurt than he was, he watched as the bitch stepped in front of the guard and kept him from hitting Quinn again. He supposed he should be grateful; another blow might have knocked him unconscious. Lucky him—it seemed Doctor Sterling wanted him awake and aware.

The prison guards all looked the same. They were all young, some not even out of their teens yet. The Rhenians liked to start military indoctrination early. All were tall and fair, in gray uniforms with tall, spit-polished boots and Old Earth military headgear that shaded their faces. There was no need for protective armor; no one here could hurt them. The prison population on Marica-3 was all like Quinn: weak, defeated, and wishing for death.

The guards were armed, though. The Rhenians hadn't gotten

where they were by taking foolish chances. And besides, it made the wet-behind-the-ears recruits feel powerful. Gave them the proper crush-all-obstacles attitude, starting with the boots, with their lead-enforced tips. They carried laser pistols in holsters at their waists and good old-fashioned batons. Quinn had gotten a rap over the knuckles with a baton a few times, and it hurt.

At the moment, he was more interested in the pistol. The med tech was standing in front of the guard reasoning with him. The guard looked down at her, into that stunningly beautiful face, and Quinn could read the young man's thoughts as easily as if they had been spelled out in a thought bubble above his head. It took one to know one, after all; he'd been in the same situation plenty through the years.

Not that the ice bitch inspired those kinds of thoughts in Quinn. No, thanks. He'd rather kiss a Marican water snake. Just as pleasant, and a faster death afterwards.

The cell was small. If he moved fast, he'd have surprise on his side. And the med tech had put herself with her back to him, providing something of a shield. Considerate of her.

He lurched to his feet. And gritted his teeth as his various injuries screamed in protest. His back spasmed, his lungs rebelled, his stomach twisted, and one of his legs threatened to give out. So much for moving fast. He was lucky he could keep on his feet at all.
Shit.

Eschewing stealth for speed, he took a few stumbling steps forward, fetching up against the lovely med tech's back and knocking her forward into the guard. The guard's arms came up automatically to catch her. At least the big bastard was predictable.

As they danced, Quinn slid an arm around her from the other side, twisting his body, ignoring the complaints from his back and shoulder—just another centimeter…and yes!—he felt the handle of the guard's laser pistol under his hand. It was the work of a few seconds to pull the pistol out, twist it sideways, and burn a hole through the guard's ribs directly into his heart.

CHAPTER TWO

The sizzle caught Elsa off guard.

One second she was standing there arguing with young Olaus about why he shouldn't hit the prisoner again—Doctor Sterling wanted Captain Conlan conscious for today's session, and besides, she didn't care how disrespectfully he spoke to her—and the next she was clutching a corpse which was sinking to the floor and pulling her down with it.

Stunned, she let Olaus go and watched as he crumpled to the concrete. His hat fell off and rolled, exposing cropped fair hair and wide blue eyes, fixed and staring. His face was surprised and very, very young. There was a trickle of blood at the corner of his mouth, and more blood flowed out of a hole in his side onto the concrete. Her right sleeve was soaked with it, clinging wetly to her arm. The smell of burned flesh stung her nostrils; mixed with the metallic tang of the blood, it made her stomach heave. Doctor Sterling always said she was too squeamish—

"Turn around."

The gravelly voice came from behind, and with the sound, the events of the past minute realigned themselves. It was as if someone had shaken a kaleidoscope, and suddenly she could see the picture clearly.

"I've never shot anyone in the back," the prisoner continued, "and I don't aim to start now." His voice hardened. "Turn around!"

The command lashed like a whip, laced with the authority of a man used to giving orders and having them followed. Instinct and training had her obeying without a thought when, amazingly, she found herself hesitating.

He had gray eyes, she knew, as cold and hard as Old Earth gunmetal, and when he looked at her earlier, they had been full of disdain. Did she really want those eyes to be the last thing she saw before she died?

"Now!"

She'd expected it, but she still jumped. And this time there was no denying the compulsion. She turned on legs that were stiff with reluctance and fear.

The prisoner was standing a few feet away, with the laser pistol in a two-handed grip, his knuckles white and his jaw clenched. Some of it may have been bravado, including the crack about never shooting anyone in the back, but some was sheer willpower as well. Elsa could see the beads of sweat on his forehead, and she knew just what effort it took for him to remain upright and in control. He shouldn't have been able to stand at all, let alone fight. Four days ago, they'd bled him dry. Two weeks before, they'd whipped the skin off his back. The week before that—

"I can help you."

She had no idea why she said it. The words just fell out of her mouth. And she knew she should be ashamed to have uttered them. She wasn't supposed to bargain for her life. Especially not with a two-bit smuggler and collaborator like this one.

But looking into the muzzle of that laser pistol, after seeing the damage it could do, all she could think was that she didn't want to die. Not today. Not like this.

Those gray eyes narrowed. "How?"

"You'll need help finding your way out of the camp. It's big. With many corridors. You could walk around for hours."

And sooner or later someone would see him. Someone who'd either kill him on sight or capture him again, and then bring him back here.

But that wouldn't help her. She'd still be dead. And while she'd been taught to face death with the bravery befitting a Rhenian woman, a descendant of the pioneers who had gone out from Old Earth a thousand years ago and begun the quest for dominance in the nexus, she wasn't ready to end her life on the floor of this cell. He had no reason to spare her life, and every reason not to want to… but surely there had to be something that would sway him.

Grasping for something—anything—that might tip the scales in her favor, she had an inspiration. "You're hurt. You'll need medical attention. I'm a doctor."

That got a reaction, but not the one she wanted. His face darkened. "You goddamn bitch. Now you're offering to nurse me through the damage you and your precious Doctor Sterling did?"

Elsa blinked. When he put it like that, there wasn't anything she could say.

"Listen, sweetheart." His voice was a little less gravelly now but no less vicious. "The only way I'll let you touch me is if my body is cold and dead and beyond anything you can do to it." He leveled the gun.

"Please!"

The word burst from her lips, and Elsa cringed as it echoed in the tiny room.

He hesitated. "How do I know you won't lead me straight to high and mighty Doctor Sterling's lab when we walk outta here?"

"Because then you'd kill him, too," Elsa said.

She cursed her stupidity the second the words escaped her lips. Now he would surely ask her to do just that. Then he would murder both her and Doctor Sterling, and it would be her fault. Every man, woman, and child in the empire worshipped Doctor Sterling. The medical discoveries he had made and the resulting improvements in people's lives had made him a hero to millions of Rhenians.

Much better if the prisoner just killed her now. Not that she could muster up much excitement for the idea. Between living and dying, she'd much rather live, even if that meant she was a bad Rhenian, unwilling to die for country and glory.

"...undressed," the prisoner said, and Elsa's eyes flew to his face in shock, even as her subconscious recognized the absurdity in thinking of him as "the prisoner" when he was the one holding the pistol. If she succeeded in convincing him to take her with him, she'd be *his* prisoner.

When she didn't immediately obey, he reiterated the order, using different words this time, and enunciating clearly, as if she might be hard of hearing or perhaps a slow thinker. "Take his clothes off."

Oh. *His* clothes. Not hers.

Relief made her tongue loose. "Why?"

"Can't walk outta here like this, can I?" He indicated the white prison-issue jumpsuit. "And my hands are a little busy. If you'll oblige?"

Elsa turned to Olaus's body, steeling herself for the task even as she told herself that it could have been worse. She would much rather remove Olaus's clothing than her own.

Starting with his boots, she tugged one off, then the other, and set them aside. Next, she crawled up Olaus's body to unfasten his trousers, taking care not to kneel in the pool of blood on the floor. As she fumbled with button and zipper, she could feel her cheeks flush and wondered if the prisoner—if Captain Conlan—noticed.

He'd been right in his earlier, crude assumption: it had been a while since she'd had the pleasure of a man's company. She'd been on Marica-3 for a year, and in that time, there had been no one who had enticed her to abandon her morals. The guards were all too young; an affair with one of them would be beneath her position, not to mention her dignity. Doctor Sterling was too old and seemed not to need or desire human contact. As he was the closest thing she had to a father figure, that was just as well.

Major Lamb had indicated an interest, but he was approaching courtship in the old-fashioned way: decorously and properly. He assured her he valued her for her accomplishments and her loyalty and service to the regime. And yes, she knew he admired her looks, but they didn't seem to inspire him to flights of passion.

As a result, she couldn't remember the last time she'd performed such an intimate act as undressing a man. Her hands were unsteady, but eventually she got Olaus's pants off and handed them to the prisoner, who began pulling them on over his overalls.

"The coat."

His voice was strained as he tried to pull the pants up while juggling the pistol and keeping an eye on her movements all at the same time. Elsa watched him, wondering if she dared go for the gun in an attempt to gain the upper hand…and then she decided she didn't. The comfort with which he held the weapon bespoke of long familiarity; he'd have it up and pointed before she could move more than a few feet.

She turned back to the corpse and went to work unbuckling the weapons belt and then unbuttoning the gray uniform jacket. As her hands fumbled over the rough fabric, she patted the pockets surreptitiously, making sure her body blocked her actions from Captain Conlan.

All the guards were armed with baton and laser pistol. Captain Conlan had the pistol, and the baton would do her no good against it. But some of the young men carried other weapons as well. Unofficial weapons: small and often deadly, concealed in their clothing. A knife or perhaps a throwing star. She had hoped she might find something when she pulled Olaus's boots off—Major Lamb kept a dagger in the top of his boot, she knew—but such had not been the case.

Now she was forced to face the possibility that young Olaus might have been too straitlaced to carry an unsanctioned weapon, and her heart sank. If she survived the next few minutes, and the prisoner actually took her with him past the prison walls and into the barren interior of the moon, a sharp knife would be a useful tool. Captain Conlan had been without a woman for more than four months; who knew what thoughts might enter his head once they were alone together? Unlike Major Lamb, there was nothing courtly or decorous about the prisoner.

Not that he seemed likely to want to ravish her, Elsa admitted, at least judging from the expression in his eyes earlier. It had been total disdain, not only for her as a woman but also as a person. They were not the eyes of a man who couldn't control his baser urges. But should he choose to try to take advantage, a knife would allow her to defend herself against him. And it would also afford her protection from the many deadly creatures that lived in the area beyond the prison walls. The venomous snakes, poisonous spiders, and flesh-eating worms Marica-3 was known for.

She had just about given up hope of finding anything useful when her hand slid over something that wasn't part of Olaus's physique. Turning her head slightly, she glanced over her shoulder to make sure the prisoner was still occupied with his new clothes. He was, balancing on one foot while he tried to insert the other into one of Olaus's boots.

Turning back to the corpse, she slipped her prize out of its inside breast pocket and inspected it, taking care that her body blocked Captain Conlan's view of what she was doing.

It was a knife. An Old Earth flick knife, small but sharp, the blade made from rare and precious steel. Carefully Elsa slid it into the pocket of her dress and returned to struggling with Olaus's jacket and its bloody, sodden fabric.

When she got it off and handed it to the prisoner, he grunted something that might almost have been a thank-you. Or maybe not. "The hat."

She crawled to where it had rolled, and turned, holding it out. Making sure to stay on her knees on the floor, non-threatening. It chafed to debase herself in front of him—one of the prisoners, and a common collaborator—but she had survived thus far; now wasn't the time to do anything stupid.

From her vantage point, she watched as Captain Conlan took the hat out of her hand and put it on his head, pulling it down to shade his face, completing the transformation from prisoner to prison guard.

He was shorter than Olaus by several inches, but with the uniform pants tucked into the tops of the high boots, nobody would be able to tell that they were too long. The bottom of the belted jacket hit too low on his hips, but it fit his shoulders well. Olaus had been too young to have filled out completely. Captain Conlan was considerably thinner now than he'd been when he first arrived in the prison colony, but his shoulders were still broad. And hunched, she noticed. He stooped, as if trying to protect his soft center from blows.

Elsa had been on Marica-3 when he arrived, and she could still remember the first time she'd seen him, coming off the transport shuttle. He hadn't looked like this then. His hair had been thick and dark, falling over his forehead, and he'd been tanned and healthy, with eyes that flashed and lips that smiled. He'd moved easily, in spite of the restraints around his wrists and ankles.

Now he looked like a different person. Thin and pale, the dark hair just a memory. The stubble covering his head held a hint of gray, at least at the temples. There were scars all over his body—she couldn't see them now, but she knew they were there—and his face was drawn, with lines of pain bracketing his mouth and nose and radiating out from his eyes. He walked like an old man, hunched and slow, as if moving was painful.

Elsa had watched the change happen gradually over months of questioning. He'd become paler, thinner, and weaker as the weeks dragged by, yet at the same time, perversely, he'd become stronger and more stubborn. Most prisoners would have broken long ago. Instead, he'd survived everything Doctor Sterling threw at him.

Or maybe *survived* wasn't the right term. They had brought him to the brink of death over and over and had lost days, sometimes weeks, of interrogation time to his recovery. He'd have been dead many times over if they'd only let him die. But Major Lamb had been adamant. Captain Conlan knew the whereabouts of the rebels, knew how to contact them, knew who was in charge of the Marican resistance and what their plans were…and the Rhenians needed that information to crush the rebellion, which had proven to be much more stubborn than anyone had anticipated. So Captain Conlan was revived and allowed to recover, while Doctor Sterling spent the downtime coming up with new and more ingenious methods of extracting information, trying them out on other prisoners first. He'd thrown all of his tricks and toys at Captain Conlan over the past four months, and the prisoner still hadn't told him what he wanted to know. Elsa didn't know whether to be amazed at the man's strength or annoyed at his stubbornness.

Didn't he realize that as soon as he talked, they'd stop hurting him?

It wasn't like Dr. Sterling enjoyed torturing prisoners. Was it?

"Up." Captain Conlan gestured with the laser pistol, and Elsa scrambled to her feet. Face to face, she was almost as tall as he was. All it took was a tilt of her chin to look directly into his eyes.

She didn't. Instead, after the first quick glance, she lowered her eyes and her head. *Look submissive. Don't give him another reason to kill you. He already wants to—he must—so don't give him another reason.*

Her heart was beating so hard she thought it must show outside her clothing. Here it was, the moment of truth. Now she'd either join Olaus on the floor of the cell, or he'd take her with him, and she'd live to see another day. Or another few hours, at any rate.

"When we walk out—"

The rush of relief was so great that Elsa missed the next few words and only came back to herself when the prisoner snapped, "Listen! I'm not gonna say this again. Are you listening?"

She nodded, heart skipping. She was alive, at least for now.

"If you do anything to signal distress, or anything to clue

someone in on what's going on, you'll be the first to die."

"I won't."

His eyes drilled into hers, the truth in his voice unmistakable. "I ain't afraid of dying. There've been times lately I've prayed I wouldn't wake up. So if they kill me, ain't no big deal. But I'll take you with me if I go. Remember that."

"I will," Elsa said.

He glanced at the door. "Open it. And remember, stay on my left."

She must have missed that the first time he said it. She wouldn't forget again.

The inner door slid back with a hydraulic hiss, followed a few seconds later by the outer.

"Check the hallway."

His voice was strained, and when she glanced over her shoulder, she saw he had the laser pistol trained on her back. Heart beating, she leaned through the door and looked right, then left, then right again. "It's empty."

"Then let's go." He tugged the hat another inch down over his face and pushed her ahead of him. Behind them, the cell doors hissed back into place.

"Which way?"

"Right." She hesitated before she added, "There are cameras. And listening equipment. It's better not to talk."

He shot her a look but didn't say anything, just took her arm and guided her down the corridor on the right.

CHAPTER THREE

Quinn had gotten only a brief glimpse of Marica-3 on arrival, as the shuttle flew over the moon and prison complex on its way in for landing. But he had heard stories about it for years. Even in the old days, before the Rhenians annexed Marica and her moons and built their prison here, Marica-3 had had a reputation as a hellhole.

The second Marican moon, a three-day shuttle ride from the host planet, was an inhospitable rock on the outer edge of the solar system. Too hot during daytime and too cold at night, it was uninhabited apart from the prison. Mostly bare of vegetation, it consisted of rock and gravel and subterranean caves, many of them home to ice-cold underground rivers and some of the most unpleasant creatures known to man. The Marican water snake was one of them, a deceptively innocent-looking reptile which rumor held could kill a man in two minutes flat.

That would be with a full dose of venom from a bite in the wild. A small dose injected by syringe just burned like the fires of hell and made you feel like your skin was melting. From the inside out.

Oh, yeah, and it caused your lungs to collapse. Eventually.

Lucky him, he'd gotten the anti-venom before that happened. He'd had all the pain and none of the death benefits.

But bad as the snake venom had been, the worst creature he'd encountered in the past few months—excepting the Rhenians themselves—had to be the worms that tunneled inside human skin and burrowed their way to the heart. Marican night crawlers. High and mighty Doctor Sterling kept a handful in the prison laboratory. Roughly the size of the earthworms Quinn used to see after a good rain on Old Earth, and the color of overripe tomatoes, the night crawlers killed you, too, but a lot more slowly, not to mention painfully. He had a spiderweb of subcutaneous tracks running up one leg almost to the groin from the time Doctor Sterling set a couple on him, and when he closed his eyes, he could still feel them burrowing around in there, the pain almost enough to make him pass out.

The Rhenians arrived on Marica two years ago, and they didn't waste any time in making use of its resources, human and animal. The prison camp had been ready a year later, built by slave labor, and the nastier creatures had become part of the camp's "medical treatment." Quinn had spent the past year and a half ferrying weapons and supplies to the insurgents. They paid well, and although he'd been aware that if he got caught he'd end up on Marica-3, it had never seemed a real possibility.

Not until Josie betrayed him, betrayed them all.

But now wasn't the time to dwell on that. On everything he'd lost, including the *Good Fortune*. On his failure to see the signs and by his mistake, putting every member of his crew into this hell.

Not when it looked like he might actually walk out of here, into the equally deadly interior of the moon. Where something—snake, worm, spider-scorpion, or the woman he was with—might kill him and put him out of his misery.

Or where he might survive for long enough to figure out how to get his crew out of prison and the *Fortune* out of impound and everyone out of orbit, far, far away from Marica and her moons.

• • •

When the ice bitch first offered to help him get away, Quinn had suspected a trap. He thought she'd walk him straight to Doctor Sterling's lab. Or if not that, straight into some other sort of situation. An ambush, a fight to the death, some sort of sick psychological torture where he was made to watch as his crew—his friends, the only family he had—was put to the question. The Rhenians had tried that once before, while they were all still dirtside on the planet. Watching Josie cry and beg him to tell them what they wanted to know had been as close as he'd ever come to spilling every bit of information he had. Even after everything she'd done.

And now fate had stuck him with another woman. Another cold-hearted, calculating bitch with ice water in her veins, who'd do whatever she had to do to get what she wanted and hurt anyone she had to in the process.

She'd help him. Hah!

When pachyderms flew.

But he had to give it to her: so far she hadn't done any of the things he expected. There'd been no traps, no attempts to tell him he couldn't possibly succeed. She'd simply walked him down deserted corridors, through doors guarded by no one, until they were here, in the sub-basement of the prison, where the laundry facilities and major mechanicals were. The heating system, the refrigeration, the ducts. If he'd had thirty minutes to spare, and Isaac and Toby with him, he could have done some serious damage down here.

The guilt slowed his steps.

Isaac and Toby. And Holden.

What kind of selfish bastard was he, to think only of getting himself out of prison? To leave them in this hellhole to rot? What if he didn't survive the outside? What if he couldn't come back for them? Would they think he'd abandoned them?

It was his damned fault they were here in the first place. If he hadn't taken the job for the Maricans, if he hadn't let Josie distract him when they came into Sierra Luz that day, if he hadn't missed the signs—if he hadn't been thinking with his other head too much of the time he'd been with her—none of this would have happened, and they wouldn't be here.

His gut twisted as the guilt bit deeper.

"Something wrong?" the med tech asked. She'd slowed her steps, too, and was looking at him with worry etched on that stunning face. Probably thinking he might off her, now that she had guided him down here.

He looked at her in silence for a moment. If he told her he needed to find his crew before he walked out, would she help him?

Was it even possible? Last he'd heard, there were a hundred thousand prisoners on Marica-3. And ten thousand guards. It was a minor miracle they hadn't run into anyone already. The longer he wandered, the more likely someone would see him. And then he'd miss his chance altogether. Both for himself and the others.

He needed time. Time to rest. To recover. To plan and prepare. If his crew were still alive, they'd have to survive a few more days on their own. He'd come back for them. If she could get him out, maybe she could get him back in, too.

"No." His voice was harsh with self-loathing. Just because it was the safest course didn't mean it made him feel good about himself.

"Just keep going."

"That's the door out." She pointed to it, at the end of the long hallway, with a finger that shook. Her voice did, too, fear skittering all over it. *Doesn't feel so good when you're on the losing end of the power play, does it, sweetheart?* "It goes to the recyclers and compactors. They're in an enclosed courtyard. There's a small gate that goes outside."

"People?"

So far they'd seen a few guards and workers at a distance, but no one up close, and Quinn would prefer to keep it that way. The borrowed uniform fit reasonably well, or as well as could be expected when the young guard he'd killed had been half a head taller than he was. Damn overgrown Rhenians. But it had a charred hole in one side, surrounded by a sizable bloodstain, and as soon as anyone got close, they wouldn't be able to help noticing. Nor would anyone be able to overlook the fact that the med tech's sleeve was soaked with blood. Or that Quinn didn't look the least little bit Rhenian in spite of the uniform. He'd feel a lot safer knowing that anyone he came across would keep their distance.

"No way to know," the med tech said. "I'll go first."

She headed for the door with Quinn just behind, remembering—and wishing he didn't—a story he'd once been made to read, about a prisoner during the Spanish Inquisition, which had been a big religious deal back on Old Earth a few thousand years ago. At least that's what the teachers said. In the story, a prisoner had been allowed to escape only to discover, just as he seemed to reach freedom, that his captors had known about his flight all along and had used his hope of escape as the ultimate torture.

Of all the things to remember right now!

But there was no way to deny hope. He did his best, in the

knowledge that outside the door might be Doctor Sterling and a complement of guards just waiting for him to walk directly into their arms, but try as he might, he couldn't stop his heart from beating faster. They couldn't have known that he'd shoot the guard and take the med tech hostage. Could they? So maybe they really weren't there. Maybe he really was on his way out.

But they were probably there. The whole thing planned, the guard a necessary sacrifice, maybe even a volunteer, and the ice bitch a willing foil. The military-crazy Rhenians were big on self-sacrifice. He knew they were probably there, had to be there, waiting, yet he couldn't keep that damnable hope from bubbling up.

And he did have the laser pistol. For some reason, she'd allowed him to get hold of it and keep it. If he walked into an ambush, at least he could turn it on himself before anyone else had time to stun him. Even if that idea held precious little appeal anymore. Amazing what just a smidgeon of hope could do. After wanting to die for months, suddenly he wanted desperately to survive.

But this was way too easy. Getting all the way here without anyone seeing them? It defied the odds. The bottom was due to drop out. Any second now.

The med tech had reached the door, and he watched as she punched the access code into the keypad. The inner door slid open slowly, and a second later, the outer door followed suit. For the first time in months, Quinn saw natural light.

And that was all he had time for, because the next second, a piercing alarm started shrieking loud enough to make his eardrums shiver, and the lights of the sub-basement flickered from dull yellow to pulsing red.

Shit!

The med tech froze, her hand still on the keypad. The look

she shot him over her shoulder was filled with panic. And then she bolted, through the open door and outside.

Double shit!

Quinn hurtled after her, as quickly as his bad leg would allow him. All around, he could hear the sounds of metal grinding and hydraulics hissing as the equipment went into alert status and the safety doors engaged with clanging thuds, and as that ear-rattling alarm kept blaring. He estimated it would only be a minute before rapid footsteps joined the fun.

The double doors the med tech had opened—the ones that had started it all—were hissing closed. If he couldn't get there in time, he'd be trapped in here.

Would that be better or worse than being trapped in the courtyard outside with the trash recyclers and the med tech?

Putting on a burst of speed, he did his best to tuck and roll the way Isaac had taught him and skimmed through the narrow opening as the second door closed, missing him with just enough room that he could feel the breath of wind going past. The door clanged into place, and he could hear the deadbolt mechanism engage. There had to be an override, but hopefully it would take the guards a few minutes at least to get the door open again. If nothing else, that might be enough time for him to find the med tech and blow her brains out.

He struggled to his feet, his battered body fighting every move he made, and looked around.

He was in an enclosed courtyard, the way the med tech had described. Electrified chain-link roof. Trash compactors and recyclers. Bins along the walls. A gate. He was so busy looking for enemy combatants—guards and officers—that the fact that he was finally outside barely registered. The air felt good against his skin, but it was hard to breathe. Marica-3 consisted of a lot of rock and not much vegetation, so the atmosphere here was thin.

There was no sign of her, of course. No sign of anyone else, either. He shifted the laser pistol to his left hand to scrub his sweaty palm against the rough fabric of the uniform pants before taking the gun in his shooting hand once more. Isaac could shoot equally well with either hand, and he'd been working with Quinn to improve his speed and accuracy, but now wasn't the time to put the training to the test.

He put some menace in his voice. "Come out, Doc."

Nothing.

"If I have to come looking for you, you won't like what happens."

There was a beat, and then a scrabble. She got to her feet beside one of the bins, a streak of dust on her cheek.

He gestured. "C'mere."

He could see reluctance clearly written on her face, along with calculation and a touch of fear, but she came, although she flinched when he lifted the pistol. "You shouldn't have done that, sweetheart."

"I didn't." Her voice hitched just a little. "I entered the code correctly. They must have discovered Olaus. The guard you shot."

"How?" He twitched the pistol just a little, menacingly.

She swallowed. "There are sensors. The cells are monitored for body heat. If he has turned cold by now, the alarm would go off."

Wonderful. So it wasn't even as simple as a tripped door alarm. That was something he could have worked around. But no, they knew he was gone. And that he'd killed one of them and taken a hostage. And he was still inside the prison walls.

There was no time to lose. None at all.

"Time to move, sweetheart." He grabbed the med tech by the

arm and swung her around roughly. She didn't make a sound, not until he let her go and pushed her toward the gate in the far wall. Then she drew her breath in on a shudder he could see vibrate through her body.

Quinn kept his attention alternately on her back and over his shoulder, on the door they'd come through, as they made their way to the gate. When she stopped, he did, too.

"There's another keypad." Her voice shook.

Quinn hesitated. The entire prison complex was likely to be on lockdown by now. There had to be an override, though. There was always an override; it just came down to who knew it, and whether that person could be compelled to use it. It would take too long to try to figure it out on his own, and if he did it wrong, the stupid keypad would likely stun him into unconsciousness.

He looked at the med tech. "Can you override it?"

She bit her lip. "I don't know."

"Why don't you give it a try? And if it turns out you can't, I'll just kill you."

She glanced at him before punching a sequence of numbers and letters into the keypad next to the lock, her hand shaking. Quinn didn't bother to memorize it. In thirty seconds, the code wouldn't matter one way or the other. He'd either be outside or he wouldn't, and the code would be useless either way.

They waited. Nothing happened.

"It's not working." There was a shrill note in her voice, of panic or fear, almost as if she'd actually thought the code would work. As if she hadn't put in the wrong code on purpose.

"Try again. And calm down first."

She muttered something, in Rhenish. He didn't understand it, but it was probably along the lines of, "*Easy for you to say.*" He lowered the pistol a few inches to see if it would help.

She tried the code again. They waited. The keypad beeped. She entered a few more numbers. Quinn glanced over his shoulder. They were still alone, and there was no sign of anyone pursuing them. So far, so good.

The gate slid open without setting off any new alarms. The inside alarms were still blaring, but faintly; out here it was silence except from the rustle of the wind. Quinn threw a last glance over his shoulder before pushing the med tech forward into the opening in the wall.

Moment of truth. If this was a setup and they were planning to stop him, now was when they'd have to act.

"There's no one here," the med tech's voice said.

He peered left and right into the barrenness beyond the prison. Along the prison walls.

No, there was no one there. And nowhere for anyone to hide. The landscape was practically flat.

Nowhere for you to hide, either, flashed through his mind.

It took a second to move the laser pistol from the med tech's back to fry the keypad beside the gate, and another to swing the gate shut behind them both. Then they were all the way outside, with the gate inoperable behind them. No one would be coming through there in the next little while. Not until they either forced the gate open or cut through the roof. After they disabled the current.

Quinn pushed the med tech away from him. She landed on her knees on the dusty ground, and he watched her brace herself, as if expecting him to shoot her now that he had no further use for her. For a second he considered doing it. He should. He owed her nothing.

He glanced around again before aiming the pistol at the back of her head. Thought about squeezing the trigger. Lowered it again. He'd never shot a woman, least of all an unarmed one. And she'd kept her word; it seemed wrong to kill her when she'd done what she said she'd do. Even if she was the same Rhenian ice bitch who had stood by and watched him scream and cry and bleed without lifting a finger to help.

He really should kill her. Stop her from doing the same thing to anyone else. To his crew, still stuck behind the prison walls until he could figure out a way to get them out. He hated to think what Doctor Sterling would do to Isaac and Holden and Toby once the Rhenians learned that Quinn was gone.

He didn't think he had it in him to shoot her, though. Not that he hadn't shot people before. But that had been in the heat of the moment, when they'd had weapons and were shooting back. Killing an unarmed woman in cold blood would make him feel too much like the enemy for comfort.

Could he knock her out? Hit her and leave her here? They'd find her when they got through the gate. Or she might wake up on her own before then. It'd buy him enough time to get away.

He raised the gun again, by the barrel this time. Looking down at her bent head, at the pale hair gleaming like moonlight, he hesitated.

Dammit, he should have just killed her upstairs. Taken his chances on getting through the prison on his own.

But the honest part of him knew he wouldn't have made it. The only reason he was standing here, in the air outside, was because of the woman crouched on the ground in front of him. The woman he ought to kill to ensure his own safety.

Scowling, he holstered the pistol and yanked her to her feet. "C'mon."

She'd asked for it. It was her own fault she was here. He would have killed her earlier if she hadn't told him she could help. Now she could damn well live with her choice.

CHAPTER FOUR

The med tech stumbled behind as Quinn headed away from the prison as fast as his legs could carry him. It wasn't as fast as he'd have liked. It hadn't taken more than fifteen or twenty minutes to navigate through the colony, but he was already limping badly, his weak leg threatening to buckle at every step. He was out of breath, too, and it wasn't just the thin air. He used to be in pretty good physical shape—Isaac didn't just know his weapons, he kept them all on their toes in unarmed combat as well—but after months of little food and no exercise, he was winded and shaky after just a few minutes of walking. His lungs burned, his back hurt, and those goddamned worms had reduced his leg to something hardly more useful than a brittle stick. He couldn't wait to see his first night crawler in the wild and stomp the little fucker into the ground until there was nothing left but a puddle of goo.

As he pulled the med tech across the dry plain, in the direction of the low hills he could see on the horizon, he expected at any moment to hear voices from behind. Demands to halt. Shots, the hissing of lasers, the heat of plasma hitting his skin. Dropping him in his tracks.

He heard nothing. Just the scuffing of their feet over the dry ground, her light breaths, his own labored ones. The wind, stirring up whorls of dust and dirt. He risked a glance over his shoulder.

Everything around him was deserted. Bare earth as far as the eye could see. And the prison.

Flying over it in the shuttle, he'd been struck by the vastness. Big as a city, it held more than a hundred thousand people. From down here, like an ant on the ground, he noticed the bulk. The walls, topped by wire, towered over him; story upon story. The buildings were even taller, and a smooth, dark gray, like enormously large building blocks haphazardly tossed by giant hands. There were no windows, no guard towers; it seemed the Rhenians, in their overblown self-confidence, had thought no one would ever get outside the prison walls. It also seemed they had no concerns about being attacked. Maybe not so surprising, since they had this small corner of the solar system pretty well locked down, but still, it seemed careless. If someone could land a small army on the other side of the moon without the Rhenians noticing, and if they could march that army over here, the people inside the prison would have no way of knowing it was coming.

Of course, getting over the walls might be a bit of a problem. And there were a whole lot of other ifs in that scenario, too.

"There are patrols," the woman next to him said, yanking him out of his reverie.

He glanced over at her. Not down, as she was damned near as tall as he was. "'Scuse me?"

"Guards. Patrolling the perimeter of the prison. Every few hours."

He looked over his shoulder again. "Soon?"

She shrugged. Either she didn't know—he saw no chrono on her wrist, so she might not be sure what time it was—or she knew but didn't want to tell him. Couldn't fault her for that. She was probably hoping the patrol would come marching around the corner any second and stop him from taking her any farther. He was frankly surprised she wasn't fighting to get away or trying to talk him into leaving her behind. Once they were out of sight, she'd be completely at his mercy, and although he knew he wouldn't touch her with the proverbial ten-foot Necklin rod, she had no way of knowing that. It was common knowledge what her fellow Rhenians, the guards and soldiers, were doing to the Marican women both here in the prison and on the planet, so why would she expect any better treatment from him?

Or maybe she knew something he didn't. Maybe she was carrying a tracker. Maybe the guards would wait until they were settled somewhere for the night and then sneak up on them.

Maybe he needed to kill her, after all. Or at least leave her right here and go on without her. The prison was visible from Marica itself, two and a half ship days away; it wasn't like she could get lost on her way back there.

Or maybe he just needed to strip her naked and make sure she wasn't carrying anything she shouldn't be.

He smiled grimly. Yeah, that'd solve the problem. And give her a little taste of what her people were doing to other people's women at the same time. Just because he wouldn't touch her didn't mean he couldn't put a little fear in her.

Plan in place, he pulled her forward through the dust, looking for a place that would offer them enough privacy to put the plan into action. From just outside the gate, the landscape had seemed as flat as the parking pad for a ground car. Now that he was a few hundred meters into it, he realized it wasn't. There were little hillocks and gullies, but the dull monochromatic sandy brown masked the ups and downs. There was vegetation on Marica-3, just enough to support the thin atmosphere, but it was sparse, and the Rhenians had situated their prison where there was very little impeding the view in every direction. Very little of anything except dirt. And Quinn and his captive were still visible from the prison, if that damned patrol were to come around the corner. He had to get them out of sight somehow.

An outcropping of rocks a little way up ahead seemed a likely place. He headed for it, med tech in tow, his leg objecting to every step.

It didn't take him long to realize that because of the thin atmosphere, things looked closer than they were, and it took a small eternity to reach the rocks. Maybe as much as an hour, Old Earth time, when he'd expected fifteen minutes or so. Each agonizing step was its own struggle not to fall flat on his face, and once they left the immense shadow of the prison, the heat kicked up several notches, causing sweat to trickle down the sides of his face.

But when he got there, the rock formation turned out to be bigger than he'd anticipated, too. Plenty big enough to hide them both and allow him to accomplish what he wanted to do. He ducked into the shadow behind it, out of sight of the prison, and sank to the ground, hoping it looked more like choice than necessity and not like his leg had folded under him. He stretched it out, taking care not to wince at the pain—*don't let the bastards see you sweat*—and conjured up a smirk before he looked up at the med tech, still standing in front of him, bathed in sunlight.

"Get undressed, sweetheart."

The first time he'd given that command, to undress the dead

guard, she'd misunderstood, and if the situation had been different, he'd have laughed out loud at her expression. Her relief when she'd understood that he didn't want *her* to undress had been palpable. There'd be none of that this time.

He hardened his voice. "For all I know, you've got a tracker stuck in your pocket, and as soon as we stop for the night, the guards'll be swarming all over everything. Before we go any further, I'm gonna make sure you don't." He lifted the laser pistol and held it on her. "Take your clothes off. Now."

She hesitated, glancing sideways. Checking her chances of escape?

If so, she must have found them lacking, because she looked back at him, and he could clearly see the reluctance with which she began removing the white lab coat.

Quinn settled back against the hard rock, doing his best to hide his own discomfort, both physical and mental. His entire body hurt, but more than that, he'd never gotten off on cruelty. Sure, she was Rhenian, and she'd cleaned up the messes after the unspeakable things Doctor Sterling had done to him and probably to the other prisoners as well, but it still didn't feel good, humiliating her like this.

And then, as she awkwardly dropped the lab coat to the ground and began to unbutton the gray dress she had on underneath, his mind slipped sideways, and he remembered the last time a woman had stood before him, taking her clothes off.

· · ·

Josie was taking her sweet time getting undressed, and Quinn could barely breathe as he watched her unbutton her top oh, so slowly, dragging out the time before she'd let him have her. She'd kept him in an acute state of arousal for more than an hour, leaning over his shoulder as he navigated the Good Fortune *toward the shipyards off Sierra Luz, her breasts brushing his arm as she whispered hot promises in his ear, telling him everything she wanted to do to him once he'd gotten them into dock and they could be alone together. He'd been so distracted he'd missed the docking clamps altogether on his first try, and he'd had to back up and go through the process again. Isaac had shaken his head in exasperation, but Josie had laughed, knowing just what her teasing was doing to him. As soon as the* Fortune *was safely docked, he'd left Isaac to organize the transfer of the weapons and supplies they were ferrying to Marica and had dragged Josie back to his cabin.*

And now he was lying on his bunk, his body at attention, watching her expose smooth skin, lush curves, and long legs. She was wearing red lace, like a crimson flame against the pale perfection of her skin, and his breath hitched in his throat as she shimmied out of her pants and kicked them aside, standing before him with her hands on her hips, black hair curling over her shoulders, and her breasts—those beautiful, perfect breasts that he loved—rising and falling with her rapid breaths. He reached for her, and…that's when all hell broke loose outside, with shouting and rapid footsteps, and the sounds of laser fire and plasma sizzling against the Fortune's *hull.*

And he'd looked at Josie, and she'd looked at him, with guilt written all over that beautiful face, and he'd known.

• • •

Quinn wrenched himself out of the memory, grimacing, just in time to see the Rhenian med tech drop the gray dress on the ground. There was no red lace here; she wore simple white synthetics under her clothes, what Josie used to call granny wear. And unlike the conniving bitch he used to bed, she also looked acutely uncomfortable.

He made sure his grin was as offensive as he could make it when he addressed her. "Keep going, sweetheart. It all has to come off. Every stitch. Even the shoes. And toss those over here while you're at it."

He used the pistol to point to the lab coat and dress on the ground.

Her eyes flew to his, and he could see the consternation in their depths. Maybe the tracker was in the pocket of the coat. Or somewhere in that sorry excuse for a dress. If so, he could make her stop now. Save them both from this uncomfortable parody of a striptease that neither of them enjoyed.

He lowered the pistol to his lap. "Tell you what. You tell me where the tracker is, and I won't make you take off any more. Just give it to me, and you can put your clothes back on."

Her gaze flickered. Surprise? Or fear?

For a second, he thought it might be easy. Then—

"There is no tracker." The med tech's voice was low, and those green eyes he'd thought were devoid of feeling were filled with resignation. Quinn felt himself waver—*just give her her damn clothes back and let her get dressed again!*—but then he hardened his resolve. He'd been fooled before; that's what had gotten him into this fix in the first place. You just couldn't trust a woman, especially a beautiful one.

"Guess you'll just have to take off the rest then, sweetheart. And toss 'em to me as you go. Starting with those."

She hesitated before bending to pick up the lab coat and gray dress lying on the ground. Then she hesitated again, holding them.

"Coat first."

She threw it from a few feet away, and it landed in a puddle at his feet. Quinn picked it up, noticing in passing the stiffness of the sleeve where the guard's blood had dried during their walk. There was a corresponding stain on her forearm, bright against the pale skin. The coat had shiny metal buttons, and he'd have to smash each one of those to make sure something small wasn't hidden inside. There was also a patch of some sort sewn to the breast pocket that he'd have to investigate further.

"Now the dress."

She didn't want to give it to him, that much was clear. She was clutching it, but not—he thought—to cover herself. There wasn't anything to cover. The underpants left everything to the imagination, while the top—a camisole?—covered her from hips to shoulders.

He laced his voice with amused contempt. "C'mon, sweetheart. You're making it harder than it has to be. Ain't like I'm enjoying the show, you know."

Her hands fumbled with the gray fabric. A moment later, the dress came flying at his face.

He got his hand up in time to bat it away at the same time as he braced himself for the expected attack.

When it didn't come, he focused his eyes on her again and saw why. She hadn't moved from her place on the dusty ground, but now she was clutching a knife, one she must have had in the pocket of the gray dress.

No wonder she hadn't wanted to let go of it.

The knife was small but looked sharp, the blade glinting in the low light. In the right hands, it could probably do some damage. But those hands weren't hers. What the hell did she think she was gonna do with it, against him and a laser pistol? She was holding it all wrong, and besides, he could burn a hole in her head from where he was sitting.

Or—if he'd been someone who got off on other people's pain—he could turn the laser on her skin, flick the setting down to low, and give her a nice little pattern of burns. Write his fucking name on her stomach if he wanted, right through the undershirt. It wouldn't be enough to kill her, not even enough to do serious harm, but it would hurt like a bitch and give her some powerful incentive to do as he said. And unless she went through more pain to have it removed, it would stay with her for the rest of her life.

"I can drop you dead from over here," he informed her, not even bothering to aim the pistol. "Not to mention the other things I could do that would just make you wish I had."

"I'm not afraid of you." But her voice was shaking.

Liar. "You oughta be. I've had a rough couple months. Maybe I'm ready for some payback."

He watched her face as that suggestion took root, then added, "Put the goddamn knife down and get the rest of your clothes off."

She didn't move. Quinn raised the pistol and took aim.

"All it'll take is a low beam right across the fingers. I'll even let you keep 'em. I just won't let you keep the knife. Either drop it, or I'll drop it for you. In five seconds. Four. Three."

By the time he got to two, she'd bent and put the knife on the ground. With the blade hidden. Quinn's eyes lingered on it. An Old Earth switchblade. Antique. Declared illegal hundreds of years ago. Everywhere except the Republic of Rhene, it seemed.

"Kick it over here."

She did, and he palmed it. Opened and closed the blade a couple of times before dropping it into his pocket. "Thanks, sweetheart. Now, if you don't mind?"

He gestured with the gun. And watched as she bent to untie both shoes before reluctantly pulling the undershirt up and over her head. The last thing she did was push those unexciting white panties down and off, throwing them to him, and then she stood in front of him as naked as she'd come out of her mother's womb. Or out of the uterine replicator, depending on how the Rhenians handled things like reproduction. He'd never bothered to find out.

Quinn did his best to ignore the stirrings of his body.

But damn, it had been a long time, and she was naked, and now that he got a good look at her, she wasn't too thin at all. Her legs went on forever, ending in a thatch of blonde curls at the apex of her thighs, and she did have breasts. Not lush ones, like Josie's, but small breasts, high and firm, tipped with pink nipples. Pebbled pink nipples, getting harder as he watched. And she was blushing, all over, which didn't help matters.

"Turn around."

He could hear the strain in his voice. When she swung and showed him her back, he took the opportunity to close his eyes for a second before opening them to look her up and down.

"Undo the braid."

And not because he wanted to see what her hair looked like unbound. Inside that tight coil was a perfect place to hide a tracker. A place most people would overlook.

She lifted her arms and removed the pins, and he watched as a long rope of flaxen hair uncoiled down her back, almost reaching her ass. Then she pulled the elastic off the end and shook out a sheet of moonlight pale silk. No tracker.

"Thank you. You can put it back up."

He averted his eyes as she got busy redoing her braid, thinking about what his next move should be. A cavity search would be customary, but damn, he didn't think he had the stomach for it. Surely the chances that she was carrying a tracker inside her body were slim. And the last thing he wanted at the moment was to put his hands on her.

Instead, he focused his attention on the plain white underwear in his lap. There was no way to hide anything in that; it was just a scrap of white synthetic material, stretchy and thin, retaining a touch of heat from her body as well as a faint womanly smell he did his best to ignore. He pulled it between his hands, scrunched it into a small ball, and then tossed it back to her, and watched as it landed at her feet. The camisole followed. The gray dress was the same, the buttons too thin to hide anything, and the pockets were empty now that the switchblade was in Quinn's possession. He fingered the hem and collar, probing for anything sewn into the construction of the dress, but found nothing. He tossed it back, as well. The lab coat…

Screw the lab coat. He could smash all the buttons and use the knife to peel off the patch, but with the entire sleeve soaked in blood, it couldn't be too pleasant to wear. The blood might attract predators. And it was white, standing out like a beacon against the dull yellowy brown of the dirt and sand. They'd be safer and less noticeable if she wore just the gray dress. With the way the heat was climbing, she'd be more comfortable without the coat, anyway. So instead of messing with it, he bundled it up and stuffed it behind his back before turning his attention to the shoes.

God, they were ugly. Brown leather, with low heels and thick laces. Not something any self-respecting woman should be caught dead wearing. Especially not one with legs like hers.

None of his business, he supposed. She could wear whatever the hell she wanted, including ugly shoes, shapeless dresses, and sexless underwear, just as long as there were no tracking devices hidden in any of it.

He felt around the shoes, inside and out, and found nothing.

Before throwing them back, he contemplated using the knife to slice the heels off, but thought better of it. If he made her shoes impossible to wear, she'd slow him down.

As if that was even possible, with the snail's pace he'd been setting.

When he looked up, she was back inside her clothes, the gray dress just dropping over her head, covering the unappealing white underwear and the not unappealing slender figure. He tossed the shoes her way. "Put 'em on. Time to move."

Much as he would have liked to have stayed where he was for a few more hours, he made himself get up, too. The worm-damaged leg threatened to buckle when he put weight on it, and he was forced to catch himself on the rock before he face-planted into the dirt.

He looked up to find the med tech watching him. She didn't speak, and neither did he, other than to tell her gruffly to get a move on.

CHAPTER FIVE

Captain Conlan's leg must really be bothering him, Elsa thought, because as they set off again, his limp was more pronounced and the tempo slower. She wondered what the problem was—maybe Olaus's boots were chafing him or he'd hit it on something along the way?—and then she remembered the Marican night crawlers. Those awful worms Doctor Sterling kept in the lab. He'd set them on the prisoner a month or so ago. She'd had to watch them make their way up his leg, bulging under the skin, while he clutched the arms of the chair and turned pale, beads of sweat springing up on his forehead. He hadn't screamed, though, or spilled any secrets regarding the Marican resistance. Just set his teeth and held on, as the tendons in his neck stood out and his knuckles turned white. She'd had to tell Doctor Sterling to stop when the worms reached Captain Conlan's groin. By then, his blood pressure had spiked into the danger zone, and she determined he was on the verge of having a stroke. And if that happened, not even Doctor Sterling would be able to revive him.

Even the thought of it now, weeks later, made her stomach turn.

At the time, the sight had made her want to retch, but she'd known if she showed weakness, Doctor Sterling would chide her for being too soft and then make her take an active hand in introducing the worms next time. Better to hide her squeamishness behind cool professionalism and save herself the knowledge that she'd been the one to actually cause him—cause any of them—such agony.

She glanced at him limping next to her. He was pale, and there were beads of sweat on his forehead, but after seeing him go through what she'd seen over the past few months, she had no doubts that whatever level of pain he was in, he'd keep walking until he couldn't walk any farther, and then he'd crawl. He wasn't someone who'd ever give up. If he was, he'd have given up the information Doctor Sterling wanted long ago.

"Why didn't you?" fell out of her mouth.

He glanced at her. "'Scuse me?"

Elsa felt a wash of color stain her cheeks. "Why didn't you tell Doctor Sterling what he wanted to know? You're not Marican." He shouldn't feel any loyalty to the citizens of the annexed planet. It was none of his concern what happened to them.

He looked at her for a second, his face unreadable, before he said, "I got paid not to."

Not enough flashed through her mind. She almost said it out loud, but bit the words back at the last moment. "You went through all of that—" the worms, the whippings, the injections, the exsanguination, "—for money?"

"I went to work for the Maricans for money. The silence was part of the contract. It always is."

"I hope they paid well."

That unguarded remark earned her another glance, one that held something akin to surprise before it morphed into suspicion and then hostility. "There ain't enough money in the world to pay for what you people did to me. But the Maricans paid well enough. And you take on the risk when you take on the job."

His tone of voice effectively closed the subject. Elsa opened it again. "But surely when you were captured…you could have saved yourself by telling the truth."

He glanced at her again. "Saved myself what? Pain?"

She nodded.

"There are worse things than pain."

Elsa blinked. He had endured enough of it in the past few months to turn his hair prematurely gray and carve deep lines on his otherwise young face. He should know. But…

"Such as?" What could possibly be worse than what she'd seen him go through?

"Watching other people suffer. And knowing you could have stopped it."

The thing she had done, Elsa thought. She had watched him—watched other prisoners too, although lately, much of Doctor Sterling's efforts had been focused on this one—being put to the question. Breaking Quinn Conlan had become a point of honor for Doctor Sterling. He had broken the prisoner's body, his strength, even his will to live, but he hadn't broken his silence, and Doctor Sterling couldn't allow that. Major Lamb couldn't allow it. The Rhenians needed the information Captain Conlan had. The Marican resistance was holding strong in spite of all efforts to eradicate it, and the information about the leaders and the strength and location of their weapons depot would go a long way toward wiping them out once and for all.

Elsa understood that. She wanted it, too. The Maricans weren't capable of governing themselves or protecting their corner of the nexus properly. They didn't even have an army. And because of their proximity to one of the major wormholes into and out of the system, their weakness put everyone else in the nexus at risk, including Rhene. Marica needed the Rhenians' help, whether the Maricans realized it or not. Once the rebels were gone, the rest of the Marican population would soon grasp the benefits of being under Rhenish protection.

But to do that, Doctor Sterling had to break Quinn Conlan and get the necessary information out of him. With Elsa's help.

And she had helped. She had monitored him, doing her best to determine how much of the torture he could take before he was of no more use to them. And she had been alternately exasperated and impressed by his strength and stubbornness. She had even lied to Doctor Sterling for once, just a little, exaggerating the imminence of a stroke to make the torture end sooner, before she embarrassed herself by retching right there in the lab. But as uncomfortable and sick-making as watching those worms tunnel through his flesh had been, she couldn't imagine suggesting that watching had been worse than enduring. She had wanted it to stop, yes—but surely she couldn't have wanted it as much as he had.

"I don't understand."

His look in her direction said plainly as words, *You wouldn't.* Still, he attempted to explain. "My pain doesn't matter. Pain ends, one way or the other. But watching someone else suffer, someone you love, and knowing that you could have prevented it but you didn't, is worse than any physical pain."

Elsa blinked, trying to imagine her reaction if she had to watch Doctor Sterling—the closest thing she had to a father—go through what had been done to Captain Conlan. If the tables were turned, and it was Doctor Sterling on the table and Captain Conlan in charge. The thought made her feel sick.

"They made me watch." His voice was tight. "I told them my crew knew nothing about the Maricans, that they had no information to give. I'd made sure of it. But they still hurt them, and they made me watch. I watched them whip Holden and beat Isaac and break Toby's fingers. I watched them rape Josie."

Josie? "Who…"

"I don't wanna talk about her."

It wasn't an answer to her question, but the finality in his voice shut the subject down flat. This time she allowed it. They trudged forward in silence.

To be honest, Elsa was amazed that they had made it this far. She'd thought they would run into someone on the way through the prison. Guards or even officers. Someone to stop their flight. She'd tried to avoid it in the sure and certain knowledge that he'd kill her if they did, but she hadn't dared hope they'd actually make it all the way outside without being stopped. Yet here they were. Outside. With the prison perhaps as much as a couple of miles behind them now. Still visible, of course, but getting farther away with every step. She wondered how far he planned to walk—they had hours to go yet if he wanted to be out of sight of the prison. And then she wondered whether he had a plan, or whether he just planned to get as far away as he could as fast as he could, and he'd worry about the rest later. And what might it mean for her, whichever the case? Why was she still here? He didn't need her anymore. Why hadn't he killed her as soon as they had cleared the prison wall? He stood a much better chance of getting away on his own.

"Where are we going?"

He shot her a look. "This way."

"Toward those hills?"

He shrugged.

"I think they're farther away than you think. Probably several days' walk."

He shook his head. "We ain't going that far. Just far enough that maybe they won't find us."

"They?"

"Guards. Your precious Doctor Sterling ain't just gonna let me walk away with you, is he?"

Lord, she hoped not! Although at this point, it was a toss-up who was more important to Doctor Sterling, the prisoner or herself. Rhene was full of young, up-and-coming doctors who would kill to work under Doctor Sterling, but there was only one Quinn Conlan.

But he was right: either way, there'd be guards searching for them. And Stephen Lamb wouldn't rest until she was back inside the prison, safe and sound. She was frankly surprised not to have heard someone behind her already. Or at least the sound of a lightflyer taking off to take a swing over the area.

Glancing back, she realized that Captain Conlan had deliberately aligned them so they were still hidden by the big rock outcropping they'd stopped behind earlier. He'd kept them walking in a straight line. She could see the dark walls of the prison on either side of the rock, but as long as they stayed right here, no one coming out of the gate would be able to see them. An attempt to veer off course made him grab her arm, hard, and yank her back to his side.

But at least he'd holstered the laser pistol. It was a little easier to breathe when it wasn't pointed at her head. And—loath as she was to admit it—the loss of the white lab coat was a relief as well. The air was hot, and the skin on her arms tingled where the sun hit it, but the stiff sleeve with Olaus's blood dried into it had chafed against her arm, and the sight had been an unpleasant reminder of his death.

Her mind shied away from thinking about the circumstances of the loss.

Not the loss of Olaus; she had come to terms with that on the walk through the prison. They were at war, and casualties were inevitable. Olaus had known the risk when he accepted the assignment. No, the loss she didn't want to think about was the loss of the coat itself. The scene behind the rock. When Captain Conlan had told her to get undressed.

Her first thought had been that she'd misunderstood. After all, back in the cell, she had misunderstood when he asked her to take Olaus's clothes off. Only this time, it hadn't been a misunderstanding. He'd pointed the gun at her and threatened to kill her if she didn't obey.

She'd thought he'd meant to rape her. Or make her do things to him.

It happened, she knew. Some of the guards boasted about using the female prisoners in such ways. Or the male prisoners, in certain instances. It wasn't officially sanctioned, of course — Captain Conlan had to be lying when he said he'd been forced to watch as "they" raped his friend Josie — but she couldn't imagine that Stephen Lamb didn't have some idea that it was going on. Stephen was too good an officer not to know what was happening in his command. But she imagined it might be difficult to eradicate something like that. There were so many of the young guards, and they were quite rowdy and undisciplined and didn't always think before they acted...

Anyway, that was what she had expected when he asked her to strip. To be used for the prisoner's needs, in spite of the disgust in Captain Conlan's voice and eyes when he looked at her.

That was until he told her that she could get out of the

humiliation by giving him the tracker she was carrying. And the unintentional cruelty of that stung. She had no tracker to give him, and no way to avoid the embarrassment.

Had he really thought this was all a big setup? That she'd allowed him to kill Olaus and allowed herself to be taken prisoner? Why would she take such a big chance? Somehow, by some insane stroke of luck or fate, she was still alive, but she knew she ought to have been dead on the floor beside Olaus. If it had been a setup, she would have refused to go along with it for that very reason: her chances of survival were slim. Captain Conlan had no reason not to kill her. She still didn't know why he hadn't, although she expected there was a reason; she just hadn't discovered what that was yet. When he had asked her to get undressed, she thought she had. Until he mentioned the tracker.

And then she hadn't been able to keep her knife—Olaus's knife—from him. And now she didn't even have that for protection.

Not that he seemed inclined to want to hurt her. He kept threatening her with the pistol, but he never actually used it. And when she was naked, standing in front of him waiting for the order to get on her knees, he'd told her to turn away instead. It was obvious he couldn't stand to look at her.

And then there had been that surprising thank-you after she'd done as he said and had undone her braid. The words had most likely slipped out without conscious thought on his part—he had no real reason to thank her for anything she did—but it was telling. He respected her, even after everything she'd done to him. She ought to be able to find a way to use that to her advantage.

And in the meantime, she should try to discover as much about his plans as she could.

"Why are we not going as far as the hills?"

Surely he'd have a better chance of getting away the more distance he put between himself and the prison. He might not ever get off Marica-3, but he could live in freedom for a while, for weeks or months, maybe, until some of the more deadly flora or fauna killed him. Or until the guards found him. And if she were dead by then, she had to trust that Stephen would keep looking for Captain Conlan until he was found.

The captain looked at her for a long moment before he answered. "The farther I go, the longer the walk back."

Back? After the trouble he'd taken to get away?

Her confusion must have been written on her face, because he added, "My crew's still there. I'll have to go back for them."

He was going to try to get a handful of other people out of the prison complex as well? How?

But he didn't explain, and eventually the need to know trumped her need to stay silent. "Why?"

"They're mine. I'm responsible for them. What kind of captain would I be if I left them to rot?"

One who looked out for his own survival. Nothing wrong with trying to survive, was there?

Except he obviously was of a different opinion. One she might have expected after hearing him say that he'd made sure his crew knew nothing about the Marican resistance. That way, if they were captured—as they had been—the focus would be on him to tell what he knew, and not on the others. A man like that wouldn't leave anyone behind.

"How do you plan to accomplish that?" Surely he must have realized from walking through the prison complex earlier that getting back inside and liberating three, or four, or five other people would be impossible.

"I haven't figured that out yet. But I will." *Or die trying.* He limped stubbornly forward.

They walked in silence for a few minutes. Elsa could hear his breaths, labored now, and the increasingly uneven rhythm of his footsteps scuffing through the dirt.

"Do you need to rest?" she ventured after a while.

He shot her a glance out of the corner of his eye. "Do I look like I'm about to keel over?"

In a word? Yes. She was amazed he was still upright and moving.

"If I stop, I don't know that I'm gonna be able to get up again. I wanna get to somewhere we're gonna be able to stay awhile first. Out of the sun and halfway safe."

Safe for him, she assumed. Safe from the guards. He must expect them to be coming sooner or later. She kept her ears peeled for the sounds of a lightflyer or groundcar, but so far there had been no sign of one.

They carried on. And on. For longer than Elsa thought possible.

By the time he finally agreed to stop, the sun was high in the sky and the heat almost unbearable. Elsa's feet hurt, and the pain Captain Conlan felt was palpable enough that she imagined she could almost feel it, too. It had drained his face of what little color it had, darkened his eyes from pewter to lead, and carved deep lines into his face. Still, she thought he would have kept going if he hadn't stumbled.

There was nothing there to stumble over, so it must be just that the leg itself gave out. And she managed to catch him before he fell flat on his face and kept him standing. It didn't come as a big surprise when he shook her off as if her touch had burned him. Elsa took a step back and kept her hands at her sides.

"You have to rest."

He looked like he wanted to argue, to insist that he could go on, but she could see the tremors running through his leg from where she was standing. If he tried to put weight on it, it would buckle, and they both knew it.

The terrain had changed now. They hadn't reached the big hills, still off in the distance, but there were shorter hills leading up to an escarpment. Big dunes of dirt and rock, bisected with tracks or trails. Animal trails, presumably, unless the guards were in the habit of venturing this far from the prison. The escarpment itself was layered with vertical shadows, fissures in the rock or perhaps even caves.

The prisoner gazed at them, assessing their potential for cover. "Up there."

Elsa looked at him, wondering what he'd do if she offered to let him lean on her. Tell her he could walk on his own, most likely. Looking into those flat gray eyes, she decided to spare herself the rejection.

What she should be doing, she knew, was running the other way as fast as her legs could carry her. He wasn't in any condition to chase her down, and she doubted he'd shoot her. By now, she was inclined to believe him when he said that he wouldn't shoot anyone in the back. And besides, he had escaped. He could afford to let her go. It would take her a couple of hours to get back to the prison and another hour, at least, to bring a search party back here. Plenty of time for him to find cover. And he had the pistol. He could shoot anyone who came close. Or himself, if he thought it necessary.

There was no reason for her to stay here.

She glanced back in the direction they'd come from, across the plain with its dips and hillocks. The prison was still visible in the distance, big and dark and imposing.

"Move." He gestured with the weapon. Elsa started climbing.

CHAPTER SIX

None of the fissures in the rock opened up into caves, but a few were big enough to enter. They ended up in one of them. After lashing Elsa's hands together behind her back and her legs together at the ankles with strips of fabric he cut from the jumpsuit he had on underneath Olaus's uniform, Captain Conlan stuffed a third piece of fabric in her mouth, murmured something that was either an apology or a warning, and curled up on the hard ground with his back to her. Elsa was amazed he had the strength to do even that much. He was clearly exhausted and dropped off to sleep, or into unconsciousness, as soon as his head hit the dirt.

She was not as lucky. They had walked for hours, and her feet were tired and sore, but it was still only halfway through the day and not even close to time for bed. So she sat there in the semi-darkness, feeling the pebbles on the ground digging into her buttocks through her dress and tasting the synthetic material he'd shoved into her mouth while she tried to wiggle her hands free from the ties around her wrists. It didn't work. He might have been exhausted, but he knew how to tie knots, even if he hadn't tied them as tight as he could have. She was uncomfortable but not in pain. But she also didn't stand a chance of getting free. All she managed to do was chafe her skin. When perspiration hit the area, it stung.

There were a few jagged rocks over on the far wall, not too far from the entrance to the fissure, and she started wiggling her way toward them. Maybe she could use a sharp edge to cut the fabric around her ankles or wrists and get free that way.

Moving on her buttocks without being able to use her feet or hands was harder than she'd expected. It was difficult to keep her balance, so she had to move at a snail's pace. If she fell over, she wouldn't be able to right herself again.

A sound from Captain Conlan halted her progress halfway to the rocks, and she twisted her head to look at him, her heart beating faster.

But no, he seemed to be asleep still. He was restless, his arms and legs twitching and his face contorting. Bad dreams, and who could blame him? Elsa continued her slow way toward the rocks.

She was there and had just discovered that it was easier said than done to tear through the stretchy synthetic material of the bonds when she heard something from outside. A rattle of pebbles in the distance, as if from underneath a foot or a paw. Possibly a claw. A creature of some sort was approaching.

She held her breath as she waited to see what it might be.

It took a minute or two, but eventually the sound of low voices reached her ear. "That look like a footprint to you?"

The voice was young, male, speaking Rhenish. Elsa's heart jumped. A few of Stephen's guards from the prison had arrived, looking for her and Captain Conlan. And she was bound and gagged and couldn't let them know they were here!

"Could be," a second voice answered, in the same language.

"Could just be an animal."

"Mmmph!" Elsa did her best to move toward the opening of the fissure, struggling to make enough noise that they'd hear her. "Mmmph!"

Outside, the first voice asked, with a hint of consternation, "What kind of animal?"

"That size track? Could be a derma-lizard, maybe."

The derma-lizard was one of the many unpleasant creatures living on Marica-3. But where the night crawler would burrow under someone's skin and the spider-scorpion would sting and the water snake would bite, just brushing up against the venomous derma-lizard would bring on blisters and open sores. It wouldn't kill you, not unless infection set in, but for the time the blisters popped and drained and the skin was raw, you would wish it had. Doctor Sterling had done some experiments with derma-lizard poison, and she had seen the damage it did. She didn't blame the young guard at all for the panic that permeated his voice.

"There are derma-lizards this close to the prison?"

"Live in holes in the rocks, don't they?" his companion, slightly older and wiser, answered.

Elsa could only imagine the young man's panicked look at the many fissures that split the rock walls. As it was, she couldn't help a careful glance around the hole she was in for the telltale dusty brown shape of the large lizard.

As she did, she met the eyes of Captain Conlan. The prisoner was awake, his eyes open and aware, and looking straight at her. As the voices continued outside, he glanced in the direction of the opening. Elsa renewed and redoubled her efforts to reach the mouth of the fissure, grunting with effort around the gag.

She was just a few feet away—if she threw herself sideways,

she might be visible in the opening—when Captain Conlan rolled her back inside the fissure and threw himself on top of her. Emaciated as he'd become, his weight was still enough to pin her to the ground. Pebbles and rocks dug painfully into her bound hands, which dug into her lower back. His knees were confining hers, holding them together so she couldn't kick or buck him off, and one uncompromising hand clamped over her mouth. Furious eyes burned into hers. Still, it wasn't until he removed the laser pistol from the holster and pressed the barrel against the soft area under her jaw that Elsa gave up the fight.

Outside, the voices continued, closer now. "There's a million and one of these holes in the rock. Are we supposed to check every one?"

"There's no room for anyone to hide in them," a second voice answered. "Look."

A powerful beam of light spilled through the opening to the fissure they were in and lit up the back wall. Elsa followed it with her eyes. So did Captain Conlan, as it skirted the area where they lay. After a second, it cut off.

"See?" the same voice said outside. "No room."

"So we tell the major they're not here?"

"They aren't here." After a moment the voice continued. "They've probably gone a different direction. Or maybe they never left the compound at all. Maybe the busted keypad was a ruse. The prisoner made it look like they left, but instead he killed Dr. Brandeis and then doubled back inside and hid somewhere in the sub-basement. There's enough space down there for a whole army. Bet you things are going to start breaking down soon. He was the captain of a freighter; he has to know how to work mechanicals."

"What about Dr. Brandeis?"

"Her body is probably stuffed in a freezer in the kitchen."

"Why the kitchen?"

"What better place to hide it? Nobody'd think to look there."

The voices faded as their owners walked away. Elsa could hear them in the distance for long minutes as the Rhenian soldiers made their way along the canyon floor. The thin air on Marica-3 didn't just skew visual perception, it made sound carry farther as well.

Captain Conlan stayed where he was, his weight heavy on top of her. His hand was warm and hard, covering her mouth, and his chest was pressed against hers. As the seconds ticked by, with no indication that the guards would be returning, Elsa found her body softening and her breath changing, synchronizing with his in a rhythm that worked for them both. Exhale when he inhaled; inhale when he exhaled…

Her hands hurt, bound underneath her, and she squirmed. As she lifted her hips to ease the pressure, she bucked against the hard length of him, and his eyes shot to hers, startled. For a second they both lay frozen, and she had just enough time to register the way his lips parted, before he rolled off her and away.

She squirmed in the other direction, as far away as she could get in the tiny space, and maneuvered her back up against the rock wall. Pulling her knees to her chest, she peered at him across them.

He stared back, and for a moment, awareness crackled in the air. Then his lips twisted. "Save it for someone who appreciates it, sweetheart."

Elsa felt the shock all the way down to her toes, and if it hadn't been for the gag, she would have gasped. As if she'd do such a thing on purpose!

But being unable to utter any of her thoughts, she had to content herself with staring daggers at him, letting her eyes speak for her.

He snorted. "Spare me. You're a woman. I know women. You're all the same."

Since there was no way for her to respond to that, either, Elsa just shot him a look that by rights should have killed him, but which just glanced off. He turned his back. "I'm going back to sleep. Wake me if anyone else stops by."

Muttering inside her head, because there was no way to mutter out loud, Elsa watched him drop back into oblivion. Like last time, she herself was too uncomfortable—and now too upset—to sleep.

The time passed slowly. The light from outside never increased, never waned, and the heat never changed. Eventually, she became drowsy, nodding off a few times, only to wake up again as her body slid sideways along the rock. Eventually she gave up and curled up on her side, closing her eyes.

When she woke, her body was stiff and her mouth dry. Her hands were numb from being tied behind her, and her shoulder hurt from where she had been lying against the rocky ground. The light through the opening to the fissure was still bright, but the shadows slanted in the other direction. Late afternoon, perhaps.

Captain Conlan was still asleep but had turned so he was facing her. His lips were slightly parted, and his eyelashes lay like dark smudges against his cheeks, his face softer in sleep than when he was awake, the pain lines less prominent. His chest barely rose at all with his breathing, and in Olaus's uniform, with the hole through the side ringed with the young guard's blood, and his face gray from exhaustion, he looked like a corpse.

What would she do if he died? Would she have to sit here until she starved to death herself? Would someone find her before then? Or might she be able to get the knife out of his pocket and free herself if he were dead?

Neither alternative was particularly attractive.

Something moved off to the side, just a glimpse of movement out of the corner of her eye, deeper in the dark. It was hard to make out in the dusk inside the fissure, and she leaned a little closer, eyes narrowed.

And then she jerked back with a strangled gurgle when she recognized the creature.

A night crawler. At least ten centimeters long, tomato red and puffy. Inching toward her. Attracted by Olaus's blood still staining her arm, probably.

Elsa tried to move out of the way, but with her wrists and ankles lashed together, it was difficult to make progress. The worm was slow but no slower than Elsa herself.

It looked deceptively innocent. If she hadn't known what it was, what it was capable of, she might have thought it pretty, with its bright color and dark markings. And it looked so gentle. When it reached her leg, it raised its head and butted against her skin for a second, almost delicately.

Elsa swallowed a sob. Captain Conlan had endured the worms burrowing under his skin for half an hour without making a sound. They'd almost killed him, and he hadn't uttered a word. Could she do the same?

The night crawler hooked its tiny feet into her skin to pull itself up, and she decided she couldn't. "Mmmph!"

There wasn't much power behind the sound; she was just too scared to muster any breath. But it was enough to wake Captain Conlan. He went from dead sleep to full alertness in the span of a heartbeat, laser pistol in his hand and his eyes darting from side to side. "What?"

"Mmmph!"

He looked at her. "What?"

"Mmmph!!!" By now her eyes were full of tears, and they spilled over and rolled down her cheeks. Another display of weakness in view of the enemy, yet Elsa couldn't find it in herself to care. If he'd just save her, she didn't care what he thought.

Captain Conlan sighed in exasperation but moved closer and removed the gag. "What is it?"

Elsa drew in a shaky breath. "W-w-worm. On my leg. Get it off!"

She could feel the disgusting creature probing her skin, and she knew it was looking for a way in: a scratch or maybe a scab. If it couldn't find one, would it make its own, tunneling through the skin?

Captain Conlan turned his head to look at it, his head cocked, an almost-smile on his face as he holstered the laser pistol. Elsa watched, dry-mouthed, as he reached into his pocket and pulled out Olaus's little flick knife.

Oh, God. What was he going to do with that?

She whimpered, and he cut his eyes to her. They were the roiling gray of storm clouds, and try as she might, she could see no trace of compassion in their depths, just bright-eyed anticipation. She had seen that same look on Stephen Lamb's face sometimes, when he had escorted Captain Conlan to the lab for "questioning." She recognized it for what it was: the excitement brought on by the prospect of watching someone else suffer.

"Please!"

He didn't speak, just lifted a finger to his lips, telling her to be quiet. Then his eyes moved back to the night crawler, and he lifted the knife.

Terrified, Elsa began thrashing, yanking against the bonds. She could feel the worm dig in deeper, but she didn't care; she had to stop him from using the knife on her. That's what the creature was waiting for, an opportunity to pierce the skin.

"Be still!" The command flicked like a whip, and Captain Conlan's hand reached over and held her leg in place. The grip was rough, stronger than she'd have guessed, given how ravaged his body was. The knife descended toward her calf. Hesitated for a second, and then moved in a lightning arc to flick the worm off and to the ground. Captain Conlan followed it down and sliced it neatly into two parts, both of which started wiggling away in opposite directions.

"Cac!"

It wasn't Rhenish, nor was it Standard, but Elsa could tell from the tone that it was a curse. He looked around frantically and came up with a rock, which he used to pound the two halves of the night crawler into shreds. The porous stone disintegrated in his hand, whether because it was weak or because of the violence of his attack, and scattered sand over the remains of the worm.

Elsa watched, shivering, with tears coursing down her cheeks, until he straightened to face her. He was shaking, too, she noticed. For a second, she thought she could see something in his eyes, but it must have been the tears blurring her own, because when she blinked, it was gone.

He wiped the knife blade against his trousers. The worm guts left a smear on the gray fabric. "Guess we'd better get outta here before the rest of the little fuckers show up."

He squatted in front of her and cut the bonds around her ankles before he moved closer and reached around her body to her bound hands, grimacing.

"Did you hurt yourself?" fell out of Elsa's mouth.

He stopped with his arm still extended and looked into her face. He was very close, so close she could see tiny flecks of gold in his eyes. Time hung suspended for a moment as her body noted his proximity and her mind turned back to those few moments earlier, when he'd had her pinned to the ground. The heavy weight of him on top of her, how his body had tightened when she struggled. Her own response to his nearness. The thought of it — and this renewed proximity — had her feeling an unaccustomed warmth low in her stomach, a warmth that was reflected in her cheeks.

He looked away. "No, I didn't hurt myself."

"What happened?" To her shame, her voice wobbled.

His eyes flicked back to hers for a second. "Don't you remember? Some of your friends took turns whipping the skin off my back a little while ago."

Lord, yes. He hadn't hurt himself; *she* had hurt him. She and her fellow Rhenians. "I'm sorry." As he cut the ropes around her wrists, she pulled her arms forward and rubbed them.

The apology made him smile, but it wasn't a nice smile. "I'll just bet you are."

Now, his voice intimated. She was sorry *now*, because she was at his mercy and didn't know whether he'd want to get some of his own back for the way he'd been treated.

Except Elsa did know, or at least thought she did. He'd stripped her naked this morning without taking advantage of her. He'd had the laser pistol pointed at her more than once and hadn't shot her. And he'd slaughtered the night crawler instead of letting it pierce her skin, when he had every reason to want to see her suffer. Allowing the worm to feast for a while wouldn't have killed her; he could have watched her writhe in pain for ten or fifteen minutes, at least, before slicing her leg open and pulling the creature back out. It would be no more than she deserved. She'd done it to him.

But he hadn't. Then, or earlier. His language might have been rough, but he had behaved decently. A lot better than she had the right to expect. A lot better than she had treated him. How could she do less?

"Would you like me to look at it? Your back?"

She could tell she had surprised him. His head tilted. After a moment he asked, "Why? You wanna admire your friends' handiwork?"

"I thought there might be something I could do," Elsa said, declining the bait. "That's why you brought me with you, wasn't it? Because you needed medical attention?"

"Was it?" He tightened the belt around the gray jacket before getting to his feet painfully. "Let's go."

He extended a hand. It must be habit, Elsa thought, more than intent. He had no reason to treat her with courtesy. Nonetheless, she took the hand and let him help her to her feet. They exited the fissure into the waning light of Marica-3 in silence.

CHAPTER SEVEN

Major Lamb gave a perfunctory knock on the lab door before pushing it open and stepping through.

"Stephen." Doctor Sterling looked up from his work, nodding politely. Major Lamb nodded back, distracted by the view.

The prisoner on the table was female. Marican by the looks of her, and not ugly, in spite of the bruises and the shaved head. Small and dark, like they all were, with big eyes and a tight little body. Doctor Sterling had her stripped down in preparation for the session, her wrists and ankles anchored to the four corners of the table, and Major Lamb gave her a thorough visual inspection. Some of the natives really weren't unattractive. Filthy little animals, of course, but good for a distraction when nothing better was available.

"Any sign of them?" Doctor Sterling asked, and Stephen Lamb turned his attention from the prisoner and shook his head.

"Not yet. The patrols have been coming and going all morning, and so far no one has reported seeing anything."

Doctor Sterling clicked his tongue, his hands busy with vials and syringes. "How could he just walk out of here, Stephen? And with my best assistant? Don't you train your guards to be on the alert for things like that?"

Major Lamb could feel himself flush and made a concerted effort to keep his temper. Losing his cool in front of the doctor—and in front of the young Marican prisoner—certainly wouldn't help matters. She seemed to have forgotten some of her fear as she listened to the exchange, and Lamb directed his next statement to her as well as to the doctor. Best not to give anyone any ideas.

"The guard made a mistake. He has paid for it with his life." Even if Lamb himself had been cheated of the pleasure of extracting that payment. "There is nothing more any of us can do about it, other than to put every effort into finding the escaped prisoner and his hostage. It won't be long. There's nowhere for them to hide, and the guards will soon catch up and bring them back here. By tonight, you'll have Captain Conlan back on the table."

"And Doctor Brandeis?" Doctor Sterling said. "You haven't found her body. That's good news, yes?"

Lamb hesitated. The fact that Elsa was out there, in the company of an armed and presumably desperate criminal, was more troubling to him than he wanted the doctor to know. If Sterling realized just how serious Stephen Lamb was about Elsa Brandeis, the doctor might interfere. Not because he wanted her for himself—the old man seemed beyond petty physical emotions such as desire or need; probably couldn't get it up anymore—but because he wanted her brains for the cause. But while her intelligence and her accomplishments certainly made her that much more attractive as a match, Stephen wanted her beauty. Her body. And her hand in marriage.

"I hope and pray that she's still alive," he said finally, "and that we can get to him before he harms her. But Conlan has a weapon and nothing to lose, and when she stops being useful to him, he won't hesitate to kill her. He's a common criminal and a collaborator, and the fact that she is a woman won't mean anything to him."

"Of course." Doctor Sterling squinted at the syringe he was holding up to the light. It was filled with clear liquid. More of the snake venom, most likely. "But for now I can hope that she's still alive and will make it back in one piece."

"Certainly." Major Lamb nodded, watching as Doctor Sterling turned toward the young woman on the table. He pinched a section of her arm and jabbed it with the syringe. The girl's body stiffened as Doctor Sterling depressed the plunger, emptying the venom into her bloodstream.

"Now where's that clipboard?" Doctor Sterling muttered, looking around. "I know Doctor Brandeis keeps it here somewhere…"

It was on a nearby shelf, and Major Lamb handed it over without comment. "Does she know something?" He indicated the girl, who had begun to breathe faster as the snake venom spread through her veins, her skin flushing. Major Lamb smiled appreciatively. No, not unattractive at all.

"Oh, no." Doctor Sterling shook his head. "She's nobody. Just riffraff swept up in the recent protests. No, I'm trying to refine the dose. To see how much someone can tolerate before they break."

"Will it kill her?" It would be a shame if she died before he could avail himself of her, but there were more where she came from. And in the dark, one Marican cunt was very much like another.

Doctor Sterling shook his head. "I'll administer the antidote before it goes that far. Unless she has a heart attack, of course. It happens."

"Naturally." And if so, Lamb would just have to find someone else to take his mind off Elsa and her predicament.

The doctor glanced in his direction. "I think this might be an opportune time to bring one of Captain Conlan's crew back to the lab, don't you?"

Major Lamb's eyes widened. "You plan to tell them the prisoner's escaped? Pardon me, doctor, but is that smart?"

Doctor Sterling smiled serenely, his eyes on the woman panting on the table before him. "I plan to tell them that he has left them here to rot. With any luck, it will cause one of them to switch their allegiance and tell us what we want to know."

Major Lamb nodded pensively. It was his opinion that the others didn't have the information the Rhenians wanted, that only Captain Conlan did. If the others knew anything, one of them would have cracked by now. Each, in his own way, lacked the willpower their captain exhibited. Lamb's own information, independently obtained, told him the same thing. However, it was important to keep Doctor Sterling happy. "Which would you like to start with?"

Doctor Sterling pondered the question, his eyes still on the girl on the table. Her body was starting to bow up, and her breaths were short and shallow. "The big one, I think. If the captain confided in anyone, it would be him."

"Not the boy?"

The young man, the ship's translator, wasn't quite a boy, but he was younger than the others by a few years and still had a sort of innocence Major Lamb would dearly love to see shattered. And he hadn't yet developed the inner strength to withstand much questioning. As opposed to the big brute, Isaac Miller. Major Lamb's face darkened. Trying to break *him* took much too much time and effort, and it left the guards discouraged with the amount of work they had to do to achieve their ends.

"The young man hero-worships Captain Conlan," Doctor Sterling said with a curl of his lip. "He won't believe the prisoner won't be coming back. And the little one, the mechanic, is of no importance, just a laborer. Captain Conlan wouldn't have confided in him. But the big one, he's a mercenary. A hired gun, willing to go to work for the highest bidder. A suggestion that Captain Conlan has left him to his own devices, and that we will reward him for helping us catch the captain and bring him back, might bear fruit."

Major Lamb's lips curved. "I'll bring him right up."

"No hurry," Doctor Sterling said as the girl's body arched off the table. "I'll be busy here for the next little while. When you bring him, she should be ready to go back to her room. If she's still alive, that is."

"Of course." Major Lamb headed for the door just as the girl started screaming.

• • •

Quinn made sure to keep the med tech in front of him as they made their slow way into the rocky canyons. That way he could scuff any footprints she left in the sandy soil. Those pointy heel marks were distinctive, and the guards would be returning at some point.

His decision to keep her in front of him had nothing to do with the fact that his body was still on high alert. Oh, no. Chances were she wouldn't have noticed the bulge beneath his zipper, anyway. Not through several layers of clothing, not to mention the loose and too-long jacket. So it wasn't like he had to make sure she didn't get a good look at him.

His thoughts circled back, like buzzards around a dead horse, to those moments in the fissure. When she'd first bucked against him, lifting her hips to nudge the hard ridge in his pants, he'd thought she'd done it on purpose. Bargaining with the only coin she had.

For a second he'd been tempted.

One look into her eyes had set him straight: she'd been as shocked as he.

She'd been in pain, he'd realized. He had tied her hands behind her, and when he rolled her to the ground and threw himself on top of her, her hands were trapped beneath her, pushed into the ground by their combined weights. She was trying to alleviate the pressure. She couldn't tell him it hurt—he'd gagged her as well—and all she was trying to do was throw him off.

It had certainly worked. He'd removed himself from the temptation…the *situation*, as quickly as possible, but the damage had already been done. He'd seen her reaction and knew she'd recognized the fact that he was turned on. And the shock and dismay in her eyes had made it clear just how unwelcome his arousal was. He thought there might have been a touch of fear, too, at the back of those green eyes. Probably thought he wouldn't be able to control himself. That he'd take advantage of her, and of the fact that she was tied up and couldn't fight him off, like some rutting animal.

Well, screw that. He had no intention of touching her. The fact that his body didn't seem to get the message was entirely incidental and purely physical. He hadn't forced himself on a woman in his life, and he wasn't about to start now. Especially not with this woman, who was nothing like what he usually liked.

And especially not now, while he was still living with Josie's betrayal every second of every day.

"Which way?"

The med tech's soft question drew him out of his thoughts, and he came back to himself and looked around. They stood at the apex of two canyons, one going left, one right. Both looked the same: dry, dusty, narrow, their high walls marked by vertical fissures.

Quinn looked at them both. Six of one, half a dozen of the other as far as he was concerned. He'd keep moving a little longer until he found a more permanent shelter than the one they'd spent the afternoon in—they'd been lucky that the two young guards had been too concerned with derma-lizards to do the thorough inspection they should have—but then he'd stop and regroup. As he'd told her, the farther they walked, the longer the walk back. What he needed now was time, time and peace, to think and plan his next move. And if he could find water and something to eat, that would help, too.

"That one." He pointed right. They trudged forward.

• • •

He looked better, Elsa thought. Still limping, of course. Still pale and scarred and bruised. But he was breathing a little easier in spite of the walking they were doing: more physical activity than he'd done since arriving on Marica-3. And some of the tension had drained from his face after the sleep. He was still keenly aware of his surroundings: any little sound—a rattle of rocks, a slither of a scaly belly over the ground, her foot slipping in the dry soil—brought his head whipping around, the laser pistol already halfway out of its holster. But he seemed more relaxed than this morning. It was as if being outside, breathing real, if thin, air and seeing real, if blazing, hot light, had lifted a metaphorical weight from his chest and made it easier for him to draw a deep breath. He even walked a little taller.

And he didn't seem to notice the fact that he hadn't eaten or drunk anything today. Perhaps the prison rations had inured him to feelings of hunger. He'd certainly lost a lot of weight in the months he'd been on Marica-3. Back before he arrived in the prison colony, she wouldn't have had a hope of keeping up with him on a cross-terrain trek like this one.

Or perhaps he was simply determined not to show any weakness in front of her.

That was silly, if so. She knew better than anyone just how weak he was, because she knew exactly the damage that had been done to his body. Knew that if it hadn't been for sheer stubbornness and will, he wouldn't have made it this far. And weak as he was, he wouldn't be able to go much farther without sustenance of some sort. Nor would she, for that matter. Her stomach was complaining loudly, and her mouth was dry as cotton. But at least she was in perfect health and well fed until today; she wasn't the one who had been living on half-rations for months.

As they continued forward, deeper into the maze of narrow canyons, Elsa began to look around for any sort of animal or plant they might be able to digest without courting imminent death.

• • •

They had walked for a few more hours by the time a high-pitched mechanical whine cut through the silence, softly at first, then louder and closer. Quinn grabbed the med tech by the shoulders and shoved her into the nearest fissure. It was smaller than the one they'd been in earlier, just a narrow crack in the rock with barely enough room for them both to stand, sufficient only if they didn't mind being close. She pushed herself into the unforgiving stone wall, away from him, so obviously she did mind.

Outside, the sound reached earsplitting proportions. A few small rocks trickled down on top of them, disturbed by the vibrations. Peering out, Quinn saw a dark shape streak across the sky—oval, like a giant insect, its six mechanical legs unfolding as it prepared to land.

"Shuttle," the med tech said.

Thank you, Doctor. He might be weak, but he wasn't stupid. "Is this the same shuttle I came here on?"

She nodded.

An eighteen-ton inner-system heavy freighter with a few passenger berths and a lot of cargo space. He'd spent the three-day trip up here chained to a hook in the floor in cargo.

"How long does it stay?" Quinn looked away from those clear, green eyes out to the bright world beyond the fissure, where the shuttle had disappeared behind the nearest rock wall, leaving nothing but a smear of exhaust in its wake. He could still hear the whine in his ears, more softly now, and slower, as the shuttle neared the prison and dropped into landing position, covering the hours they'd just gained in a matter of minutes.

God, what he'd give to be able to fly out of here!

"Just long enough to drop off prisoners and supplies," the med tech said, "and to pick up anything going back down planetside."

"A day?"

"Less. A few hours only. Prisoners are marched off—"

Quinn nodded; he remembered his own first meeting with Marica-3.

"—supplies are unloaded and reloaded. It doesn't take long."

"Who does the loading and unloading? The guards?" If so, a large number of them would be occupied in the same area for a bit of time. Then again, if it was the same area where he wanted to be, that wasn't necessarily a good thing.

"Prisoners," the med tech said. "The ones that are considered strong enough for the task."

He'd been strong enough. Before Doctor Sterling went to work on him.

She must have read his mind, because she added, "Your information was too valuable to allow you to be used that way."

Wonderful. Not that he blamed them. Given the opportunity, he'd have been off this godforsaken chunk of rock in a matter of hours. Flying an eighteen-ton inner-system freighter would have been no problem. Obviously they'd realized it and made sure he wouldn't get the chance. "Does it always come at the same time?"

She shook her head. "Different days and times each week. No set schedule. Up and straight back down. Sometimes there's a stop on Marica-2, but only when the second moon is in this quadrant."

"What goes back to Marica on the shuttle?" Quinn asked.

For a second, he wasn't sure she'd answer. Then she sighed. Guess she'd decided it wouldn't hurt to let him know; he'd never get the chance to use any of the knowledge he was gaining. "Staff, sometimes. The guards rotate out every six months. The ones that don't choose to stay here go back planetside. Sometimes the officers and medical personnel have business off-moon that they have to attend to. And then there are the prisoners."

The prisoners left Marica-3? How?

"The dead prisoners," the med tech clarified.

The back of Quinn's neck prickled, and he arched a brow. "How many prisoners do you kill a week, sweetheart?"

If he put her back up sufficiently, maybe she wouldn't realize where this line of questioning was leading. For being the personal assistant to high and mighty Doctor Sterling, she seemed remarkably free of guile.

Or maybe she just played her part remarkably well, he reminded himself. There had to be something about her that appealed to the doctor. Something other than the fact that she was extremely easy on the eyes.

She flushed. "Not many."

"How many's that? Two? Five? Fifteen?"

"Most of the time none at all. Sometimes one or two. And we don't kill them all. Some die from natural causes. Sometimes they kill one another. Or themselves."

Just as he'd have done if he'd ever had the chance. "So if you woulda just let me stay dead one of those times you killed me, I woulda been off this rock by now?"

Her voice sounded piqued. "You might have been off Marica-3, but you also would have been dead."

"Mighta been better than this." Quinn looked around, at the barren landscape, the endless sky, and the seemingly never-ending rock walls.

"I'll be happy to shoot you right now," the med tech said, in a voice as if she were gritting her teeth. "Just hand over the pistol."

Quinn grinned. So she had a little bit of personality, after all. It just took getting to know her. "Nice of you to offer. But when I'm ready to end it all, I'll do it myself. So what happens when someone dies? Actually dies, I mean?" As opposed to dying and then being brought back to life the way he'd been. Over and over again. "Cryo-freeze?"

That would effectively kibosh the tentative plan that was starting to form in his head. Killing and cryo-freezing his entire crew in order to get them off Marica-3 was a little drastic, even for him. And besides, he needed them alive and awake. He'd be able to fly the shuttle—he'd never flown anything that big on his own before, but he'd make it happen if it would get them all off this hunk of rock—although he'd need a little help hijacking it first. The four of them against the Rhenian guards were bad enough odds; alone, he didn't stand a chance.

The med tech shook her head.

"Incineration?" Even worse. There was no coming back from that. At least you could thaw out someone who was cryo-frozen. But he couldn't create humans from ashes.

Another shake of her head. She hadn't done a sufficiently good job of pinning up her hair after he made her take it down earlier, and between that and the restless hours they'd spent in the fissure, flaxen wisps had escaped the braid and were framing her face. They made her look softer, more like a woman and less like a droid. "The bodies are just sent off-planet the way they are. And handed over to the families."

Egads. Quinn tried not to let the statement affect him, but he felt like he failed. By the time the dead got downside, after three days in the shuttle, they'd be ripe, even with refrigeration. And if they weren't black and oozing by then, the families who received the bodies would no doubt be able to see just exactly what had killed their loved ones. The burns, the injections, the bruises and flayed skin…

Who would have been the lucky recipient of *his* body, had he been allowed to die? He had no family, no one he was close to apart from his crew, and for the first time, he was glad for it. At least no one would receive his bloated, rotting corpse as a gift.

Of course, knowing the Rhenians, they'd stick his head on a spike in the town square in Calvados as a message to anyone who thought of getting involved with the resistance. It'd make a compelling argument, for sure. And would send a fairly demoralizing message to the insurgents, too, while they were at it.

Bastards.

Putting the thought aside, he turned his mind back to more important matters. He was alive, at least for the time being, and while he had his life and freedom, he intended to make the most of it.

"Guess we'll have to find a way to stay out of sight when it comes back."

The med tech didn't answer.

"C'mon. You said it'll be a couple hours before it's ready to take off again. We'd better make tracks."

"I'm thirsty," the med tech said petulantly.

She wasn't the only one. Quinn's mouth was so dry, he had a hard time talking. It was time to find something to drink somewhere. Maybe they'd run across some kind of succulent plant he could slice open for the liquid it hoarded. Something like the prickly desert plants back on Old Earth, the ones that conserved liquid inside their trunks because it never rained where they grew.

He'd also heard that there were underground rivers on Marica-3. Rivers that fed into the prison colony, where they needed water for drinking and washing. Although the Marican water snake lived in those rivers, or so he'd been told. But if the water was free of snakes, and free of venom, maybe it'd be safe to drink. And whether they died from dehydration or from drinking poisoned water came to much the same thing in the end, didn't it?

Trudging forward into the darkness creeping across the horizon, he kept a sharp look out for any plants that looked like they might contain liquid and any hints of vegetation that might indicate groundwater.

CHAPTER EIGHT

Isaac Miller was just as combative as Major Lamb had expected, and having expected it, Lamb had armed himself with two of the guards for the trip into the cell block. Between the three of them, they took great pleasure in subduing the prisoner and in walking him, bruised and bleeding, through the corridors up to Doctor Sterling's lab. Any other prisoners they encountered took one look at Miller's countenance and, wincing, reconsidered any ideas they might have had of resisting the next time someone came to fetch them.

The young Marican woman was dressed by the time Stephen Lamb pushed open the door to the lab and maneuvered Isaac Miller through.

"You." He turned to one of the guards. The young man immediately stood up straighter.

"Sir."

"Take this woman back to her accommodations. And do not touch her. Or I will personally whip every inch of skin off your back. Do I make myself clear?"

"Sir!"

Major Lamb nodded. "Dismissed."

He watched as the young man approached the woman and ushered her toward the door. Without touching her.

"I'll see you later, my dear," Major Lamb called after her and had the pleasure of seeing a flash of trepidation in her eyes when she looked at him.

As the door closed behind her, he caught Isaac Miller's eye. "Pretty thing, isn't she?"

"I've seen prettier," the big man said with a shrug of those massive shoulders. He licked away the bead of blood that had appeared on his lip from speaking and didn't say any more.

"Of course you have." Stephen Lamb smiled. "What was her name? Josette, wasn't it?"

There was a flash of something in Miller's eyes, but his voice was even. "I never had nothing to do with Josie. She belonged to Quinn."

"To Captain Conlan?"

Miller inclined his head.

"And the captain didn't share?"

There was a sound that might have been laughter, and Miller licked away another bead of blood. "You ain't figured that out yet?" He shook his head. "Listen, friend. If I knew the information you're looking for, I'd give it to you. I didn't sign on for this."

Major Lamb was almost certain he heard a trace of resentment in the big man's voice. Just to be sure, he asked, "If you knew the information about the Marican resistance, you would give it to us?"

"Sure," Miller said. "I ain't Marican. Why'd I care what happens to 'em?"

No reason Major Lamb could think of.

"If you don't care about the Maricans," Doctor Sterling said, "why did you agree to ferry a shipload of weapons to their aid?"

Miller turned to him, and there was a slight pause before the big man spoke. "We went where the money was good, doctor. Don't make no never mind to me who wants what, so long as they're willing to pay."

"You like money?"

"You know someone who don't?"

Major Lamb was of the belief that duty was more important than recompense, but he supposed he shouldn't expect any better from a gun for hire, a mercenary with no allegiance and no code of honor.

"You seem like a reasonable man, Mr. Miller," Doctor Sterling said, peering myopically up through round glasses. The doctor was a tall man, taller than Major Lamb himself, but he looked puny next to the muscular prisoner. "I wonder if we might be able to work something out."

The big man tilted his head and contemplated the doctor in silence for a second. "What kind of something?"

"Well," Doctor Sterling said, "Captain Conlan left us yesterday."

There was a pause, while Major Lamb watched Isaac Miller closely for any sign of shock or excitement. Or worry. There was none. The man's broad, brown face retained the same lack of expression, and his voice was level. "Dead?"

"Oh, no." Doctor Sterling shook his head. "He killed a guard, took a hostage, and broke out of the complex."

Miller's eyebrows rose, and after a second the big man grinned. "Too bad."

The temptation to knock the irreverent expression off Miller's face was almost irresistible, but Major Lamb restrained himself.

"He won't get far. We have guards out looking for him. However, someone who knows him and knows his habits might be able to point us in the right direction. And at the same time make things a little easier for themselves."

He waited to see whether Miller would take the bait. Of course they had no intention of actually letting him go, but it wouldn't do to reveal that. And he doubted Miller would think of it. These inferior races never seemed able to comprehend the finer points.

"Sure," the prisoner said.

Doctor Sterling blinked, and even Major Lamb was aware of a sensation of surprise. Wasn't Miller even going to pretend to think about it?

The mercenary turned to him, and Major Lamb found himself looking into a pair of eyes, flat and void of expression. "Not like I owe him, is there? I told you, I didn't sign on for this. Why should he be allowed to walk outta here while the rest of us are stuck in this hellhole?"

There was no arguing with that, but it seemed Doctor Sterling still felt compelled to try. "Don't you think he'll come back for you?"

There was another noise, but this one wasn't laughter.

"You crazy?" Miller said. "He don't care about us. He coulda told you what you wanted to know any time since we got here, and he didn't. That sound like he cares to you?"

Perhaps Captain Conlan had recognized the fact that telling the Rhenians anything wouldn't get his crew off Marica-3. But if Isaac Miller was too stupid to realize it, then Major Lamb certainly wasn't the person to point it out. "Have a seat, Mr. Miller," he said instead.

Isaac Miller surveyed the lab, and chose to remain standing. "What d'you want from me?"

"Why don't we start with a little background," Doctor Sterling said, making himself comfortable with his clipboard on his lap. "How long did you travel with Captain Conlan?"

Isaac Miller focused his attention on the doctor. "Year or two. Give or take."

"That's enough time to get to know someone quite well."

Miller shrugged. "Guess I know him as well as anyone. As well as he lets anyone know him, anyway."

Major Lamb nodded. This coincided with his own impressions. Captain Conlan was someone who understood the concept of command. He kept the crew of his ship at a distance. Except the woman, but she didn't count. Major Lamb already knew Quinn Conlan hadn't confided in her; she'd been a convenience, there to attend to his needs, but nothing more. No, Conlan didn't share important information with anyone, even his most trusted lieutenant. It was how Lamb handled his own business. It made things simpler. If he gave an order and it wasn't obeyed…well, then there were no messy personal connections to worry about as he dealt the appropriate punishment.

"So it's your opinion he won't come back to try to free the rest of you."

"Would you?" Miller said.

Stephen Lamb certainly wouldn't. Nor would Doctor Sterling, it seemed, because the doctor saw no need to argue the point. "What will he do?" he asked instead.

Miller didn't hesitate. "Get as far away as he can as fast as he can. And stay there."

"And Doctor Brandeis?"

"'Scuse me?"

"He killed a guard," Major Lamb said again, "and took a hostage."

Miller shook his head. "SOB don't stand a chance. Probably dead already."

"It's a female doctor."

Miller's eyebrows arched.

"Does that make a difference?" Major Lamb asked.

Miller contemplated him in silence for a moment. "You oughta have figured him out by now. You think he'd kill a woman?"

"What will happen to her?" Doctor Sterling asked, a faint wrinkle between his brows.

Miller turned to him. "Knowing the captain, she'll be leading him around by the nose in no time. Right back here, belike. What's she look like?"

Major Lamb looked at Doctor Sterling. "Very attractive," the doctor said. Lamb nodded.

Miller shook his head. "He don't stand a chance. Fool's fair game for any decent piece of ass that comes along. Just look at what happened with Josie."

"Do you think she'll find a way to lead him back here?" Doctor Sterling seemed satisfied to disregard, for the moment, the prisoner's description of his most valued research assistant as a decent piece of ass. The derogatory address made Major Lamb bristle, but he resisted the temptation to teach Miller some manners. And the man did have a point. Just look at what had happened with Josie.

"She's one of you, right?" Miller's dark eyes moved from one to the other of them. "And she's a doctor. So she's gotta be smart. She's probably got a plan. Unless she's just gonna let him do what he wants to her 'cause she thinks he'll hurt her if she don't. Depends on what she's like, I guess."

Doctor Sterling glanced at Major Lamb. "She's committed to the cause."

Lamb nodded. Elsa Brandeis was beautiful, intelligent, educated, and aloof, and she had ice water flowing through her veins. Captain Conlan would get nowhere with her.

"Well, then," Isaac Miller said and spread his hands as far as they'd go. It wasn't far. The chains holding his wrists together clanked as they moved. Major Lamb assessed him for a moment. Aside from the damage the guards had just inflicted in transporting him to the lab, he looked strong and fairly healthy. Unlike some of the prisoners, he hadn't wasted away in the time he'd spent on Marica-3. And if they didn't have to worry about him turning, he might be useful to them.

Lamb made a decision.

"Why don't you come with me, Mr. Miller? I can hear the shuttle arriving. We could use someone of your stature for the unloading."

"Happy to help," Miller said as he shuffled toward the door, as if Major Lamb had offered him a good time instead of hard work. Lamb shared a look with Doctor Sterling behind Miller's back, as he reflected that these inferior races were so pathetically easy to manipulate.

· · ·

The day had almost passed by the time they found water, and by then they were both at the ends of their respective ropes. Quinn's bad leg had once again endured all the motion it could stand without buckling, and the med tech was probably not used to this level of activity, especially on an empty stomach, because her movements were becoming slow and lethargic.

The shuttle had left Marica-3 again. They had stood pressed up against the rock wall in a narrow canyon watching it streak across the sky, folding its legs as it went. Quinn had been aware of a sense of mingled anger and hopelessness as he watched it disappear out of sight. It wouldn't be back for days, and by then, any manner of things could change. For him to remain free that long would require something akin to a miracle, and he'd stopped believing in those awhile back. He'd stopped believing in anything at all, if it came to that.

He thought they might have to stop for the night without any water, when a patch of green caught his eye. It was a pale and dusty green, dull and unexciting, but after the desolation of the unrelieved dirt, it gleamed like a beacon.

Grabbing the med tech by the arm, he turned her in the direction of the plants and gave her a push. She stumbled forward.

Like anything else on Marica-3, the vegetation was farther away than it looked. It took them, he thought, the better part of an hour to get there. But when they did, the plant did turn out to be succulent and yielded enough liquid for them both to quench their thirst. Quinn would have been happy to have more, and so he assumed would the med tech, but one plant was all there was: something a little like an Old Earth aloe plant, with spikes and a whitish liquid inside.

It wasn't until after he'd cut every part of the plant off at ground level and drained its spiky leaves that Quinn realized he'd left any guards who happened by a clear indicator that they'd been here. It was almost as good as scratching his initials in the crumbling rock wall. *Quinn Conlan was here. Med tech…*

"What's your name?"

The question took both him and the med tech by surprise, and she froze with a pale green stalk held to her lips, matching green eyes peering at him over it. Then she lowered her hand, and he watched as the tip of her tongue darted out to lick the last of the liquid from her lips before she spoke. "I'm Doctor Brandeis."

"Your first name's Doctor?"

A hint of color came up to stain her cheeks, and she shook her head. "Of course not. My first name is Elsa."

Quinn nodded. He had no idea why he'd asked, beyond thoughtlessness, and he couldn't come up with anything to say. So he began gathering the stalks of plant together instead and looked around for somewhere to put them. The best thing might be to bury them in the sand. That way, if a patrol happened by, they might not notice that someone had been here.

While he crouched to suit action to words—his bad leg complaining loudly—the med tech wandered off. He could hear the scuffing of her footsteps in the dirt, so he knew she hadn't gone far, and when he glanced over his shoulder, he could see her, a few yards away, staring into the gathering darkness.

"You see something?"

She glanced at him but didn't answer.

Quinn went back to burying the remains. When the stalks and roots were invisible, covered over with dirt, he got up and stomped the hard-packed ground with his foot for good measure. Through it all, the med tech stood frozen in the same place, like the statue he'd compared her to. The setting sun gilded her hair and gave that alabaster complexion a hint of color.

"Something there?"

She shook her head and put a finger to her lips. Arching his brows, Quinn limped over and stood behind her, peering over her shoulder in the same direction. Close enough that he caught a whiff of some floral scent from her skin or hair. He ignored it, focusing instead on the patch of geography she was watching. There was nothing there that he could see. Just dirt and more dirt.

He glanced sideways at her and got another noseful of flower scent. "What?"

"Shhh."

Okay, then. It wasn't something she'd seen but something she'd heard.

He conquered his first instinct, which was to grab her and push her into a mad dash to safety. She'd let him see that she was listening; that must mean what she'd heard wasn't the guards. If they were coming, she wouldn't have let on but would have waited for them to descend like the wrath of God. Quinn sharpened his ears and listened for the telltale rattle of loose pebbles or the slither of a scaly body nearby.

He heard nothing. Just the wind rustling the dirt and an underlying lower-pitched sound, like a rumble or low roar.

Another shuttle? Or some other kind of craft?

Not a lightflyer, their engines were smaller and the pitch higher. Same for a hopper. And it wasn't a groundcar. Nobody would drive a groundcar in this environment.

Neck prickling, he focused on the roar. It wasn't changing in volume. So whatever was making it wasn't coming closer or for that matter moving away. The sound stayed at the same level: a dull sort of rumble. If he didn't know better —

"I hear water," the med tech announced.

Quinn nodded. He heard it, too. Unless his ears were playing tricks on him.

"This way." She wandered off. Brows arched, Quinn limped a few steps behind, hand on the handle of the laser pistol just in case she was planning something.

Behind him, Marica's sun was beginning to set. Letting the med tech walk ahead, he slowed his steps to watch the sunset, his first in months.

Okay, yeah, and maybe she was walking too fast to keep up with, and he didn't want her to see how painful each step was for him. It had been a long day, with more activity than he'd had in months. If he was honest, he was surprised he was still moving.

The sunset didn't take long. Less than a minute from the moment the lower rim of the sun hit the horizon, causing molten gold to bleed into the sand and dirt of the landscape, staining the ground red, until the entire flaming globe had sunk out of sight. At first, the sky was brilliant orange and red, darkening to blue and purple, like a candle flame. But by the time the sun was gone, purple had faded to black, and stars were appearing above him. When he turned on his heel, Marica-2, the second moon, was just beginning to peep over the horizon, an enormous disc in pale pink, almost as big as Marica itself.

And the med tech was gone.

Damn.

CHAPTER NINE

"Doctor!"

Quinn looked around, telling himself not to panic while feeling panic creep into his voice nonetheless. Where the hell could she be? He'd only looked away for a minute; it shouldn't have been enough time for her to vanish from sight.

Dammit, didn't she know how dangerous Marica-3 was?

Bad enough when they could see where they were going and what they were doing, but in the dark, anything could sneak up on them. And he wasn't thinking of the guards. Unless he was asleep, he'd hear them coming, and if they had any sense, they'd be safely tucked away inside the prison by now, avoiding the chance of an encounter with any of the small but deadly Marican critters that prowled the night. Spiders, scorpions, snakes. Not to mention those damned worms.

For a second his mind flicked back to the scene in the fissure that afternoon, when the med tech woke him from dead sleep for the second time. At first he'd thought the guards were back, that she'd been trying to catch their attention again. He'd gone for the pistol without thinking.

And then the terror in her eyes had hit him like a punch in the gut. And the tears.

He'd always been a sucker for a woman with tears in her eyes. Dammit.

Not that she hadn't had reason for the fear. When he'd seen the night crawler, he'd felt bile rise in his own throat.

Thank God it had been alone. He tried to imagine wading through a writhing tangle of the little fuckers—dozens, maybe hundreds of them—to get to her and shuddered, not sure he could have done it.

It had been attracted by the dried blood on her arm, he supposed. The damn things had the noses of bloodhounds. Good thing he'd gotten rid of the lab coat. The sleeve had been soaked in it; with that much blood, there might have been more of them.

Come to think of it, maybe he'd be better off ditching the uniform, too. Plenty of blood on that. And with the heat on this godforsaken hunk of rock, he'd be more comfortable in just the jumpsuit, anyway. Maybe there was some way she could wash her arm before they bedded down for the night, to get rid of the dried blood.

If he could find her again, that was. If she wasn't running headlong toward the prison as fast as she could go.

"Doc!"

Christ, after this afternoon, could he even blame her? The fear in her eyes when he'd pulled out the knife had slapped at something deep inside him. He knew he'd scared her earlier—had done his best to scare her, to tell the truth—but had she really thought he was about to cut her open?

"Captain?"

Her voice came out of the darkness, much calmer than his had been. Relief he didn't want to examine too closely flooded his body as he turned in the direction of the sound. "Where the hell are you?"

"Just on the other side of the rocks."

Which rocks? There was nothing but rocks anywhere he looked. "Keep talking."

Her disembodied voice floated back to him. "What do you want me to say?"

"I don't care what you say. Just keep making noise."

Quinn shuffled in the direction of her voice, the reinforced toes of the guard's boots kicking at rocks and clumps of earth along the stony ground. After a few yards he saw the rest of her, that pale hair gleaming with lavender-pink highlights from the second moon.

He came out into something like a valley, dry and dusty as everything else around them. The mountains were still off in the distance. A little closer now than this morning but still farther away than they looked. Between him and them were more foothills and this valley.

"There." The med tech pointed.

"What?" Nothing there that Quinn could see. Just more dirt and rocks.

She glanced at him. "That's where the sound's coming from."

The sound. The water. Quinn focused his ears. The roar was a little closer now. And he could feel a sort of vibration in the ground under his feet.

He glanced at her. "What do you know about the underground rivers, Doc?"

"Not much," she admitted, following as he made his slow way into the valley. "I read up on the topography of Marica-3 when I was assigned here last year. And the fauna. But…"

"But?" He shot her a look over his shoulder.

She shrugged. "There isn't much known about Marica-3."

"Didn't you people do a survey before you decided to snatch and grab a whole planetary system?"

It was too dark to see, but Quinn would have bet good money she was blushing. Her voice was stiff, and so was her posture. "Of course. But the military surveys aren't available to civilians."

And they probably dealt more with military tactics and layout, anyway. Although the Rhenians weren't stupid, even if they were idiots. They'd been traveling the nexus for centuries by now. They would have built their prison in the best possible place for it. And that included easy access to water. With more than a hundred thousand people inside the walls, they'd go through a lot of it on a daily basis. Chances were, somewhere in the sub-basement, in a part of it he hadn't seen on his way through this morning, there was access to one of the underground rivers.

If he could figure out where and how, it might get him back into the prison. And back out again, with the rest of his crew.

"One of 'em runs underneath the prison complex, right?" The question was, which one? Not like they were marked, so how would he find it?

The med tech shot him another look, this one full of suspicion.

Quinn shook his head, exasperated. "It ain't five space math, sweetheart. You don't smell too bad, so I gotta figure you've had a bath in the year you've been here. The water had to come from somewhere. I doubt it came in on the shuttle."

If it came to that, he'd been hosed down a couple times himself. They'd shaved his head and pushed him into a makeshift sort of shower, and he'd stood there, shivering, while ice-cold water cascaded over his head. The only good thing about it had been the rinsing away of dirt and blood and other things. Then they'd given him a towel the size of a handkerchief to dry himself with before tossing him back into his cell, chilled to the bone.

'Course, for the med tech, they would have heated the water first.

For a second, his mind slipped sideways again as he tried to imagine her lounging in a tub with bubbles up to her neck, the steam turning her skin pink and curling her hair…but he couldn't. The tight-assed Dr. Brandeis had probably taken her showers the way he had, standing straight up while ice-cold water soaked her skin and plastered her hair to her head and tightened those pink nipples—

Cac!

Shaking his head to dislodge the image, he wrenched himself out of the fantasy. What the hell was wrong with him? Bad enough that he was remembering making love to Josie, after what she'd done, but naked fantasies about the ice bitch? He must have lost what little was left of his mind.

"Yes," she said stiffly. Back in the present, he tried to remember what question she was responding to. She continued, "One of the rivers runs underneath the prison complex. There's a pump in the sub-basement. Why do you ask?"

"No reason." He gave her an easy grin. "Just interested, is all."

"Of course." Her tone made it clear she didn't believe him, but she was too uptight to actually say so. "Are you ready to go on?"

He supposed he ought to be. But the truth was, every time he stopped it was harder to get going again. As long as he was moving, he'd keep moving, but once he stopped and that damned leg stiffened up, it took twice as much effort to get himself back into motion.

Then again, they couldn't stay here. Not out in the open on the floor of this valley. They had to find a place to spend the night. When the sun was too warm in the middle of the day, they'd had to take a break so they wouldn't fry to a crisp, but now that the sun had set, it was quickly becoming too cool for comfort. He'd thought that maybe they'd keep moving through the night, when there was less chance that the guards would find them, but as the warmth from the sun faded and the air turned colder, it was quickly becoming evident that they'd freeze to death out here. Not to mention that in the dark, they could run into God only knew what—or who—much too late to avoid it. Or them. The Rhenian guards probably had night vision equipment. Maybe they weren't back at the prison, asleep.

No, the two of them had to find somewhere to spend the night until the sun rose and they could see what they were doing again.

"After you."

Her lips tightened—maybe she thought he'd be watching her ass if she was ahead of him—but she just gave a tiny shake of her head and walked off. Quinn gathered what he had of resolve and kicked himself into gear. Leg complaining loudly with each step, he set off down the canyon floor, his eyes on the back of the woman in front of him.

· · ·

As the door hissed shut, Major Lamb stopped for a moment to adjust his uniform. He enjoyed a certain reputation among the guards, who admired his prowess and success with the opposite sex, but it wouldn't do to look disheveled.

All in all, his visit to the cell had been a fairly pleasurable interlude. The young Marican woman hadn't been as spirited as he liked, but maybe she'd been worn out from the session with Doctor

Sterling earlier. Perhaps if he gave her a day to recover, she'd afford him more amusement tomorrow. Conquests were a lot more satisfying when he had to work for them, after all, and bending this one to his will had been all too easy. She'd hardly put up a fight at all. In fact, she'd seemed almost too willing to be accommodating.

Feeling marginally cheated by that, he looked around. The hallway appeared just as it had when he arrived an hour ago: white and empty, the doors blending so well into the walls it was hard to see where one ended and the other began. No guards anywhere that he could take out his dissatisfaction on.

Perhaps he'd make a visit to the young translator from Captain Conlan's ship on his way back to his quarters. That might make him feel better.

Doctor Sterling had seemed satisfied after his conversation with Isaac Miller this afternoon, as if the mercenary's opinion that Dr. Brandeis would return with the prisoner in tow was all the doctor had been waiting for. He was busy preparing for Captain Conlan's return, refining his doses of venom and coming up with new and more efficient methods of extracting information.

Major Lamb wasn't as sanguine.

Oh, he shared the doctor's high opinion of Elsa Brandeis. She was brilliant, beautiful, and totally committed to the cause. Now *there* was a woman worthy of conquering—and he would, he promised himself. He had made a few strides in his suit since she first arrived on Marica-3, but Doctor Sterling kept her so busy in the lab, monopolizing most of her time, that it had been difficult to make any real progress. If she wasn't careful, she'd turn into a female version of the famous doctor: old, shriveled, and alone, all that beauty and breeding wasted.

In any case, he agreed that Captain Conlan hadn't a hope of

subverting her. But while Lamb tended to accept Isaac Miller's description of the captain as pussy-whipped, he also knew the other man couldn't possibly be led entirely by his dick. Conlan had run a successful smuggling operation for years, and that took discipline. The weapons run to Marica hadn't been his first; the Rhenians just hadn't caught up with him before.

Until Major Lamb had taken a personal interest. He permitted himself a small congratulatory smile as he contemplated his brilliance in targeting the weak link in the captain's chain of command.

Just as he was about to do now.

Yes, a talk with the young translator might be just the thing he needed to make himself feel better.

Stephen Lamb set off down the corridor, a spring in his step.

• • •

Elsa wondered how much longer Captain Conlan would be able to keep going. She'd thought he'd been near the end of his rope in the middle of the day, when they'd stumbled into the fissure and he'd dropped off to sleep between one heartbeat and the next. Now it was eight or nine hours later, and he was still moving. One agonizingly slow step at a time, true, but moving. Each time he put his weight on the weak leg, she saw him hesitate, and she held her breath, too, while she waited to see if this would be the step that felled him. So far the leg had held, and he'd kept upright, but she couldn't help but wonder how much longer that would last. Sooner or later the leg wouldn't be able to support him anymore, and then what would they do?

Would he accept her help if he had no other choice?

Or would he be stubborn and sit in the same place until he either froze to death or had rested enough to be able to get up and get going again under his own steam?

He was infinitely stubborn, she knew that. He was more than capable of refusing help even when he needed it.

Perhaps she ought to nip the argument in the bud before it started. Take his arm now and insist that he lean on her. After all, he was slowing both of them down, not just himself. If he'd been faster, they might have reached the water source by now.

They were getting closer. She could tell. The roar in her ears was louder and the vibrations in the ground stronger. Yet there was no visible evidence of water. And they'd been walking for at least an hour. The distances in this horrible place were so much greater than she'd anticipated.

She'd only ventured outside the prison once before in the whole time that she'd been on Marica-3. And that had been on the opposite side of the complex, where the main gate and landing pad were. Major Lamb had invited her for a ride in his lightflyer a month or two ago. They'd driven for a few minutes, not far enough to lose sight of the prison, but enough that the sounds of it faded, and had sat in the lightflyer to watch the sun go down.

There'd been no indication of water on that side of the prison. She hadn't heard the roar or noticed the ground trembling the way it was now.

Then again, Major Lamb hadn't taken her very far. Since this morning, she and Captain Conlan had covered kilometer upon kilometer of dusty terrain, to where they could no longer see the prison in the distance. They were farther into Marica-3 than she'd ever been before.

And they'd die out here if they couldn't find water. The vegetation Captain Conlan had found earlier had helped for a few minutes, but not enough. And besides, she was a little concerned about just how good it had been for them. The prisoner had explained that it was a succulent plant, like the ones he'd seen on Old Earth, which hoarded water in their leaves, and she'd taken his word for it, but she hoped they wouldn't be paying for it later.

All along they'd passed tiny skulls and bones, bleached by the hot sun, of animals that had breathed their last out here in the unforgiving desolation. She hadn't wanted to end up like them, so she'd drunk from the plant. But in order to survive, they'd need water. Real water. And come tomorrow, they'd also need food. One day without sustenance was one thing; another would make them so weak they'd have to stop walking. And after that, there was nothing for them to do but to give up.

Would Captain Conlan consider going back to the prison if it came down to a choice between that and starvation?

Not likely, she thought. But he might be willing to let her go. And then he'd probably kill himself rather than running the risk of being recaptured by the guards.

Perhaps there was some way she could get the pistol away from him—

On her next step, the ground gave a little when she put her foot down, shaking her out of her reverie and bringing her to an abrupt halt. Captain Conlan must not have been paying attention, because he walked into her, knocking her forward with his momentum. For a second they teetered, as the movement upset his equilibrium and caused his bad leg to give way. His arm came around her waist to help keep himself—or maybe her—upright. The strength of it, and the feel of his hard body pressed up against hers, caused an instinctive recoil.

Stiffening, Elsa pushed his arm away and stumbled forward, her only thought to put some distance between them. One step, then two. On three, just as she turned to face him, the ground gave, this time all the way. A scream ripped from her throat as she dropped into nothingness, amidst a cascade of dirt and soil. The last thing she was aware of before going into freefall, was the shock on Captain Conlan's face.

· · ·

"Shit!"

Quinn flung himself flat, reaching out. The med tech scrabbled wildly for the edge of the hole, for something solid to hang on to. For a second he grasped blindly at the air before snagging one of her wrists. "Gotcha."

Locking both hands around it he held on, grimly.

But stopping her descent was just the beginning; dragging her up to the surface again was something else. He wasn't as strong as he used to be, and the scars on his back and shoulders protested the rough use. She wasn't heavy, but he didn't weigh as much as he did before, and the combined weight of her body and the natural pull of gravity dragged him forward along the rocky ground, causing stones and pebbles to scrape painfully against his stomach and thighs. Good thing he hadn't taken off the uniform yet. The thick wool afforded him a bit of protection from the sharp ground that otherwise might have cut his skin to ribbons.

The med tech's other hand fumbled for his arm and latched on, slender fingers wrapping around his wrist. The sound of the water was much louder now, roaring from the hole in the ground. Over the deafening sound he could make out her voice, shrill with terror. "Don't let go!"

Not if he could help it.

But holding on was easier said than done. Fighting against the pull of her weight, he squirmed back, froglike, trying to drag her up on solid ground. It didn't work. Not only couldn't he lift her, but the maneuver ate away at the edge of the hole. The rim was corroding, sending loose rocks and dirt raining down on top of her. He felt it hitting his hands and knew it had to be striking her. He could hear her coughing, and then her hand slipped off his arm again, so the only thing holding her up was his death grip around her wrist.

He set his teeth. "Hang on, dammit!"

"Can't…" She coughed again, the vibrations making it that much harder to maintain his grip, "…can't help it!"

"Yes, you can! You wanna fall?"

She didn't, because she tried to reach for his arm again, to help him help her. Her hand found his, but as more rocks and dirt parted from the edge and trickled down on her head, another coughing fit racked her body and her arm dropped back down.

"Cac!"

There shouldn't have been enough moisture in his body for actual sweat, not with the perspiration he'd given up that day, but Quinn felt her hand slipping through his grip. He tightened his hold to the point of feeling her bones grind together as the rim of the hole crumbled under his chest.

He held on all the way down, with her terrified scream ringing in his ears as they both dropped into stygian blackness.

He held on as they hit the underground river with a splash.

He even held on as the water closed over his head and the mind-numbing cold drove every ounce of breath out of his lungs and every coherent thought out of his head.

As he clawed his way to the surface with one hand, gasping from cold and lack of breath, her wrist was still clutched in the other, and when the current grabbed them both, tossing and turning them like twigs in the rapids, carrying them downstream at breakneck speed, he did the only thing he could, and kept a tight grip on the one solid thing in the world.

CHAPTER TEN

The current was swift and vicious, and the water cold enough to numb his fingers and toes in a matter of seconds. Quinn's wool uniform became unmanageably heavy, and the tall boots quickly filled with water, threatening to drag him down below the surface. Fumbling with one hand and the other foot, he managed to get one boot off and felt it being yanked away by the current.

The other was trickier. Maybe it fit differently, or maybe he just couldn't get a good grip on it. Maybe it was the leg itself that didn't respond right. Maybe it really was brittle from those damned worms, and it actually soaked up the water, swelling. At this point, he'd consider any explanation. Whatever the reason, the boot wouldn't come off. Twisting and turning in the rapids, tossing from side to side, grabbing breaths of air whenever he could, he scrambled to kick the boot off while maintaining his grip on the med tech.

He had no idea how she was. She wasn't screaming anymore or trying to communicate with him, and there was too much movement in the water itself for him to be able to determine whether she was trying to fight the current. Was she conscious? Was she even alive?

At the moment, they were both just borne along by the river. It was pitch black around them, and he had no idea how wide the river was or what the edges of the water looked like. Were they in a smooth tunnel, a sort of natural pipe through the ground, or were there rocks sticking out into the stream? Maybe places he'd be able to latch on and drag them both out? Paths, even?

The second boot came off finally and was sucked away, and the pull of the water decreased marginally. Making sure to maintain his viselike grip on the med tech's arm, he struck out for the left, towing her behind him. He had no idea which side of the river was closer, but he had to choose one, and his left hand was free while his right was holding on to her. It seemed the logical choice.

Fighting the current was also easier said than done, and it took much longer than he wanted it to take before his hand slapped against something hard. It hurt, even through the numbness from the ice cold water. *Go ahead, genius, break a couple fingers while you're at it; that'll really help!*

When it happened again, he tried to hold on, digging his nails into the porous surface of whatever he'd gotten hold of, but his fingers wouldn't respond. Another rock slipped out of his grasp, and he was borne another few yards down the tunnel. It was damned hard work just keeping his head above water, and the med tech was no help at all. For all he knew, she was dead, and he was wasting his time and resources trying to save a corpse. Maybe he oughta just let her go, and concentrate on saving himself.

Up ahead, he caught a glimpse of light. As he passed directly under it—another rip in the ground, like the one they'd fallen through—streaks of pinkish moonlight from Marica-2 illuminated his surroundings for just long enough to give him an impression of the space he was in. The ceiling curved high over him, wet with spray from the rapids, and huge rocks stuck out into the water on either side. They were lucky they hadn't bashed their brains out on one of them. His heart jumped as he realized another one was coming closer, impossibly fast.

Determined, he stretched for it. The impact of flesh against stone felt like it would tear his arm right out of the socket, but he hung on grimly, his whole arm wrapped around the rock this time. The current yanked at him, threatening to rip the med tech out of his grasp, and he had to fight to keep his hold on her while at the same time scrabbling to find purchase on the slippery stones.

The struggle for ground seemed to go on forever. Minutes, hours. Eons. He'd gain a couple centimeters, only to slip back when the water dragged at the med tech, as if deliberately trying to tear her away from him. The rocks were slimy under his hands, covered with lichen or seaweed or something else slippery and oily. But eventually he managed to drag himself up onto semi-dry ground beside the river, a rocky sort of ledge. With water streaming from his clothes, he turned and yanked at the med tech.

"C'mon, sweetheart. Help me out here."

There was no response, and also no movement from the limp body he towed. Reaching out, he wrapped a fist in the fabric of her dress and hauled with what little strength he had left. It wasn't much, but enough to drag her halfway out of the water.

She didn't move when he dropped her on the rocks, did nothing to help herself or him, and the water still tugged at her legs, as if trying to recapture its lost quarry. After a moment spent facedown, panting, Quinn got his hands under her arms and hauled.

Christ, for a skinny woman, she sure weighed a lot.

Dead weight, the back of his mind supplied.

"Shut up." He got her out of the river and onto the ledge.

Ignoring the water that streamed from his clothes and hers, he fumbled for her heart, not even pausing when his questing hand brushed across a hard nipple.

There.

Marking the shallow valley between her breasts, he leaned down and pressed his ear to it, against the sopping wet, cold fabric of the ugly dress.

Nothing.

Dammit!

Sitting back on his heels, he ran a cold, wet hand over the top of his equally cold, wet head, feeling razor stubble in place of the hair he used to have. Now what the hell was he supposed to do?

Old, half-forgotten knowledge bubbled up from the murky depths of his memory. Push on her chest, right? Massage her heart or something, to try to get it to start? And breathe air into her lungs?

Lips twisting, he got to his knees, the strain and narrow escape combining into a snort of slightly manic laughter. Here he was, really needing a med tech for the first time since they'd left the prison this morning, and his med tech was the one who needed the help.

And who the hell was he to help her? It'd been years since he'd even thought about needing to keep someone alive, and longer than that since he'd had to. For the most part, the *Good Fortune*'s runs had been business as usual, at least until he took on the Marican resistance. And Josie.

First things first. Ignoring the button closure of the soaking-wet dress, he grabbed the edges of the fabric and pulled. The dress ripped down the middle, and he spread the edges apart. There was no need to remove the top she had on underneath; the synthetic fabric was too thin to be a hindrance to anything he tried to do.

As he put his hands together in the middle of her chest, one on top of the other directly between those small breasts, it occurred to him to wonder why he was taking the trouble to try to revive her. He didn't owe her anything. Now she was out of his hair—what he had left of it—and he didn't have her death on his conscience. He hadn't killed her. Hell, he'd done his best to stop her from going into the water, and he'd kept a tight hold on her the whole way down the rapids. He was the one who'd hauled her out. So maybe he should just leave well enough alone and let her stay dead, the way he'd wanted her to do to him.

Even as the thoughts chased one another through his head, he was thrusting against her breastbone, counting in his head while trying to remember how many times he was supposed to push before breathing into her mouth.

Or—*shit!*—was he supposed to do that first?

Moving from her chest up to her head, he fumbled for her nose. Finding it by touch, he pinched it shut and fitted his mouth over hers. Her lips were cold and slack, and the parody of a kiss was even more uncomfortable than that joke of a striptease he'd made her go through earlier.

Christ, he'd been a bastard.

Yeah, he'd had reason. No question about that. But now that she was dead, he kinda wished he'd been a little nicer. She'd spent her last day of life scared shitless because he had a score to settle.

And yeah, maybe she'd deserved some of what he'd dished out. She'd deserved most of it, if it came to that. She'd probably deserved worse. But he must have scared her more than he realized. The last thing she'd done before the earth swallowed her had been try to get away from him. All he'd done was grab her around the waist to steady himself as well as her when he stumbled into her. That was all he had tried to do; it hadn't been a cheap attempt to cop a feel. But she had pushed away from him as if his touch had burned her. That initial look on her face, when she turned toward him, had been one of sheer panic. And that had been *before* the earth opened under her feet.

And if he couldn't bring her back to life, he'd have to live with that image in his head for whatever amount of time he had left.

After breathing into her mouth once, twice, three times for good measure, he crawled back and started pushing on her chest again. Her ribcage felt so fragile under his hands, he was afraid what he was doing might hurt her. Then again, it wasn't like he could kill her any deader than she already was. And he didn't think he was breaking any of her bones. That'd be bad, if he succeeded in getting her back, only to puncture one of her lungs in the process.

Not that there seemed much chance of getting her back. Her body stayed cold and limp under his ministrations. The only good thing about it was that it got his own blood pumping again. He was frozen all the way through, the wet clothes clinging to his skin like sheets of ice. It was almost like being back inside the prison again for another damned shower. They'd left him wet and shivering then, too.

Maybe he should take the time to stop and strip. The air was cold, and the idea of sitting around underground in nothing but his skin wasn't appealing, but the sodden, chilly fabric wasn't doing him any good, either. He'd probably be better off without it.

After the next time you blow into her mouth.

He was okay for the moment. She was not. When he'd done everything he could for her, he'd deal with himself. He'd survive another few minutes in wet clothes.

And she was already dead.

Maybe not. Maybe not quite.

Crawling forward, he sought her face again and, finding it, pinched her nose shut with two fingers before taking a breath and leaning down, seeking and finding her lips again. They were still cold and flaccid.

He breathed once. Twice. Three times.

C'mon, damn you! Breathe!

Only to rear back when her body convulsed under his hands.

. . .

The young translator from Captain Conlan's ship had always annoyed Stephen Lamb.

Oh, they all annoyed him in their own ways. Miller, the mercenary: so inferior to the Rhenians in every way that mattered, yet so big and strong physically, it was hard to squash him like the vermin he was. Toby Flatt, the mechanic, the total opposite: small, skinny, and nervous. A sniveling weakling in Lamb's opinion, and quite possibly a halfwit, too. At least Major Lamb had never managed to get anything halfway coherent out of him. And of course there was the captain, with his arrogance and his stupid refusal to give the Rhenians the information they needed.

Now he'd even managed to do what no one else had ever done and escaped.

With Elsa Brandeis. For whom Stephen Lamb had had intentions.

Swallowing the spasm of rage that shook him at the thought of Captain Conlan daring to defile the Rhenian doctor—the rage he thought his interlude with the young Marican woman had partially defused—Major Lamb contemplated the young man in front of him instead.

Holden Sinclair, translator for the crew of Quinn Conlan's ship.

Older than most of the guards on Marica-3 but still in this twenties. And soft, his face almost pretty, which made him look younger than he was. Some pampered namby-pamby mama's boy. He'd probably grown up with the proverbial Old Earth silver spoon in his mouth. Private schools, tutors, the whole nine yards. He spoke better Rhenish than most of the guards, with an upper-crust accent that rubbed Major Lamb raw. No one should speak Rhenish that well unless he was a Rhenian.

And Sinclair was unfailingly polite. When Lamb walked through the door, instead of cowering the way most of the prisoners did, the young translator greeted him with a civilized, "Good evening, Major Lamb."

As if he imagined they were on the same level. As if he thought he had any business greeting anyone at all.

Backhanding the young man was automatic. Lamb's hand hurt from the impact, but it was worth it to see the tears swimming in Holden Sinclair's hazel eyes when he sat up, a pale hand cradling his cheek.

Major Lamb smiled. If the young man hadn't yet learned to respect authority, it was high time he did.

However, the news he was about to impart would rub the shine off better than most anything else he could do to the young man, he figured, pleasant though it would be to sink his fist into that too-pretty face.

"Now that I've got your attention—" And there was no doubt that he had; Sinclair was watching him like a mouse with a cat, waiting for the other shoe to drop. "—I have some news you'll find interesting."

He waited to see whether the young man would open his mouth again or whether he'd learned his lesson. When Sinclair didn't speak,

Major Lamb continued. "Captain Conlan left us this morning."

Earlier, when he'd said those same words to Isaac Miller, the mercenary had been disappointingly matter-of-fact in his response, his flat black gaze betraying none of whatever emotions he may have felt. The same could not be said for Holden Sinclair. The young man's reaction was immediate and transparent. A quick blink as if Major Lamb had hit him in the face a second time, then an expression of shock he made no attempt to hide. The only similarity to Miller's reaction was that they both asked the same question, Sinclair in a voice that shook. "Dead?"

Major Lamb smiled. "Oh, no. He walked out under his own steam."

The young man blinked again, in confusion this time. "Walked out?"

Lamb allowed his smile to broaden. "Straight through the doors and onto Marica-3."

"You mean, you let him go?"

"Well, no." Lamb feigned a sorrowful tone. "He took a hostage and broke out."

He watched the young man, but this time Sinclair didn't react beyond a slight widening of the eyes. Lamb added, twisting the metaphorical knife, "So he's gone. And you're still sitting here. After he got you into this mess in the first place."

"He didn't get us into it."

The denial was quick and probably automatic. From the young man's expression, Lamb rather suspected the words had surprised him, too. He waited, and after a moment Sinclair added, almost reluctantly. "It was *her* fault."

Of course. "Her being Josette? Josie?"

Sinclair glanced up for a moment, his eyes confirming the

statement even as his lips were clamped tightly together. One cheek was still red from the contact with Lamb's hand.

"It's hard to blame him for being distracted," Lamb said pleasantly. "I've met Josette. And I imagine she'd be able to wrap most men around her finger."

Not him, of course. And obviously not Isaac Miller, who hadn't risen to the bait at all. But Major Lamb had always suspected young Sinclair idolized Captain Conlan. He had probably jacked off in his hole on the ship imagining he was banging the captain's girlfriend.

"I'm surprised Quinn's still alive," Sinclair said. "I'd have thought you'd have killed him by now."

"We have," Major Lamb informed him, smiling. "Several times. Just never quite dead enough."

Something flickered in Sinclair's eyes for a moment. "I don't think he'll be back. There's nothing he can do for us, and he'd have to be stupid not to realize it. He's not."

"So you think he'll stay gone?"

"I think he wants to die in peace," Sinclair said bluntly. "Somewhere private. Where nobody's going to revive him again."

"What about the hostage?"

Sinclair hesitated. "Quinn doesn't always play fair, but he isn't cruel. I guess it depends on who the hostage is and how that person has treated him. What goes around comes around, and all that."

Which didn't, Major Lamb reflected, say a whole lot about Elsa Brandeis's chances of survival.

CHAPTER ELEVEN

Coming back from the dead hurt.

As many times as she'd seen it done to others, Elsa hadn't ever thought she'd be in the position of experiencing it firsthand.

Now that she was, she had a new appreciation for the pain Captain Conlan had gone through at Doctor Sterling's hands. At *her* hands.

Everything hurt. Her insides, every inch of her skin, her ribs, her heart, and her head. Her brain felt as if it was about to explode out of her skull. Little flickers of light burst in front of her open eyes, but since they were still there when she closed them, the flickers must be in her mind and not in reality.

Slitting her eyes open once more, cautiously, she tried to focus, but saw nothing. Everything was pitch black. Impenetrable. And loud. Her ears were roaring. Or maybe the roaring—at least part of it—came from outside herself.

Where was she? And how had she gotten here?

When she first came back to herself, she'd thought she was dead. She'd come to with a convulsion and coughed up what had felt like gallons and gallons of slimy water. Once her stomach had settled down and she'd managed to catch a breath again—a chore in itself when her lungs felt like they were on fire, and were fighting against her—she'd found herself in this no-man's land of sound and pain.

The afterlife wasn't supposed to be painful, was it? Wasn't there supposed to be soft wind and flowers and music? Everything full of peace and beauty?

There was nothing beautiful here. Nothing peaceful, either. Just earsplitting sound and darkness. And pain. The whole world had narrowed to those three things.

So perhaps this was Purgatory. She was paying for her sins. Those sins of omission Captain Conlan had talked about, the things she had seen and hadn't lifted a finger to stop.

Except…hell was supposed to be hot, and this place was bone-chillingly cold. And speaking of Captain Conlan…where was he?

Casting her mind back, she struggled for clarity. For… something. Some memory of what happened, how she came to be here. Wherever here was.

She remembered falling. The ground giving way. And the hands wrapped around her wrist, hurting her, but holding her up, keeping her from going into freefall. Until…had he let go, eventually? Had he tried to hold on, but couldn't? Opened his hands deliberately, or tried and failed?

She remembered dropping through the air before hitting the water. The icy impact of it freezing both body and soul. The darkness and the roar of the river. But she couldn't remember anything after that. Until here and now.

Lifting a limp hand to touch herself, she realized she was wet. Still mostly wearing her dress but soaked through. Shivering, with long, cold shudders passing through her body. And everything hurt, from her feet all the way up to the top of her head.

She'd been dead, hadn't she? There'd been a tunnel, and a light, like in the stories…and someone's voice from very far away. *C'mon, damn you! Breathe!*

That voice…

She coughed, and her body clenched with pain. Moaning, she lifted both hands to press against her head, as if physically trying to hold it together.

"Hurts, don't it?" that same voice said, not too sympathetically, close to her ear.

For a second, she couldn't breathe. Then, "Captain?"

"Didn't think you'd get away from me that easy, did you?"

She thought he might have chuckled, but it was hard to be sure over the roar of the river.

Her throat was raw from the purging and probably from lack of breathing. She swallowed and tried again. "What happened?"

She coughed again, a little more easily this time. Turned her face to where she knew he was, to see if she could see him, but couldn't. There was nothing there but inky black.

"You drowned," his voice said, from out of the darkness. Judging from the sound, he was sitting a few feet away. "I had a hell of a time bringing you back."

"Why did you?"

She held her breath while she waited for his answer, not sure what she expected to hear and not sure why it mattered, but waiting nonetheless.

"You think I shoulda let you die?"

It would have made his life easier if he had. However much of it he had left. Yet he hadn't. He must have gone into the hole with her and held on all the way down the river, and when he'd pulled her lifeless body out, instead of leaving well enough alone, he'd brought her back from the dead. She'd done her own fair share of that, so she knew the effort it must have taken.

"Thank you," she managed.

He chuckled. This time she was sure of it. "Not sure I did you any favors, sweetheart. Drowning or poisoning comes to much the same thing in the end."

"Poisoning?"

"Marican water snakes, remember? They live in the rivers."

Lord, yes. She remembered the Marican water snakes. Doctor Sterling used their poison in the lab. Yet another "treatment" Captain Conlan had been subjected to. She'd have shuddered, had her body not already been racked with spasms.

He added, "I got you back from drowning, but if the water's poisoned, ain't much I can do about it. How d'you feel?"

"Bad," Elsa said, taking stock. Everything still hurt, and she'd had no idea it was possible to be this cold. "What does Marican snake poison feel like?"

She couldn't see Captain Conlan, but she could picture his face, and the expression on it, from the tone of his voice. That twisted half-smile. "Good thing I've been through it and survived, ain't it, sweetheart?"

There was nothing she could say to that, of course. Except another "I'm sorry." And she was. Deeply.

"It burns," he said. "When the poison goes in the blood, it takes a minute to get around. Your body gets warmer and then really hot, and then you start feeling like you're boiling. Like your skin's melting from the inside. And I hear it makes your lungs collapse. 'Course, I didn't get that far."

No, he hadn't. She'd monitored his vital signs, and when his heart rate spiked into the danger zone, she'd administered the anti-venom, her ears ringing with his screams and curses. The antidote had taken a minute or two to kick in, but when it had and he'd gotten his breath back, he'd looked at her with so much loathing, it ought by rights to have brought her to her knees.

But of course it hadn't. Instead, she had given him a tight smile and walked away, leaving him there, no doubt wishing he could kill her. Instead of which he'd just saved her life. She'd gotten so much more—or less—than she deserved.

"I don't feel anything like that." That kind of heat might actually feel nice. At least for a little while. She was so cold she felt numb.

"That's when the poison goes directly in the blood," Captain Conlan said. "Maybe digesting it's different."

"Or maybe if I did digest it, I got rid of it again."

He might have shrugged, but she had no way of knowing. "How d'you feel, otherwise?"

"Cold," Elsa said, teeth chattering.

"I figured that. Think you've recovered enough to get up and walk? It'll help to move. And we can't stay here."

"Walk where?" But she made an effort to sit. Her head swam, even as it continued to pound, and every muscle in her body screamed in protest.

"There's another crack in the ceiling back that way a bit."

He was probably gesturing, but it was too dark for her to see. His voice was moving, however; he grunted, and then she heard scuffling as he got himself to his feet. "Need a hand?"

"Please." She was too cold and in too much pain—and feeling much too humbled—for pride.

"C'mon, then." She heard shuffling, and then there was the sensation of him stopping beside her. Even so close, she couldn't see him. He grabbed her under the arms and lifted. "Up."

"Thank you." But her legs were a lot less steady than she'd expected, and she'd have landed back on the ground if he hadn't braced her with an arm around the waist.

"This way." He nudged her to the right, his body still up against hers. "Keep your hand on the wall, and be careful where you put your feet. If you go into the river again, I ain't jumping after you."

At this point, she wasn't sure whether to believe him or not. Anyone with sense wouldn't jump after her, but he'd gone in with her the first time rather than letting go of her arm. She wouldn't put it past him to do it again.

Overdeveloped hero complex. Or something.

But since she didn't much fancy going back in the water herself, either, she did as he'd said. Kept one hand on the cold rock of the wall as she crept forward. Shudders racked her body every few feet, and progress was slow when she had to test the ground for every step she took. Captain Conlan kept his arm wrapped around her waist, using the other to guide himself along the wall. He was as cold and wet as she was, and shivering, too.

It took a small eternity to navigate just a few yards through the dark, the blackness pressing in and down on them like a living thing. The roar from the river was deafening, and the thought of falling in again played merry hell with her mind. Although Elsa had never considered herself particularly afraid of the dark before, she was afraid now. She couldn't see where she was going, had no idea what might be two feet in front of her, and wasn't sure she could trust the man at her back. It seemed wrong to question her survival, yet she couldn't help wonder…why had he saved her life? Why hadn't he just let her drown? He didn't owe her anything.

Oh, yes, he did. He owed her pain and suffering in equal measure to what she'd given him.

So had he, perhaps, something more sinister in mind for her? He'd revived her after the drowning only because he planned to kill her in some more heinous way later?

Or because there were things he wanted to do to her first?

She stumbled and would have pitched forward if not for his arm around her waist.

"Watch it."

The arm tightened and kept her standing. For just a second she returned, in her mind, to the seconds up above, before she'd fallen through the earth and landed them both in this predicament. He'd walked into her and grabbed her to steady them both...and that had been the catalyst for her stumbling forward onto the thin crust of ground above the river.

Her fault. All of it.

Her voice broke. "I'm sorry."

His came back, calm and even in spite of the shivers racking his body. "We're all right. Just watch where you're going."

As if she could see her hand in front of her face.

But he had no idea what she was going through in her mind, and she didn't think she wanted to tell him. So she did her best to empty her mind of anything but the need to move forward, to keep a hand on the wall, to test the ground before putting her weight on it, and they continued on at a snail's pace.

• • •

Christ, it was cold.

Quinn tried to hold back a snort but couldn't quite manage. What was it they used to say back on Old Earth? Colder than a witch's tit?

From personal experience—the woman in front of him—a witch's tit was plenty cold.

A chuckle passed through his body, ending in a shiver.

All joking aside, they'd both die if he couldn't get them warmed up soon. The walking helped to keep the blood pumping, but they were both getting colder and stiffer with each step, their movements slower and more lethargic.

What was it called, when you froze to death?

The med tech would know. He cleared his throat. "Hey, Doc."

"Yes?"

He could hear her teeth chattering on just that single syllable and knew the difficulty she'd had in getting it out.

"What's it called, when you freeze to death? Hypo-something?"

"Hypothermia," his med tech managed.

"Right. You think we need to worry about that?"

There was a pause during which he figured she was debating whether to curse him or not. Because—hell, yes—it was obvious they had to worry about it. He wasn't stupid. If he couldn't get them both out of their wet clothes and get some body heat going soon, they wouldn't last the night. He could feel his internal temperature dropping with every minute that passed, and holding her was like embracing a frozen slab of meat.

He thought about trying to talk her out of her clothes, and grimaced. *Good luck with that.* Threatening her with the laser pistol probably wouldn't do the trick this time. She must have figured out by now that he wasn't gonna shoot her. Not unless she gave him no choice.

Could he strip her himself if she refused to undress? Just peel her clothes off and try not to get maimed in the process? She was pretty weak right now—he'd been in the position of having been brought back from death's door enough to know how it felt afterwards—so he might escape unhurt.

Then again, maybe not. This whole mess had started because he'd grabbed her around the middle. He was frankly amazed she was allowing his touch at all right now, although she probably knew she didn't have much of a choice. But if he tried to take her clothes off, she might turn on him again. And he was weak, too. A lot weaker than he wanted her to know.

"Listen, Doc."

It took a second. "Yes?"

"We're gonna have to find a place to hole up for a while. Get warm and dry."

There was another pause. Then, "Where? How?"

"Don't know yet." But it would have to be underground. He didn't have the strength to figure out a way up right now. And besides, it might actually be warmer down here. Marica-3 could be bitterly cold at night, or so he'd heard. "But you're a doctor. You know how."

Her spine stiffened. "I'm not taking my clothes off in front of you."

Her tone of offended dignity, especially coupled with the chattering teeth, would have been funny had the circumstances been less dire.

"Ain't like I'll be able to see you, sweetheart." Or like he hadn't seen her already.

She didn't respond, and he added, "You stay in those wet clothes, you're gonna freeze to death. I'll take 'em off you myself if I have to, but you're getting naked."

A minute passed, while they made their slow way forward. He tried to take her silence for tacit agreement but figured she was just trying to come up with a counterargument. To forestall her, he hardened his voice a little—not easy to do with his teeth knocking together.

"I ain't above hogtying you, sweetheart. I did it earlier. And I ain't about to die of hypothermia just cause you're too prissy to share. You wanna survive the night, you'll do as I say."

There was no answer again, but this time Quinn felt reasonably certain he could count on her cooperation when they got to the place he decided they'd spend the hours until dawn.

Chapter Twelve

The darkness was the only thing that made it bearable. Elsa was certain that if it hadn't been for that, she would have died of mortification.

By the time they made it to the part of the river where pale pinkish moonlight shone down on them through a hole in the roof, she could barely move from the cold. All she wanted to do was curl up against the wall and fall asleep. And she would have done it if it hadn't been for Captain Conlan, telling her sternly to strip.

She squinted at him. It was nice to be able to see again, however poorly, after all the time spent in pitch blackness. He looked almost as battered as she was, and if she'd felt a little better herself, she'd have been tempted to refuse the order. His hand wasn't even on the pistol. Maybe he didn't dare touch it for fear it would go off; he was shivering as violently as she was, and if he tried to handle a weapon, she wouldn't put it past him to slice his own toes off by accident, especially now that he was barefoot.

"What happened to the boots?"

He glanced at his feet, as if he hadn't realized the boots were gone. It took him a second to answer. "Lost 'em in the river." His voice was uneven with chills.

Something seemed to be wrong with his arm, too. He kept it close to his body, favoring it the way he did the bad leg. And he was just as wet as she was, just as beaten and battered, just as in need of rest and warmth.

He'd saved her life earlier. And now he was trying to keep her—and himself—alive through the night. He wasn't looking for a groping session. If he felt even half as bad as she did, sex was the last thing on his mind. So she should, perhaps, cut him a break and do as he asked without further argument, however embarrassing it would turn out to be. Embarrassed was better than dead.

"Turn around, at least."

He managed a grin, a pale shadow of the one from earlier in the day, yet still wolfish. "I've already seen what you've got, sweetheart."

So he had. And if she hadn't been chilled to the bone, the reminder would have caused her to blush. "Then you shouldn't need to watch again. Please."

He looked at her for a second, steadily, before he turned his back. "I'll be down here. Just walk this way when you're done."

Elsa nodded and watched as he limped away, unsteadily, into the shadows. Just before the darkness swallowed him, he told her over his shoulder, "No peeking. Fair's fair."

She answered without thinking. "I've seen what you've got, too, Captain Conlan."

There was a touch more real amusement to the smile this time, and a lot more cynicism. "I guess you have, Doc. Don't take too long. I don't wanna lose any parts while I wait."

He didn't wait for an answer, just faded into the shadows. Elsa got busy peeling her sodden and clingy clothes off.

The dress seemed to have taken quite a beating from her trip down the river. It was ripped almost in two, from the top all the way down past her waist. But her underthings were still intact, and she slipped them off, shivering, not entirely certain whether it was better or worse wearing nothing. It felt good to get the cold fabric off her skin, yet there was a distinct chill in the air, and a breeze whistling down the tunnel that her clothes, however wet, had thus far protected her from. Now it caused her skin to draw tight, tiny goose pimples cropping up everywhere.

She hesitated for a second over her hair. It was wet, too, of course, still braided and coiled at her nape. It would dry like that, eventually. But would it dry faster if she let it down? Or would the cold tresses against her skin make it even more difficult to get warm?

She tried to picture it in her mind—her own cold and naked body coiled next to Captain Conlan's—but her mind rebelled against the image. *Better not go there until you have to.* But at least if she let her hair down, long as it was, it might offer her an illusion of defense, a shield of some kind between her and him.

She slipped the pins out, most of them dropping through her frozen fingers onto the floor of the tunnel. She was too cold to get on her knees to look for them, so she just let them lie where they fell. The band at the end of the braid she slipped over her wrist before shaking out her wet hair. It settled around her shoulders like an icy shroud, bringing on yet more chills. The cold strands hitting her breasts caused her nipples to tighten almost painfully.

Dear Lord, how was she supposed to get through this night?

• • •

Quinn couldn't see the med tech very well, and he was glad for it.

He'd managed to strip off his own clothes by the time she slipped through the darkness to stand in front of him. He'd been wearing more clothes than she had, and he also had more injuries, so by rights it should have taken him longer; she must have spent the time talking herself into coming back here, he figured. He was halfway surprised she was here at all. She could have just walked away in the opposite direction and kept her clothes on. She'd likely have died of—what had she called it? Hypothermia?—before the night was out, but she could have done it. He didn't have it in him to chase her down. After walking all day, his leg had had enough.

He'd found a semi-comfortable place to sit, on the lee side of a couple big rocks that afforded a little bit of protection from the wind whistling down the tunnel and the occasional spray of water from the river. The ground was hard, but no harder than anywhere else, and there was enough room for him to stretch out his aching leg. He hoped that the small space between the stone wall and the rocks would retain a little heat from their bodies once they curled up together. Surely huddling here made more sense than staying out in the open, where the wind would whip any heat away.

The med tech stopped next to him, just a white blur in the darkness. Not that it mattered. She'd stood naked in front of him that morning, in blazing sunlight, and he could still see the picture when he closed his eyes. Long legs, slender body, small breasts. He didn't need to see her now to know what she looked like. Good thing he was too cold to even consider doing anything about it.

He patted the ground next to him. "Have a seat."

She hesitated. Probably wishing she could tell him she'd stand. Quinn sighed. "Listen, Doc. I'm too cold and too tired and in too much pain to even think about copping a feel. I just wanna survive the night. After all this, it'd be a damn shame not to. For both of us."

She didn't answer, but after a second she stepped forward and folded herself down next to him. About a foot away. Not close enough that their bodies touched. And she was curled so tightly into herself it was a wonder she could breathe. Still, it was progress. He'd give her a minute or two before he insisted she move closer. Put her at ease a little more before he had to touch her.

"How're you feeling?"

She cleared her throat. "Uncomfortable."

Hah.

Her voice was still a little uneven but not as shaky as it had been. Getting the wet clothes off must have helped. Quinn felt the same way. The ground was cold and hard, the air was chilly, and the river wind nipped at his tender skin, but being naked was better than wearing wet clothes. If he'd had some sticks, he could have used the laser pistol to start a fire. Of course, wood was in short supply on Marica-3, so they'd have to do without. But if they could make it through the night and figure out a way to get back up to the surface, the sun would warm them up in the morning. Dry their clothes, too.

If they could figure out a way back up to the surface.

But maybe they shouldn't. They were down here. Safe for the time being. The guards wouldn't think to look for him here. If they followed the river down to the prison, he might make his way inside and find the others. Somehow. Maybe he could get them back into the tunnel, and together they could figure out a way up and, eventually, away. If anyone could come up with a way off this godforsaken rock, it was the crew of the *Good Fortune*.

He tried to picture the med tech's expression when he told her they were headed back into the prison and couldn't.

He cleared his throat. "Tomorrow morning we'll figure out a way up to the surface. Get warm again."

His med tech didn't answer.

"If we survive the night."

Nothing.

"I need you to help me out here, Doc."

He thought she might have sighed, but she turned to him. "What do you want me to do?"

Quinn suppressed the first couple of suggestions that came to his mind. While they might get his blood pumping, and hers too, now wasn't the time to make jokes. "Gimme your hand."

A hand ought to be safe. As long as he was careful where he put it.

The same thought must have crossed her mind, because she hesitated. But eventually she reached a pale hand toward him. He took it in both of his. It was freezing. Colder even than his own, those long, slender fingers like ice. He rubbed them, trying to get some friction going. For a minute, they were both silent. As the time passed, he thought he sensed a lessening of tension in her body.

"Where'd you grow up, Doc?" That oughta be safe enough to ask and easy to answer. Might put her at ease.

Her voice was soft and sounded farther away than it was. He had to concentrate to hear it over the rushing of the water. "Republic of Rhene. You?"

"Old Earth." Ought to be safe enough to admit that, too. She probably already knew the basic information about him. "Ireland. Town called Dublin."

"I've never been to Old Earth."

"I've never been to Rhene."

She didn't answer, and he added, "Is it cold there? Or warm?"

"It's a planet," his med tech said.

"I ain't stupid, Doc. I know that." But not all planets were like

Old Earth, with its winters and summers. It all depended. He'd seen a lot of planets in his travels that were more one way than the other. "Sumatra's warm. Krai is cold. Old Earth is both."

"Rhene's both, too. It's located far enough from our sun to have seasons."

"So you're used to the cold."

"Not like this," the med tech said. "We dressed for it. And we didn't go swimming in the winter."

There was a...tone to her voice. Was she blaming him for their involuntary dunking?

"I tried to hold on, Doc. Not my fault the ground gave way."

There was a pause.

"Is that what happened?" Her voice was soft. "I wondered."

Her hand was getting a little warmer, and so were his. He moved on to her wrist. Not the one he'd clasped earlier. That one probably had bruises. "It's a much bigger hole now. Should make it easier to get out tomorrow." If they survived the night and could make it up there.

"That one?" She gestured to the rip in the ground just up ahead, where beams of pink moonlight shone through.

Quinn shook his head, focused on rubbing some warmth back into her skin. Her pulse beat against his fingers, sluggishly. "We floated a long way. You fell in farther up."

"How much farther?"

He shrugged. "We were in the water a couple minutes, at least. And it's moving fast. We'll have a ways to walk tomorrow morning."

"If we survive."

He grinned. "Yeah. If we survive."

She was quiet for a while. Quinn thought he might have to come up with something new to say when she opened her mouth.

"Do you think we will?"

"I hope so."

She didn't answer, and he added, "We're both hurt. It's nighttime, cold and getting colder. We haven't got clothes or blankets or a fire. I wanna think I didn't go through today just to drop dead of cold tonight, but yeah, there's a chance we won't make it." A pretty good chance from where he was sitting, though he didn't tell her that.

Silence reigned again, only broken by the roar of the river.

"I don't want to die."

No shit. And after months of hoping, wishing, *praying* for death, neither did he.

"You wanna come a little closer, then? Give this bundling thing a try?"

He tugged on her arm. Felt resistance at first, and then she gave in. He wasn't sure whether to breathe a sigh of relief or yell when her chilled body aligned next to his, and he contented himself with trying to catch his breath instead. Christ, she was cold! Having her next to him was almost as bad as plunging back into the river again. And she was as rigid as the marble she resembled.

Exasperated, he reached out an arm and draped it over her shoulder. Dragged her all the way into his side, ignoring the chill. "Been a while, hasn't it, sweetheart?"

"Excuse me?" Her voice was, if possible, even more frozen than her body.

"Try to relax. Melt a little."

"Excuse me?"

"You won't feel as cold if you relax."

"I'm relaxed." But her clenched teeth belied the statement.

"Sure." Sick and tired of coddling her, and frozen almost all the way through, Quinn shifted his grip and hauled her onto his lap, trying not to flinch when the cold strands of her hair got trapped between his chest and her arm. Ignoring her weak struggles, he wrapped both arms around her and held her there. "Just pretend you're comfortable. We're both gonna die if you can't."

She fought against him for another few seconds, her body stiff and unyielding, before she gave in. A shuddering sigh passed through her, and she relaxed against him.

Finally. "There you go." Quinn tightened his arms a little more and settled his back against the cold stone of the tunnel wall, wishing for the miracle of peaceful rest but knowing the best thing he could hope for was to spend a cold, uncomfortable night on the hard ground.

But that'd be okay, he told himself; he'd take a little discomfort now as long as he could make it through till tomorrow.

The time passed slowly. They spoke at first: he teased out answers to questions about her life on Rhene and—later—on Marica-3, but didn't think he learned much he could use. She wasn't stupid, so he had to be careful about the questions he asked; anything too specific, and he figured he'd put her back up. The air got colder as the night deepened, but the med tech's body gradually became less chilled with their proximity. She still wasn't warm, but she became less flaccid. As a result, he became a little warmer, too.

After a while, she dozed off, her head on his shoulder and her shallow breaths puffing against the side of his neck. He thought about waking her up again so she could keep him company but decided he might as well let her sleep. When she asked him questions in return for the ones he'd asked her, he had to stay alert, mentally on his toes, so he didn't accidentally let slip some bit of information she didn't already know, and he wasn't feeling up to it. So he leaned his head against the cold stone wall and closed his eyes, trying to remember what feeling warm was like.

It'd been a while. The Rhenians kept the cells just barely comfortable, but at least he'd had clothes on inside the prison. It hadn't been like this.

Growing up had been one cold night after another, holed up in corners of Dublin's back alleys, scrounging for food. And the orphanage and foster homes he'd spent time in in between… there'd been precious little warmth there, too. He oughta be used to this by now.

So when was the last time he'd felt warm?

Grimacing, his mind slipped back where he didn't want it to go. To the *Good Fortune*, his quarters…and Josie. The two of them sated and satisfied, with legs entangled and arms wrapped around one another under downy blankets. Warm curves fitting themselves to his body, his nose buried in her riot of black curls, drinking in her scent, while her hands covered his, keeping his arms snug around her. Keeping his mind and his body focused on her, so he wouldn't think too hard and realize that she was getting ready to stab him in the back.

"God dammit!"

The med tech stirred on his lap, and Quinn clenched his teeth, soothing her back to sleep. She hadn't broached the subject of Josie, and Josie was the last thing he wanted to discuss.

Willing his mind to go blank, he pulled the med tech carefully down on the cold ground and wrapped himself around her, one arm holding her snug to his chest. Doing his best to push what he had of warmth into her and taking back out what he thought she could spare. At this point, she was more important than he was. Getting her through the night was just as pivotal, if not more so, than surviving himself. He needed her information to get him back inside the prison. Without that knowledge, he had no way of getting the rest of his crew out, and if he couldn't, he might as well be dead.

CHAPTER THIRTEEN

Quinn went from dead sleep to wakefulness in a heartbeat, his breath caught in his throat, eyes open and scanning their surroundings.

What?

Something had woken him. And it wasn't the woman in his arms. She hadn't moved. For the first second or two, he couldn't tell whether she was alive or dead. Her body was chilled, motionless. It wasn't until he felt her back rise and fall against his chest that he knew he wasn't holding a corpse.

Something else, then. A sound? He concentrated, sharpening his ears, but couldn't hear anything above the rushing of the water.

It was still dark where they were, but the light up the tunnel, shining in from above, had changed from pink-tinged moonlight to pale sun. *Early morning*, his mind supplied. Looked like they'd both survived the night.

But there was another light, too. Down the tunnel in the other direction. A flash of illumination, and a hovering ball of yellow light brighter than the sun.

"Shit!"

The realization hit him at the same time as the med tech's eyes opened. She blinked those long lashes, her body stretching catlike against his…until something of their situation must have come back to her. Maybe it was the feel of him against her back. He was up, in more ways than one. She turned as stiff as a statue, her breath exiting her body on a gasp.

Quinn didn't hesitate, just flipped her over on her back and covered her body with his, his hand hard over her mouth.

She blinked at him over it, shocked and still a little sleepy.

"Sorry, Doc." The water was more than loud enough to cover anything he said; he wasn't worried about anyone hearing him. Seemed there was a patrol coming, shooting off flares to light their way up the tunnel, but he didn't need to worry about them hearing her, either, even if she screamed at the top of her voice. The water was loud enough to drown out any number of sounds either of them could make.

Nonetheless, he kept that hand over her mouth and her body pinned to the ground. No sense in taking chances, and he definitely couldn't afford to have her jump up and down and wave. They may not hear her if she screamed, but there was no way they'd be able to ignore a naked woman bouncing up and down on the other side of the river. Not once they got up this far and shot off a sphere that would light up this entire section of river. Instead, he spoke directly into her ear. "We're expecting company."

Her eyes shifted sideways, and he saw the light from the hovering sphere reflected in them, like tiny suns.

"Looks like a couple guards out for a stroll," he added, since he figured she couldn't see them from where she was. Under him. "We must be pretty close to the prison." Somehow they had managed to fall into the right river. What were the odds?

Or maybe there was just one river in this area. It didn't matter, anyway; the important thing was that Rhenian guards were on their way in this direction. With a supply of light-spheres—another arced up under the ceiling as he watched and hung there, casting a wide glow. The next one, or the one after that, would illuminate the area where they lay.

The med tech didn't answer his statement—couldn't, with his hand covering her mouth—but her body tensed. He tensed his own, waiting for her to try to buck him off. On the other side of the river, the shadows separated themselves into two guards in gray uniforms.

The edge was wider on the other side, he saw, and smoother. The guards could walk without having to worry about stumbling over rocks or slipping into the river. The path looked manmade, like the Rhenians had been through here at some point, leveling it. The next sphere they shot cut through the darkness, lighting up the ceiling of the tunnel, the rocks on the other side, the water itself. The glow came perilously close to where they lay, and Quinn held his breath, wondering what the hell he'd do if the guards noticed them. On the one hand, they were on the other side of the river, with no way across. They couldn't grab him even if they wanted to. Nobody could swim these rapids, he'd stake his life on it. And it may come to that, since some of these war-crazed puppies might be stupid enough to try.

On the other hand, they had laser pistols in their belts and plasma rifles over their shoulders that could drop him from where they stood. And if they were down here specifically to look for him, they might even have stunners. Doctor Sterling wouldn't risk Quinn's life—or, he assumed, the med tech's—but the guards could stun him and pick him up at their leisure, once they figured out a way across the river.

Hell, they wouldn't even have to cross. All they had to do was mark the spot in the ceiling where the hole was, then go there on the surface and lower a sling and a couple of burly guards to haul him up.

He turned his attention back to the woman beneath him. The very naked woman whose body he'd held all night. Whose eyes were looking at him now with a mixture of trepidation and worry. "Might be a good idea to be quiet so they don't notice us, sweetheart. Easy to misunderstand the situation. Us both being naked and all."

He watched as the suggestion took root and saw the horrified realization in her eyes at the same time as her cheeks flooded with color. She must be feeling better—warmer—if she could blush like that. And it wasn't just her cheeks that flushed; her entire body got a degree or two warmer. All the way down.

Because he could, he grinned at her. "You just stay right there and don't fight me, like a good girl. They'll be gone in no time."

He hoped.

Unfortunately, best he could figure it, unless he'd gotten turned around somehow on the way down the river, the guards were on their way away from the prison, not toward it. Which probably meant they'd be back. They'd walk however far they had to, to complete their patrol—or whatever the hell they were doing down here—and then they'd turn around. He just hoped there wasn't a bridge farther up. Then they'd come down on *this* side of the river, and all hell would break loose.

Except—dammit—they stopped. Just across the river and downstream a few yards, on the edge of the light cast by the sphere. Close enough that he'd have been able to hear what they were saying, had it not been for the rushing water—and the fact that they probably spoke Rhenish. Thank God it was still dark over on this side.

But soon he realized he didn't need to hear them to understand what they were talking about, though. A few yards beyond where they stood was that hole in the ceiling he and the med tech had floated under last night, the one that had allowed him to see the big rocks on the edge of the river. The guards were pointing to it and babbling, and then they ventured closer, until they were directly across the river from where he and the med tech were tucked away, halfway behind their big rock.

Quinn raised his head carefully and watched. Something about that hole seemed to be of interest to the guards. And that'd make sense if it was a new hole—say, the one he and the med tech had made last night, falling through the crust of the earth—but it wasn't. This hole had already been there when they came rushing by.

So why would the guards care about it?

Unless…

He'd had to kick off his boots in the river last night.

What if they'd been carried downstream to the prison, and someone had found them? Maybe they'd gotten caught in the pumping mechanism or something. And then someone had realized whose feet they'd fallen off of?

That'd explain why there were patrols down here. It wasn't like the Rhenians would normally patrol the river, was it? There was nothing down here except water and those damned snakes. The guards might be harvesting snake venom for high and mighty Doctor Sterling to use in his lab. But if so he'd expect them to be watching the ground or the water, not the ceiling.

Or they could be looking for him. Or his body.

The med tech squirmed under him, drawing his attention. The ground must be hard and cold against her bare backside. But at least her hands weren't tied behind her this time. He didn't have to worry about her lifting her hips to nudge against him, however accidentally.

He should be grateful. He hadn't a hope of hiding his reaction from her, not stark naked. Not that he thought he'd hid it very well last time, even through his clothes. Or that he imagined she hadn't noticed the state he was in right now. Morning wood, a naked woman in his arms, adrenaline…whatever excuse he might come up with, she wouldn't have been able to ignore the blatantly obvious. He had the mother of all hard-ons, and any woman alive, no matter how frigid, would have noticed.

But she wasn't fighting him. She squirmed, but it was a small squirm, an *I'm uncomfortable and you're heavy* sort of squirm. She wasn't trying to kick him off.

Why not?

Last time the guards had come close, she'd damned near gotten them both caught. Yet this time she was making no attempt to get anyone's attention.

He looked down at her, but she was no longer looking back. Her head was turned to the side, baring that long, elegant neck. There was still a touch of heightened color in her cheeks, best as he could see in the low light, and her teeth were sunk into her bottom lip. The expression in her eyes was worried. And Christ, that face… still perfect, still stunning, but soft, like a living, breathing woman instead of a marble bust, surrounded by yards and yards of soft, silky hair. A living, breathing woman whose naked body was stretched out under his, all soft skin and slender curves and long limbs.

Yeah, it might look kinda bad if the guards noticed them. She must just want to avoid getting caught with her panties down. Or off. Couldn't fault her for that.

Across the river, the Rhenian guards finished their discussion and went off down the tunnel toward the prison. Without shooting off another sphere. Without noticing the two of them lying here. Must have been looking for the new hole in the ceiling. Quinn wasn't sure whether to be happy that they were leaving or worried about their interest in the hole.

He waited until the guards were out of sight before taking his hand off the med tech's mouth. "Time to go, Doc."

For a second she didn't speak. Then, "Go where?"

"Up and out." He pointed over her shoulder up the tunnel. "Just in case they come back."

Her eyes flickered. "Will they?"

"Gotta figure they might. And I don't think we wanna be here when they do." He rolled off her and sat up. She watched him for a second and then seemed to realize what she was doing, because she blushed and looked away.

Quinn grinned. "Sorry, Doc. Been a while since I woke up naked on top of a woman, you know what I mean?"

"Urk," his med tech said, or something like it, as she flushed an even more painful shade of crimson.

He took pity on her. "I'll just go over here and put something on. What d'you do with your clothes last night?"

She waved a hand up the tunnel.

"Why don't you go see if any of it's dry enough to wear? I don't think you oughta be walking around like that. Don't want nobody to get the wrong idea if they see you."

And he didn't want to deal with the distraction she presented, either.

She scrambled off on long legs, her cheeks hot. Both sets. Quinn went in the opposite direction to rustle up his own clothes. What he needed was a cold shower, but since he didn't want to risk another trip into the current, putting on cold, wet clothes might be the next best thing in order to try to get his body under some semblance of control.

• • •

Good Lord, Elsa thought, as she trailed Captain Conlan up the tunnel toward the spot where they'd fallen in last night, *what was wrong with her?*

He was wearing his prison-issue coveralls, a little worse for wear and with the bottoms of the legs cut off to fashion restraints for her yesterday. Olaus's uniform was slung over his shoulder. Like her dress, the wool was too wet to wear.

She herself was dressed in nothing but her synthetic underthings. They were damp but not too uncomfortable, and as he'd mentioned last night, once they got out of the tunnel and up to the surface, the sun would be warm. She'd be dry in no time.

Elsa still had no idea how he planned to accomplish that feat, and she didn't want to ask. The less said between them right now, the better. At least until she figured out what was wrong with her—or him—and exactly what had happened last night and this morning.

The night had been awkward, but less so than she'd feared. He hadn't been able to see her—or she him—which had helped. And he'd tried to put her at ease with his questions about her background and childhood. He'd even answered a few questions of his own, even if his answers had been evasive at best and possibly untrue. She was pretty sure she hadn't learned anything from him she didn't already know. He'd told the truth when he'd said he was from a town called Dublin on Old Earth—that had been in the information packet they'd received from the Rhenish military base on Marica—but she had no way of knowing whether it was true that he hadn't been back there since he was seventeen.

At any rate, he'd done his best to make the experience as comfortable as possible for her. It wasn't his fault they'd fallen in the water and needed each other's warmth to survive. Judging by the way he'd looked at her yesterday, he hadn't been any more eager to bundle up than she'd been.

But he'd been a gentleman about it, she'd give him that. In spite of his assertion that he was too cold and tired to think about violating her, she'd been a little worried that, once they were both naked, he'd let his baser instincts rule. Men did, after all. But he'd kept his word. He hadn't—as he so crudely put it—copped a feel.

She should be thankful. After all, it wasn't as if she had wanted him to touch her beyond the strictly necessary. The thought was disgusting, abhorrent. He was a criminal, a collaborator, inferior in every way that mattered, and probably a cad and a womanizer as well…she shouldn't want anything to do with him—and she didn't, of course not. She was just a little surprised that, given his obvious physical reaction to her, he hadn't chosen to take advantage.

But perhaps he was telling the truth and that reaction was just simple biology, the male animal's automatic response when faced with a female animal in a copulatory setting. Perhaps it wasn't her at all. He would have reacted the same way to any naked woman.

And probably had, a voice at the back of her head informed her. *Often.*

Elsa did her best to ignore it. Her own reaction had been far more disturbing. Captain Conlan had been weak—possibly even weaker now than he'd been yesterday, not to mention the obvious physical disadvantages of being aroused and distracted—yet she hadn't taken advantage of those vulnerabilities to hail the guards.

He'd told her to lie still—like a good girl!—and she'd obeyed. When she should have fought him, and fought dirty, to get the guards' attention. If she had, she might be on her way·out of the tunnel by now, back to the prison.

And so would he. Back to another session with Doctor Sterling and the doctor's "toys."

A poor way to repay him for saving her life.

She had to admit, she hadn't relished the idea of getting caught in such a compromising position. Naked, her hair unbound, with the prisoner on top of her, also naked and obviously aroused… after spending the night sleeping next to him. It was a legitimate concern. The guards wouldn't have been able to keep such juicy gossip to themselves. It would have spread like wildfire among the staff, ruining her reputation as well as her peace of mind. And she could tell herself all day long that it was the reason she hadn't taken the opportunity to set up a hue and cry…but the truth was that she hadn't been able to bring herself to do it. And not because she was afraid of looking stupid, but because she wasn't ready.

He'd saved her life. When he owed her nothing but disdain.

He'd endured months of torture instead of telling Doctor Sterling what he knew about the Marican resistance, although he owed the Maricans nothing.

And he'd made it out of the prison, to freedom, yet the only thing on his mind was going back to save his friends.

He was a riddle, an enigma, and she wanted to understand what made him the way he was. If she gave him up to the guards, she'd never have the chance to figure him out.

Yes, she'd have to give him up later. She was resigned to that. They wouldn't survive out here for very long, and whether he believed it or not, there was no way off Marica-3. He might think he could rescue his crew and make it off the moon, but he was wrong. Sooner or later, he'd be back in Doctor Sterling's lab again. But not today. Not after he'd saved her life. The least she could do for him was give him one more day of freedom. It would be taken away from him soon enough.

. . .

Like Holden Sinclair and Isaac Miller—and Captain Conlan himself—Toby Flatt was an annoyance to Major Lamb. A sniveling weakling, his compact body barely reached Stephen Lamb's nose, and the look in his eyes was one of mingled fear and confusion. Lamb suspected him of being simple, so he kept his words short and easy to understand.

"I'm sure you've heard that Captain Conlan left us yesterday."

Flatt blinked. "No." After a moment's pause, he added, "Nobody tells me anything."

Lamb smiled. "Of course. Well, he took a hostage yesterday morning and broke out. Leaving you all here."

Flatt blinked again. It was the only response he gave, and the look in his eyes didn't change. All Major Lamb could see in their depths was bovine stupidity. He sighed.

"It seems he fell in the river and drowned."

"River?" Flatt asked.

"There are rivers under the prison. Where did you imagine the water and power comes from?"

"Didn't think about it," Flatt said, confirming Major Lamb's suspicions that he was an idiot. Really, as a mechanic, shouldn't he know better?

"Of course. Well, the rivers are cold, so even if he'd made it out of the rapids—a highly unlikely event—his chances of having survived the night are slim."

Major Lamb's concern now was for Elsa Brandeis, whom he hoped had escaped the captain's fate. Patrols were coming and going, on the surface and down below, but so far no one had seen any sign of her, alive or dead.

They hadn't recovered Captain Conlan's body, either, but that was just a matter of time. They had his boots; the rest of him would follow in due time.

"What's it gotta do with me?" Flatt wanted to know, and Major Lamb turned his attention back to the mechanic.

"With Captain Conlan gone, Doctor Sterling will be looking to the rest of you for answers about the Marican resistance. I thought you'd like to know what to expect."

"But I don't know nothing!" Flatt protested. He'd turned a shade paler, Lamb noted, and was twining his fingers together. They'd healed crookedly after being broken, and Lamb imagined the man wasn't looking forward to another session with Doctor Sterling's equipment.

"Of course not," he said. "You're just a mechanic, right?"

Flatt nodded.

"Captain Conlan wouldn't have confided anything important to you."

Flatt shook his head, and didn't even seem to notice the insult. Lamb sighed.

"Why don't you give it some thought, Mr. Flatt? Maybe you can come up with something to tell Doctor Sterling when the time comes. Before he pulls out the thumbscrews again."

Flatt nodded, but his eyes were worried. Major Lamb withdrew, a smirk on his face. He may not have Captain Conlan, but at least he could take his frustrations out on the other prisoners. Perhaps he'd pay another visit on the young Marican woman from yesterday, too. She might have recovered enough by now to present more of a challenge.

Whistling, Lamb set off down the hallway in the direction of the women's wing.

CHAPTER FOURTEEN

They were running out of options faster than he liked.

Quinn stood in the tunnel for a long time, looking up at the hole they'd made yesterday, trying to come up with some way to get up there. But if he leaned too far to his left, he'd fall in the river. It was too high to jump. He had nothing to climb on and no tools at his disposal.

Thoughtfully, he put a hand on the grip of the laser pistol. Out of the corner of his eye, he saw the med tech take a step back.

"I ain't gonna shoot you, Doc. You being dead won't make it any easier for me to get up there."

There was another pause, while he contemplated the hole and she contemplated him. Probably trying to decide whether he meant it.

"You could lift me," she said.

Oh, sure. "Not unless you want me to drop you in the water again."

She gave him a slanted look out of the corner of her eye. "You didn't drop me the first time."

True. "I'd drop you this time. The angle's wrong."

The opening was directly above the water. He'd have to hold her up and out, over the rushing waves, and there was no way he'd be able to do that without letting go. They'd both overbalance and fall back in the water. Although he supposed he should be grateful the hole was where it was; if they'd broken through anywhere else, they'd have fallen through and busted their heads open on the rocks instead of landing in the river.

Would the laser beam from the pistol be strong enough to cut through the earth? Would the charge last long enough? If he could widen the hole in this direction, he might be able to get her up there without giving her another bath. Then she might be able to get him out.

Or she might leave him down here, with a laser pistol that was out of power, while she ran like hell. He'd be stuck like a rat in a barrel, just waiting for the guards to pick him off. He still had the knife, sure, and if it came to it, he'd cut his own throat before letting himself get recaptured, but the thought held little appeal.

What were their other options?

They could explore further. Walk up the river past this point, see if anything changed up there. Maybe there was another way out, more easily accessible.

Or they could head back down the tunnel toward the prison. There'd be guards there, too, but he'd be closer to where he wanted to be. In a position to rescue Holden, Isaac, and Toby. Always assuming Holden, Isaac, and Toby were still alive and able to be rescued, of course, and he should probably ask the med tech first before he did anything stupid. It'd be a damn shame to go back only to learn that they were dead and he'd risked himself for nothing.

A chill ran through his body, and he did his best to shake it off. It was cold down here, even with the sun blazing above, and his coveralls were still damp. By now he wished they weren't. He had other things on his mind than the med tech in her granny panties, so he no longer needed that pseudo cold shower, and the damp fabric clung uncomfortably and slapped against his legs with every step. He was cold, he was tired, his entire body ached from the buffeting in the rapids and the night spent on the cold, hard ground…all he wanted was to curl up somewhere warm, to sleep and think.

But first they had to get up and out.

Pulling the laser pistol from the holster he told the med tech to step back. "Might be rocks flying in a minute. You don't wanna get hit."

She shook her head and flattened herself against the wall. Quinn aimed the pistol at the ceiling and squeezed the trigger, watching as a beam of light cut through the twilight and sizzled against the rocks. Slowly, he carved a line through the ground above. Pebbles and dirt rained down into the water, followed by a chunk of earth the size of a small groundcar. If he'd been standing under it, he'd have been flattened. As it was, it hit the river with a mighty splash. The med tech shrieked as a wave of cold water cascaded out of the river and splashed them both.

"Cac!"

Quinn stepped back, slipped on the wet rocks, and almost dropped the pistol. The only thing that saved him was the med tech's hands at his waist.

He froze and felt her do the same. After just a second her hands dropped, and she stepped away, back against the wall, leaving him to find his balance on his own. He wondered whether she'd make reference to it. But no, she didn't say a word. Probably afraid he'd take her head off, after that crack yesterday about not wanting her to touch him.

What was it he'd said? *Unless I'm cold and dead and beyond anything you can do to me…?*

"Thank you." He didn't bother to glance over his shoulder to see how the tacit apology was received, just braced his legs and lifted the laser pistol again. If she answered, he couldn't hear it over the rushing of the river and the sound of pebbles and dirt dropping.

The second big chunk of earth hit the path, and they both had to jump out of the way to avoid getting hit. Even so, rocks and gravel sprayed, and Quinn felt the impact when something sharp struck his cheek. His eyes stung from the dirt and debris in the air, but when the dust had settled and he'd blinked his eyes clear, Marica's hot sun flooded into the tunnel.

The med tech stepped forward and squinted up at it, her lips curving as the warm rays hit her. For a second, all Quinn could do was watch as the sun gilded that perfect alabaster face, making her skin glow and her hair light up like a halo. She'd braided it again this morning, and it hung in a long rope down her back, but as it dried, soft tendrils had pulled free to frame her face. Her eyes were half closed, those long, curving lashes lowered, and her expression was one of pure bliss.

Look at me *that way*.

The thought was unbidden and—he reminded himself—unwanted. This was the Rhenian ice bitch, Doctor Sterling's assistant. The queen of the clipboard, buttoned to the neck with no trace of humanity or normal feelings hidden beneath that exquisite exterior. Just because she looked human now didn't mean she was, ultimately. Bedding her would be like bedding a pleasure droid: physically complete but emotionally unsatisfying.

However, his body didn't seem to get the message, probably

because he couldn't bring himself to look away. She was like a marble statue in an old holovid he'd once seen, a perfect work of art come to life, and the illusion of warmth imparted by the sun only served to make her more stunning. She looked soft, warm and touchable, and at that moment, it was all he could do not to reach out and do just that.

Until she opened her eyes and looked at him. And whatever she saw on his face—and he had a pretty good idea what—caused her cheeks to flush. Those soft lips parted on what might have turned out to be a gasp had he been able to hear it over the rushing water, and her eyes got wider and darker. With awareness…or fear?

Must be the latter, because she took an involuntary step back, away from him, and would have toppled backward into the river had he not reached out and steadied her. "Careful."

His voice was rough, a husky growl, and he could feel her tense under his hands.

For a second they stood frozen, while his fingers flexed on her upper arm. He wondered whether she had any idea how close he was to yanking her up against him and taking some of his frustrations out on her.

Then she blinked, and the spell was broken. Biting back a curse, Quinn pulled her away from the edge of the river and propped her against the wall. "Watch where you step!"

He dropped his hand off her arm, and she immediately folded both across her chest. A physical barrier between them as well as an emotional one, which also served to hide those pert nipples poking at the damp fabric of her top.

Just as well. If she'd been able to burrow into the wall, he thought she would have. He was frankly surprised she wasn't running down the tunnel as fast as she could to get away from him.

To give her — and himself — a chance to regroup, he turned his back, half expecting a push between the shoulder blades to send him headlong into the river. It didn't come. When he glanced at her over his shoulder, after he thought he could deal with looking at her again without disgracing himself, she was standing in the same spot staring straight ahead.

"You ready?"

She jumped and flushed. "What?"

"You ready to try this?" He gestured at the hole, now extending above them. Through it he could see blue sky and bright sunshine.

"Oh. Um…" Her eyes flickered. "I suppose."

"C'mon." He gestured for her to join him and couldn't help but notice the reluctance with which she came forward. "Looks to me like it's about ten or eleven feet up there. What do you think?"

She looked up, gauging the distance from where they were standing to the ceiling, and nodded.

"I'll try to lift you. But in order for this to work, I think you're gonna have to stand on my shoulders."

She shot him a look, one of mingled surprise and clear unwillingness.

"How tall are you, Doc?"

She gave him her height in centimeters, and it took him a second to convert into feet and inches. Bottom line, she was just an inch or so shorter than him.

"If it's eleven feet up there, the only way you'll reach is if you stand on my shoulders. You'll just have to be careful so you don't fall in the river."

She gave the frothing water a wary look.

"You'll be fine. I'd do it if I could, but I don't think you're gonna want me climbing on you."

The double entendre didn't strike him until the words were out, and by then it was too late. She blushed again.

"C'mon." He braced himself with both hands against the wall. "See if you can get up."

There was more silence, with nothing happening. Eventually, she stepped up behind him and put her hands on his shoulders. "How?"

"I don't know. Just…climb."

She tried, he'd give her that. And damn near killed him in the process. In more ways than one. Especially when—frustrated by the lack of progress—he turned and grabbed her and lifted, almost burying his nose in her crotch.

"Get your knees on my shoulders!" His voice was strained, and not just from the effort. He knew he should probably hold his breath, so he wouldn't come across as some pervert sniffing her panties, but he needed to breathe, dammit. Oxygen was already in short supply here on Marica-3. And she was heavier than he'd expected, or maybe he was just weaker than he thought. His arms were shaking with the strain of holding her aloft.

"I'm trying." She huffed, finally managing to fling…not a knee but her whole leg across his shoulder. Now his nose really *was* buried in her crotch.

"Sorry! Sorry…"

She wiggled, which only made it worse. Biting back a curse, Quinn did his best to shift her to the back, where, eventually, she ended up sitting on his shoulders.

"Now…"

They both needed a moment to catch their breaths. The med tech seemed to have a hard time hanging on; her hands were shifting over his head, trying to find purchase. At one point, she even grabbed his ears. If his hair had been longer, he had a feeling her hands would have been fisted in it by now. And Christ, the mental holovid *that* thought brought on…!

Shaking his head to clear it of sexual images, he almost unseated her, and she shrieked. It was his turn to apologize. "Sorry…"

And his hands on her thighs didn't help. Her skin was smooth, soft, a little cool, but not flaccid, not the way it had been last night. There was an underlying warmth now. He tried to imagine those thighs spread open for him, with her fingers threaded through his hair and her breath coming on little pants and squeaks…and then he tried not to imagine it, tried *hard*, but the image was lodged in his head and wouldn't go away.

"Cac!"

"What?" her voice said above him.

He glanced up, and caught a glimpse of her face upside down. "What?"

"You keep saying that. What does it mean?"

The expression was such a part of him now, he had to think about it. Go back to childhood, to when he'd heard Gaelic spoken in the streets. The shipyards and alleys had been rife with curses, and that one still rang in his ears to this day.

"Shit."

"Oh." She blushed, her teeth worrying her bottom lip. Upside down. "I thought it would be something worse."

He grinned. "Sorry. I can get more inventive when I want to, but that's the standby. You ready to get up higher?"

She nodded, a little reluctant. He took his hands off her legs and moved them up to brace her waist. "Get on your knees. One side at a time."

It took a minute or two, and a few more curses, but eventually she got there and gained her balance. From there, it was easier to get all the way up. Quinn kept his hands on her ankles, although how that was supposed to help if she fell, he had no idea. Maybe he ought to reach higher instead. That'd give her more support, wouldn't it?

Skimming his hands up her calves, he changed his mind by the time he got to her knees. The feel of her was just too damned distracting—*when had that happened?*—and he needed to keep his wits about him. If she fell, she'd either bash her brains out on the rocks, or he'd lose her to the river again. He'd have plenty of time to fantasize about her if they got up and out.

Correction: he'd have plenty of time to remind himself why fantasizing about her was a bad idea if they got up and out.

"Can you reach?"

His voice was strained, even in his own ears.

"A little to the left."

He shifted a few inches, careful not to jostle her or upset her balance. "How about now?"

"Just a second." He felt her move, and tilted his head back, carefully. And immediately wished he hadn't. Not only was it bloodcurdling to watch her stretch for the edge of the hole, her body swaying, but with his head between her legs, the view was damned near blinding.

Gritting his teeth, he focused on the wall. And waited. Not watching, not asking about progress. Just waiting. Until the pressure on his shoulders eased. Then he looked up, in time to see her long legs scramble up over the edge of the hole and out of sight.

Now a moment of truth. Would she come back? Or was she already on her way toward the prison as fast as those legs could go?

A few seconds passed, and then her head came back, blocking out the sun's rays. "Now what?"

He hadn't thought that far. He'd just focused on getting her up and out. Now he considered their next move. And realized that again, his options were limited. She couldn't reach him. And she probably couldn't lift him even if she could. And they had no rope, let alone a ladder, and no wood with which to make one.

"Don't know."

She was silent for a moment. Then she reached a hand down. "Throw me the clothes."

He scanned the ground and saw the wet uniform and dress they'd put aside when they started their acrobatics. She probably wanted to lay them out in the sun to dry. The sooner her dress was wearable, the sooner he could stop looking at her underwear, so it was fine with him. Maybe if she put on the ice bitch dress again, he'd be able to see her as the bitch she'd been in the lab and not as the woman he'd held all night because she'd have frozen to death otherwise.

He gathered the clothing and tossed it to her, one piece at a time. It took a few tries, but eventually she had all three. She scrambled out of sight again without a word. And didn't come back. A minute passed, then another.

Great. She probably hadn't wanted to run back to the prison in her panties. If she put on the dress now, it'd be dry by the time she got there.

Quinn shaded his eyes against the glare of the sun and peered up at the opening. "Doc?"

Nothing.

"Elsa!"

Still nothing.

"Dammit to hell!" He kicked at a rock on the ground. It skipped once before it landed in the river and sank.

"What?"

She was back. Quinn decided it was safer not to examine the feeling of relief that accompanied her face staring down at him.

"Where'd you go, Doc?"

Was there something going on up above? Like, she'd crawled out into a contingent of Rhenian guards? And now they were all standing there with their stunners out, surrounding the hole, ready to tag him the second his head breached the surface?

"Just up here." She gestured over her shoulder. "I made a rope."

It dropped as she spoke: a makeshift string of their clothes knotted together, sleeve to pant leg to sleeve, dangling just out of reach.

"Anyone else up there with you?"

She glanced over her shoulder. "Who'd be here? We're in the middle of nowhere."

True. But the fact that there was now a big hole in the ground that hadn't been there yesterday might have gotten someone's attention. Given that he—that they—were still out here, the guards may have been a little more diligent than usual when they made their rounds this morning.

"Is that a no, Doc?"

She blew her breath out, exasperated. "Yes, Captain. It's a no. There's no one here but me."

He looked up at her, trying to determine whether he could trust that she was telling the truth. She looked back, those pale green eyes clear.

He hadn't much choice but to trust her, really. Or at least he hadn't much choice but to try to climb out. Wasn't like he could stay where he was. He was cold, too, chills running through his body with regularity, his clothes still damp. He needed to get up into the sun to get dry and warm. The only way there was up. Whether guards were ringing the hole or not.

"What did you fasten the rope to?"

Best as he could recall, there wasn't much up above. No trees, certainly. Not much in the way of big rocks or boulders, either.

"Me," his med tech said.

"'Scuse me?"

"I tied it around my waist."

Quinn shook his head. "Nuh-uh. Ain't no way you'll be able to haul me out."

"You don't have a choice," the med tech told him, her voice calm. "And you don't have far to go. Just climb quickly, and get to the edge of the hole. Then you can let go of the rope."

Like hell. "I don't think that's gonna work, Doc."

"It has to. There's nothing else you can do. Unless you want to sit down there until the guards come up the tunnel a second time."

The threat in her voice was subtle but real. And she was right. He'd have less of a chance getting out without her help. He should be grateful she was willing to extend it.

This makeshift rope wasn't gonna cut it, though. Especially not wound around her waist. He was more likely to pull her back into the hole than he was to get out. She'd end up back in the river. And he'd hurt her in the process. He'd lost a few stone in the time he'd been on Marica-3, but he was still too heavy for her to pull up. And the "rope" would damn near cut her in half once he started climbing.

"Maybe there's another way."

She shook her head. "There isn't. At least not until we've tried this." And then the clincher. "Please, Captain."

Christ, he was a sucker.

"Fine. I'll try. But don't blame me when you end up back in

the river." He looked up at the uniform jacket dangling above him. Hesitated.

"What?" the med tech asked, a touch of impatience in her voice.

"One second."

Stepping over to the edge of the river, he unhooked the canteen from the gun belt and unscrewed the lid. Might be a while until they saw water again. And it seemed to be safe to drink. The med tech had certainly gulped down enough of it last night to kill her, and she was still breathing. He'd had his own share, for that matter, and it didn't seem to have hurt.

Once the canteen was full and he'd tightened the lid, he went to hook it back on his belt and paused. The less he weighed, the better.

"Here." He tossed the canteen up to her. She caught it and put it out of the way. Quinn's hands hesitated for a second on the belt itself, and the pistol it held. It was extra weight. Yet he wasn't sure he trusted her enough to hand it off.

"Just climb," the med tech said, an echo of his own earlier words to her.

He supposed he'd better. Looking up at the rope, he gauged distance and how fast he'd have to climb. Took a breath. "Brace yourself, Bridget." And jumped.

CHAPTER FIFTEEN

Bridget? Who was Bridget?

And then he jumped, and every other thought flew out of Elsa's head. As soon as he grabbed the pitiful excuse for a rope she'd made, his weight yanked her body at least a foot closer to the edge of the hole.

Good Lord! Elsa strained in the other direction, trying to roll away, but it was no good. The "rope" wasn't very long, and he weighed more than she'd expected.

She should have known better. He'd had no problem holding her down the two times he'd tried. He was much heavier than she was. Why had she thought she had any hope of lifting him? Now they'd both end up back in the river, and it'd be her fault.

And it hurt! The makeshift rope cut into her waist with every movement he made, and she was slowly, inexorably, dragged closer to the edge of the hole. Sand and rocks must be raining down on him—she could hear him cough, and that hurt, too.

Last night, the edge of the hole had given way and dumped them both in the river. If it happened again, they'd land in a heap on the rocks. They'd probably break limbs, and then they'd be stuck down below. He'd take the brunt of it, being on the bottom. She'd land on him. She tried to imagine dealing with a man with a broken leg. She'd learned how to set broken bones in medical school, for emergency situations such as this, but there was nothing here she could use for a splint, let alone anything he could take for the pain. And what would they do if he couldn't walk?

Another shower of dirt and pebbles scraped away from the edge of the hole, and Captain Conlan coughed again.

He'd called her Elsa earlier. It had been a while since anyone had called her by her first name. Even Stephen Lamb, in his courting, hadn't gotten past calling her Doctor Brandeis. And it had sounded strange in Captain Conlan's Standard, without the guttural Rhenish pronunciation she was used to. Softer, more lyrical.

And then he'd called her Bridget.

"Who's Bridget?"

He didn't answer but saved all his breath for climbing.

It seemed to take an eternity, every second sending stabs of pain through her—she'd have bruises from this—while every yank of the rope brought her closer to the edge of the hole. By the time his hands became visible, she was teetering, trying to hold on, to lean the other way, but desperately close to losing the fight.

She held her breath, watching. One more time…just once more!

His hand moved, then the other…and he transferred his grip from the rope to the edge of the ground. Elsa watched breathlessly, waiting to see if it would crumble under his weight.

It didn't. A few chunks of dirt and more dust and pebbles rained down, but the ground itself held. As the pull on the rope ceased, she scrambled around, out of the way, and threw herself flat, facing the hole. The rough ground dug into her exposed skin, but that was of secondary importance right now.

Slowly, he pulled himself up. Got one elbow out of the hole, then the other. He was breathing hard, with drops of sweat forming on his forehead. Something must have struck him earlier, because there was a cut on his cheek, oozing blood. His jaw was tightly clenched, and the look in his eyes was almost feral.

The first thing he did was glance around. Maybe he really had been afraid someone else was here.

She reached for him, but he gritted out a "No."

"You don't want help?"

"Bad enough if I fall. Don't need you to."

He heaved, grunting, and got a knee up on the ground. It still held, although more dirt trickled down.

"Now can I help?"

"No."

But when she reached for him anyway, he didn't tell her not to.

She kept her body flat to the ground, legs and arms extended. If the ground was thin and might break, behaving as if she were on ice might help. She'd gone skating as a child, on the lake by the Rhenish state school she'd attended, and she'd had the safety measures drilled into her at an early age. If the ice cracks, flatten out. Take up as much space as possible. Distribute the weight. Move slowly.

Another eternity seemed to pass until she had worked her arms under his. Then, if he slipped back, he wouldn't fall far. She'd hold him. At least long enough for him to catch another grip on the ground.

It turned out not to be necessary. The edge crumbled, and dirt fell, but the ground held. Captain Conlan got his hips up onto the surface, the muscles in his arms quivering with the strain, and then the rest of his body followed.

Nervously, Elsa watched as he just lay there for what felt like a long time, trying to catch his breath. He looked dangerously close to exhaustion: motionless, his breathing rapid, with his cheek against the dirty ground and his hands limp, lightly curled. There were rope burns across the center of each palm, she noticed, and she had no doubt there were matching burns around her waist. The scratch on his cheek wouldn't get any better from being ground into the dirt, either.

"We should move."

"In a minute." He didn't turn to look at her, just spoke to the ground, his voice ragged.

"You're bleeding."

There was a pause. "You've seen blood before, ain't you, Doc?"

Lots of blood. Including his. It was just a week since she'd watched him bled dry. What was coating the scratch on his cheek right now, mingling with the dirt, was mostly synthetic.

"At least turn this way so I can look at it."

She waited to see whether he'd tell her—again—that the only way he'd let her touch him was if he were cold and dead…but he didn't. After a moment he shifted, with a muffled groan.

The right side of his face was a mess. The blood and sweat had combined with the dirt to create a rusty brown paste that streaked his cheek in grainy rivulets. He'd already closed his eyes again, the lashes spiky against his pale skin. When she opened the canteen and turned it, and the freezing water splashed his cheek, he jumped like a scalded cat, eyes flying open.

"What the hell…!"

"Sorry." But at least now she could see the problem. And it wasn't as bad as she'd feared. A cut, maybe an inch long, not deep, scoring his cheek. It'd heal on its own. He'd probably end up with a scar, but it wouldn't be a bad one. Not compared to some of the others he had.

That was assuming he'd live the couple of days it would take for the skin to weave back together, of course.

Their clothes were still tied around her waist, fashioned into their makeshift rope, and she untied them and used a sleeve to wipe his cheek clean, or as clean as she could. She chose her own dress for the job; the fabric was a little softer and less scratchy than the rough wool of the uniform. He let her minister to him without protest, although he watched, the expression in his eyes unreadable.

Elsa was a little unnerved herself. *This* was the reason she had wanted to become a doctor all those years ago. To heal, and to help. Not to hurt.

Captain Conlan was watching her face. He couldn't know what was going on inside her—of course not—but something of her sudden despair must have shown on her face, because he asked, "You okay, Doc?"

She nodded and cleared her throat. "Fine. You?"

"Better." He moved to sit up, wincing as he did it. "Christ."

"Did you hurt yourself?"

He glanced at her. "No more than usual."

Certainly nowhere near as much as Doctor Sterling and the guards had hurt him.

"I'm sorry about your hands."

He looked at them, as if he only now had noticed that they were abraded. "I've had worse."

No doubt. Looking at his face, she noticed again the beads of sweat on his forehead.

The sun was well up now, but after the hours underground, and the dunking in the subzero water, Elsa felt pleasantly warm. She'd have thought it would be the same for Captain Conlan. Yet he was perspiring. Heavily. He was pale, too, his eyes sort of sunken. And he was shivering.

Impulsively, she reached out and put the back of her hand against his forehead. She half expected him to jerk away from the touch. He didn't. Instead, his lashes lowered, and he leaned in. Almost as if her still-cool hand felt good against his skin.

And no wonder.

"You're burning up!"

For a second, the corners of his mouth curled up. "No kidding?"

"No. You have a fever." She moved her hand to cup his cheek. The uninjured one. It was also warmer than it should be.

"Huh." His eyes drifted shut, and he leaned into her palm.

"You can't stay here," Elsa said, dropping her hand to her lap. It was tingling, probably from the heat of his skin.

He blinked his eyes open, with some difficulty. "Why?"

She glanced around, at the wide open, shallow valley, surrounded by dusty hills. "Because we're out in the open. Next to a big hole in the ground. With the sun beating down on us. We'll fry to a crisp. You need somewhere shady, where you can rest."

He managed to rouse himself. "You got somewhere in mind?"

She didn't. She just felt very exposed out here. And the fact that he seemed perfectly happy to stay, with no concern for the guards who may be on their way out here as they spoke, was disconcerting. He really must be feeling bad if personal safety was so far from his mind.

She got to her feet and put out a hand. "Come on."

He looked at it for a second before he took it and let her haul him to his feet. It was easier said than done, and when he finally got there, he was swaying. His hand was dry and burning hot in hers.

"You'll have to lean on me." There was no way he'd be able to walk on his own without support. She hadn't noticed how pale he was down in the tunnel, or how sluggishly he moved. Yes, it had been dark, and she'd had other things on her mind...but that last climb on top of lifting her must have really taken it out of him.

He didn't move, just stared at her, but when she made a move to put an arm around him, he stepped aside. And almost stumbled. Heart thudding against her ribs, Elsa lunged for him and yanked him back to safer ground.

"Careful!"

And then she realized he'd drawn the laser pistol from his belt and was holding it in a shaking hand.

Elsa forced herself to calm down, to keep her voice even. "You won't need that, Captain Conlan."

He blinked at her, and she realized his addled mind had thought she was going for it, that she'd been trying to reach around him to where it was holstered.

She added, her voice slow and soothing, "I don't want the pistol, okay? Just put it away. And let me help you. We'll find somewhere to lie down."

There was a pause. Then he nodded. "Yeah. That'd be good." He holstered the pistol again, a little awkwardly, as if he couldn't quite get it into the holster on the first try. Or the second.

"Lean on me."

Heart thudding, she moved to slip an arm around his waist. This time he allowed it. His coveralls were still damp, but it was hard to tell whether they were wet from their dunking in the river or whether the fever had contributed to their current state.

"Come on, Captain. Let's go." She gave him a gentle nudge forward, back into the low foothills they'd spent most of the day navigating the day before. There was shade there, and little cracks and crevices where they could rest, out of the sun and away from anyone walking by.

And he needed rest. A couple of days' worth, really, to do even the minimal of good, although he'd be lucky to get a few hours. The guards would be out looking for them again now that the sun was up, and the sooner they could get under cover, the better. Elsa kept a keen eye out for resting places as they moved, agonizingly slowly, through the narrow canyons. They were both barefoot by now. The hot ground burned the soles of her feet, so she knew it must burn his as well, and he kept stumbling, as if he couldn't quite get the hang of putting one foot in front of the other. The longer she held on to him, the more obvious his fever became: he was almost uncomfortable to touch, his skin heating hers even through the layers of clothing.

It must have taken a couple of hours of slow but determined movement to get to a place where Elsa felt comfortable stopping. They were deep into the canyons by then, with tall rock walls on either side. Nothing about it was familiar, so she thought they must not have come this way yesterday. Then again, everything was the same dull, monotonous tan, so it was difficult to be sure.

At any rate, there were fissures in the rock, just like yesterday. And a few big boulders that offered the promise of shade. No water, of course, and no vegetation, but she still had the canteen and planned to use some of the water as soon as they stopped. Their clothes, which she was also carrying, were dry by now, but she hadn't bothered to put the dress on. The sun was scorching her exposed skin, but additional clothing would only serve to make her feel warmer.

When she saw the narrow fissure in the rock wall, it called to her. Something about it was different from the others. At first it was hard to tell what, but she knew it didn't look the same.

When she slowed down to look at it, Captain Conlan did, too, his head tilted. She didn't know whether it was deliberate or whether he just couldn't hold it up straight any longer.

"Deep," he said eventually, his speech slurred.

"Excuse me?"

He glanced at her, gray eyes under lowered lashes, like he couldn't quite keep his eyes open, either. "'s deep. Deeper'n the others."

"Do you think so?"

"See for yourself." He dropped his arm and stood there, swaying. After a worried look—hopefully he wouldn't fall flat on his face—Elsa removed her arm from around his waist. She waited a few seconds, just to be sure he was capable of keeping on his feet without support, and then scrambled up the gravelly incline toward the fissure.

When she got there, she saw he was right: this fissure was even deeper than the one they'd spent the afternoon in yesterday. Enough room for him to lie flat. And although it was hot, as everywhere else, it was dark and at least a few degrees cooler than outside, away from that searing, unrelenting sun. Perhaps he could get some rest, finally. Maybe sleep off some of the fever.

She waved to him to join her, and he did, stumbling in the loose gravel. She had to catch him and pull him the last meter into the fissure.

They were up above the canyon floor by two meters, safely out of the line of sight of anyone happening by. She scanned the path in both directions, looking for any sign of life, but saw none. That done, she examined the fissure itself. No derma-lizards that she could see, and they were big enough that she ought to notice if one was there. No spider-scorpions. And no tomato-red worms. Thank the Lord for that, because they were both battered and bruised from the trip down the river and the climb out of the tunnel. Any night crawler would have an easy time penetrating either of their bodies. As usual, Captain Conlan was in worse shape than she was, and Elsa determined to keep a close eye on him for the next few hours.

"Come on, Captain. Lie down. Get comfortable. As comfortable as you can."

The clothes they'd had on last night when they fell in the river—the clothes that had enabled them to climb back out of the tunnel—had dried on the walk here, and she fashioned them into a makeshift pillow she could put under his head while he lowered himself to the hard ground, wincing. After a second or two of moving around, he grinned up at her.

"This ain't so bad. No worse than that sorry excuse for a bed I slept on in the prison."

"I'm sorry." It seemed to be her new refrain. He didn't respond, but at least it seemed as if he no longer doubted her sincerity. He'd stopped commenting on her apologies.

"Here." She cupped the back of his head and lifted to shove the folded-up uniform underneath.

He looked at her for a second, his expression unreadable. "Thank you, Doc."

"You're welcome, Captain."

Another weak grin lit his face. "I think you should probably call me Quinn. Seeing as we spent the night together and all. Wet and naked."

Elsa could feel the blush creeping up but could do nothing to stop it. Hopefully the light was too low for him to notice. "I'm not sure I feel comfortable doing that."

He looked at her for another long moment. "Doctor-patient issues? Or prisoner-jailer ones?"

"I'm not your jailer, Captain Conlan."

"No," he agreed. "Out here, I figure I'm yours. As long as I've got the pistol, anyway."

"You won't shoot me." She wasn't quite sure where the words came from, but she was sure she was right.

"You don't think so?"

"You haven't so far."

"Don't mean I won't."

"You're more likely to shoot yourself than me."

He didn't answer, and she added, "You could have let me fall in the river last night, and you didn't. You could have left me for dead when I drowned. You didn't have to resuscitate me. And you certainly didn't have to hold me all night so I wouldn't freeze to death."

"I did it so *I* wouldn't freeze to death."

Hah, Elsa thought. "You did it so we both wouldn't freeze to death. And after all that, you won't just shoot me for no reason."

"I'll shoot you if you get in my way." There was no mistaking the sincerity in his voice, and this time she believed him.

"I'll try to make sure that doesn't happen. I'm not ready to die. For right now, just try to get some rest. Would you like a drink?"

His eyes fell on the canteen. "How much is left in there?"

She tilted it, gauging the contents. "Half?"

"Maybe just a bit, then."

Elsa unscrewed the cap and held the bottle to his mouth, dribbling a tiny stream of water between his lips. He swallowed and nodded. "Thanks." The tip of his tongue came out to lick the last drops of water from his bottom lip. When she went to cap the bottle again, he added, "What about you?"

"I'm…" She stopped short of telling him she wasn't thirsty, since that would be patently ridiculous. Her throat was practically parched.

"Go ahead. If you die of heat stroke, I can't carry you." And although he didn't say so, she knew he wanted her to get him back inside the prison so he could try to get his people out. She still thought it was an impossible task, but she wasn't going to tell him so. At least not yet.

"Maybe just a little." She lifted the canteen, then hesitated. He'd just drunk from it. Maybe she should wipe it first before drinking herself? Sharing the bottle seemed a very intimate act. And if he was getting ill, it was probably a good idea to take precautions.

Then again, he must have had his lips all over hers last night. She hadn't really thought about it until now, that he must have given her the breath of life, but for her to have survived, it was the only possibility. No resuscitation machine down in the underground tunnel last night—he had to have done it manually. Pushing on her chest with his hands, pushing his own breath into her lungs.

The thought was…she probed inward, gauging her feelings the way she'd gauged the contents of the bottle…a little disturbing, perhaps. Or perhaps distracting was a better word, but it wasn't horrible. In fact, if she had to be beholden to someone for saving her life, she'd almost rather it was him than someone else. Even if the irony was intense. She had revived him over and over, only so Doctor Sterling would be able to torture him to death again.

He had revived her so she could live.

He was watching her, and she wondered if he was thinking about the same thing. She ignored him as she lifted the canteen to her lips and took a sip. The water was warm now, after hours in the sun, but the liquid went down her throat like the finest wine, clearing away dust and sand. It would have been so easy to keep drinking, but there was no telling how long they'd have to make the water last. Better not.

She went to cap the bottle, but hesitated.

"Something wrong?"

"I need a piece of cloth."

He didn't ask what for, just lifted his head long enough to reach behind him for her dress and pull it out. "Here."

"Thank you." She examined it. One sleeve was still dirty and stained with blood from when she'd wiped his cheek earlier. The other was clean. She dribbled a little of the water onto it. "Close your eyes."

He looked at her for a second before he obeyed. Elsa waited until his eyes were closed before she began wiping his face with the wet fabric. The cut on his cheek looked like it would heal all right, she noted. The synthetic blood had clotted the way it was supposed to on the walk, and the bleeding had stopped. She made sure to avoid that area with the sleeve, just wiped around it.

Slowly, over the next few minutes, the tension in his face lessened, and he began to breathe more easily. He didn't fall asleep, but he was able to rest more comfortably. Elsa continued south, moving the wet fabric under his jaw. His pulse was beating in the hollow of his throat, a little faster than it should be. She brushed the wet fabric over it.

When she flicked open the top button of the coveralls, his eyes opened. "You trying to get me naked again, Doc?"

She made sure her eyes didn't meet his. "I'm just trying to make you more comfortable, Captain. You're too warm."

He managed another tired grin, but his eyes drifted shut again as soon as she began to wipe his chest, his breath leaving his body on a sigh.

He had a tattoo, Elsa knew, from seeing him undressed in the lab, and as she moved the damp cloth over his chest, she kept her eyes on it, trying to make out the words. It had always intrigued her, but of course she hadn't been able to give it much attention on the other occasions she'd seen him like this. A couple of lines of script, faded almost to illegibility, snaked across his left pectoral. *Bráithre thar gach ní*, best as she could make out, with allowances for some of the more faded letters.

She wasn't thinking when she reached out to trace the words with her finger. He must not have been expecting it either, because he jumped, and his eyes opened again, sluggishly.

"Sorry. I was just trying to…" She trailed off.

One of his hands was on the grip of the laser pistol and had been there since he lay down. She assumed he was worried she'd try to make a grab for it if he fell asleep. The other had come up to cover the tattoo, almost protectively. "It's Gaelic."

"What does it mean?"

He contemplated her for a moment before he answered. "Brothers above all."

"Do you have brothers?"

He shook his head.

"Why do you have it written on your chest?"

He hesitated. "It's a long story."

"I'm not going anywhere," Elsa said, rather surprised to find that it was true.

"It ain't that interesting. When I was seventeen, I got a job on a ship running contraband out to New Jericho. They were in the middle of a siege, kinda like what's going on here. They needed supplies, and they were willing to pay for them."

"Your family allowed you to go off into a war zone?"

Elsa had left her own family at six, to enter one of the Rhenish state institutions for learning, and she hadn't really had much contact with them since. It was the way things were done on Rhene: the resources, including the human ones, were there for the good of the republic, their own lives and desires secondary to the needs of the Rhenish society. But not everywhere was the same, and she had heard that on Old Earth children actually lived with their families until they were adults and able to take care of themselves.

The fever must be affecting his brain, because he was answering her questions more candidly than he'd done before. "Ain't got no family. I grew up in an orphanage, and by seventeen I'd been on my own for a couple years already. Wasn't nobody who cared what I did."

Also unlike Rhene. There, someone always cared what you did. Even if it was less out of concern for your personal well-being than the well-being of the republic.

"So you hired onto a smuggling ship. Did they make you get the tattoo?"

He shook his head. "The marking came later. Couple years. We ran into a bit of trouble on a run. Got hailed just off Fontaine. First rule of business was to protect the cargo at all cost. Dump anything else, but keep the cargo. The cargo was money in the bank, and the employer got right pissy if we lost it."

Elsa nodded.

"One of the men was hurt in the fighting, and instead of taking care of him, the skipper made tracks. Leaving Sean there."

Elsa blinked. "What happened to him?"

"The Kedarii got him." His voice was matter-of-fact, but with a tight undertone.

The Kedarii. Elsa had no personal knowledge but had heard the residents of el-Kedar were vicious. "What happened?"

He met her eyes, his own steady if overly bright from the fever. "Don't know exactly. Though I can guess."

Based on his own recent experiences, she assumed, and felt sick all over again. The Kedarii had a well-earned reputation for brutality and viciousness. Was he saying that the Rhenians were just as bad?

Considering some of what she'd seen, some of what she'd done, could she argue the point?

He continued, his voice controlled. "In the end, they killed him. By then, he probably wished for it." The look in his eyes told her he was intimately familiar with the feeling.

There was a pause.

"And the tattoo?"

He glanced down at it. "A reminder. And a promise that I won't make that mistake again. I don't leave people behind."

Hence his need to go back inside the prison to find his crew. Didn't he realize how unlikely it was that he'd succeed?

"Are you sure you want to risk your life to try to get the others out? You've gotten away." For now, anyway.

He stared at her for a moment without speaking. "Better to try and fail, and die in the process, than live with the knowledge that I didn't try."

"But what if you don't die? What if you're recaptured?"

She had no conscious memory of deciding to say the words; they just spilled from her mouth.

He gave her another long look. "I'll have to try to avoid that. But I can't not try. I owe it to them to do everything I can. It's my fault they're there. I gotta try to get them out."

The tone of his voice effectively closed the argument. Elsa turned her attention back to the wet fabric in her hand. When she lowered it to his chest a second time, he shivered. Maybe he'd had enough. She put it aside and brushed the edges of the coveralls back together. "Why don't you get some rest, Captain? Try to sleep off some of the fever."

He blinked at her, his eyelids heavy. "You planning to run, Doc?"

She shook her head. "I'll stay with you. And make sure you survive."

"Why?"

"You did it for me."

It wasn't much of an answer, but it seemed to do the job. He nodded and closed his eyes. Elsa leaned back against the hard rock wall of the fissure and prepared to wait.

Chapter Sixteen

The hours dragged by. Elsa sat in the twilight of the fissure dividing her attention between Captain Conlan and the deserted, sunlit canyon outside. Her stomach felt hollow and strange. Every once in a while, it would give her a jab of pain. If there'd been anything edible anywhere around—even a night crawler—she would have eaten it, but there was nothing. Just rocks and dirt, and she wasn't quite at the point yet where she wanted to try chewing on that.

How long could they hope to survive without food? Yesterday hadn't been so bad, between the adrenaline and the fact that she'd eaten breakfast in the morning, but today she was nearing the end of her rope.

Outside the fissure the light moved from left to right. Inside, nothing changed. Captain Conlan dozed. Occasionally, Elsa would dribble a little tepid water between his lips or onto the sleeve of her dress to wipe his face and throat. It gave him momentary relief, but nothing lasting. Best as she could tell without the proper instruments, his fever kept rising. Toward the end of the day, his skin was almost blazing. He was shivering with cold in spite of the hot, still air. She did her best to cover him with Olaus's uniform, but it was a poor effort, not helped by the fact that he got more and more restless as the day went on and kept throwing it off. Whenever he managed to fall asleep for a bit, he had bad dreams, which made his features contort as if in pain and caused him to whimper and moan.

Watching him was heartbreaking. To see all his strength and that stubborn determination reduced to such utter weakness touched something deep inside her. She hadn't known he had it in him, to be honest. She'd assumed he was always strong, always determined. Through everything Doctor Sterling had thrown at him, she'd never seen him so broken as he was now. And the knowledge that she had been a party to reducing him to this, that this was her doing, twisted her insides into knots. The hunger pains were nothing compared to the realization that this was her responsibility.

She'd never been someone who enjoyed pain, her own or other people's. She had wanted to heal, not hurt. She had specialized in research, imagining herself finding cures for the blue plague and the swamp fever that plagued her fellow Rhenians. Doctor Elsa Brandeis, making great discoveries, saving lives and making Rhene a better, safer place to live.

Until Doctor Sterling came along and turned her head.

Not in a romantic way, but with his reputation and his interest in her talents and abilities, his tutelage and mentorship. She had come to Marica-3 at his request after he was asked to head the medical team here. To be his personal assistant, his second-in-command of the lab.

By then, she was already too far gone down the road of hero worship and admiration. Somewhere in the back of her head, a small voice told her that what she was doing was wrong, that hurting people wasn't what she was meant to do…but the admiration and honor she received from being Doctor Sterling's chosen right-hand researcher drowned that small voice out. What Doctor Sterling was doing was more important than her small plans: he was working to further Rhene's reach in the nexus, to help her home planet conquer worlds.

And so she had stood by and watched Doctor Sterling inflict horrible tortures on Captain Conlan, ignoring the voice in the back of her head. Shutting down all of her emotions to be able to function. Building a shell around herself so thick and impenetrable that nothing could get through. She had monitored his vital signs, determined how much more of the torture he could take, with his screams and curses ringing in her ears…and she had justified it as necessary to obtain the information the Rhenians needed.

She could no longer justify it. Not when she watched him like this, so defenseless, so broken, stripped of any strength or dignity by the fever. The fever he'd caught saving her worthless hide.

And then her heart almost stopped when he choked, his body bowing up as he struggled for air.

"No!"

She threw herself at him, pushing him back down into the ground. "Breathe!"

He tried, she'd give him that. His fists clenched as he labored to draw breath.

"Breathe!"

She drew back and did the only thing she could think of: lifted her hand and slapped him, hard, across the cheek. The impact stung her palm and snapped his head to the side, but he did suck in a breath. And then another. And then—*God!*—it was Elsa's turn to choke as she found herself flipped on her back with his weight on top of her.

It wasn't the first time she had been in this position during the past two days, but this time he had both hands wrapped around her throat. His eyes were feral, beyond reason or recognition as he looked at her, his teeth bared. His voice vibrated with barely leashed fury. "You goddamn bitch! Did you think you could hide from me forever? I swore if I ever got my hands on you again, I was gonna kill you!"

He looked like he would do it, too, his eyes blind with fever and rage, the gray almost black. His hands around her throat were so hot, they felt like a brand.

Who did he imagine she was?

Not herself, obviously. Not Elsa Brandeis. He'd held Elsa in his arms all through the night. If he had wanted to kill her, he could have done it then, more than once.

No, he wasn't seeing her. He was looking at someone else. Hatred was coming off him in waves, stronger than the fever.

Thank God he's weakened by the illness, flashed through her mind. If it hadn't been for that, she would have been dead already. He had the determination, but at the moment, thankfully he lacked the strength.

Gasping for air, Elsa managed to get her own hands up to his chest. "Captain…"

Her voice was no more than a whisper. His skin, even through the fabric of the coveralls, was uncomfortably hot to the touch, and the feel of his muscles against her palms was distracting. Surprisingly so, given the circumstances.

He must have noticed, because he laughed. "That ain't gonna work, sweetheart. Not this time. I know you now. Two-bit whore."

"No…" Struggling for breath, she moved her hands up to his cheeks, forcing him to look at her, pushing her voice past the hands wrapped around her throat. "Captain. It's me. Elsa. Not…"

He blinked, and for the first time, a touch of doubt crept into those gray eyes. "Josie?"

"No! Elsa. I'm Elsa. Doctor Brandeis." He'd mentioned Josie before. Was she his girlfriend? Or wife?

The possibility that there was a Mrs. Conlan somewhere was surprisingly disconcerting.

The grip around her throat slackened. "Doc?"

She could breathe again, and immediately speaking became easier. "Yes, Captain." *Thank the Lord.* "It's me."

"Christ." He moved away, up on his knees, and looked at his hands as if he hadn't seen them before. Elsa carefully sat up, too.

"You need to lie down, Captain. You're ill, remember? You fell in the water?"

"Water?" He looked around, confused.

"Just rest. I'll get you something to drink." She crawled over to where the canteen lay and brought it back to him. "You have a fever, Captain. That's why you're feeling this way. You need to sleep."

He nodded. "Sleep."

"Lie down. There you go." She got him arranged again on the hard ground. Now that the adrenaline had left him, he was as docile as a child, and back to shivering violently.

"Have a drink." She dribbled some of the tepid water between his lips. "Close your eyes. I'll wipe your forehead."

He closed his eyes obediently, and then opened them again. "Sorry, Doc. Don't know how that happened. You don't look anything like her."

"No?" She poured a few drops of water onto the yet-again dry sleeve of her gray dress.

He managed a headshake. "She had dark hair. Sort of curly.

And she was a lot smaller than you. And more—"

He made a wilted movement up around his chest.

More buxom. Well endowed.

Of course, Elsa thought sourly. He was a common, garden-variety smuggler who'd grown up parentless on the streets of Dublin; what did she expect? He probably spent any money he made at the pleasure palaces on Avaris, gambling, drinking, and wenching. Naturally he would appreciate women with obvious physical assets. Men like that always did.

"Close your eyes." Her voice was short, even to her own ears. She waited until he obeyed before she began mopping the sweat off his forehead. "Who was she? A girlfriend? Your wife?"

"Never had a wife. And she's nobody. Less than nobody."

Elsa wrinkled her brows. Whoever else Josie was, she'd been someone important enough that he wanted to kill her. "What happened?"

Captain Conlan opened his eyes again. They were a clear gray now, still overly bright from the fever, but awake and aware. "Don't you know?"

"I have no idea," Elsa said. He had a medical file in the lab, and she'd read it, but there'd been nothing in it about anyone called Josie. And although she knew he and his crew had been picked up on Sierra Luz for carrying weapons the Rhenians thought were intended for the Marican resistance, she knew nothing about his life before then. Not apart from what he'd told her. There'd been three others sent to Marica-3 along with him: all crew on his ship, and all male. If Josie had been on the ship, she'd been left behind on Marica.

"I met her on Avaris the end of last year. Most beautiful girl I'd ever seen."

Something inside her bristled. "Really."

He smiled. "Don't be a bitch, Doc. That was before I ever laid eyes on you."

Elsa flushed. Not only was it embarrassing to get caught being so obviously resentful of another woman's looks—more so when she had never put much stock in such things before—but to have him suggest that Josie had been the most beautiful only because he hadn't seen her, Elsa, yet…

Did he really think so?

Her face was all right, she supposed. It had all the right features in mostly the right places and proportions. It might even be a trifle more attractive than most. Her eyes were nice, but she'd been told they could freeze a man's gonads off, which couldn't be good. And she was a bit too tall, almost as tall as he was. If Josie had been smaller, he probably liked short women. With dark hair.

Her own hair was practically colorless, like pale wheat, and it didn't have much body, either. When she was a very little girl, her mother used to curl it into ringlets and fasten them with big bows. When she got a few years older and went away to school, where she had to take care of herself, it was easier just to grow it long and keep it braided and tucked out of the way. These days, it was less likely to be a distraction to herself or to any of the men she worked with. It was hard enough being a professional woman in male-dominated Rhenish society.

In any case, when left alone, she supposed her hair was nice enough. But it was fair. And she was skinny and flat chested. If Josie had been buxom, Captain Conlan probably liked his women well endowed. And short. And dark haired.

Elsa stopped herself before she could meander further down the tortuous paths of inadequacy. It didn't matter what he thought of her. He was a two-bit smuggler and collaborator. There could never be anything between them. Even if he were willing to put aside his preference for small, dark women with big breasts, she couldn't in good conscience go against her Rhenish upbringing to become involved with him. No matter how enticing the prospect sounded.

Ruthlessly she squashed the thought process. "So she joined your crew?"

"Not so much joined," Captain Conlan said, "as she came onboard to keep my bed warm."

Ouch.

It was difficult to keep her face under control. On the one hand, she wanted to dislike him for the way he said it, as if women existed only for his pleasure and convenience. She'd fought against that same attitude her entire professional life, and it was annoying that he should share it.

On the other, it gave her a guilty sort of satisfaction to hear him describe this Josie so callously. She might have been beautiful, but he clearly didn't think very highly of her. So maybe he did prefer his women to have more to offer than warm bodies.

But none of that explained why he wanted to kill her.

"What happened?"

He shifted on the hard ground. "Couple months went by. We got to Sierra Luz. Josie dragged me off to bed as soon as I'd pulled the *Fortune* into dock. We were still there when your people came knocking. She dragged it out as long as she could."

He swallowed painfully, and she tilted the bottle to his lips and poured another trickle of warm water into his mouth.

"So you were arrested. What happened to Josie?" Because to the best of Elsa's knowledge, she wasn't on Marica-3.

He laughed. It was remarkably ugly, everything considered.

"Turns out she'd been playing me. She's probably living high somewhere in Calvados right now, courtesy of some big-wig Rhenian bastard. No offense."

"None taken." For him to spend months with the woman, to share his bed with her, share his body, his life, his home and probably his wealth…and then have her turn on him like that—well, it wasn't surprising he was bitter.

And if it was Josie's actions that had landed him here on Marica-3, small wonder he wanted to kill her. She'd been responsible for everything that happened to him, including what had been done in Doctor Sterling's lab. And not just to him, but to the rest of his crew as well.

Bitch.

Elsa blinked, frankly surprised at the level of indignation she felt.

You're not without blame, you know.

No, she wasn't. And for her to sit here, outraged at Josie's betrayal, when she herself had stood by and watched him be beaten, whipped, poisoned, and exsanguinated without lifting a finger to stop it, was hypocritical at best, and at worst, dangerously self-deluded. No, she wasn't without fault. She was just as responsible as Josie.

Nonetheless, if she ever came face to face—or nose to forehead—with the other woman, Josie had better watch out.

Captain Conlan settled back into uneasy rest and left Elsa alone with her increasingly uncomfortable thoughts. She kept a keen eye on him, however, and made sure to wipe his forehead more frequently. She had no idea what good it would do, when the water in the canteen was as hot as his skin by now, but she wanted to avoid another instance of choking, and doing something—anything—was better than doing nothing. Next time, she might not be able to shock him into breathing again, and she didn't want him to die.

Funny what a difference a day could make. It was just yesterday she'd sat in a fissure much like this one, watching him sleep, and wondering what she'd do if he died. She'd been trussed like a Longnight goose, bound and gagged, and concerned that she'd be left to starve if he didn't wake up from his nap.

She was still concerned that she'd starve, but not because she was bound. She had the use of all her limbs as well as her mouth, and if he died, she'd be able to make it back to the prison.

She could go right now. He wouldn't miss her until it was too late, and he'd have no way of following her. She doubted she could get him upright and moving to save his life.

The problem was that she didn't want to go. He'd saved her, and abandoning him now seemed wrong. The least she could do was make sure he was back to full strength first.

Before turning him over to Doctor Sterling?

She pushed the thought aside.

Was there anything on this horrible hunk of rock that was edible? The animals must eat something, surely, and they seemed to flourish. But they probably ate one another. Perhaps each was so venomous the poisons simply canceled one another out. The spider-scorpions ate the derma-lizards, and the derma-lizards ate the spider-scorpions—and probably the night crawlers, too. The Marican water snakes must eat something, and surely the night crawlers did as well. Unless they ate themselves. The bigger, stronger night crawlers ate the smaller and weaker ones. Elsa wouldn't put it past them. Marica-3 was the sort of environment where something like that would happen.

Captain Conlan muttered and shifted in sleep, and Elsa whipped her head around to look at him. But he seemed to be all right, with no obvious problems. Just another bad dream, twisting his features as phantom pain flickered across his face. Nonetheless, she dribbled more warm water on the sleeve of her dress and crawled closer to wipe his forehead again. Better safe than sorry.

It was while she sat there, on her knees, that she became aware of sounds outside. Just like last time, there was the trickle of sand and rocks in the distance, as something—human or animal— approached.

Stealthily, Elsa dropped to her stomach and crawled toward the entrance to the fissure.

They were well up above the canyon floor, so if she stayed low, there was a chance whoever was out there wouldn't notice her. Hopefully it would turn out to be a derma-lizard or something equally noxious in an intellectually simple way. The derma-lizard wouldn't care that they were here. If it came into the fissure, she'd do her best to avoid it and to ensure that it didn't touch Captain Conlan, but beyond that, it wasn't worth worrying about. The lizards weren't known to be aggressive; the blisters and burns were just an unfortunate side effect of coming in contact with their bodies, and sharing the space with one might actually be helpful. The guards would think twice about approaching the fissure if there were derma-lizard tracks heading inside.

On the other hand, it might be guards outside. They'd still been patrolling as of this morning, down in the tunnel, so chances were they were still on the surface as well. And would continue to be until they'd either found her and Captain Conlan alive or found their dead bodies.

The sounds were getting louder as they came closer, and Elsa held her breath as she crouched there at the entrance to the fissure, staring down the canyon.

There! A shadow across the ground, long and low…a lizard?

No, dammit! The shadow may have been long and low, but the man who cast it wasn't. Taller than her by a half a head, he had broad shoulders and golden hair he kept brushed back from a high and noble forehead. The hair was longer than the prison rules dictated — all the prisoners had their heads shaved, the women as well as the men, while the guards were expected to keep their hair military short. Those rules didn't apply to Major Stephen Lamb, who was vain about his appearance. He exuded arrogance as he strode up the narrow canyon, trailed by one of the guards, a boy even younger than Olaus, who was half-skipping in his wake. As they came into view, Elsa could see the young man swallow nervously.

She shrank back, paling. Major Lamb was a far worse opponent than one or even two of the guards. They were young and unproven, unused to being out here in the desolation. They were frightened of the wildlife and quite possibly of Captain Conlan, too. An escaped prisoner with a hostage and a gun, with nothing left to lose and no qualms when it came to shooting to kill…it was enough to make anyone nervous.

For a second — just a second — she considered making her presence known. Standing up and stepping out of the fissure. Major Lamb would take her back to the prison. He probably had a lightflyer nearby. His boots weren't dusty enough for him to have walked the distance from the prison, and knowing him, she rather thought he would consider it beneath his dignity.

If she hailed him, she could ride back. There'd be clothes to wear. Salve to put on her burnt skin. Food and water, as much as she wanted. Soap for her face and hair.

All she had to do was give up Captain Conlan.

And then she jumped when the major's voice rang out and echoed off the walls of the canyon. "Elsa! Dr. Brandeis! Can you hear me?"

CHAPTER SEVENTEEN

The prisoner woke up with a start and looked around, disoriented, as loose rocks and dirt from the ceiling rained down on him. He opened his mouth.

No!

Elsa abandoned her vigil at the entrance to the fissure and scrambled across the ground as quickly and quietly as she could, to throw herself on top of him before he could speak, her hand cutting off the words. He stared up at her in shock, his eyes still overly bright with the fever.

With Major Lamb so close, Elsa didn't dare make a sound as sand and dirt still drizzled around them. Instead, she lifted her free hand to her own mouth to signal the need for silence. Captain Conlan watched her lips even after she removed her finger.

However, when he felt her fumble for the laser pistol at his side, he moved as quickly as a snake to trap her wrist in his hand.

Ow!

The flicker of pain across her face made him relax his grip, but he still kept his fingers wrapped around her wrist. His hand was big and hard, the palm hot, and Elsa became acutely aware of the fragility of her bones in his grasp. Just a quick twist, and she'd have a broken wrist to worry about.

Outside the fissure, Major Lamb was still calling her name, and stones and dirt skittered all around from the vibrations. She risked a quick whisper. "I need it."

He grabbed her other wrist to drag it away from his mouth to answer. "Sorry, Doc."

"I wasn't going to shoot you."

"You weren't gonna shoot him, either." His eyes flickered to the entrance to the fissure.

Well, no. She probably wouldn't have been able to do that. In truth, she wasn't quite sure what she'd wanted to do with the laser pistol. She just knew she'd have felt better—safer—with it in her hand.

Outside in the canyon, Major Lamb's voice had become more distant. He was moving away, still calling her name.

Captain Conlan's eyes came back to hers, those flecks of gold in their depths set off by the fever brightness. He didn't speak again, just looked up at her. Into her eyes at first, searching, as if trying to read her thoughts. Yesterday, when they'd been in this position, in another fissure with the guards outside, he'd been the one on top of her with his hand over her mouth. She'd fought him, desperate for the chance to give him away.

Now the tables were turned, and he had to wonder why.

Elsa wondered, too, distantly. She was a Rhenian woman, a doctor, holding an important position in the new regime, working directly under Doctor Sterling himself…her task, an important one, to aid the empire in every way she could.

When had her allegiance changed from that to keeping this

scruffy smuggler alive? He was a traitor, a collaborator. Her enemy. He should mean nothing to her, nothing but a means to an end.

And yet…

Was it when he'd brought her back from the dead, when he could have just left well enough alone and been free of her? Or was it when he'd held her all night, so she wouldn't freeze to death in the chill underground?

Or was it even earlier, when he'd allowed himself to fall into the ice cold river with her, instead of letting go and saving himself?

For *her*. When he owed her nothing. Less than nothing.

The outside was silent, save for a few last skittering stones. The danger had passed. For now.

Inside the fissure, time stood still as Captain Conlan's gaze moved from Elsa's eyes down to her lips and back up again. Her breath caught in her throat at the look in his eyes. When his hand came up to cup the back of her head and pull her down to him, she didn't resist.

His lips were soft, hot and dry. The fever, she supposed. Or maybe not. Her stomach tingled, and heat flooded her own body. Maybe this was the way it was supposed to be, when it was right. When it meant something beyond the purely physical.

It's never been this way before.

The kiss was gentle. Tentative. Just a soft brush of his lips against hers. An unspoken question. The opportunity to say no, to push away from him.

She didn't. The response rang through her entire body. A single word: *more*.

His mouth came back to hers, less tentative this time, and Elsa felt her body melt against his. His hand left her wrist, disappeared for a moment, and then came back to slide up her arm all the way to the shoulder, his touch leaving fire in its wake. He caught her braid in a firm grip and let it slip through his fingers until he found the elastic at the end. The quick tug to free the band stung her scalp, and Elsa gasped, her lips parting under his. He drove both hands into her hair and shook it loose, to fall forward on both sides of her face and hide them behind a curtain of shimmering silk before he cupped her cheeks and deepened the kiss.

• • •

It had to be the fever.

Just another of the dreams that had plagued him most of the day, or however long he'd been fighting this illness.

Nightmares of being back in the lab at the prison, strapped to a table with snake venom running through his veins, setting his body on fire, melting him from the inside out, his throat sore from screaming. Dreams of stumbling through the desert under the unrelenting Marican sun, his skin blistering, his throat parched, dragging his feet toward the water in the distance…only to find, when he got there, that it was all a mirage, just more sand and rocks and dirt as far as the eye could see. Under that searing, never-ending sun.

Interspersed with the nightmares had been dreams about other kinds of heat, of Josie driving him to the ragged edge of sanity, his body precariously balanced on a knife's point between pain and delirious pleasure, his skin on fire, burning with the need for relief. Only to have her leave him unfulfilled, in agony, unable to move or follow when she walked away, begging her to come back until his throat hurt.

And now it was his med tech. That slender body twisting in his arms, her mouth hot against his, while that fall of corn silk hair flowed like water through his fingers.

It had to be the fever. No way was it real.

But he could enjoy it while it lasted.

And it was glorious, every damn second of it, everything he could have imagined and more. There was nothing cold about her now. Gone was the stiff-backed Rhenian ice bitch with the imploder lance stuffed up her ass, and in her place was a warm, willing, living, breathing woman. Her skin was like satin under his hands, and her mouth was avid against his. She was thrumming with need, her body writhing restlessly, as if determined to get closer to him. When he dragged his lips away to skim down that long, slender neck to the pulse beating double time at the bottom of her throat, she arched her back to give him access, her breath reduced to shallow pants. He groaned as her pelvis pressed against the hard ridge of his erection, and she froze.

"Don't stop." His voice was ragged. To make sure she knew he meant what he said, he ran his hands down her back to cup that firm ass through the fabric of those unexciting white underpants, and pushed her down, grinding against her. The agony was exquisite, and the soft sound of desperation that escaped those perfect lips was like music to him.

Emboldened by the implicit encouragement, he slipped his hands under the synthetic material and caressed her skin, and when she whimpered and moved restlessly against him, he lost his last pretense of control. If it was a dream, anyway, what the hell was the point in holding back?

Flipping her to her back on the rough rock floor, he settled into the cradle of her thighs, his hard length against her softness. Rocking his hips against her, he watched those even, white teeth sink into her bottom lip. Her normally cool green eyes were liquid now with heat and arousal, and she made no attempt to hide her desire from him. He'd swear he grew another inch just from looking into her face.

When he pushed the skimpy top up above her breasts, she didn't protest, although he could see her cheeks flush.

"You're beautiful, Doc." And more responsive than he'd thought possible. He kept waiting for her to turn on him, to turn into Josie—driving him crazy with need while holding herself aloof and in control had been Josie's stock in trade—but it never happened. The med tech—Elsa—stayed warm and open, her response to his touch too urgent, too awkwardly untutored to be feigned. When he closed his mouth over the crest of one firm, pink-tipped breast, her body arched up to meet him, her hands holding him in place as her breaths turned into needy whimpers.

"Please…more…"

Her desperation transferred itself to him, and he stripped her panties off with hands that shook. Although there was no real question of whether or not she was ready for him, he touched her, anyway, and found his fingers slipping through the slick wetness he expected, reaffirming that yes, she did want him, just about as desperately as he wanted her. Her hands shook, too, when she fumbled with the buttons on the coveralls, and her touch on his bare skin came close to undoing him.

"Touch me," he ground out.

"I am." Her soft hands pushed the coveralls off his shoulders, down his arms, and then went on to slide over his chest.

"Not there." He grabbed one of her hands and pulled it down to where he wanted it. The feel of his hard shaft in her hand caused her to gasp—hopefully that meant she was impressed—but Quinn didn't have time to worry about it. The sensation of her cool hand wrapped around him, sliding up and down his length, was almost enough to throw him over the edge.

He slid a finger inside her, up into that wet heat. Damn, but she was tight! Looked like he hadn't been far wrong in his quip about it having been a while since she'd had a man. Not in recent memory, if the feel of her body—and her responses—were anything to go by. She was so damned desperate for release her body was vibrating with it.

What the hell was wrong with the Rhenians? She was here on Marica-3, possibly the only woman on the entire moon excepting the few female prisoners, and there weren't enough of them to go around. She was surrounded by ten thousand guards and officers… how could she be lacking for sex? Were they all blind as well as stupid?

And then he imagined her in some Rhenian officer's arms, rolling around on the bastard's bed—just like Josie—and a red haze filled his head. Was she fucking that old goat Doctor Sterling? That'd explain what she was doing here on this godforsaken chunk of rock. No wonder she was the old man's favorite assistant.

Or maybe it was that big blond ox with the smirk and the riding crop…the son of a bitch calling her name outside earlier. Some innocent-sounding bastard… Fish? Swan?

"How long has it been, Doc?"

He had to force the words out, and his reluctance was painfully obvious in the tightness of his voice. She stiffened, and for a second he was afraid he'd ruined the mood. Then her body softened against his again, her voice barely more than a whisper. "Three years."

Shit.

No sex since before she came to Marica-3, then. None of the men here had gotten what she was offering him. But hell, if it had been that long, maybe he should try to slow down a little.

He slipped his finger out of her, and she whimpered in protest.

"You're too tight, Doc."

Her body tensed again. For a moment before she asked, softly, "Don't you like tight?"

Hell, yeah. The thought of plunging into that slick, narrow sheath, to feel her convulsing around him, was almost enough to make him lose it then and there.

"I don't want to hurt you."

"You won't. Please, Captain…" Her hand flexed on his shaft, tugging gently. "Now…"

He'd never really had a chance, and as he knelt between her legs, he admitted it. It had been too late two days ago. The moment he'd watched her strip and felt his body tighten at the sight, this had been inevitable.

"I'll be gentle."

If he could. It was a slim chance, he knew that going in, and it shrank to none at all when he positioned himself at the entrance to her body and pushed inside.

His eyes practically rolled back into his head from the sensation. She was so slick, and so exquisitely tight, and he was so overdue that just that first heady feeling of being enveloped threatened to undo him.

Grimly, he held on. After three years, she deserved better than that. Better than six seconds of being pounded into the ground before he couldn't restrain himself any longer.

Not that she was complaining. She was clutching his shoulders, arching up into him, meeting each of his thrusts with one of her own, while small squeaks and needy whimpers escaped her lips. "Oh… yes…please, Captain…"

"Quinn," he ground out. If she wanted him to show her paradise, she could at least use his name for the ride there.

There was a pause, then, "Quinn."

Her voice was soft, maybe even shy, the word almost a verbal caress. Or maybe that was just in his head. But he liked the sound of his name on her lips.

Fool.

"Again." To emphasize the request—or demand—he surged into her as he said it. She gasped, clutching at his shoulders.

"Oh! More…please…"

"Quinn."

"Yes. Yes, Quinn. More, please!" She pulled his head down to kiss him, her mouth hot against his, those tightly-budded nipples scraping against his chest, and her hips arching up to take him deeper. Her voice whispered in his ears through the pounding of his blood. "Please, Quinn…"

It all became too much, much too soon, and he lost what little control he'd started with. As his careful rhythm dissolved into jagged thrusts, and his climax started building, he cursed himself for failing her, for leaving her behind.

"Sorry, Doc…"

"Elsa," she managed.

"Elsa. God, you're beautiful. I don't think I can—"

But then she clenched around him, her body arching up with a cry before dissolving into spasms. She shuddered, flying apart in his arms. And as his own climax roared through him, Quinn was pretty sure he'd died and gone to heaven.

A damn shame it was just the fever, because he'd definitely like to do this again.

Chapter Eighteen

That was the most incredible experience of her life.

Elsa stretched like a cat, not caring about the hard ground under her body, or the rocks digging into her skin, or the various muscle aches and pains she'd somehow managed to pick up during the interlude. She felt incredible, a brand-new woman.

Unable to stop smiling, she turned to look at Captain Conlan—at Quinn—still stretched out next to her, limp and boneless on the rough floor of the fissure, still deeply asleep.

Fine doctor you are. You wore him out. And the exertion probably didn't do his fever any good.

Maybe not. Heat was still rolling off his body. But she couldn't find it in herself to feel guilty. Not when she felt so good.

Had this been what she'd been missing during all those years of celibacy? Could she have had this all along?

But no, surely not. Her early experiences with sex had been as different from this as…well, as different as she was now from the woman she'd been before today.

Sex had never transformed her before.

Sex had never done much of anything before. Mostly, it had left her cold. Brian, her companion in medical college, had fumbled his way into her underpants and out again, without setting the world on fire. And more recently, a colleague in the laboratory where she worked before being recruited by Doctor Sterling had talked her into going home with him. He'd done all the requisite things and had brought her to some sort of climax, but it hadn't been like this. She had never *needed* in quite the same way before.

Perhaps it was the concept of the forbidden fruit that had added that extra layer of perceived need? The knowledge that she shouldn't have him, that he was the last man on Marica-3 she should be having these kinds of thoughts about…?

Or perhaps it was just him. He was obviously very good at sex. Much better than her previous lovers.

He's probably had a lot of practice.

A mental image of him with another woman beneath him—a woman with dark, curly hair and a lush figure, quite unlike her own—flashed into her mind, and she flinched. On the heels of the visual came the sickening thought that maybe he'd even imagined someone else while he made love to her.

But no. He'd used her name. Insisted that she use his. He knew who she was and wanted her to acknowledge him. It hadn't been impersonal. And he'd told her she was beautiful. He'd had his hands and mouth all over her body. The size of her breasts hadn't been a problem, not judging from the way he'd touched and kissed them. And if the way he'd loosened her hair and run it through his fingers had been any indication, he was fine with that, too, even if it was neither dark nor curly. She could trust that he'd enjoyed this, with her.

As she'd enjoyed it with him. Perhaps a lot more than she

should have.

Sitting up, cross-legged, she ran her gaze over him, taking stock, trying to determine whether the interlude had done him more harm than good. The fever was clearly still ravaging his body, eating away at whatever reserves he had left. He was too thin. The months in prison, and the poor rations, had made him lose more weight than he should have. She could count his ribs, and his hip bones jutted out a little too sharply, too. But once he got off Marica-3 and had the chance to eat normally again, he'd gain back what he'd lost.

If ever, her treacherous back brain whispered.

She did her best to ignore it. He'd be fine. He'd gain the weight back. And become the man he used to be. Strong, healthy, confident. She just had to figure out a way to keep him alive until then.

There was nothing she could do about that pattern of subcutaneous tracks from the night crawlers. They went all the way up his leg to the hip, like a pale web under the skin, and she knew it had weakened him. But with time and rest, and by building the muscles up again, it would bother him less. The lash marks across his back…there was nothing she could do about those, either. They'd fade with time but would never go away completely. Not on their own. But there were solutions for that. Skin grafts. Peels. Injections.

Having gotten to know him a little, she doubted he'd want anything done to remove the marks, however. He'd probably prefer to keep them, as a reminder of where he'd been and what had landed him there. A reminder of Josie, of why he shouldn't trust women? Just like the tattoo on his chest was a reminder of Sean, and why on his ship, saving lives was more important than saving the cargo.

Putting it aside for the moment, she continued her survey. His hair would grow out. At the moment, it was just dark stubble covering his scalp, scratchy and rough against her palms earlier, but it would get longer. And if it turned gray at the temples, it wasn't the end of the world. Everyone got older. The lines on his face would fade. They might never go away completely, but once the fever left him, he'd look less ravaged. And with rest, and time, and food, and more rest, he might get back to something of what he'd been when she first saw him. Before Doctor Sterling went to work on him.

If she could keep him alive. And get him off Marica-3.

To do that, she'd have to make sure he stayed away from the prison. If Major Lamb got hold of him, there was no telling what the major would do in retaliation for the murder of Olaus.

But with the rest of his crew still inside the prison, nothing would keep Quinn away.

Unless she lied. For his own good. If she convinced him his friends were already dead, he might see the futility in going back.

She glanced over at him. Would she be able to do that? To lie? After what had just happened between them?

But perhaps it wouldn't be a lie. They might be dead. With so many prisoners, how was she expected to know? People died all the time. And to be honest, she wasn't sure she even knew who they were. She remembered Quinn himself, mostly because Doctor Sterling had spent so much time working on him. He'd been in and out of the lab almost every week. The others might have come through once or twice in the early days, when they first arrived on Marica-3, but she couldn't remember seeing them. Couldn't match faces to names.

So yes, perhaps she could get away with telling him they were dead. For all that she knew, they were. And if it would keep him away from the prison and safe, then it would be worth it.

He cleared his throat. "Morning, Doc."

She glanced at the opening of the fissure. "It's still evening." The light outside had changed, turned to dull orange as the Marican sun sank toward the horizon.

Although there was undeniably something of that awkward morning-after feeling about this. After that disappointing experience with Niels Alden, the laboratory technician on Rhene three years ago, she had waited for him to fall asleep before gathering her clothes and leaving his quarters as quickly and quietly as she could. Only to endure the most uncomfortable conversation in the lab the next morning, when Niels wanted to do it again and Elsa had to explain that she'd rather endure her annual gynecological checkup than go another round with him. His efforts had been no more enjoyable than her gynecologist's.

The captain's…Quinn's eyes seemed to search her face for something. She wondered if she was as unreadable to him as he was to her.

"Did you sleep?"

She shook her head. Thought about telling him that she'd felt too good, her body too energized, and her spirit in the grip of a strange sort of fey happiness, to be able to settle down. "How do you feel?" she asked instead.

He stretched tentatively. Grimaced. "I've felt worse."

She hadn't hurt him, had she? "Um…I didn't…?"

He grinned quickly. "No."

"Oh." Elsa could feel hot color seep into her cheeks. She bit her lip.

"You did everything right."

"Oh." She blushed again, but for a different reason this time.

"I was the one who screwed up."

She looked up at him, shocked. "No! You did everything right, too."

He chuckled. "If I'd done everything right, it woulda lasted longer than fifteen seconds."

"It did last longer than fifteen seconds." An eternity. Long enough to change her life. Maybe not that last part, but by then she'd been beyond caring. She'd been so desperate for release, had waited for what felt like hours to reach that elusive peak, that she didn't care that it had come quickly. And what came before it had certainly been thorough.

He didn't answer, just looked at her, but there was warmth in his eyes. Unless she imagined it. Because it flustered her, she looked away, out at the darkening world outside the fissure. "Do you think we'll be safe here tonight?"

He glanced around, too. It was quickly becoming too dark to see much. "Safer than outside. Warmer than where we spent last night."

There was no arguing with that. Although it would get colder here, too, after the heat of the day had dissipated from the rocks and sand.

He added, "We probably won't have to worry about freezing to death."

No. So did that mean he wouldn't want to hold her? It had been strange when he did it last night, but now she thought she would enjoy it.

He was watching her face, and her thoughts must have been plain to see, because he grinned. And held out a hand. "C'mere, Doc. Before you can't see where you're going. Don't want you getting lost in the dark and ending up with some other guy."

As if there was any chance at all of that. But since that wasn't really the problem, anyway, she just gave him a smile of surprised delight and scrambled across to slide into his arms again.

He added, into her hair, "And maybe this time I can make it last more than fifteen seconds."

"It lasted more than fifteen seconds last time!"

"Prove it," he said, and kissed her. And it started all over again.

• • •

"I need you to do something for me, doc."

It was the next morning, and Elsa was getting dressed. She'd survived another night, wrapped in Quinn's arms, and had woken up feeling amazing, in spite of the aches and pains in her body both from sleeping on the hard ground and another enthusiastic round of lovemaking. He'd obviously felt the need to prove to her that he was a better lover than their first encounter might have led her to believe, and although she'd had no doubts whatsoever, she'd been happy to let him try to convince her. Which he had. Beyond a shadow of a doubt.

As for herself, she'd had three years of abstinence to make up for, so this morning she was pleasantly sore in a lot of places, but otherwise on top of the world.

Her underwear was fine; the synthetic material had survived the water and the resuscitation and Quinn's treatment no problem. Her dress was another story. It was torn down the front all the way to the waist.

Elsa fingered the rip, frowning.

"Sorry, Doc." He was sitting on the ground a few feet away, already dressed in the prison jumpsuit with his arms wrapped around his knees, watching her. "I did that. After you fell in the water."

She smiled at him. "It's no problem. I have others."

He didn't smile back. "I need you to do something for me."

"What's that?" She slipped the dress over her head and so didn't see his face when he answered. On the upside, he didn't see hers, either.

"We gotta figure a way to get back into the prison."

And there it was. The topic she'd been dreading. Far worse than the awkward morning-after conversation.

She managed to school her face into passivity before she had settled the dress around her hips, and could look at him again, blandly. "Why?"

"I told you. My crew's in there. It's up to me to get 'em out."

She glanced at him for a moment. It was all she dared to do. A longer look would be beyond her. "Are you sure they're there?"

"We came up in the shuttle together."

Elsa took a breath. And had to force the words out past a lump in her throat. "That doesn't mean they're still here."

He didn't answer, and she stole another look at him, in time to see an expression of utter devastation in his eyes.

I can't do this.

"What happened?" His voice wasn't much above a whisper, and her heart clutched at the sound. He sounded...lost.

"Nothing. I mean, I don't know. I'm not sure that anything happened. All I'm saying is that even if you came up together, it doesn't mean they're still here."

He looked up at her, his eyes steady but with a hint of fear lurking in their depths. "You told me the only way off Marica-3 is the shuttle. And the only way the prisoners leave is if they're dead. So are you telling me my crew's gone? I failed them?"

She hesitated. But she just couldn't bring herself to meet his eyes and lie, and so she settled for the truth. Hoping it would be enough. "I don't know."

"How can you not know?"

"There are a hundred thousand prisoners here. I can't possibly know everything about all of them."

"You knew me," he said.

"You were special." And not just because of Doctor Sterling's attention. He'd caught her eye the moment he stepped off the shuttle. And he had stayed on her mind because of his frequent visits to the lab.

A smile flickered across his lips, but only for a second. And it was bitter more than it was sweet. "There are three of them. Holden Sinclair is our translator. He's young, still in his twenties. Tall, light brown hair. Looks younger than he is. He's been traveling with me for six years. Helped me negotiate for the *Good Fortune* when I bought her. He's the closest thing to a brother I've ever had."

He looked at her. Elsa tried to keep her face neutral but wasn't sure she managed. They were his family. Not just crew, not just friends, but family. She could hear it in his voice.

"Isaac Miller's our security. Big black guy. A mercenary I picked up off Sumatra a year and a half, two years ago. He wanted a ride home in exchange for some protection along the way, but then he ended up sticking around. I guess he got used to us." A faint smile curved his lips for a second, as if at some private joke, or memory. Then he continued. "And Toby Flatt's the monkey."

"Monkey?" Elsa had never seen one except in vids, but weren't they small brown or black simians that swung through the trees on Old Earth? They ate some sort of strange yellow Earth fruit, if her memory served. The hot Marican rain forests had something similar.

"You never done ship duty, Doc?"

Elsa shook her head. Her only experience with space travel had been the trip from Rhene to Marica and from there to Marica-3 on the shuttle. Just because humans had now conquered space—to the degree that space had allowed itself to be conquered—didn't mean that most people traveled through it a lot. Most Rhenians had never been off Rhene, just like—she was willing to bet—most of the people on Old Earth had never left their home planet. He was the exception, not she.

"The space monkey's a mechanic. The man crawling around the outside of the ship making sure it's space worthy."

Oh. She amended her mental picture from a small furry creature with a human-looking face to a man in coveralls swinging through zero-gee. "I'm sorry. I don't know them. Any of them."

"Damn." He bit his lip and looked away from her, out into the daylight beyond the fissure.

Elsa watched him, waiting. This was a lot harder than she'd imagined. The expression on his face, the look in his eyes—it made her want to say something, anything, to make him feel better.

But she had to keep him safe. It was the only way.

He looked back at her. "We still have to try."

"What if they catch you again?"

"I'll risk it." He grinned. "Besides, I've got you, right? You'll make sure nothing happens to me."

That's what she was trying to do, dammit. "There are a lot of things I can't control. That's one of them. It's better if you just leave things the way they are."

He shook his head. "Sorry, Doc. Can't do that."

"What if I won't help you?"

He looked at her in silence for a moment. "Then I'll go back by myself."

"You can't do that!"

He nodded. "Yes, I can. I have to. They're mine. My responsibility.

I took the job for the Maricans. *I* trusted Josie. I wasn't there for them on Sierra Luz. It's my fault they're here now."

"You'll die." Her voice was flat. Deliberately so—if she didn't control it, it would shake and give away just how much that possibility frightened her.

"That's all right. I'm prepared for that. But I have to do it. And I need you. You know how to get back inside and find them. I don't. And if something goes wrong…"

He hesitated and looked away.

"Yes?" Elsa asked, her heart thudding. What if something went wrong?

He looked back at her. "I need you to do something for me."

"I know. Get you inside the prison so you can find your crew." An impossible task.

He shook his head. "That'd be great, but it isn't what I was gonna ask. If I get there, and I get recaptured…"

"Yes?"

He took a breath. "I need you to kill me."

"What? No!"

He scooted a little closer and fumbled for her hands. She pulled them away, and he dropped his own hands in his lap. "You have to, Doc. I won't have the chance to do it myself. And I don't think I can live like that anymore."

She shook her head, mutely.

He forced a smile. "It's just a matter of time, anyway. You know it. One of these times Doctor Sterling goes to work on me, I'm gonna die for real. You'd just make sure it happens sooner rather than later. Don't work quite so hard at reviving me next time."

"I can't do that." She was a doctor. She didn't kill people.

And what a lousy, hollow excuse that was. If she were a doctor, her focus should be on helping people, not hurting them. He wanted her help, so he wouldn't be hurt again. She didn't want him hurt any more than he did.

Nonetheless, every fiber of her being rebelled against his request. She loved him. She couldn't kill him. Couldn't watch him die without doing everything to keep him alive.

"I can't. I—"

She stopped before blurting it out. It was much too soon for love. Love didn't happen like this. Especially not between two people as different as they were. All it was, was infatuation. And sex. Really good sex. And gratitude, because he'd saved her life.

That gratitude should compel her to honor his request. She owed it to him. If he wanted to die, she should let him die. They had no future, anyway. Not even if by some miracle they got off Marica-3. He would never truly love her back. He might enjoy her body for a day or two, but she was still the woman who had stood by and watched him be tortured. He should want her dead, like Josie. She was amazed he had brought himself to touch her.

"Please, Elsa." He reached for her hand again, and this time she let him keep it, just because it was a miracle that he wanted to. A miracle she couldn't hope would last. His fingers twined through hers. "If you feel anything at all for me, please make sure I die. If there's no other way out, please just kill me."

"I don't want to."

Her voice was tiny. He smiled. In spite of everything that was going on, he managed to smile at her. "I know. Thank you, Doc."

She hadn't promised. But somehow he knew that when—if—it came to the worst, she'd do what he wanted. And as he pulled her in for a soft kiss, sealing their bargain, Elsa closed her eyes on the tears that threatened and prayed that if—when—the time came, she'd have the strength to deliver on the promise. To kill the man she loved, even if everything in her wanted to keep him alive.

CHAPTER NINETEEN

By the time they got back to the hole in the ground, with the water rushing underneath their feet, they were still arguing. Quinn knew what he had to do, and his med tech wasn't happy about him doing it. And he could understand that. If the situation had been reversed, he'd have done everything in his power to stop her from going back to a place where she'd most likely get recaptured, tortured, and killed, too.

But it wasn't like he had a choice, was it? His crew was there. He had to get them out. And if the only way off this godforsaken rock was the shuttle, then he had to figure out a way to get everyone on the shuttle.

A way that didn't involve killing everyone first.

And the only way to do that was if she'd help him. Which she seemed disinclined to do.

"It won't work."

"You have a better idea?"

She hadn't. Just more—or the same—excuses. "There are cameras. And patrols. Even if we can get back inside the prison, someone will see us walking around."

"Nobody saw us on the way out."

"We were lucky. We can't expect to be that lucky twice. And they didn't know you had escaped then. Not until the last minute. Now they do. They'll be looking for you."

"To come back? They can't think I'm that stupid."

"You *are* that stupid," she pointed out—a little unnecessarily, he thought.

"Yeah, but they don't know that." And hopefully wouldn't expect it.

"It's a suicide mission."

"Let's hope not. I know you said the only way off this rock is if I'm dead, but I'd like to avoid that. All we have to do is get in, find the others, get them out of their cells, and walk back out. And up the tunnel to the hole. And up to the surface. And then figure out a way to get on the shuttle when it comes back."

All right, so it sounded difficult. But not impossible. Nothing was impossible.

Her voice was flat. "You forget that we have to spend another day somewhere before the shuttle comes back. With a lot of people looking for us. And then somehow get on the shuttle without anyone noticing, and spend three days there. And then—"

"Yeah, yeah." They had to get off the shuttle again, too. Unless they hijacked it and took off. But a shuttle was an inner-system craft, not built for deep space. The furthest they could hope to get was somewhere else on Marica or possibly Marica-2, if the second moon wasn't on the other side of the planet. If it was, they'd run out of fuel before they got there. Either way, they couldn't get out of Marican space. Not on the shuttle. And the Rhenians had Marican space locked down. Anywhere they went within the Marican planetary system, there'd be people looking for them. Hard enough once they got out, since the Rhenians had a lot of the space in this entire nexus locked down.

"Any idea where my ship is?"

She shook her head. "No."

The Rhenians had probably sold her for scrap. *Bastards.*

"Who would know?"

"I have no idea," his med tech said. "I assume it was impounded."

"She."

She glanced at him. "Excuse me?"

"She. A ship's a she. Not an it."

There was a moment's pause. "Is there a particular reason men call their vehicles 'she'?"

He couldn't resist. "I guess cause we ride 'em."

She looked shocked for a second, and then she smiled. "What about guns? You call your guns 'she' as well, don't you?"

Quinn had never been particularly prone to call his gun—the weapon he used to keep strapped to his hip—anything at all. He'd carried one for a long time, but had no particular relationship with it. Isaac, on the other hand, loved his weapons. And—yes—called them by the female pronoun. He might even have named them.

"Not sure. I guess maybe we like to touch 'em?" Isaac certainly touched his enough. He called it maintenance, but Quinn had always suspected he just enjoyed fondling the hardware.

"I see," his med tech said. "I'm sorry. I don't know where your ship is. If you were berthed at Sierra Luz, she might still be there."

It was possible. Sierra Luz was the biggest shipyard in Marican space. The Rhenians might just have decided to keep the *Good Fortune* there. It'd be easier than moving her anywhere else.

So if the *Fortune* was at Sierra Luz, and they could get to Sierra

Luz and find her, and she was space worthy, and that was assuming he had gotten into the prison to find the others and they had gotten off Marica-3 in the first place…they had a chance to get out of Marican orbit.

Those were a hell of a lot of ifs. Made him think it'd be easier just to give up.

And do what?

There was that, of course. Nothing to do on Marica-3. Nowhere to live. Nothing to eat. And sooner or later the patrols would catch up with him. He might as well be proactive. Strike a blow for freedom. He might die in the process, but then he hadn't had much of a life lately, so it wouldn't be a huge loss.

And her?

He glanced at her, trudging next to him through the dirt and dust.

When he kissed her last night, he hadn't expected much. Certainly not that immediate, almost desperate response. Connection. That she would not only welcome his touch, but that she'd meet him halfway, and give him not just body but soul, had floored him. He'd experienced not only the temporary oblivion of losing himself in a warm, willing woman, but rest, and solace, and peace.

He'd spent the night holding her in his arms, her body wrapped around his, feeling at home and at rest for the first time in months.

And then this morning he'd asked her to kill him.

Way to go.

He'd had to, though. He knew the odds going in, and they weren't good. Soberly, his chances of making it into the prison and out again with his crew were close to nil. And when he got recaptured, which he was pretty sure he would be, he needed a way out.

There would be no more chances to escape. They'd make sure

of that. Once he went back, he'd be there until he died. If he was lucky, they'd just decide to kill him outright and be done with it. An eye for an eye; maybe they'd execute him for the murder of the guard he'd shot. But if they didn't, if they decided to keep him around awhile, he needed a way to end things. On his own terms.

And for that he needed her.

Much as he'd hated to ask it of her. Much as he hated the idea of making her do it. It had to be done.

And so did this.

The hole they'd made in the ground yesterday was just up ahead. He could hear the roaring of the water coming up from the earth. As they stepped out from the canyon into the valley, he turned to her. "Take your dress off, Doc."

He could tie it with the uniform into another rope, and lower her down into the tunnel. Then he'd take his chances on dropping after her himself. Hopefully his bum leg wouldn't break when he hit solid ground below.

She stuck her bottom lip out truculently, but he knew the edge in her voice was tears, not anger. "I don't want to do this."

He hardened his heart against it. "Don't be difficult, sweetheart. We've talked about it. There's no other way." Going through the tunnel and trying to get inside the prison through the pumping station in the sub-basement was a far better plan than walking across the plain where anyone could see them. He'd take any advantage he could get. He was no more eager to brave the river again than she was, but he'd do what he had to do. And he wasn't afraid to die. Maybe that was the difference. She was still hoping to stay alive. To keep him alive.

He gentled his voice as much as he could. With fear and anticipation jangling along all of his nerve endings, it didn't do much good. He still sounded impatient and demanding. "C'mon, Doc. Just do it. Ain't like I haven't seen your underwear before."

She pressed her lips together but began pulling the dress up over her head. Quinn watched her. "At least I didn't have to make you strip at gunpoint this time," he offered.

She shot him a jaundiced look as her head appeared from out of the dress, but she didn't speak. Instead she simply handed it to him. And looked at him, those beautiful lips quivering as her eyes filled with tears.

"Ah, dammit! Don't cry. It'll be all right."

He dropped the dress on the ground and took a step forward, pulling her to him. His moves were a little rougher than necessary, with the guilt stabbing through him. He was just about to capture those soft lips in a kiss, something to take her mind—and his own—off his impending death, when—

"I think that's enough," a voice said.

Quinn froze, his lips a scant inch from the med tech's. She froze, too, the body that had been in the process of melting suddenly stiff and unyielding in his arms, her eyes wide.

For a moment, no one moved. The seconds ticked by in utter silence. Then her eyes shifted, and Quinn's world snapped back into focus. Keeping her up against him—for luck, for cover, in instinctual protection of her, not himself—he dropped one hand from her back to the handle of the laser pistol, still hanging from the belt he'd taken off the uniform yesterday down in the tunnel. After cutting through the ground with it to get them up and out, the charge was a little low, but there was probably enough to shoot someone. Himself, if there was no other choice.

He had the pistol halfway out of the holster when the med tech moved, her voice shrill. "No!"

She pushed away from him. He stumbled back, his bad leg protesting the rough treatment, but managed to stay on his feet and keep hold of the pistol. Until she threw herself at him, knocking it out of his hand.

Deliberately knocking it out of his hand.

He went down hard, and then a hundred and ninety pounds of Rhenian guard landed on top of him, snapping and growling like a rabid dog. The last thing he saw before the guard's fist connected with his chin and snapped his head back, was the sight of his med tech—*his* med tech!—turning into the arms of that bastard Finch and hiding her face against his shoulder while the son of a bitch smirked and put his hand on her ass.

• • •

It was like déjà vu all over again.

He woke up in his cell inside the prison, flat on his back on the same hard cot, looking up at the same smooth white walls with the same blinding light shining down on him, breathing the same stale, filtered air.

His chin hurt; the only proof he had that the past three days hadn't been a dream.

What the hell happened?

They'd been on their way to the entrance to the tunnel. She'd given him a hard time...

No, he corrected himself, she'd been afraid. He'd stopped what he was doing to comfort her, but just before he could kiss her, that bastard Swan had stopped him. It was almost like the son of a bitch thought Quinn had been about to hurt her.

Shit.

Going over the conversation in his head, it seemed as if maybe the son of a bitch *had* thought he was about to hurt her. And that maybe he'd had reason to think so. Not because Quinn would have done anything to her, but because the way he'd behaved might have given that impression.

Elsa had known better, though. She'd just about melted against him before she'd realized they weren't alone.

But then she'd gotten in his way when he tried to get the laser pistol out of the holster. She'd knocked it out of his hand. *Deliberately* knocked it out of his hand. And she'd turned to Finch for comfort while the guard flattened Quinn.

The bastard had held her in his arms. With his hand on her ass. *His* med tech.

And she'd allowed it. Had seemed to welcome it. She'd been the one who had flung herself in Swan's arms in the first place. After making sure Quinn couldn't use the laser pistol on anyone. Including himself.

Including Finch. Or whatever the hell the guy's name was.

So had all of last night been a sham?

It wouldn't be the first time he'd been taken in by a pretty face. Josie had played him like a goddamn *clàrsach*. The ice bitch could have done the same. Fed him a pile of lies while using his own body against him. Maybe it really hadn't been three years for her. Maybe she'd been screwing Swan the whole time she'd been here on Marica-3. So what if she'd been tight? Could be the bastard just had a really small pecker. Those shiny boots and that riding crop had to be compensating for something.

And the fact that she'd climaxed didn't count for shit. She'd probably closed her eyes and imagined Swan while Quinn fucked her. That's why she'd been so reluctant to use his name. And why she'd acted so strange this morning.

Guilty conscience. For cheating on her lover.

The thought left a nasty taste in his mouth, where things didn't taste so good to begin with. He was going on either three or four days with no food, and nothing to drink save the river water. His gut roiled with pain, although he had a feeling it was just as much mind as body.

You failed.

He'd gotten out. He'd had a chance to save everyone else. To right the wrong he'd done when he'd landed them in this mess in the first place. But no. He'd thought with his other head again and ended up bedding another duplicitous, mind-fucking bitch.

You'd think after what happened last time, he'd have learned his lesson.

There was a scraping sound over by the door, and he looked up in time to see a rat bar slide out of the food slot. Right behind it came a tube of water.

Dinner.

Rolling off the cot and getting to his feet, he shuffled over to it. It was edible. Better than nothing. And it seemed he was in here for the long haul. Might as well keep his strength up.

As he limped back to the cot, rat bar in one hand and water in the other, he wondered what the ice bitch was having for dinner. Something a hell of a lot better than this, he didn't doubt. Champagne and caviar in the major's bed, belike.

The thought turned the rat bar to sawdust in his mouth.

Then again, rat bars tasted like sawdust, anyway, so that didn't mean much.

Or so he told himself.

CHAPTER TWENTY

"I'm not hungry," Elsa said, not for the first time. "I've had enough. Thank you." She pushed the plate of sweet rolls toward Major Lamb.

He was sitting on the other side of the table beside Doctor Sterling, and they were both looking at her with concern. The doctor's eyes kept snagging on the bruises around her throat, while Major Lamb's gaze drifted farther south.

He'd noticed the bruises, too, of course. When he'd first came upon them, out in the desert, she'd been in her underthings, with all her injuries on display. Including those accidental strangulation marks around her throat. And the abrasions around her wrists from that first afternoon when Quinn…

She caught herself and deliberately put some mental distance between them in light of what she had to do soon: when Captain Conlan had tied her up while he took his nap.

As soon as she had removed herself from Major Lamb's embrace and pulled the remnants of her dress over her head as a shield against his obvious regard, the major's attention had been caught by the rip down the front. Naturally, he had jumped to the conclusion that Quinn had forced himself on her, much against her will.

She hadn't corrected him. He'd wanted to execute Quinn right then and there for daring to lay hands on her, but she had managed to talk him out of it, her heart beating wildly in her throat the whole time. Doctor Sterling would want him back in one piece. The doctor would not be pleased if Captain Conlan came back in a box. He had ways to make the captain suffer for what he'd done. She thanked Major Lamb very much for his offer to uphold her honor, but it was unnecessary. She would take care of Captain Conlan herself.

Major Lamb had smiled with acid appreciation at that and told her she was a woman after his own heart. Elsa had simpered and feigned weakness and leaned on him and requested to be taken home. The guard had fetched the lightflyer that had brought the two men out to the desert in the first place, and they had dumped the unconscious Quinn in the back of the vehicle. Elsa had managed not to wince at the rough treatment. The major had handed her tenderly into the front and taken off, leaving the young guard to hoof it back to the prison. Elsa couldn't muster up much sympathy for him, even after having spent a couple of days out there under the burning sun. He had water in the canteen at his belt, and the jog wouldn't scar him permanently.

Once they reached the prison, she had seen to it that the captain was deposited in his cell, with the door securely locked and a different guard posted outside. She had given the guard strict orders to let no one in and hoped he understood that that included his own superior. To increase her chances of success, she did her best to keep Major Lamb with her for the remainder of the day, so he wouldn't have a chance to drop in on Quinn and make good on his threat. The major stayed in her quarters while she bathed and changed, ostensibly to make sure no one came in unannounced. After her terrible ordeal, Major Lamb was very understanding of her fear of attack and her need for protection. It made him all the more determined to retaliate against Quinn at some point, but there was nothing Elsa could do about that. Her main concern right now was keeping Quinn alive and unharmed until she could kill him herself. Properly.

When she came out of the bathroom, Doctor Sterling had arrived, and both men got busy trying to make sure she ate. It wasn't until she pushed the food aside and informed them that she'd had enough that they stopped badgering her.

"Do you need medical treatment, Doctor Brandeis?" Doctor Sterling asked, his expression fatherly and solicitous.

Elsa shook her head. "I'm fine, thank you."

The two men exchanged a look.

"Really. I don't need anything." The last thing she wanted was for Doctor Sterling to insist on examining her.

Not that she was concerned about what he'd find. Her body showed plenty of evidence of trauma, evidence that could be interpreted in a lot of different ways according to the viewer's prejudices. An examination would in no way prove that Quinn hadn't raped her.

"Would you like something to help you sleep, then? We don't want you to wake up with nightmares."

Elsa had her mouth open to say no, when she changed her mind. "That would be helpful. Thank you."

She forced a smile. The main thing right now was that they believe she was back, just as she had been before she left. If they knew, or even suspected, that her giving herself to Captain Conlan hadn't been forced, they'd send her away in disgrace. Or worse, put her in a cell and make her one of the prisoners. For the guards to have sexual relations with the inmates was one thing; for Elsa to do it was something very different.

The doctor beamed. "I'll just go to the lab and get something."

"I'll come with you." She got up too quickly and swayed. Major Lamb put out a hand to steady her, and Elsa had to fight against the inclination to throw it off. The only chance she had of getting away with this was if she acted as if nothing was wrong. As if she were still the same woman who had left the prison three days ago.

She made herself smile at him, even more warmly than usual. "Thank you."

He clicked his heels together. "A pleasure." The way his gaze lingered a second too long told her he meant it.

Doctor Sterling headed for the door, the tails of his white lab coat flapping behind him, and Elsa hurried to catch up. Major Lamb fell in behind as they exited her quarters and made their way down the hall to the lab.

Once there, the doctor went to a locked cabinet on the far side of the room. Elsa, meanwhile, stopped in the middle of the floor and looked around.

She'd only been gone three days. The lab looked just as it had the last time she saw it. White walls, scrubbed tile floor, metal tables with wrist and ankle restraints. Trays of syringes, vials of various liquids, and containers of synthetic blood.

The room hadn't changed in the time she'd been gone. The only thing that had changed was her.

"What are you thinking about?" Major Lamb wanted to know, his eyes fixed on her face.

Elsa forced another smile and did everything she could to make it look genuine. "Just that it's good to be back. I'm looking forward to getting back to work."

He smiled, obviously pleased with her ability to bounce back from tribulation. His eyes lingered appreciatively on her face.

"Here we are." Doctor Sterling came trotting across the floor with one of his beloved vials in his hand. "A simple sleeping draught." He put it in her hand and wrapped her fingers around it. "A spoonful before bed, and you will sleep the sleep of the righteous." He beamed.

Elsa smiled back and refrained from telling him that it would take a lot more than a simple sleeping draught to accomplish that feat. The sleep of the righteous was something she imagined would elude her for the rest of her days. "Thank you, Doctor Sterling."

"It seems the least I can do," Doctor Sterling said and put both hands behind his back, rocking backward and forward. He wasn't a very emotional man, had never seemed to want or need human contact, but Elsa could tell that he was genuinely distraught at what had happened to her. Or what he imagined had happened. "I am so sorry, my dear."

There wasn't much she could say except, "Thank you."

"Rest assured," Major Lamb said, his voice grim, "I will make sure he pays. For everything."

A chill went down Elsa's spine. "Thank you, Major, but…" She cast about for something to say, something that would make sense. "I think I would like to take care of that myself. With my own hands. If Doctor Sterling approves?"

She turned to the older doctor.

Sterling beamed, his voice delighted. "But of course, my dear Doctor Brandeis! I knew you'd get over your squeamishness sooner or later."

Elsa forced another simper, even as her stomach did a slow roll.

"We'll do it together," Doctor Sterling said. "First thing tomorrow morning." He rubbed his hands together in anticipation, like an evil villain in an old holovid.

No!

She managed to bite back the word but couldn't control the involuntary movement. Major Lamb looked at her, brows raised, and she managed a smile. "Of course." After a second, she added, "I hope you will let me take a more active role this time, though, Doctor Sterling. After what happened, I think I would like the reins. In this particular case."

"Of course." The doctor radiated approval.

Elsa suppressed a shudder, but just barely. It was a lifetime ago, yet only a few days, that she'd wondered why Quinn hadn't just told Doctor Sterling what the Rhenians wanted to know. It wasn't like the doctor enjoyed hurting people, she'd reasoned, and if Quinn just told the truth, the torture would stop.

Now she saw that she'd been wrong. Doctor Sterling's childlike delight in her plan to put Quinn through the most heinous of pains was chilling—and eye opening. And although some of it was undoubtedly due to the fact that both men thought Quinn had defiled her and by old-fashioned Rhenish law should die for it, she recognized that some was just plain anticipation of someone else's suffering, too.

I have to keep him away tomorrow morning. If I have to kill him in his sleep to do it.

"May I have a look at the cabinet?" She gestured to the one in the corner, where Doctor Sterling kept his favorite potions.

"Of course, my dear!" He beamed at her.

Major Lamb was right on her heels when she opened the door,

his gaze avid. "What's here?"

She glanced at him over her shoulder, disturbed by the question as well as by the proximity—a little too close for comfort—but forced herself not to let it show. Instead, she made herself show him the contents of the cabinet.

"Synthetic blood." A lot of it. Then again, a human body held a lot of blood, and when they had to replenish a whole supply, like they'd had to do after exsanguinating Quinn, it took a few bottles. And the captain wasn't the only one they'd bled in the time she'd been here.

"Lizard dermis." The skin of the derma-lizard, ground into coarse dust. When mixed with liquid, it turned into a grainy paste that burned the skin and caused blisters and open sores, same as if the victim had brushed up against a derma-lizard in the wild.

"Marican water snake venom." Vials of clear liquid, a half dozen or so, to be injected into the bloodstream. Once removed from the snake, it didn't last more than a few days, so Doctor Sterling frequently had to drain the snakes of more.

At the back of the cabinet she spied two small vials of spider-scorpion venom. Just two; it wasn't something Doctor Sterling used frequently. He preferred his "patients" to be aware during the sessions, able to feel every jab and burn. For research purposes.

"What will you be using tomorrow?" Major Lamb wanted to know.

Elsa hesitated. It had to be quick and painful. Painful wasn't a problem; everything in the cabinet produced pain at sufficient levels for her needs. But it wasn't all quick.

"He responded well to the night crawlers," Doctor Sterling opined. He had joined them at the cabinet doors, peering nearsightedly at the contents. And although he looked myopic and distracted, like an absentminded professor in a holovid, Elsa could tell that his brain was spinning, cataloging the contents of the cabinets and coming up with a plan of attack. One that included those terrifying worms.

Lord, no. If she had to spend another half hour watching the worms burrow through Quinn's body before he died, she'd kill herself while she was at it. The fact that Doctor Sterling equated responding well with causing the most pain had her stomach clenching.

She swayed. "I think I need to lie down."

"Of course." Major Lamb was quick to take her elbow, and then, when she didn't object, the opportunity to slip an arm around her waist. He held her a little too tightly, but Elsa let him, even as the touch caused her to want to flinch away. "I would be happy to assist you tomorrow, Doctor Brandeis," he told her, his breath moist against her cheek. "Perhaps even make sure the prisoner is in the proper condition for the worms. A few strokes with a whip would open him up nicely."

"No," Elsa managed, fighting back nausea and dizziness at the thought. "That's not necessary. I'll manage without that."

Major Lamb didn't answer, just continued to guide her down the hallway as Doctor Sterling exited the lab behind them. Elsa stopped and with effort faced Major Lamb.

"This is for me to do, Stephen. Not you. If you want to watch, I won't stop you, but I don't want anyone's help. I have to do this myself. My way."

He looked obstinately disinclined to agree, and she stepped closer, into his personal space, and lowered her voice, using his first name again for added familiarity. "Please, Stephen. Promise me."

"Of course, Doctor Brandeis," Doctor Sterling said soothingly and stopped beside them. He glanced at Major Lamb. "You'll have your chance with Captain Conlan, Stephen. But first we'll let Doctor Brandeis have her turn."

Elsa started breathing again. "Thank you, Doctor."

He smiled at her. "A pleasure, my dear. I can see how much this means to you. And Captain Conlan will be with us for a long time yet. There'll be plenty of time for Stephen to get his wish."

He trotted off down the hallway toward his quarters, humming. Elsa kicked back into motion and forced herself to put one foot in front of the other until she'd reached the end of the hallway and her own door.

She stopped to face him. "Thank you, Major Lamb. For everything."

The major clicked his heels together and bowed. "My pleasure. Will you require my services further tonight?"

Elsa shook her head, then thought better of it. "What plans do you have?"

The major smiled. "I thought I might let Captain Conlan's crew know that the captain has been recovered."

The crew? "Perhaps I should come with you." And learn where they were held.

The major looked her over carefully. "Are you sure you feel up for it?"

"I'll manage. I managed out there for three days."

"So you did." His expression was approving.

"And I'd like to see them for myself. See the kind of crew Captain Conlan surrounded himself with."

Major Lamb nodded, as if the request made perfect sense. "Come along, then, Doctor Brandeis."

"Please," Elsa said, and tucked her arm through his, "call me

Elsa."

Lamb smiled and stroked her fingers. "It will give me great pleasure."

They headed for the lift tube.

. . .

Elsa was up bright and early the following morning, her heart beating so hard in her chest she was afraid it would show on the outside. Her stomach was churning, and given what she had to do shortly, it was probably best if she didn't eat anything, anyway. She got up and put on her best dress, she braided her hair as usual and coiled it at the nape of her neck, and she finished with a fresh lab coat atop. When she looked at herself in the mirror, she looked the same as she always did. Only her eyes betrayed her: they were shadowed with fatigue but bright with excitement. She'd spent most of the night awake, going over and over the plan in her head, doing her best to plug any holes, dreading what she knew she had to do. Praying for the strength to do it. But now that morning was here, all she wanted was to get started. The sooner she started, the sooner it would be over.

She got to the lab before Doctor Sterling, and when the doctor ambled through the door at his usual hour, she had a pot of coffee brewed and ready.

"Good morning, Doctor Sterling." She handed him his mug and spared a thought for how he'd managed for the past three days while she'd been gone. Perhaps he hadn't ingested any coffee.

"Thank you, Doctor Brandeis." He lifted the mug to his lips and took a sip, grimacing as the liquid went down his throat.

Elsa's heart slammed against her ribs. "Something wrong?"

He smiled. "Not at all. You make a stronger brew than I do

myself." He took another sip, without grimacing this time. Elsa started breathing again. She even managed a smile.

"I would hate for you to fall asleep in the middle of this session, Doctor."

"Have no fear," Doctor Sterling said and lifted the mug, "this will keep me awake." He wandered off toward his desk, mug in hand. Elsa picked up her tea and followed.

After putting his stack of paperwork on the desk, the doctor turned to her. "How can I be of help to you this morning, my dear?"

"I'm ready." Elsa glanced at the table, where everything was laid out in neat rows. Anything anyone could possibly need to give someone else pain. Vials of snake venom. Syringes. Extra needles. Razor blades. Rags and wipes. A bottle or two of synthetic blood.

"Are you planning to bleed him?" Doctor Sterling asked, a wrinkle between his brows.

Elsa was glad to hear her voice was steady. "I don't know yet what I plan to do. All I know is I want him to suffer. But I want to be prepared for all contingencies."

"You ought to prepare a couple of the worms," Doctor Sterling said, rubbing his hands together. "In fact, I'll just go ahead and do that now."

He executed a neat turn and stumbled. "Dear me."

Elsa rushed to his side, taking his elbow to support him. "Something wrong, Doctor?"

"No, no." He shook her hand off. "Just a momentary aberration. A bit of dizziness. I'll be all right in a moment."

"Perhaps you ought to sit down," Elsa said, watching as the doctor made his way toward the table against the wall where the night crawler habitat stood.

"Nonsense. I just need to work. It will pass." He stumbled just as he passed her teacup and narrowly missed knocking it over. Elsa rescued it and brought it over to the sink by the wall. Her stomach was too queasy to be able to process the liquid, anyway. "Perhaps I'd better just get this out of the way, too." She reached for the doctor's coffee mug.

"Perhaps that's best." When she turned to look at him, his eyes were out of focus. "I'm sorry, my dear. I don't know what's come over me."

Elsa sent him a sweet smile, one that made him blink. "I'm sure it's nothing, Doctor Sterling. It's been a difficult few days for all of us. Why don't you sit down and rest, and I'll get the worms?"

Doctor Sterling nodded and made himself comfortable on a wooden chair not too far from the table where Elsa planned to put Quinn. Just as the door from the hallway to the lab opened, Doctor Sterling leaned over to tick one of the restraints at the head of the table. "Are you sure this will be enough to hold him?"

"It'll be fine. He's in pretty diminished condition already. Being outside was hard on him." Elsa turned her gaze to the newcomer. "Good morning, Stephen." She smiled.

"Good morning." The major inclined his head. "Everything all right here?" His gaze lingered on the doctor.

"Fine, fine," Doctor Sterling said, waving the concern away. "A momentary weakness, nothing more."

Major Lamb nodded and turned to her. "Are you ready to get started, Elsa?"

Please. "The sooner the better."

"Would you like for me to have the prisoner brought up?"

"I think," Elsa said, "I would prefer to fetch him myself." It would give her a chance to prepare him for what she planned to do. And to make sure no one else had a chance to hurt him first. He was hers, and only hers. "Why don't you stay with Doctor Sterling and have a cup of coffee?"

"When we return," Major Lamb said firmly. "I couldn't possibly let you fetch the prisoner on your own, Doctor Brandeis. Not after what happened last time."

Doctor Sterling nodded agreement. He looked exhausted, his skin pasty and his eyes dull, but he was adamant. "I'll be fine right here, Doctor Brandeis. Go with Stephen."

There was no way around it. Elsa turned to the major. "With your assistance, then."

Lamb clicked his heels and indicated the door. "After you."

She crossed the threshold into the corridor with him a step behind.

"Is he all right?" Major Lamb wanted to know as soon as they were outside the lab with the door closed.

"The last few days have been difficult for all of us," Elsa said again. "I'm sure, by the time we get back, he'll be fine."

Lamb nodded and put a possessive hand on her back as they walked down the hallway toward the lift tube.

CHAPTER TWENTY-ONE

The door to his cell hissing open came as no surprise. Quinn had been expecting them ever since he woke up. Figured it was just a matter of time before they came.

Even so, his chest tightened at the sight of her.

And then a second later, it was his stomach that clenched at the sight of the man trailing her through the door.

Goddamn Lark. Come to rub his face in it.

He guessed he couldn't blame her. Or Lark, either. Last time she'd come to his cell with one of the guards, the guard had ended up dead. That wouldn't happen this time. Lark was too smart for that.

He could have kept his mouth shut, he supposed. It just didn't seem worth it. "Morning, sweetheart. Back for more?"

Just like the guard had done last time, Lark lashed out. But instead of a fist to the chin, the bastard backhanded him across the mouth. "Curb your tongue, or I'll cut it out!"

Elsa took an instinctive step forward and just as quickly aborted the movement. He could see her jaw tense. Quinn ran his tongue over his bottom lip, tasting blood. For a second, he thought he'd seen something move in her eyes, but he must have been wrong. They were cool and clear when she looked at him, devoid of expression. Same with her voice.

"You'll have to come with us, Captain Conlan."

"Sure, Doc." He got to his feet, more easily than the last time she'd been here. "Time for another visit to the lab?"

"I'm afraid so." She gestured for him to precede her out of the cell.

"And don't try anything," Major Lark warned. "Or I'll shoot you dead!"

Quinn stopped in the doorway to look back at him. "Is that supposed to scare me, Lark?"

"Lamb," the major snarled, and Quinn could see his hand tightening on the weapon. It might almost be worth it to push him, just to see if he could be made to make good on his threat. Being shot dead in the hallway outside the cell would be better than going through another session with Doctor Sterling.

But his goddamn med tech got in the way. She put a hand on Major Lamb's arm—Lamb, not Lark. Or Swan or Finch or anything else. Lamb. She put her hand on his arm, those cool fingertips against the back of his hand, and the major simmered down.

Quinn watched, eyes narrowed.

She was back to being the ice bitch again. Hair perfectly groomed, yanked back from her face and braided at the nape of her neck, with no stray strands escaping. Another ugly dress, this one a muddy sort of greenish tan, and another pair of clunky lace-up shoes. There was probably another pair of overlarge granny panties underneath the dress, and another undershirt.

And dammit, the idea of that should not have his body reacting.

Especially not with what he knew about her.

Get a grip, fool. This isn't the woman you made love to yesterday. That woman doesn't exist. This is who she really is.

"Let's go."

She couldn't even bring herself to touch him but let Lamb grab his arm, a little too hard, and march him down the hallway. Quinn went along without a fight, doing his best to ignore the med tech's presence.

If only it could be as easy to ignore the memories of her.

• • •

As expected, they ended up in Doctor Sterling's lab. Quinn's home away from home on Marica-3. If he wasn't in his cell, he was here, strapped to a table or chair, going through some "treatment" or other.

The only difference this time was that when they walked through the door, the old goat was sitting in a chair next to the table, his chin on his chest, rattling like a malfunctioning rear thruster.

Major Lamb's steps faltered, and for a second, his grip on Quinn's arm slackened. Quinn tried to take advantage of it to yank away, but the major held on.

"Oh, dear," the med tech said; her voice calm, as if this happened all the time. "He must have been more tired than he let on."

Major Lamb was still staring. "I've never seen him like this before."

She spared him a glance out of those cool green eyes. "He's getting older, Stephen. And it's been a stressful few days. For everyone."

Her glance brushed over Quinn when she said it, but didn't linger.

"After you get Captain Conlan situated on the table," she added, with no change of inflection, "you can help me take Doctor Sterling back to his quarters. Let him get some rest."

The major nodded and yanked on Quinn's arm. It didn't seem worth fighting, so Quinn allowed himself to be stretched out on the metal table, his clothing removed down to his underwear, and his ankles and wrists strapped down.

The med tech, meanwhile, was working on getting Doctor Sterling up and moving, her voice steady and her hands brisk as she woke him and got him to his feet. "Major Lamb and I will escort you to your quarters, Doctor. You need to lie down."

"Oh, dear," the doctor murmured as he weaved back and forth. "Don't know what's wrong…"

"I'm sure it's nothing, Doctor Sterling." Elsa's voice was soothing, like it had been when Quinn was ill and feverish back in the fissure…was it yesterday? Or the day before? "You just need to rest. Once we get there, I'll check your vitals and make sure everything is all right."

The doctor nodded and continued his stumbling way toward the door, with the med tech holding his elbow. At the door she turned. "Are you finished, Major Lamb?"

"Finished." Lamb secured the last strap around Quinn's wrist—a lot tighter than necessary—and grinned down at the captive. "Don't go anywhere, Captain."

Quinn shook his head, the one part of his body he could still move. "Wouldn't dream of it, Lamb. The doc and me, we've had some good times. Don't wanna miss another."

The major's eyes narrowed, and Quinn braced himself for another slap, or maybe a punch this time.

It didn't come.

"Stephen?" the med tech prompted from the door, a hint of impatience to her voice. "Your assistance?"

Major Lamb hesitated. After a snarled, "You'll pay for that," he stalked away. The three of them passed through the door into the hallway, leaving Quinn alone.

Contrary to what he'd told the major, of course he tried to get free. But it was no use; the restraints bit into his wrists and ankles, and twisting only made it worse. He kept at it until he could feel the flesh around the restraints beginning to swell, and only then did he give up.

Next he turned his attention to the table next to him, trying to figure out what he might be in for.

It was filled with all sorts of interesting items. Syringes and spare needles. Vials of clear liquid, some big and some small—more of the snake venom, most likely. So he should expect to feel like he was being cooked, then.

Some sort of paste. Derma-lizard stuff, probably. That hurt like hell, too, but it got worse the second or third day, when the blisters popped, leaving the skin raw. Maybe today wouldn't be too bad.

There were knives and razor blades. Bottles of synthetic blood along with plastic tubing. And rags and wipes. She must be planning on making a mess.

And—his stomach clenched—a small container inside which something wiggled and squirmed.

Night crawlers.

His stomach lurched at the thought. Of all the horrors of the lab, that was the one he least wanted to experience again.

And she knew that, didn't she? She'd seen him turn one of the little fuckers into nothing but a smear on the ground. She wasn't stupid; she'd have recognized the fear the creature inspired in him, as well as the anger.

For a second, desperation welled up inside him. Why was she doing this? He hadn't done anything to her. Nothing she didn't want him to do.

But maybe she was punishing him not for what *he* did, but for what he made her do. For what he made her feel. Enjoyment. Making her want him. For inciting her to let her body rule her, even for just a few hours.

She wasn't someone who'd enjoy that feeling, he imagined: the feeling of losing control, of losing herself. So yeah, she'd want to make him suffer for it.

There was a sound over by the door, and they were back.

"...fine," his med tech said, obviously continuing a conversation they'd started earlier. "You saw him, Stephen. There was nothing wrong with him. I checked his vital signs. He just needs to sleep."

"It's not like him," the major insisted.

"I know it isn't. But he's getting older. And the last few days have been stressful. I'm sure he'll be fine by tomorrow."

Major Lamb glanced over at Quinn. "Should we postpone this session until he's back to normal?"

Yes.

The med tech shook her head. "I need to take care of this today." Her gaze flickered over Quinn, expressionless and cool. "Is he ready?"

"As ready as I can get him," Major Lamb said, "under the circumstances. Are you sure...?"

"Are you questioning my expertise, Stephen?" She didn't wait for an answer. "I've been working under Doctor Sterling for a long time. I'm his most valued assistant. He agreed to let me do this myself. You heard him. The fact that he's not here to observe shouldn't make a difference."

The major looked mutinous, but he didn't actually object.

"Why don't you pour yourself a cup of coffee," the med tech suggested, her tone conciliatory, "and get comfortable. I'm sure you'll enjoy watching."

The major nodded, and with a look at Quinn took himself off toward the corner. Elsa, meanwhile, turned to him.

"How do you feel today?"

Quinn grinned. "Not too bad, Doc. Though I'm sure you're aiming to change that."

She didn't deny it. "Fever all gone?" Her fingers were cool against his forehead, and for a second his eyes drifted shut with the memory. Hot air, hot ground under his body, and a soothing touch on his face.

He fought his way back. For just a second, he thought he caught a glimpse of that same memory drifting through her eyes, but then it was gone, so he must have just imagined it. "Seems so."

She nodded. "I guess we can get started, then. If you're ready?"

She was asking him?

He set his teeth. "Just get it over with, please." No sense in waiting. Sometimes the anticipation was worse than the torture. Not often, but he might get lucky.

She nodded and turned to the table. Quinn watched as she prepared one of the syringes. "More of the snake venom?"

She glanced at him. "Your last experiment with it showed you responded well."

"You mean I lasted a long time without passing out?"

She smiled, a flash of even white teeth, just as Major Lamb came back, a steaming hot cup of coffee in his hand, and took up position on the other side of Quinn. "Exactly."

"I'll try to do better this time, Doc."

He braced himself as she slipped the needle in. The bite was almost imperceptible. As she stepped back, Quinn tried to force his body to relax, but he knew what was coming, and it was difficult not to fight against it.

The med tech kept her eyes on the chrono strapped to her wrist. He'd like to think it was because she didn't want to watch him suffer, but he figured she was just counting seconds, waiting for the venom to make its way through his body.

It started with a flush of warmth. Gentle at first, but it was just a few minutes before his body was hotter than it had been during the fever. Breathing became painful; each mouthful of air burned going down. His blood bubbled through his veins as if on the boil, and he felt like his skin was melting, sliding off his bones.

Through it all, Major Lamb watched avidly, his eyes bright and interested. Under other circumstances, Quinn would have said something to him, but it was all he could do to stay conscious.

By the time the med tech administered the anti-venom, he could have kissed her. Even after everything that had happened.

However, his relief wasn't long lived.

"Is that it?" Major Lamb asked, disappointed.

Elsa smiled. Tightly. She was pale, or maybe he was imagining it. He wasn't seeing too clearly, probably. "Of course not. It's just the beginning."

"Good. Cause I think I coulda done a better job myself."

Even through the haze of pain, Quinn noticed the major's pedantic diction slipping. Elsa must have noticed it, too, because she wrinkled her brow. "Are you feeling all right, Stephen? Feel free to leave if this isn't keeping your attention."

"Apologies," Major Lamb said and straightened his back. "Just a momentary weakness, Doctor Brandeis."

"Perhaps another cup of coffee would help?"

"Still got some." The major lifted the cup, unsteadily. Some of the contents splashed out and onto his hand. He looked at it, stupidly. "How did that happen?"

"Go run your hand under cold water," Elsa said. "And get yourself another cup. I'll apply the lizard dermis while I wait."

Lamb hesitated, but then he nodded and ambled off, unsteadily. Elsa put the container of paste back down and ran a hand down Quinn's body. Even the light touch hurt, and he sucked his breath in sharply, but at least it wasn't as bad as the derma-lizard paste would have been.

Major Lamb stumbled back to the chair and sat down, a full cup of coffee in his hand. "All done?"

Elsa nodded, wiping her hand on a towel. Trying to wipe away the feel of him?

That wasn't how you felt two days ago, Doc. He thought the words but didn't say them. No sense in inviting another slap across the face, after all.

"Whatcha gonna use next? How 'bout them things the old man likes so much?"

Elsa hesitated. Even through the haze of pain, Quinn could see it. But eventually she nodded and turned to the table. When she turned back, something small wiggled between her fingers.

Quinn tried to swallow, but his mouth was too dry.

Three days ago, she had begged him to save her from a night crawler. She'd been crying, terrified. How could she handle it so carelessly now?

Had she been deceiving him then? Or was she doing it now?

She paused beside him. He looked up at her face, searching for something, anything. Some flicker of emotion, of feeling. "Please, Doc."

His voice was just a hoarse whisper, his throat raw from the screaming. But she heard him. So did the major, who chuckled.

For a second—less—he thought he might have gotten through. Something moved in her eyes. Pain? Sorrow?

Then it was gone again, her voice steady. "I'm sorry, Captain. You responded well to the crawlers, too. Doctor Sterling was most impressed with your endurance. However—" She looked him over. "—we'll start a little closer to the heart this time, I think."

Major Lamb snickered. He sounded drunk, Quinn thought distantly. Maybe he'd laced his coffee with something.

Quinn wouldn't have minded a bit of false courage himself right now. His worst nightmares were about those damned worms.

His body tensed as Elsa's hands descended toward his abdomen. She hesitated for a moment, then deposited the night crawler gently beside his navel. With his skin already sensitized by the snake venom, even the slight weight was painful. The lizard dermis would have made it worse, though, so he could only be grateful she had changed her mind about using that. With Lamb off treating his hand, unable to see what she was doing, maybe she'd decided to spare Quinn what she could.

For the next eternity—a few minutes, or hours—silence reigned, only broken by his increasingly ragged breaths. The crawler made its slow way across his stomach, prodding the sensitive skin. Major Lamb kept his eyes on it, eagerly awaiting the moment when the creature broached the skin. He was a little flushed himself and looked like he had a hard time keeping upright on the chair.

Elsa was watching Quinn's face. Every once in a while he'd look over and meet those clear, unblinking, green eyes, but mostly he kept his own gaze aimed at the ceiling.

The nick of the blade came out of the blue, a sharp instant of pain cutting through the haze. He looked over in shock, in time to see Major Lamb fall back down on the chair unsteadily. "Speed things up a little," the major muttered in explanation.

Elsa made a move forward before checking herself. "Thank you, Major Lamb." Her voice was cool and pleasant, although for a moment, Quinn could have sworn he'd seen fury in her eyes.

"Pleasure," Lamb slurred and slipped the knife back into the top of his boot. On Quinn's stomach, the night crawler paused, sniffed the air, and then started its slow trek toward the cut. Elsa's hands fisted at her side, so hard the knuckles showed white, but she didn't move.

The pain when the worm burrowed under the skin was almost enough to pull him down into unconsciousness, but he clenched his jaw and held on, determined not to break. He'd endured before; he could do it again.

The pain was excruciating, though. Bad enough last time, when the night crawlers had been all he'd had to bear. With his body already agonizingly tender from the snake venom, with his veins on fire and every nerve ending screaming, the movement of the crawler just underneath the skin was intolerably painful.

He felt himself slipping into darkness and welcomed it. But just as he was about to let it take him under, Elsa's face appeared above him. She had another syringe in her hand and another ampoule of clear liquid.

"More venom?" Major Lamb's voice inquired, from far away.

No. Please. The agony was already more than he could bear.

She nodded, seemingly in slow motion, and reached for him. The pinprick of the needle was lost in the sensory overload of everything else. As this new venom flooded his body, the darkness that had threatened to swallow him turned to blinding light. The pain lessened, and he could feel his body begin to shut down. His heart slowed, and although he tried to draw breath into his lungs, he couldn't.

I'm dying.

Above him, Elsa leaned in, her head for the moment blocking out the light, which gave her a wholly undeserved halo. His eyes were failing, but he was sure, for just a second, he saw tears in hers. Her face was soft, lit from inside like an angel's.

The last thing he heard before the vortex claimed him was her voice, sweet and distant.

"Good-bye, Captain."

And he understood. Too late to thank her, to tell her he forgave her for the pain. As he slipped away, his last coherent thought was hoping she knew that he was grateful for his death.

CHAPTER TWENTY-TWO

Elsa turned away from the lifeless body on the table and walked to the rubbish bin on legs that felt weightless. She watched her own hands distantly, looking at them as if they belonged to someone else and weren't attached to her body, yet amazed at how steady they were when she dropped the syringe and the small vial, now empty, into the bin.

"Whatcha doin'?" the major slurred from behind her.

She turned to face him. "It's done."

"Whass done?"

"He's dead."

"What?" Lamb lurched to his feet and stumbled the few steps over to Captain Conlan's body, catching himself on the edge of the table. "Can't be." It took him a few tries to find the right spot for a pulse check. Elsa held her breath as he fumbled, afraid he'd knock Quinn onto the floor. Afraid the sleeping draught in the coffee hadn't been enough to dull his senses sufficiently. Doctor Sterling was asleep. Major Lamb was still upright when she'd counted on them both being out of her way.

Lamb kept his hand on Quinn's pulse point for a few very long seconds before straightening. Bracing himself with both hands on the table, he stared at her across the body, his expression muzzy. "Doctor Sterling ain't gonna be happy."

No, he wouldn't. But he was the least of her concerns right now.

She firmed her voice. "It had to be done. I couldn't let him live after what he did to me. And you know as well as I do, Stephen, that he wouldn't have given up any information. If he could keep his tongue through this, he would have kept silent through anything."

Major Lamb didn't disagree. Elsa wasn't sure he was awake enough to truly understand the ramifications of everything that had happened, but at least he agreed with her on this point.

Outside, a sharp whine cut through the air.

Yes. Right on time.

"The shuttle's here," Elsa said.

Major Lamb tilted his head to the side and tried to focus his eyes. "Gotta go."

She nodded. "I'll take care of him. Prepare him for departure."

"Departure?" If nothing else, that supposedly simple sleeping draught had done a number on his cognitive abilities. That was one thing to be grateful for. With luck, he wouldn't realize what had happened until they were safely onboard the shuttle and away from this awful place.

She made her words simple, to make up for his lack of understanding. "Since the shuttle is here, we may as well ship him out. No point in letting him stay here and rot."

Major Lamb thought about it. It seemed to take considerable effort. Finally he nodded. "Gotta go."

Elsa nodded. "I'll get one of the guards to help me." Starting with the one who had hit Quinn yesterday. A little payback seemed in order.

. . .

The young man, Thorsten by name, was by her side thirty minutes later, when she stopped outside a cell door in the E-block. In fact, he was so nice and solicitous, it made her feel just a little bit guilty about what she was about to do. Not guilty enough to abort the plan, but enough to thank him very nicely, again, for accompanying her.

He clicked his heels together. "A pleasure, ma'am!"

She gave him her most dazzling smile, and while he was still blinking from the impact, hit the button to open the cell door. The outer door hissed aside, followed a moment later by the inner. Elsa stepped through, with Thorsten scrambling on her heels.

It was just a day since she'd been in this cell, and it hadn't changed since then. Same white walls, same white floor, same bright light. Same uncomfortable cot against the wall. Same young man sitting on the cot.

Aside from the fact that he was in here and they came from the outside, he might almost have been one of the guards. Taller than her by a couple of inches, and older than the guards by a few years, but still young enough to look boyish. Handsome, with high cheekbones, long-lashed hazel eyes, and a hint of softness to his mouth that even the time spent on Marica-3 hadn't been able to eradicate.

Elsa nodded cordially. "Good morning."

He nodded back warily.

"I'm Doctor Elsa Brandeis. We met yesterday. I'm afraid I'm going to have to ask you to come with me."

He turned a shade paler. "Where?"

"I'm Doctor Sterling's assistant. We'll be going to the lab."

She nodded to Thorsten, who took a step forward. Holden Sinclair got to his feet, and she could see his hands curl into fists, but before anything could happen, she jabbed a needle into Thorsten's backside and pressed the plunger.

He half-turned. "What—?"

It was all he got out before his eyes rolled back in his head, and he crumpled. Elsa moved to catch him, trying not to think about Olaus dying at her feet less than a week ago, in a cell very like this one.

Holden Sinclair watched her suspiciously, keeping his distance. She huffed at him. "I could use a little help."

He didn't move. "What's going on?"

His Rhenish was flawless. She had noticed as much last night and had counted on it when she made her plans.

"Help me lay him down. And then we have to take his clothes off."

He hesitated. But eventually he assisted her in lowering the unconscious body onto the floor. As soon as it was laid out, he stepped back, away from her. Elsa left him alone to think things through. She wasn't afraid he'd attack her. He didn't seem the type, and besides, she kept him in her line of vision.

Undressing Thorsten was eerily similar to undressing Olaus's corpse. The only difference was that Thorsten was still alive. Unconscious, but alive. Living and breathing, with a heartbeat and color in his cheeks. And he would remain so. He'd stay unconscious for the next three or four hours—long enough for the shuttle to get airborne—but he'd be awake after that. And unharmed, aside from a headache. But he'd be stuck in this cell with no way out. It'd be interesting to know how much time he'd have to spend here before anyone realized where he was—but she didn't ultimately care. He'd get food and water through the slot by the door. He'd be fine.

He kept a knife in his boot. Emulating his mentor, probably. Stephen Lamb was an idol to many of these boys, poor role model though he was.

For a second she thought about Lamb's knife slicing through Quinn's skin, opening him up for the night crawler, and a red haze of anger descended over her eyes. Then she shook it off. No time for that now. She had too much to accomplish before the shuttle took off to plan revenge on Stephen Lamb.

And if she could pull off what she was trying to accomplish, it would be the best revenge anyone could hope for, anyway.

After putting the boots aside—and the knife in her pocket; better not to take any chances, plus it might come in handy—she removed Thorsten's trousers and tossed them in Holden's direction. "Put these on."

He didn't move. "Why?"

"Because you can't walk out of here in that." She gestured to the white jumpsuit, the same suit all the prisoners wore. In the back of her head, she could hear Quinn's voice telling her the same thing. *Can't walk outta here like this, can I…*

"I thought I was going to the lab."

"You are." She spared him a glance. "And then you're going to the shuttle."

He blinked. "Why?"

"Accompanying a corpse."

He turned another shade paler. "Anyone I know?"

"You'll see." No time to explain right now. Especially since the explanation was complicated and would take time. Time she couldn't spare. "Please just do as I say. I'm trying to help you."

He opened his mouth—possibly to ask why again—but seemed to think better of it. Bending, he lifted the trousers.

"Take the jumpsuit off first."

When she and Quinn had made their way through the prison that first day, the fact that he'd had the jumpsuit on under the uniform had made no difference. If anyone came close enough to notice, it was too late to matter. But if Holden would be walking among the guards, he had to look the part.

Glancing up, she noticed he was blushing, and it was almost enough to make her smile. Almost. "I'm a doctor, Mr. Sinclair. I've seen naked bodies before."

And his was of little interest to her. However, in deference to his feelings, she added, "I'll be busy down here. I won't look."

She went to work on Thorsten's weapons belt and uniform jacket. After a few seconds, she could hear Holden begin to unzip the jumpsuit.

By the time Thorsten was stripped of jacket and shirt, Holden had pulled the trousers on and was in the process of fastening them. Like Quinn, he was too thin from the poor rations, but Holden was younger and must have been more slender to begin with, so it was less noticeable. Rather more conspicuous were the stripes across his back and shoulders, evidence of floggings in the not-too-distant past.

"Here." She handed him the shirt. "When you're finished changing, I'll need your help moving him onto the cot."

He didn't respond, just nodded. She checked Thorsten's vital signs to make sure the young man was holding up well—his heart rate was normal, and so was his breathing—and by the time she was done, she looked up in time to see Holden complete the transformation from prisoner to guard.

He put Thorsten's cap on his head and looked at her from under the brim.

Excellent.

The uniform fit him well. He was perhaps a fraction shorter than Thorsten but not so much that anyone would notice. The tops of the trousers disappeared into the boots, and the jacket hit at roughly the right spot on his hips. The weapons belt sat snugly around his waist, and the hat shaded his face well. With ten thousand guards on Marica-3, he stood a good chance of passing unnoticed.

"Here." She handed him the laser pistol, identical to the one Quinn had carried for three days. "Do you know how to use it?"

He weighed it in his hand, looking at it for a few moments before moving his gaze up to hers. Suddenly he didn't look as young. "Yes."

"Put it in the holster. Don't shoot anyone unless I tell you to."

He nodded.

"Let's go."

She opened the door and stuck her head out. Looked both ways. Was reminded vividly of doing this with Quinn, a lifetime ago, last week.

The hallway was empty. Elsa stepped outside. Holden followed, and she sealed the door behind them, locking Thorsten in.

Before they could put the next part of the plan into motion, they needed another guard. Elsa eyeballed the ones they passed and finally settled on one she decided would best suit her needs. He was shorter than Holden by almost half a head, the smallest of all the guards she'd seen on Marica-3. Shorter than her by a centimeter or two as well. She might have felt sorry for him and the inferiority complex she assumed he must carry, had it not been for the fact that when they came upon him, he was hassling one of the female prisoners, someone even smaller than himself. Hand at her throat, holding her against the wall, he was letting his other hand explore her body.

"Soldier!"

Her voice lashed like a whip, and he snapped to attention, his back ramrod straight. The young woman took the opportunity to slip away down the corridor. In a few seconds she had disappeared around the nearest corner.

She shouldn't be out and about on her own, and for a moment Elsa wondered if she should dispatch Holden to bring her back. For her own safety more than anything. A female prisoner alone was fair game for any of the guards. But then she thought better of it. She didn't have time to be sidetracked by stray prisoners. The girl was all right. They had come upon the situation before the guard had had time to do anything but feel her up. And someone else would find her and bring her back to her cell eventually. If not, she'd make a useful distraction.

She turned her gaze to the young soldier. "Come with me."

He swallowed but fell in behind when she set off down the corridor. She could hear his whispered request for information, with nerves laced through this voice, and Holden's curt response in perfect Rhenish. "Corpse transport."

It wasn't necessary to see the guard's face to know his reaction; she could feel dismay rolling out from his compact body in waves. Elsa permitted herself a tiny smile, since he couldn't see her face, anyway.

After making their way through the warren of corridors, they stopped outside another cell. Manipulating the buttons beside the door, Elsa opened it and stepped through. It looked just like the other one, except for the fact that here, the prisoner was curled up on the bed, his hands tucked into his armpits. When they walked in, he scrambled into a sitting position, his back against the wall. His eyes were a pale sky blue, wide with fear, his gaze flickering from one to the other of them. "What do you want?"

Holden made an instinctive move forward, until Elsa shot him a look that stopped him in his tracks. Instead, she nodded to the small guard, who was smirking in anticipation, watching the prisoner. "Go ahead."

He grinned. And took a step forward, his hand already on the baton hanging from his belt. When she jabbed him with the needle, he crumpled so quickly she didn't have time to catch him. Somehow she couldn't work up much regret over that.

"I'll get his uniform," she told Holden. "You explain."

He nodded and, removing his headgear, addressed the prisoner still cowering on the bed in Standard. "Toby. It's me."

It took a moment before the words penetrated, but then Toby Flatt straightened. "Holden?"

"Yeah. We're getting out of here."

Toby shook his head. "I don't trust her. She was here yesterday. With that bastard Lamb."

"I was making sure I knew where you were," Elsa said, in her own less perfect Standard. She was kneeling on the floor, stripping yet another guard down to his underthings. It didn't even faze her this time.

"He has a point, though," Holden said. "There has to be a reason why you're doing this."

She looked up to meet two pairs of eyes. One blue, one hazel, both watching her intently. "There is. Quinn."

Both pairs of eyes blinked. "What about the captain?" Holden said, his tone suspicious.

Elsa sat back on her heels. There wasn't much time, and she

didn't know how much to tell them, but they needed some kind of explanation. "He escaped. A few days ago."

"They told us," Holden said. "Or Lamb did. Said Quinn shot someone and took off. With a hostage."

Elsa nodded. "Me."

"You helped him escape?"

Not exactly. "Not at first. But we spent three days together out there. He saved my life." More than once. And in more ways than one.

"That sounds like something he'd do," Toby murmured. Holden nodded.

"He could have kept walking. He might not have gotten off Marica-3, but he could have stayed away long enough that the patrols stopped looking for him. It's a big moon. But the only thing he cared about was going back here to find the rest of you. And in going back, he got caught."

They exchanged a glance. "So he's back here."

"Not…exactly."

There was a pause.

"He's dead," Holden said, his voice flat. "That's the corpse you want us to put on the shuttle."

She nodded. There was more to it than that, but just in case she was wrong, better not to get their hopes up.

"What happened?" There was a catch in his voice, making him sound even younger than he looked.

"I killed him." Her voice was clear and amazingly steady. "He said if he got recaptured, he wanted me to. He didn't want to live like this anymore."

They both nodded.

"The last thing I can do for him is get him and you off Marica-3.

If I can get you onto the shuttle without mishap, you stand a chance of getting away."

"What about him?" Toby asked, looking at the guard laid out on the floor.

"He'll wake up in a few hours with a bad headache and no way out of this cell."

She finished stripping the guard's pants off and handed them to Toby along with the tall boots. "Take the jumpsuit off before putting these on."

"There's a guard in my cell, too," Holden told him, and turned his attention to Elsa. "Why are we leaving guards in the cells? Wouldn't it have been easier just to get a couple of uniforms from the laundry?"

She answered without looking up from unbuttoning the guard's uniform jacket. "There are over a hundred thousand prisoners on Marica-3. Too many to keep up with. So the cells are wired for body heat. If there's no living, breathing creature inside, an alarm goes off. By leaving the guards in your cells, it looks as if you're still here. If we're lucky, no one will realize for a few days that the warm bodies in these cells aren't your bodies."

They exchanged a glance. "Smart," Toby said.

"Thank you." She handed him the uniform jacket and shirt and sat up to face them both. "We have to talk about Isaac Miller."

There was a pause.

"What about him?" Holden said.

"Do you trust him?"

The young man's eyes narrowed. "Why wouldn't we?"

"You know I came to your cells yesterday, with Major Lamb."

They nodded.

"We also went to Mr. Miller's cell."

"And?" Holden said.

"He and the major seemed to be friendly. Major Lamb thanked him for his help with unloading the shuttle last time it was here and told him he'd be doing it again today."

They looked at one another for a few seconds.

"He's a mercenary," Elsa prodded. "Quinn said you picked him up off Sumatra a couple of years ago. He agreed to provide security in exchange for passage home."

Holden nodded.

"Could he be working for Major Lamb in an effort to buy his way off Marica-3?"

"Anything's possible," Holden said. "But I don't think so."

Toby shook his head. "He wouldn't leave the captain here. Holden and me either, I don't think, but definitely not the captain."

"Are you sure?" Elsa said.

Toby looked at her, in the process of buttoning up the guard's white shirt. It was taking a while, as his fingers fumbled with buttons and tiny buttonholes. "Isaac woulda been sitting in a Sumatran prison if it hadn't been for the captain. He ain't gonna leave him here."

Holden nodded. "Especially not here, I would think."

"We'll have to find him, then." If Miller wouldn't have left Quinn behind, she wouldn't leave him. Even if having him along would make everything they had to do that much harder. They'd have to figure out a way to get him onto the shuttle and find a place to hide him. There was no conceivable way the big black man could pass as a Rhenian guard. Nor would she be able to find a uniform big enough to fit him.

She just hoped the other two weren't wrong about him. If they were, Isaac Miller could blow her plan wide open before they even got off the ground.

Toby shrugged on the jacket and began buttoning it. It fit him well. Elsa turned to Holden. "Help me get this one on the bed."

He nodded. Between them, they lifted the unconscious guard onto the cot and stepped back. Toby finished dressing and looked from one to the other of them. "Now what?"

Holden, too, looked at Elsa.

She swallowed. "I guess it's time to go get Quinn."

CHAPTER TWENTY-THREE

He was where Elsa had left him, on the table in the lab, motionless and cool to the touch. She had closed the cut in his side with surgical glue and snapped the restraints off his ankles and wrists before leaving, placing his hands in a more decorous position on his chest, but otherwise he looked the same. It hurt her heart to look at him, and in glancing at the faces of the two men, she saw she wasn't alone. Both of them had removed their headgear upon walking into the lab. Toby looked like he was trying not to cry, his face pale and sort of pinched, and Holden swallowed hard, and then swallowed again. "He looks different."

"He's had a rough few months," Elsa said. "When we realized he was telling the truth, and no one but him had the information about the Marican resistance, Doctor Sterling made it his mission to break him."

Holden glanced at her. "Did he succeed?"

She shook her head. "Whatever Quinn knew left with him."

"Good." Holden moved his attention back to the lifeless form on the table. Nobody spoke for a minute. Then it was Toby's turn to glance over at her.

"What do we do?"

"I guess we move him onto a pallet for the trip down to the shuttle. But first we have to put him in a body bag. I'll get one."

She headed for the cabinet, leaving the three of them there in the middle of the room. By the time she turned around, body bag in hand, the two that were conscious had pulled out their laser pistols and were pointing them at her.

I should have seen that coming.

"Why should we trust you?" Toby asked.

She looked from him to Holden down to Quinn, on the table. "He did."

"No offense," Holden said, "but that's not a recommendation. You killed him."

"He asked me to."

"So you say. But how do we know you're telling the truth?"

"I gave you the guns. I could have kept them." She had thought that might sway them. However, their expressions didn't change. "I need your help."

"With what?"

"Him." She looked at Quinn.

"He's dead," Holden said. "You could wheel him down to the shuttle yourself."

She didn't answer, and he looked at her, intently. And switched over to Rhenish. She wasn't sure whether it was to make explaining easier for her, in her own language, or to keep Toby from understanding what they were saying. "What is it you're not telling us?"

She glanced up and met his eyes once before going back to looking at Quinn. "If I get him on the shuttle soon, there's a chance

I can get him back."

There was a beat.

"I thought you said he was dead," Holden said. "People don't come back from the dead."

She nodded. "It's complicated. But he's not so dead—not yet—that I can't get him back." She'd done it before. Although not after this long. She added a qualifying, "Maybe."

Holden glanced at Toby. She didn't know how much Toby had understood, but something passed between the two men, some form of communication. Holden turned back to her. "We'll help you. If we don't get caught, we'll see if you can do what you say you can. But if you don't, just be warned that Toby might shoot you."

Elsa's lips twitched. "Not you?"

"I'm reserving judgment," Holden said.

Very well. "I need one of you to go get a float pallet. Through that door right there." She pointed to it. Toby trotted off and came back a minute later, pallet in tow.

"Thank you. We need to get him into the bag and onto the pallet."

"The easiest is to put the bag on the pallet and move him into it," Holden said. "You hold the pallet steady. Toby and I'll move the captain."

Two minutes later, the table in the lab was empty. Quinn was on the float pallet, inside the body bag. Elsa had made sure that it wasn't sealed all the way. His body had slowed down to where he only took a breath every few minutes, but it was best not to take any chances. And making sure he got enough oxygen to his brain was vital.

As they maneuvered the float pallet across the room toward the door, she sent a prayer heavenward that she hadn't miscalculated the spider-scorpion venom. To the best of her knowledge, this had never been attempted before. And Doctor Sterling had done very little experimenting with the spider-scorpion venom. The creature used it to paralyze its prey, leaving it immobile and unfeeling, but alive and aware, while the spider-scorpion devoured it. Doctor Sterling—and this should have tipped her off to the doctor's true nature a long time ago—wasn't interested in a venom that caused the victim not to feel.

The spider-scorpion usually feasted on snakes or lizards, while Quinn was considerably bigger. But she'd thought if she could recalculate the dose, she could put him into a sort of induced paralysis, to make him look dead enough to pass muster with Major Lamb. But something had gone wrong. Quinn wasn't aware. His body was alive, hanging on by a thread, but he'd gone somewhere she couldn't reach him. After Stephen Lamb had stumbled out of the lab earlier, she had tried to talk to Quinn, had searched his eyes for any flicker of awareness, of response. But had seen none. For all intents and purposes, he might as well be dead.

What had happened? She had calculated the dose carefully. Had spent most of the night going over and over the numbers to make sure she gave him enough to shut his body down but not enough to kill him.

What had she done wrong?

And how long could he stay like this before he just slipped away? A body couldn't sustain itself on a heartbeat and a breath every couple of minutes. Not for long.

Her mind churning, she followed the float pallet into the hallway in the direction of the lift tube.

• • •

Downstairs on the shuttle pad, there was considerable activity. The shuttle itself squatted at the end of the landing pad like some enormous prehistoric insect, all six legs bent and its jaws open, a long tongue reaching toward the ground. Up and down this tongue—or ramp—tiny figures moved.

As Elsa and her companions got closer, the figures separated themselves into two groups: gray-clad Rhenian soldiers with laser pistols at the ready, barking orders and directing traffic, and prisoners in white jumpsuits, trotting up and down the ramp, hauling boxes and crates. They must have unloaded what was staying on Marica-3, because all the boxes and crates were going onto the shuttle.

Good. Closer to departure.

"Do you see him?" Elsa asked Toby under her breath as they made their way across the tarmac with the pallet.

He shook his head without looking at her. He looked nervous, and she wished she could tell him not to be, that the guards didn't look nervous, they looked like they owned this moon and knew it… but he didn't understand much Rhenish, and there were people all around them, so she didn't dare speak in Standard any more than she had to.

Holden twisted his head a half-turn. "Over by the crates."

Elsa followed the direction of his gaze and saw the big man laboring over the boxes. Head and shoulders taller than the other prisoners, most of whom were Marican, he was distributing cargo to them. The crates he so easily picked off the top of the pile often buckled the knees of the prisoners he gave them to.

As she watched, a small, white-clad figure trotted up to him. It was hard to tell at a distance when they were all wearing the same white coveralls and had shaved heads, but Elsa thought this one was female. There was a certain grace to the movements the others lacked. Isaac Miller picked up and discarded a couple of boxes before he found one that would pass muster, and he handed it to her carefully. For a second Elsa caught a glimpse of white teeth as he smiled. Then the girl turned and hurried off, but not without a glance over her shoulder at him.

At the bottom of the ramp, a Rhenian soldier stood guard, plasma rifle in his hands. Elsa stopped in front of him. "Soldier."

He nodded, his eyes still on the prisoners going up the ramp with boxes and coming back empty-handed. "Doctor."

"Body transport."

"Tag him with final destination and put him in the cooler."

Final destination…

"He isn't Marican. He'll be moving off planet."

The guard looked dismayed. "He going to Sierra Luz?"

"Is that a problem?"

The guard straightened his back, his face turning impassive. "No, Doctor." After a moment he added, as if he couldn't help himself, "It's just that the second moon isn't in the quadrant. It'll take a while to get him there."

And during that time he'd be rotting. It was understandable that the guard wanted the corpse off his hands sooner rather than later.

Sierra Luz was a shipyard. They'd have an easier time losing themselves on Marica itself. If they managed to get there.

Elsa shook her head. "He can go to Calvados first. In fact, maybe I should accompany him there myself. And make sure he gets where he's going."

The guard looked surprised for a moment before his face slipped back into immobility. "Yes, Doctor."

She glanced around. "I should tell Major Lamb. Have you seen him?"

"Over there," the guard said, gesturing, a tiny wrinkle between his brows. Elsa turned, and after a bit of searching, spied Stephen Lamb sitting on a crate with his back against several others. His legs were stretched out in front of him, and his head was tilted back, his mouth open and his eyes closed. She was too far away to be able to hear and probably wouldn't have been able to, anyway, over the din of scuffling feet and yelling, and the low hum of the shuttle's engine, but it looked like he might be snoring.

She turned back to the guard. "Has he been like that for long?"

"Ever since the shuttle touched down," the guard said.

"Goodness. Obviously he isn't feeling well. He should go to his lodgings and lie down. Come with me, soldier."

"I'm on duty."

"I'm reassigning you. Temporarily. Thorsten—" Her glance brushed Holden's. "—will stay here in your place. And you," she nodded at Toby, "take the body inside."

They both nodded back. At least Toby understood that much Rhenish.

"May I?" Holden reached for the guard's plasma rifle. The guard hesitated but ended up relinquishing it, if with clear reluctance.

"You'll be back on your post in fifteen minutes," Elsa told him bracingly. "And Major Lamb will appreciate your assistance. As do I." She smiled.

The guard blinked and then smiled back, visions of Major Lamb's appreciation no doubt dancing in his head.

She wished she could give Holden some instructions before she went back inside the prison, but with the guard standing right there, she had to trust that he'd figure it out on his own. He'd have to stand guard while Toby went inside the shuttle with Quinn's body and found a place for it and himself. While she and the guard were gone,

Holden would also have to make sure that Isaac Miller got onto the shuttle and into hiding. It would be up to her to get Holden and herself onto the shuttle once she got back.

She nodded to him. "Carry on, Thorsten."

He nodded back. "Ma'am." His eyes were clear and steady. He was intelligent; he'd do what was necessary.

Her gaze brushed Toby's. There was still a hint of suspicion lurking in the man's eyes, but she didn't suppose she could blame him for that. He'd learn that he could trust her eventually. Or they'd get caught before they made it off the tarmac, and then it wouldn't matter.

She made herself face the young guard. "Come along, soldier. Let's get Major Lamb up to his bed."

The guard nodded and followed her across the tarmac to the sleeping major.

The next few minutes were difficult. The major did not want to go inside and to bed. As he explained, in a voice garbled with sleep, it would be a dereliction of duty. She tried to reason with him, to tell him that he wasn't doing anyone any good sitting on the landing pad sleeping—that, in fact, he was damaging his reputation and making his subordinates question his abilities to lead—but it only made him more belligerent, and more determined to stay. He became combative, and the young guard seemed disinclined to want to wrestle with him.

By that point, they had variously coaxed and coerced him into the building and were on their way to the lift tube.

Elsa fumbled in her pocket. "I'm afraid this is necessary. If he won't listen to reason…" She nodded to the guard to hold the major steady.

The guard looked like he wanted to argue, but she stared him down. She was Doctor Sterling's assistant, second-in-command to the doctor himself; on medical matters, her word was law. Even when it came to Major Lamb.

Lamb bellowed when the needle plunged through the fabric of his uniform and into the flesh, and he bucked and tried to throw off the guard. The young man held on for all he was worth.

"Hold him," Elsa gritted out as she clung to the major from behind, trying to still his flailing fists. "He'll stop any second now…"

And just like that, the major slumped.

"Hold him!"

The guard tried, but the major's dead weight was heavy. Between them, they managed to drag him into the lift tube, where they propped him against the wall with the guard holding him steady. Elsa took his wrist and checked his pulse. It was normal.

Upstairs in the guard wing, she overrode the keypad beside the door to open the major's quarters. They were similar to her own flat beside the lab, but the major favored darker, more sumptuous fabrics and antique carved furniture he must have shipped in all the way from Rhene. Elsa chastised herself for being unkind, yet couldn't help but feel that his bedroom looked like something out of a house of disrepute in an old holovid, the bed enclosed by heavy velvet curtains and the coverlet slippery satin. He liked blacks and deep reds. A pair of restraints dangled from one of the bedposts, and Elsa eyed them, perplexed for a moment, before realization dawned.

Flushing, she turned away, only to be faced with the guard, who stood in the middle of the floor, still supporting the major and looking around with a mixture of interest and dawning fascination.

"Put him on the bed." The curtness of her tone snapped him out of whatever fantasy he was entertaining. Cheeks flushed, he moved to do as she said. Between them, they got Major Lamb arranged on the bed. Elsa removed his boots, weapons belt, and jacket but decided anything else was beyond the call of duty. She left him in his trousers and shirtsleeves and pulled the hangings closed around the bed, wishing she dared make use of the restraints.

"He'll wake up in a couple of hours," she told the guard, who looked a little worried. "I knew he wasn't feeling well. Doctor Sterling is under the weather, too, but at least he had enough sense to go to bed. The major just needed a little push." She smiled tightly.

The guard smiled back, tentative.

"Don't worry. None of this was your fault. I'll make a note in your file."

She crossed her fingers in her pocket and tried not to feel too guilty when she saw the look of relief on the young man's face.

"If you don't mind, I'd like to make another stop while we're here. It'll only take a minute."

He nodded, of course. What else could he do?

So she took him up to her own quarters first, and picked up the small carry-on bag she'd packed last night in the event that they got this far. It contained a few changes of clothing and all she had been able to scrape together of money. It wasn't much, but enough to get them into hiding for a few days once they got downside to Marica. Assuming they weren't caught on the way there.

Next, they stopped in the lab, where she added a small case to the carry-on bag—all she could carry of venoms, anti-venoms, and synthetic blood, along with syringes, needles, and assorted paraphernalia. Just in case.

That done, she gave the guard a big smile. "Just one more thing. We have to go into the prisoners' block for this."

He nodded, too dazzled to protest. After trailing her down to the cells, she led him to one of the doors and keyed the code into the keypad. "After you."

He stepped inside and glanced around. And looked nonplussed when the cell turned out to be empty. When he turned back to her, Elsa said sweetly, "Get on the cot, please."

The guard's eyes widened, and he swallowed convulsively. But he scrambled to do as she asked, his eyes hanging on her every move as she stepped up to the side of the bed and smiled down at him, hands in her pockets.

"You were a great help. I appreciate it. I'll make sure to make a note in your evaluation."

"Thank…" He had to clear his throat and try again. "Thank you."

"My pleasure. Now close your eyes." She smoothed one hand over his cheek while the other stayed in her pocket. Only when his eyes were closed, pale lashes resting against smooth cheeks, did she remove the other hand. He jerked when the needle jabbed his thigh, but by then it was too late.

"I'm sorry," Elsa told his startled eyes, "but it's necessary. And this way Major Lamb can't blame you for what happened."

He was already fading, but she thought that last sentence might have made sense to him. And really, he had been very helpful. She had no desire to make his life any more difficult than it was. He didn't deserve to suffer for what she'd done or what she'd made him do.

Leaving him in Isaac Miller's cell with the door securely sealed behind her, she lifted her carry-on bag and rushed back to the shuttle pad.

CHAPTER TWENTY-FOUR

Holden was still standing at the bottom of the ramp, clutching the plasma rifle in a white-knuckled grip. When he saw Elsa coming, his expression registered a relief totally unbecoming a Rhenian guard. Luckily, no one important was there to see it. The other guards were busy directing prisoner traffic in the other direction. Rather than loading the shuttle, the task had now become moving the boxes that had been unloaded the last step of the way into the prison. Lines of prisoners filed in and out of the front doors; she'd had to squeeze past them on her way out. The tower of crates that Isaac Miller had been handling were all gone, loaded onto the shuttle while she'd been inside. Miller was gone, too.

"I was getting worried," Holden muttered when she got close enough to hear him. "You were inside a long time."

A shade of that worry still lingered in his eyes, and Elsa realized he'd been waiting for the guards to drag him back inside, to strip him and whip him for attempting to escape. He'd thought she'd set him up.

She gave him a smile and a deliberate caress on the arm. "Sorry,

Thorsten. I didn't change my mind. I just stopped at the comconsole in the lobby and got you your leave pass. A week downside before you have to come back." She glanced around. There was no sign of Isaac Miller or Toby Flatt.

After the initial surprise, Holden's expression lightened. "Thank you, Doctor Brandeis."

"If we're going to be spending the next week together," Elsa said and smiled up at him, coquettishly, "I think you'd better call me Elsa. Don't you?"

His eyes widened for a moment, before he started playing along. "Right. Elsa."

"Are you ready? Is everyone on board?" Everyone that mattered?

He nodded. "The shuttle is almost ready to take off. I told them to wait for you."

"Thank you." She took his arm. "Shall we?"

"Yes, ma'am." He smiled as he escorted her up the ramp, a hint of proprietary pride on his handsome face. Elsa thought about dropping her hand, to make it clear to him that she was behaving this way solely for the benefit of anyone watching, not because she intended to give him access to her bed or her body during the flight. But then she saw the guard standing just inside the shuttle door, ready to pull the ramp up as soon as they were safely inside, and she realized that Holden had no illusions about her feelings; he was just playing to their audience.

The guard leered, and she gave him a cold stare as she took the necessary paperwork out of her carry-on bag. "Leave passes for Thorsten Anderton, Edmund Newsome, and Elsa Brandeis. One week downside."

The guard inspected them carefully. "You're Thorsten?" He

glanced at Holden, who nodded. "Where's Edmund?"

"I sent him onboard earlier," Elsa said. "With a corpse."

The guard grimaced and handed the passes back rather quickly, as if afraid they were contaminated. "We only have two passenger cabins. This is a freight transport."

"We'll manage." She glanced coyly at Holden, who blushed on cue.

The guard grinned. "Up one level, first and second door on the right."

"Thank you." She smiled at him and turned to Holden, giving him another stroke along the arm for good measure. "You go on up. I want to check in on…"

For a second her mind blanked on Toby's identity, and she saw her own consternation reflected in Holden's hazel eyes before it came to her. " —Edmund first. And tell him where the cabins are."

"I'll come with you. Keep you warm."

He tried to leer and couldn't quite pull it off, but it got the point across.

"Leave the rifle here," the guard said, holding his hand out. "You won't need it."

"Of course." Holden handed the rifle over, a little reluctantly, and the guard opened a cabinet in the wall beside the door and put it inside.

"You won't need it for the next three days."

"Of course not." Elsa glanced up at her companion. "Let's go. The sooner we finish, the sooner we can go to our cabin."

"Yes, ma'am." Holden grinned and took her arm to escort her down the hallway.

"Ten minutes to takeoff," the guard called after them. "Make sure you're buckled in when we lift, or you'll regret it later."

"Do you know where to go?" Elsa asked Holden as soon as she estimated they were out of range of the guard. Just in case there were microphones, she kept her voice low and spoke Rhenish.

He sent her a look that belied his years. "I came up on this shuttle."

So had she. But she hadn't ventured below cabin level. Hadn't wanted to. It was easier to feel nothing when you didn't see anything to upset you.

"Where are the prisoners kept?"

"Cargo hold," Holden said, his voice tight. "Like cattle. You'll see."

He headed toward a set of doors at the end of the hallway. When he pushed them open and stepped aside so she could go in first, Elsa bit back a sound of dismay.

The room was big, but hardly cavernous. Not big enough for the numbers of prisoners the shuttle sometimes carried. The boxes from earlier were stacked along the walls of the big room, fastened with hooks and straps so they wouldn't shift during takeoff or landing. And all across the rest of the room, in rows along the floor, were embedded hooks. For more straps, or...

She shot a look of horror at Holden. "Are those what I think they are?"

He nodded. "When I came up, there were more than fifty of us, fastened hand and foot to the floor. For three days straight."

"What about eating? Or bathroom breaks?"

"They didn't feed us," Holden said. "No bathroom breaks necessary."

And Quinn had still managed to walk off the shuttle smiling. Elsa swallowed. "I'm sorry."

He smiled, but it didn't reach his eyes. "I'd tell you not to worry, that it wasn't your fault—"

"But we both know better." She looked around. "I don't see anyone."

"They're here somewhere. We just have to let them see us. The cold storage is through here." He headed toward a door on the other side of the room. "That's where we'll find Quinn. Probably Toby and Isaac, too."

He pushed the door open and waved her through. Elsa walked in, straight into the crosshairs of a laser pistol.

"Whoa!" The gun looked like a toy in Isaac Miller's hand, but there was no doubt the big man knew how to use it, or that he would, given the circumstances. Elsa raised her own hands slowly. "It's us."

"It's all right," Holden added, following her inside. His voice made clouds in the frosty air. "You won't need that."

Isaac Miller's dark face split in a grin. "Kid. Glad you made it."

Holden nodded. "This is Elsa Brandeis. Don't shoot her. She's the one trying to get us out of here."

"She's the one killed Quinn," Isaac retorted, without lowering the pistol, "and I for one'd like to know why we're being nice to her." He turned his attention to her, dark eyes drilling into hers.

"He asked me to," Elsa said. Her voice shook, but she wasn't sure whether it was from fear or the chilly temperature. Probably a bit of both. Her breath made clouds in the air in front of her face, and already she could tell that Isaac was cut from a different material than Holden and Toby. There was a ruthlessness to him, an edge of violence the other two lacked. It wasn't surprising that he had been able to trick Stephen Lamb into the almost sort of camaraderie she'd noticed when she'd gone with Stephen to Miller's cell last night. The major had probably recognized some of himself in Miller.

If it had been a trick.

Miller's eyes narrowed. "Not sure I believe it. Don't sound like the man I know."

"He isn't the man you know," Elsa said. "He's been through a lot. A lot more than any of you. He'd have been dead many times over if we hadn't always managed to get him back at the last minute."

She lowered her hands. Even if Isaac decided to shoot her, there wasn't anything she could do about it. "When we were out there, wandering, he made me promise that if he got caught again, I'd let him die next time. Really die. So I did."

"Except he may not be dead," Holden said. "Really dead. She thinks she can get him back."

Isaac shook his head. "He's dead, all right. We've been sitting here with him for twenty minutes. He ain't waked up yet."

"He wouldn't wake up," Elsa said, her voice still shaking, "not without help. Is he breathing? Have you checked for a pulse?"

"'Course. I'm telling you, the man's dead!"

"Let me see." Heart slamming against her ribs, Elsa brushed past him to where the pallet floated against the wall, occasionally bumping into the curved bulkhead. Toby moved out of the way as she approached. The holster in his gun belt was empty; his laser pistol must be the one in Isaac's hand.

"Any problems getting here?" Holden inquired of the other two. Elsa ignored them. They were here, so obviously everything had worked out all right. She had more immediate worries.

Someone had opened the body bag, exposing Quinn's face and throat. Her heart clutched as she stopped beside the pallet and looked down at him. He did look dead, didn't he? His face was beyond pale, his cheeks gaunt and his eyes sunken. To the friends who hadn't seen him for four months, he must look beyond recovery.

To her, he didn't look that bad. It had been a few hours since the events in the lab, and he looked no worse than he had then. There might yet be hope.

Reaching out, she placed both hands on his cheeks, feeling for warmth, for breath, something to indicate that he was still in there.

Isaac made a move toward her but subsided when Holden gave him a headshake. "She says she can do it. Maybe. Let her try."

Elsa shook her head. "There's nothing I can do for him right now. There's no time. The shuttle's about to take off. We have to strap in, or we'll all get hurt."

The gun came up to point at her stomach again. "You ain't going nowhere until you do whatever it was you were gonna do for Quinn!"

Holden reached out a hand to push the gun down, but Elsa shook her head at him before addressing Isaac. "I understand how you feel. I want him back more than any of you. But we have to get airborne first. He's lasted this long. He'll be all right a little longer."

Isaac looked at her for a second, his face a mask, devoid of expression, and his eyes the flat black of a water snake about to strike. Elsa resisted the temptation to wrap her arms around herself for warmth.

Finally he nodded.

"There are two cabins upstairs," Holden told Toby. "Elsa'll take one and you and I the other. Isaac—" He turned to the big man. "I don't guess it'd be a good idea for you to start walking around. Someone might see you."

Isaac nodded. "I'll stay down here with Quinn. Cold don't bother me much."

"You won't be spending much time in cold storage," Elsa told him. "Once Quinn wakes up, he'll need to get warm. We have to find somewhere else for the two of you."

The shuttle lurched, and everyone staggered.

"After we're airborne. For now, just stay with him and make sure he doesn't get hurt. More hurt."

"Better sit down and find something to hold on to," Holden added.

"Out." Isaac pointed to the door, and they all scrambled out into the main storage room. Elsa shut the door to the cold storage behind her. She hated to leave Quinn there, but he was supposed to be dead; she couldn't leave him in the cargo hold. If one of the shuttle crew came by, and they might, they'd wonder what he was doing outside cold storage. At least until they got him back to life and consciousness, he was better off where he was. The cold would retard any breakdown taking place inside him as well.

"Two minutes to takeoff!" an automated voice announced. Glancing up, Elsa saw a register in the ceiling above her head. Above the door to the corridor, a red light had started blinking.

"Come on!" Holden grabbed her hand.

He pulled Elsa across the floor of the storage room with Toby on their heels. Outside, he pushed her back up the corridor to where the ramp was now sealed, and from there, up the narrow stairs to the top level. They were about halfway there when the automated voice came back with another warning. "One minute to takeoff!"

"Hurry!"

Elsa hurried. Up ahead was a row of seats with lap belts, and she flung herself into one and pulled the belt across her body, snapping the buckle shut just as the countdown began.

"Thirty seconds to takeoff."

Holden fell into the seat beside her and strapped himself in.

"Twenty seconds to takeoff."

Toby dropped into a seat opposite and did the same, fumbling with the belt and buckle.

"Ten seconds to takeoff. Nine. Eight. Seven…"

The voice faded into the background as Elsa gripped the edges of her seat hard enough that her knuckles showed white.

"Not used to traveling?" Holden asked.

She shook her head. "This is my only trip off Rhene. My third time in a spacecraft."

Toby smirked.

"You'll be all right," Holden said. "Just relax. Think about something else."

Like what? All the other ways they could die? And might, before this was over.

Elsa's response was lost in the roar as the shuttle blasted off from the ground, straight up into the air. A second later it was streaking above the barren landscape of the moon, covering in seconds what it had taken her and Quinn hours to traverse. She remembered standing with him that first day, pressed up against the rock wall of a narrow canyon, watching the shuttle flash by overhead. Just three days ago. And a lifetime.

The body of the craft vibrated against her back and feet, sending shivers up her legs, making her stomach twist. She could feel the jolt as the shuttle's six legs folded and tucked themselves away inside its metal shell.

They sat without speaking for the next ten or fifteen minutes. The engine was loud, and they'd have to yell to hear one another. For a lot of different reasons, that seemed like a bad idea. So they sat in silence. To Elsa, it felt as if the shuttle was being ripped to pieces beneath her, and all she could think about was poor Quinn, downstairs in the cold room, unable to hold on to anything. They'd fastened the pallet to the wall, but they hadn't fastened Quinn to the pallet. He could have been jolted off and might be tossed around on the floor right now. And what about Isaac? Had he found something to hold on to?

To keep her mind occupied, she went over their situation again and tried to think of anything she might have missed or should have done differently.

She'd taken every precaution she could think of so no one on Marica-3 would realize they were gone. She'd made sure the men's cells were occupied, so the sensors would register warm bodies. She had arranged leave passes for Holden and Toby, or rather, for Thorsten and Edmund, so they were accounted for. She had killed Quinn dead enough to pass muster with Major Lamb, and she had marked him as deceased in the prisoner base. No one should be looking for him.

She had incapacitated all three guards, along with Doctor Sterling and Major Lamb. All five should wake up in a few hours with nothing worse to show for their adventure but a splitting headache. Hopefully they'd just go back to sleep at that point. Of course, the three guards would be stuck in their cells when they woke up, with no way out and no way to let anyone know where they were. Unless someone specifically went to open those particular doors, it could be awhile before anyone realized they were there instead of the prisoners who were supposed to be.

Sterling and Lamb would be the biggest problem. None of the guards were independent thinkers; they were unlikely to figure out what had happened. But Doctor Sterling was a very intelligent man, and Major Lamb, for all his strutting and posturing, wasn't stupid, either. She had left a note for each man explaining how, after her terrible ordeal, she had decided to take advantage of this inexplicable illness that had struck them both down, along with the fortuitous arrival of the shuttle, to spend a few days in Calvados. Hopefully it would be enough to allay any suspicions either man might have, at least for long enough to get down on Marican soil and into hiding.

Once they got to Calvados they'd be safe. Or as safe as they could be on a Rhenian-occupied planet.

The shaking of the shuttle intensified for a moment, until Elsa felt as if her teeth were being shaken loose. Then, as suddenly as it had started, the rattling ceased, and the shuttle settled into smooth flight. The vibrations in the ship's hull became a barely noticeable hum, and Holden and Toby both straightened in their seats and visibly relaxed. Toby rolled his neck while Holden turned to Elsa.

"That was the shuttle passing through the atmosphere. We're out of Marica-3's space. It should be a smooth ride from here. Until we enter the atmosphere around Marica itself, anyway."

"So can we go back down to the cargo room?" The sooner they went, the sooner she could start work on bringing Quinn back to life.

Holden nodded. "I'll go with you. Toby…" He turned to his friend and switched into rapid Standard. "You should probably spend most of your time in the cabin. We'll make up some excuse. Motion sickness, or something."

Toby snorted, and Holden grinned back.

"I know. But you don't speak Rhenish well enough. If someone corners you, you won't be able to talk your way out of the situation."

Toby nodded.

"Try to come up with a plan for something we can do when we get downside to Marica. Some idea for where we're gonna go from there."

"Ain't much of a planner," Toby said. "The captain was the one making the plans."

"And hopefully he'll be awake by then and can figure something out. But you know he'll want to find the *Fortune*. Give some thought to where she might be and how we can get her back."

Toby nodded. He gave Elsa a brief glance. "Good luck."

"Thank you." It was the first time he'd looked at her with anything but suspicion and hostility, and she was absurdly touched.

She unzipped her overnight bag and took out the small case of vials and syringes she'd brought from the lab. Tucking it in the pocket of her dress—it really wasn't very big; hopefully the contents would be enough to do what she needed—she handed the bag itself to Toby. "Would you take this to one of the cabins? I won't need it down there."

"I'll let you know if anything happens," Holden promised and turned to Elsa. "Ready?"

She nodded. The sooner she got back to the cargo hold and Quinn, the sooner she could start the work of dragging him back from death's door. The more time a man spent in that vicinity, the more difficult rescue became. Quinn was already past his limit. If she didn't get to him soon, she could kiss him good-bye. Forever.

CHAPTER TWENTY-FIVE

Cold.

So damn cold.

He couldn't feel his fingers or toes, and he wasn't too sure about his arms or legs, either. And it was hard to breathe with the weight of the air on his chest like this. It was like drowning, only in air instead of water. He tried to claw his way to some sort of surface but couldn't. His body wouldn't cooperate. Nothing worked. Everything was too cold, too heavy to lift.

And through it all he could hear her voice. Calling his name. Begging for him to come back. To stay with her.

He fought his way toward her, toward the voice, through the cold air, like slogging through snow up to his armpits. And when he reached her and gathered her in his arms, she was frozen, her skin marble pale, hair like icicles, and those green eyes as cold and clear as glacier water, expressionless when they looked into his.

"No!"

He did the only thing he could think of: pulled her close to his body and kissed her. Tried, so desperately, to push some of his warmth into her. To thaw that frozen body and cold heart.

But he was so cold himself, and her chill was creeping into his bones, and she wasn't responding, although he could still hear her voice calling to him inside his head, from so far away. "Come on, Captain! Help me!"

• • •

"Damn," Isaac said and stepped back from the pallet. "I thought we had him that last time."

Elsa nodded, wiping her forehead. She'd thought so, too. For a half a minute at least, she'd been sure he was just a heartbeat away from opening his eyes and looking at her.

She'd been laboring over him for more than an hour. He was still alive. By now, even Isaac had to admit it. There was a heartbeat and a pulse. It was slow, much slower than it should be, but it was there. His blood pressure was dangerously low, and his body temperature was ten degrees below where it should be. When his skin took on a blue tint, they had made the decision to move the pallet and its burden out of the cold room and into the regular cargo hold.

Now Holden stood guard in the hallway and would let them know if any of the shuttle crew was on their way down, while Isaac had said he would take care of any intruders. Elsa wasn't looking forward to the bloodshed—she would much prefer to get through the trip without anyone being the wiser as to their presence—but if it came down to a choice between Quinn's life and someone else's, she knew which way she'd vote.

She just hoped he wouldn't decide to kill her instead, if she couldn't bring Quinn around. None of them felt any loyalty to her, and she wouldn't give much for her own chances of survival if she were unsuccessful in rousing him.

"You okay?"

She looked over into Isaac's flat black eyes and managed to dredge up a semblance of a smile from somewhere. "Yes. Thank you. Just thinking."

Focus. Try again. He's in there; you know he is. You just have to get to him and make him listen to you, so you can draw him back out.

Taking a deep breath, she bent again over the pallet and placed both hands on Quinn's cheeks.

"Come on, Captain. I know you're in there. Open your eyes and look at me."

• • •

"Come on, Quinn. I know you can hear me. Open your eyes."

Quinn fought his way from the depths of nightmare up to the surface. Forcing his gluey eyelids open, he struggled to focus on something, anything.

Cold.

So damn cold.

Hell wasn't supposed to be cold, was it?

So where was he, if not there?

He looked around, searching for anything familiar. And saw white walls and bright lights. He was lying on something cold and hard. Everywhere he looked was white, bright, and icy.

A face swam into view above him. Pale, gorgeous. The most beautiful face he'd ever seen. Hair the color of wheat pulled straight back from perfect features, eyes the color of glacier ice under bird-wing brows.

His sweetest memory and his worst nightmare rolled into one.

"Ah, shit!"

He wasn't dead, after all. He was back in his cell in the goddamn prison on that godforsaken moon. Again.

She smiled. "Oh, good. You're awake. Finally."

"I'm supposed to be dead, damn you! I asked you to kill me!"

He was pretty sure it came out garbled, since his vocal chords didn't seem to want to cooperate. When he lunged for her, wanting nothing more than to wrap his hands around her throat for being a lying, duplicitous bitch, he only managed to throw himself half off the cold metal table.

She caught him before he could go far and put him on his back before speaking to someone over her shoulder. "He's going to hurt himself. We'll have to sedate him again. Hold him down, if you will."

A young man in a gray uniform stepped forward. Quinn couldn't see his face clearly under the brim of the headgear, but he recognized the uniform. Another goddamn Rhenian guard.

He tried to fight, but it was laughably easy for the young man to place his hands on Quinn's shoulders and push him down into the cold metal table. "Easy, Captain. You don't want to hurt yourself. Not now."

That voice…

Quinn stared up at the young man's face, struggling to focus. But it was cold, and his head was fuzzy, and he couldn't seem to get rid of the mist over his eyes. He didn't notice the needle until it went into his arm, and then he jerked against it.

"Hold him down," the med tech warned, her voice strained. "If he gets violent, the tip of the syringe can break off. If it does, we'll have a hard time getting it out without the proper equipment. And I would prefer not to have to slice him open to get to it. He doesn't need any more complications."

The guard nodded, pressing down on Quinn's shoulders.

He waited for the pain to start—for the snake venom or spider venom or some other type of poison to make its way through his bloodstream, leaving burning agony in its wake—but nothing happened. After a bit, he started to feel warmer, his body more relaxed. The guard kept his hands on Quinn's shoulders, but lighter now, no longer actively restraining him.

"Better?" his med tech asked. She was leaning over him again, her face concerned. The guard let go of his shoulders and came around the pallet to the other side.

Quinn did his best to focus on Elsa's face. She looked tired, with deep circles under her eyes. And she was pale. Paler even than usual.

He managed a whisper. "You didn't kill me."

She nodded. "Yes, I did. Just not quite dead enough."

He could feel his lips twitch involuntarily. "Story of my life."

She bit her lip, those white teeth sinking into the plump softness. "I was worried. You were gone for a lot of hours. Deeper than I thought you'd go. For a while I wasn't sure I'd be able to get you back." And she looked miserable about it.

He wet his lips. "I'm glad you did." Even if she'd just have to try again later. At least this way he got to see her one more time.

"Why?" There were tears in those green eyes now, turning them to liquid emerald.

He tried to smile. "Get to thank you."

Now her lips were quivering, too. "I hurt you."

"'s all right." He'd asked her to kill him. She'd had to make it look good. That bastard Lamb had been there, and he wouldn't have been satisfied with less than excruciating agony.

"I'm sorry." Her eyes overflowed, and tears ran down her cheeks. A few dropped and landed on him. He was too weak to lift his hand and brush them off.

Instead he moved his eyes to indicate the ceiling and walls, to give her something else to think about. "Where?" It wasn't his cell. Nor the lab. Not if they were speaking this candidly.

It was the guard who answered, while Elsa was busy wiping her eyes on her sleeve. She was still wearing the same God-awful ugly dress as earlier—yesterday?—whenever she and Lamb had brought him up to the lab. "The shuttle. We're on our way to Calvados."

That voice…

Quinn squinted and managed to get the face under the brim into focus. "Holden?"

The young man's face split in a grin. "Evening, Captain. Good to have you back."

It was good to see him too, but Quinn couldn't find the strength to say so. "How?" he managed instead.

"She did it." Holden indicated Elsa. "She found us all and got us onto the shuttle. Including you. That's why you're so cold. We had to put you in the cooler."

Because he'd been dead. Right.

"The others?"

"Toby's upstairs," Holden said, "keeping an eye on the shuttle crew and staying out of trouble. Isaac is standing guard outside the cargo hold."

"How long?"

It took a moment for Holden to figure out what he wanted to know. "Since we took off? Six hours, give or take."

They had two days then, roughly, before the shuttle touched down on Marica. Two days for him to regain his strength and get back on his feet. Two days before the chase began again. And that was if they made it off the shuttle, if the crew didn't realize they were here and killed them all before they got that far.

Not much time to come up with a plan to save everyone's life.

Then again, he'd had some thoughts on the subject during the time they'd been tramping through the sand hills. Once he remembered what he'd thought about, they'd be all right.

And two days was an eternity. Enough time to change someone's life forever. They were alive. They were off Marica-3. They were safe for now. It was enough. The rest of it would come later.

Moving his head on the table, he shifted his attention from Holden back to Elsa. She wasn't crying anymore, but her face was still wet. He made a superhuman effort and managed to get a hand up to brush over her cheek once, feeling soft skin against his fingertips.

Never figured I'd have the chance to do that again.

He found enough strength for another smile and a whisper. "Thank you, Doc."

She sniffed. "You're welcome, Captain."

"Stay with me?" He fumbled for her hand.

"Always." She found his, wrapped her fingers around it, and held on.

· · ·

Of course, "always" had the potential to stop real soon, unless they got some sort of game plan together. And they didn't have much time to do it.

Quinn drifted off to sleep again pretty quickly, and when he woke up, Elsa was gone. So was Holden. Instead, it was Isaac sitting on the floor a few feet away, with his legs crossed and his eyes closed. Until he heard Quinn move, and then his eyes opened. When he saw that Quinn was awake, his face split into a broad grin, and he got up on his knees next to the float pallet. "'Morning, boss."

Quinn looked around. Just like in the prison, there was no

way to tell day from night here. White walls, bright lights. Boxed cargo along the walls. Nobody in sight except for himself and Isaac. "Morning?"

"The shuttle runs on prison time," Isaac said. "You slept through most of the night."

Damn. "Everyone else asleep?"

Isaac shook his head. "There's you and me. We're awake. And Toby's having a look at the machine and engine rooms. Figured he'd take the opportunity while two of the guards were abed. The only guy awake is the second pilot."

Made sense. If Quinn had felt better, he would have joined Toby in exploring the shuttle. But just the motion of trying to lift his head from the pallet had dizziness setting in, and he put it back down. "This sucks."

"Nah," Isaac said. "This is awesome. We're alive. We're out of prison. We're off that goddamn hunk of rock. We'll be all right."

True. "Elsa asleep?"

Isaac nodded. "Must be. She's been here the rest of the time. If she ain't here now, I figure it has to be cause she's sleeping."

There was silence for a moment, and then Isaac added, "She worked hard. Guess she figured if she couldn't wake you up, I'd shoot her." He grinned.

Quinn squinted at him. Sometimes it was hard to be sure whether Isaac was joking or not. "She only killed me in the first place 'cause I asked her to."

"That's what she said," Isaac nodded.

"I couldn't get you out. I tried, but when I went back for you, that bastard Lamb was waiting."

"She took care of him," Isaac said.

"'scuse me?"

"Your woman. Gave him something that made him act like a damn fool. He came staggering out on the shuttle pad looking like he was on a bender." Isaac grinned at the memory, white teeth flashing. "Jacket misbuttoned, zipper down, the whole thing. And then he damn near stumbled over his own feet, and a couple of the guards had to help him sit down. He fell asleep after that, snoring up a storm. Just sitting there while everything was going on around him."

"No shit?"

"No shit," Isaac said. "It was beautiful."

They sat in silence for a moment, Isaac no doubt savoring the memory and Quinn wishing he could have been awake — or alive — to see it.

"How'd she manage all this?" he asked after a minute, gesturing to the shuttle, himself, Isaac, the missing Holden and Toby and everything else.

"I wasn't there for part of it," Isaac informed him. "All I know is, she came by my cell last night. With the bastard."

"Doctor Sterling?"

"He's a bastard, too," Isaac said, "but no. Lamb."

"Why?"

"Said she wanted to be sure she knew where we were. Course, the bastard only came to gloat about getting you back behind bars."

Of course.

"Me and Lamb have gotten close," Isaac continued. "Best buds. So very civil to each other on the surface. Course, he thinks I'm a savage, and I know he's a sniveling pussy, but we've gotten oh, so friendly. He's been letting me out to help unload the shuttle the last few times it's been up."

"Have you learned anything useful?"

"Not much," Isaac admitted. "But the shuttle's the only way off the goddamn moon, so I figured I'd better learn what I could."

"And?"

"There's a crew of three. Pilot, copilot, monkey. All armed with the usual stuff. Pistol, baton, and whatever little toys they've hidden in their boots and pockets."

Like the guard's flick knife and Lamb's dagger. Quinn nodded.

"There are tools, of course, for the monkey to use. And a couple plasma rifles in the cabinets outside." Isaac nodded to the door to the hallway. "Holden brought one onboard, but he had to give it up. It's in a cabinet out there."

"What about the shuttle itself?"

"You'd know that better than I would," Isaac said. "I know hand weapons. You know ship specs."

True. "This is an eighteen-ton Class 2 inner-system freighter. Rhenian make. They're usually not equipped with much. A laser bank on each side is probably the most we can hope for."

Isaac nodded. "Not much help."

No. "There's no point in hijacking the shuttle," Quinn said, staring at the whiteness of the ceiling arching above him. "I thought about hijacking the shuttle, and I guess you must have thought about it, too—"

Isaac nodded.

"But there's nowhere we can go. If we try to hit deep space in this thing, we'll break apart. She isn't made for it. And that's if the Rhenians don't blow us out of the air first. If the only place we can go is Marica, we may as well let the Rhenians take us there."

"Sure," Isaac said. "If you don't mind exiting right into the military shipyards."

There was that. "We'll have to work around it. But our chances are better on the ground than up here."

Isaac was quiet for a few moments. "I guess we're gonna be looking for the *Good Fortune*, then?"

"We're gonna be looking to save our skins," Quinn said, "but yeah, eventually we'll need to get out of Marican space. Rhenian space. That means either our own ship or someone else's. One we borrow, or one we buy. I doubt there's much tourist traffic into and out of Marica these days, so the chances of us finding passage on a cruise ship are slim to none."

Isaac ran a broad hand over his bald head. Of all of them, he was the least changed by his time in the prison colony. He was thinner but still muscular and strong, and since he'd always kept his head shaved anyway, his outward appearance had changed less than Holden's. Quinn had yet to lay eyes on Toby.

"I have a friend in Calvados," Isaac said. "Inez Borges. She might be able to help."

"Can we trust her?"

"Don't see why not, when it's her home planet the Rhenians are trying to gobble up."

Quinn nodded. "When we get downside — if we get downside — we'll try to contact her. But first we have to figure out a way to get off this ship without anyone noticing."

"Your girlfriend might have a plan," Isaac said with a glance over his shoulder. "She figured out how to get us all on the shuttle. She might have a plan for getting us off, too."

He turned, gun in his hand, up and pointed, at the sound of the door opening.

CHAPTER TWENTY-SIX

The panel slid back a crack, just enough for a small body to slip through, before it closed again. Isaac relaxed, and Quinn tilted his head to look at Toby Flatt.

If Isaac had changed the least in the past four months, Toby had changed the most, unless that honor went to Quinn himself. He hadn't had the chance to look in a mirror and didn't know if he wanted to. At least not after seeing the damage the past four months had wrought in his mechanic.

Toby had never been big; that was the point of a monkey. He was an inch or two shorter than Quinn, who was about average, and lean more than muscular. But he'd always looked healthy, whereas now he was both too thin and too pale, his compact body almost frail looking and his normally rosy cheeks a distant memory. But he was smiling when he stopped beside the pallet and put both hands behind his back. "Captain?"

"Toby." Quinn grinned at him. "Good to see you."

"You, too." But Toby wasn't quite adept enough to hide the shock that flickered in his eyes upon seeing Quinn.

"That bad?" Quinn said.

Not that he could blame Toby. If he looked as bad as Toby did, he must look pretty damn awful, and since he was the one on the pallet, while Toby was upright and walking around, he probably looked worse.

"You look like you've been through hell and back," Isaac said bluntly, never the guy to pull any punches.

"Thanks ever so."

Isaac grinned. "Don't matter what you look like, boss. Don't matter what any of us look like. We survived. And got out on the other side."

"Not quite yet." Quinn turned back to Toby. "Find anything interesting?"

Toby shrugged. "Just the usual."

"No hidden deep space powers?"

Toby shook his head. "Sorry, Captain. She's just what she looks like. Inner-system freighter. All the usual capabilities. Decent repair. Some wear and tear on the flaps. One of the thrusters is gonna need replacing soon."

"But she can't get us out of Marican space?"

"No, sir. She can get us to Calvados, or Sierra Luz if we want to go there, but no farther."

Quinn nodded. "In that case, I think we're probably better off not rocking the boat. Just let the pilot take the shuttle where he wants to go."

Isaac and Toby exchanged a look. "That'd be the military shuttle port, Captain."

Yes, it would. Talk about going from the frying pan, on Marica-3, into the fire.

They sat, lay, and stood in silence for a minute. "There are escape pods," Toby offered.

Of course. Spacecraft. There would have to be. Even the Rhenians weren't stupid enough to construct a freighter without an escape pod for emergencies. "How many? How big?"

"Two," Toby said. "Small. You can run a Class 2 freighter with three people. Don't need much space to bail out if something goes wrong."

No. Not if you didn't mind abandoning the cargo. Quinn imagined the shuttle spinning through space, its cargo hold full of prisoners fastened hand and foot to the floor, while the crew made their escape in the pods. He swallowed the resulting bile and said, "That's enough room for all of us." Him and Elsa in one, Toby, Isaac and Holden in the other. "If we're lucky, they may not turn the lasers on us and blow us outta the sky."

There was a beat of silence. "Not sure that's a chance I wanna take," Isaac said.

Quinn shook his head. Him, neither, under better circumstances.

There was another pause.

"If we can make the shuttle malfunction," Isaac said with a glance at Toby; Toby nodded, as if to say that yes, he could manage that, "the crew might get into one of the escape pods and leave. We could land the shuttle somewhere. Somewhere that isn't the military base. Make it look like a crash landing." He looked at Quinn. "You know how to fly this beast, don't you, boss?"

He did. And under normal circumstances he wouldn't hesitate. But— "I'm not exactly in great condition right now. Not sure I want everyone's lives in my hands."

Neither of the other two said anything, but the silence spoke volumes. *Too late.*

He'd gotten them out of prison and off Marica-3. Or rather,

Elsa had, but in the crew's minds, she was probably an extension of him. Now he had to get them safely to Calvados and from there home. Their lives were in his hands whether he wanted them to be or not. They had been long before this started.

But he still didn't want to risk piloting the shuttle. Not unless there was no other choice.

"You and I could get into the pod," he told Isaac. "As long as Marica-3 hasn't discovered that we're missing, Toby and Holden—and Elsa—can walk through the military base and out into Calvados with no problems."

Isaac nodded.

"If Toby can make the pod look like it's malfunctioning, like it just jettisoned on its own, they may not turn the lasers on us." Maybe. If they had the devil's own luck.

"Big chance to take," Isaac said.

No question. But maybe preferable to having to make it through the military shuttle port, surrounded by a few thousand Rhenian guards and officers.

Toby cleared his throat. "We could make a lot of things look like they're malfunctioning. Take most of the day to get there. Just small stuff, nothing serious enough to make them decide to bail out, but attack the nonessential functions. The pods, the door seals, the refrigeration in the cooler. Send distress signals from everywhere to the helm. Once they've looked into it a few times and found nothing wrong, they'll probably just assume they've got a systems malfunk. We're just a day and a half from Calvados. If it isn't gonna hamper their ability to navigate or breathe, I doubt they'll abandon ship. They'll probably just decide to push through and get her to maintenance as soon as they hit planetside."

That was a lot of words coming from the usually taciturn Toby.

"Can you do that?" Isaac asked. Toby shook his head.

"It has to be systemic. I can't break anything, because when the shuttle monkey goes to look at it, it has to work right. It just has to look like a malfunction. If enough stuff looks like it's malfunctioning, but it's actually working fine, they'll probably just decide to ignore anything else that happens. We may be able to disable the lasers, too, while we're at it. Just in case they do decide to fire at the pod. That's something I'll have to do manually. But most of this has to happen in systems, not mechanicals."

"Can you do it?"

Toby shook his head. "Not alone. With access to systems, I can maybe finesse some of it. But I don't do systems. I do mechanicals."

"Go wake Elsa," Quinn said. "If there isn't a comconsole in the guest cabin, Holden will have to see what he can do about getting access to one of the helm coms."

Toby nodded.

"Do it now. Before anyone else wakes up."

"Yessir." Toby turned to the door and then turned back. He put a hand awkwardly on Quinn's arm and then immediately snatched it away, but not before Quinn noticed the new crookedness of his fingers. *Damn Rhenians.*

Toby didn't give him a chance to speak. "It's good to see you, Captain. I'm glad you made it out all right."

He didn't wait for an answer, either, just turned and walked toward the door.

"Don't do anything that'll make 'em come down here to check cargo," Isaac called after him. "Better if they stay busy on the upper level."

Toby lifted a hand to signal that he'd heard, but he didn't turn or speak. A moment later, the door slid aside and he disappeared into the hallway. Isaac turned to Quinn. "What about me?"

"We could use somewhere to hide if they come down here."

Isaac nodded. "I'll see what I can find."

"In a minute. Tell me something first."

"Sure." Isaac settled back down on the floor, laser pistol still loosely held in his hand. His air of relaxation didn't fool Quinn for a second. The moment anything threatened either of them, Isaac would be up and firing. And hitting what he shot at dead center.

"How come the two of you still do what I say?"

"You're the captain," Isaac said.

"Yeah, but…haven't you gotten into enough trouble doing what I say?"

Isaac shrugged those massive shoulders. "You usually manage to get us out of trouble again, too. Like now."

There was a moment of silence. Quinn didn't know what to say. Forgiveness shouldn't be this easy. After what he'd done, what he'd failed to prevent, his crew should at least be a little bit reluctant to follow him into danger again. Not jump onboard with both feet like this.

"Besides," Isaac added, "it was her fault. Not yours."

"Her?" Elsa?

"Josie," Isaac said. "You weren't the only one didn't see it coming, boss. We all trusted her."

Right. He hadn't thought about Josie for a few days. Now he found that most of the emotion was gone.

Sure, maybe he still wouldn't mind wrapping his hands around that beautiful throat and squeezing all the life out of her…but if it hadn't been for Josie, he wouldn't have ended up on Marica-3, and he wouldn't have met Elsa. And where he wasn't about to say that it had been worth it—it would never be worth it—he also wouldn't trade Elsa now that he had her. Not for anything.

"I'll go look for a hidey-hole," Isaac said and rolled to his feet. "Don't go nowhere."

Quinn shook his head. "Not sure I could stand up if I had to. Hopefully it won't come to it."

"Let's hope so." Isaac wandered off. Quinn closed his eyes and thought about Elsa.

. . .

When Elsa walked into the cargo hold and saw Quinn lying there on the float pallet, for a second or even two, terror gripped her heart. Then she saw his chest rise and fall, and relief flooded her as she realized he was only asleep. And that was when he opened his eyes and looked at her. And smiled.

She smiled back, a little giddily. Part of her had been worried that yesterday had been a fluke. That the previous three or four days had been a bigger fluke. That he'd want nothing to do with her now. He'd gotten what he wanted—out—and he had no more need for her.

When he reached for her hand, all the worry evaporated under the warmth in his eyes. "Doc."

Not heat—it wasn't that kind of a look. She knew he could look at her that way if he wanted—he had, back in the desert—but this was a different kind of warmth. This was joy and love, not heat and lust. He was happy to see her. He'd missed her. Maybe he'd been worried, too.

She took his hand and twined her fingers through his. "How do you feel?"

"Like death warmed over."

If he could joke, he couldn't be feeling too bad, she reasoned.

Then again, he'd managed to joke when he was bleeding to death, too, so maybe he could. She lifted her other hand and put it on his forehead. It was cool. "No fever."

He shook his head. "I feel fine."

"Really?"

"Well…" He dragged it out. "Other than that I can't move."

What? "You can't move?"

"I can move. I just can't stand. Or sit. Or walk. Or lift my head from the damn pallet."

Oh. Another wave of relief swamped her. "Don't worry. Remember all the other times you were dead, and I revived you? It always took a few days before you were back to normal."

"That's all it is?"

She nodded. "I promise."

"Good," Quinn said and squeezed her hand, "'cause there are things I wanna do that I can't do when I'm like this."

Of course. He wanted to be up and moving around. Organizing his troops. Saving the world, or at least the planet.

Or not. The look in his eyes suggested that there was something else he wanted to do more. Elsa blushed, and Quinn grinned. "C'mere, Doc."

"I'm already here," Elsa pointed out.

"Closer." He waited until she was bending over him, and then he reached up and pulled her down to where he could kiss her. She let him, even though she knew it would take it out of him. And sure enough, when his lips parted from hers, reluctantly, he was out of breath and flopped back down on the float pallet as if he had no strength left to keep his head up. But he still managed to grin. "Thanks, Doc."

"You're welcome." She should be thanking him. The fact that

he still wanted to kiss her, still wanted her near him, was a miracle.

He reverted to business soon enough, though. "Were you able to do anything about the systems?"

"We got in," Elsa said. "Good thing, too, because it turns out the whole shuttle is wired for heat signatures. The three of you showed up on the schematic like little hotspots."

"Shit." He looked around as if the hotspots were there for him to see.

"There's a comconsole in the guest cabin," Elsa said. "Holden was able to go from the public comconsole into ship's systems. He started by disabling the heat signature scan down here. Now he and Toby are setting up malfunctions all over the shuttle. Where's Isaac?"

"Looking for somewhere to hole up in case they come down here," Quinn said. "We have to expect that once things start to look like they're falling apart, the monkey will stop by to have a look around. After the first few times, hopefully they'll just chalk it all up to a systems failure and leave it at that. We just have to get through the next eighteen hours. Tomorrow night we'll move into one of the pods, and as soon as we're through Marica's atmosphere, we'll jettison. Hopefully they'll think it was slicing through the atmospheric barrier that cut the pod loose, and they won't bother firing at it."

Hopefully.

"Toby will fix it to make it look like there's no one onboard, right?" Because the idea of standing on the bridge, watching the shuttle turn her laser banks on the plummeting pod and the man she loved, didn't sound like much fun. "If the whole shuttle is wired for heat signatures, the pods probably are, too."

"Sure," Quinn said. "But that's no guarantee they won't blow it to smithereens on departure. It'll look like a loose pod. SOP in cases like that is to neutralize it before it can crash into anything. At least that's the way it was when I ran contraband for Hector Vega."

"The man who left your friend Sean for the Kedarii?"

He nodded grimly. "Protect the cargo at any cost. Shoot anyone who stood in your way. And if someone looked like they were trying to get away with something—like a stray shuttle—blow it to hell before it could get away."

"Same thing in any army I've ever been a part of," Isaac's voice said, and Elsa turned toward the cold room in time to see the big man exit and close the door behind him. He flapped his arms a couple times. "Cold in there."

"Any hidey-holes?" Quinn wanted to know.

Isaac shook his head. "'fraid not. If they come down here, you'll probably just have to pretend to be dead. It'll be cold, but it won't kill you. Or I can take care of whoever comes through the door before he can see you. But then we have to worry about someone discovering the body."

"Or missing whoever you kill," Elsa murmured.

Quinn nodded. "Try not to kill anyone. If you have to, you have to, but do your best."

"Sure, boss." Isaac looked up as the lights flickered. The hum of the refrigeration stuttered before kicking back on. "That us?"

"Probably. Maybe you should wheel me into cold storage and zip this thing up." Quinn plucked at the body bag. "If the lights go, they'll be down to check on us."

Isaac nodded.

"I'll go see what's happening on top," Elsa said, as the lights flickered off and on again. She glanced from Quinn to Isaac and back to Quinn. If anything happened to him… "Be careful."

"Always." He grinned at her. "Before you go, see if you can find that laser rifle of Holden's in the cabinet out there. Isaac can take it. That way I can keep the pistol. If anyone decides to open the body bag to make sure the corpse is really dead, at least I can shoot him before he shoots me."

"Sure." She hustled into the hallway and over to the cabinet where she'd seen the guard stash Holden's rifle the day before. By the time she got back, Isaac had towed the float pallet with Quinn on it into the cold storage. "Here." She handed Isaac the rifle and watched him give Quinn the pistol. Then Isaac melted into the shadows and Elsa moved to pull the zipper up over Quinn's face. "I love you."

He smiled. "I love you, too. Go up on deck and keep everyone occupied."

"How?"

"By being there," Quinn said.

Elsa frowned—how would being there keep everyone occupied?—and Quinn continued, "You're the most beautiful woman they can ever hope to see. As long as you're there, they'll not want to leave. They'll want to keep looking at you."

She stared at him for a second—surely he wasn't serious?—until he smiled. "Get outta here, Doc. As long as you're here, it's all I can do to stare at you, too."

A blush crept up in her cheeks. "I'll be back later to check on you."

"Send Holden," Quinn said. "I'm serious, Elsa. Leave your hair down. Open a couple buttons on your dress. And stay up there. If you do, they will, too. And if they have to leave, they'll be eager to get back to you. Please."

When he put it like that, how could she refuse?

"I'll miss you." All she wanted was to be where he was.

"I know, Doc. I'll miss you, too. But once we get off this goddamn ship and onto our own, we'll be together every day for the rest of our lives. We just have to get there first."

Right. She squared her shoulders. And pulled the zipper up to cover his face.

CHAPTER TWENTY-SEVEN

It turned out to be the longest day in Quinn's memory. Eternal and never ending. He tried to sleep as much as he could, to regain as much of his strength as possible, but as the cold seeped into his body and bones again, even that became impossible. He had no idea how Isaac managed to keep from freezing to death, although he was aware how, occasionally, Isaac would take the float pallet out of the cold storage and into the cargo area to give them both some time to warm up.

About halfway through the day, the temperature rose. It went from freezing to merely cold. Around the time when it went from being cold to almost bearable, Quinn heard footsteps outside in cargo. A sound from inside the cold storage told him Isaac had heard the same thing and was getting ready to deal with whoever was coming.

If they were lucky, the crew would content themselves with checking that everything was working all right in the cargo area and wouldn't bother to come inside cold storage. If they did…well, all hell was about to break loose.

There was a sound over by the door. He heard the hiss of the double doors opening, and then a man's voice, speaking Rhenish. The inflection made it sound like he was asking a question, and the answer, also in Rhenish, was obvious, even to someone who didn't speak the language. "*Not on your life.*" Then Quinn heard a light laugh that had all the hairs on the back of his neck standing up. Elsa's voice was amused, and her heels clicked on the hard floor of the cold storage as she came closer. The body bag opened into stygian blackness, and her fingers brushed his cheek. The pad of her thumb found his bottom lip and lingered there for a second before she withdrew. She said a few words, and he heard the sound of footsteps coming closer. He shut his eyes just as a torch turned on and illuminated his face. The hand holding it must be shaking, because the light moved up and down. Quinn held his breath and did his best to look dead.

"See?" Elsa said. Even with his lack of understanding of her native language, he could understand that. And the Rhenish word for *dead* was one he'd heard often enough over the past four months to memorize it.

The light disappeared, and the bag closed back up again. Elsa's heels clicked toward the door along with the set of boots. The seals hissed closed.

He waited until he'd heard their footsteps cross the cargo hold and the other door close behind them as well before he raised his voice. "What was that about?"

"Best as I can figure," Isaac's voice came back out of the blackness, "they came down because cold storage is malfunctioning. It's getting warm in here. I think the doc wanted whoever was with her to see that you were still in the bag and dead."

"I'm not dead."

"No," Isaac said, "but you look bad enough to fool someone. Especially some green kid who didn't really wanna look at the bad corpse, anyway."

Great. He must look even worse than he'd thought.

"Relax," Isaac said; Quinn could hear him coming closer. "This probably means the doc is keeping them occupied. And we'll be a bit less uncomfortable."

Hopefully so. Quinn closed his eyes again and focused on trying to make the hours pass faster.

The next time someone came by, it was Holden. "Quick," he said into the darkness in the no-longer-cold cold storage. "Time to go to the pod."

"It's been a day?"

"As near as makes no difference," Holden said. "The crew's in bed. Only the second pilot is on the bridge. Elsa just brought him some hot chocolate to help him stay awake. We'll be in Calvados in about eight hours."

"That soon?" Quinn stretched. A second day of enforced rest had allowed his body to regenerate just a bit of necessary strength, although large parts of him still hurt like the devil.

"We've been making tracks," Holden said, making his way toward him by sound. "Can you walk?"

"If I have to." He'd managed to walk around Marica-3 for a couple days. He could walk to the escape pod.

"Here." Holden took hold of him on one side and Isaac on the other. Between them, they slid him out of the body bag and off the float pallet. His legs were weak—hell, his entire body was weak—but with help, he could stand.

They moved toward the door at a snail's pace, Quinn's feet dragging with each step.

"Fuck." He was out of breath, too, just from trying to walk across the cargo hold. "This isn't good."

"You're doing fine," Holden said. "Just hang on to us. Isaac can carry you if you can't make it on your own."

Isaac chuckled.

"Over my dead body," Quinn said.

"It may come to that. You gonna be okay, boss?"

Quinn gritted his teeth. "I'll be fine. Just don't talk to me. I need my breath for walking."

That shut them up. They crept toward the door.

Finally they made it there, and out into the hallway. After another eternity, they were at the bottom of the stairs looking up.

The staircase consisted of nine steps. Not very many in the scheme of things. The man Quinn used to be would have taken them two at a time and made it to the top in a second or two. The man he was now looked at the top of the staircase and thought it appeared as far away as the top of Olympus Mons. The way he felt, his chances of making it there were about equal to his chances of climbing the tallest mountain in Old Earth's solar system, too.

"Need a rest before we start?" Holden asked diplomatically.

Quinn shot him a glare. "Don't patronize me. The less time we spend hanging out here, the better."

No arguing with that, and Holden didn't try. "Wanna crawl?" he asked instead.

"Fuck you! No." Quinn shook off the hands helping him and reached for the railing to pull himself up on the first step. Dammit, he wasn't a cripple! He could do this on his own.

Except he couldn't. His body wouldn't cooperate. He made it three steps before he turned around. "All right."

Neither of them said anything. They didn't look at him like he were a failure, either. Isaac just moved up beside him and practically lifted him the last six steps, with Holden bringing up the rear.

"Thank you." Quinn couldn't quite bring himself to look at either of them when they stood in the upper hallway.

"Don't mention it," Isaac said in a tone that warned Quinn he meant it.

Holden added, "You'd have done the same for any of us, Captain. Don't think we don't know it."

There was nothing to say to that, either, so they just made their way to the pods as quickly as possible. In other words, at a very slow shuffle.

There were two, one on either side of the shuttle, each with its own little alcove for access. "We've disabled heat signatures on both," Holden told him softly. "Which do you want? Left or right?"

He and Elsa had taken a right out of his cell the first day and had gone down the right-hand canyon later. Things had turned out all right. Stick with what worked. "Right."

They turned right. A minute later, he and Isaac were inside the pod with the double doors sealed behind them. "You're armed?" had been the last thing Holden asked.

Isaac had brandished his plasma rifle, and Holden's eyes had snagged for a second on the laser pistol weighing down Quinn's pocket, the one he lacked the strength to lift at the moment.

"We'll hit Marican atmosphere in less than six hours," Holden continued. "Hopefully it'll still be just the second pilot on the bridge by then. Toby has disabled long range on the lasers, but if we disable the laser banks altogether, they might suspect something's going on. We'll do our best to make sure they don't fire on you. Including shooting them if we have to."

Quinn nodded. "If that happens, get in the other pod and bail out. It'll be easier to maneuver than the shuttle."

"Right," Holden said. "You know I'm not a pilot, right?"

"You've watched me for six years. You musta picked up something. And Toby can pilot a little. Between you, you'll figure it out."

"Sure," Holden said, but he didn't sound like he meant it. "Assuming we all make it downside in one piece, where do we meet up?"

There was a pause while they all thought about it.

"There's a little village," Isaac said finally, "about thirty minutes outside Calvados on the south side. Vargas. There's a little wood behind it, with a stream. We can meet there."

"You've been to Vargas?"

Isaac turned to him. "I told you I have a friend on Marica."

Right. Inez something. "She lives in Vargas?"

"Not when I met her," Isaac said. "She lived in Calvados. But her family's from Vargas."

Good enough. "The wood outside Vargas it is. Tell the others." He glanced at Holden, who nodded.

"Good luck."

"You, too," Quinn said, and watched Holden duck outside and seal the pod doors. The pod illumination flickered on faintly, and he looked around.

It looked a bit like the *Fortune's* two pods, like a very small ship consisting of just a bridge and a few seats with straps. There was plenty of room for him and Isaac, even given Isaac's size. There would have been enough room for the other three as well, and for a second he thought about calling Holden back and asking him to gather Elsa and Toby so they could all get the hell outta here together.

But he didn't. The three of them could walk through the military spaceport unaccosted on arrival, and his and Isaac's escape would be aided by leaving them here, to ensure that no one fired on the pod when it dropped. Just in case Rhenish SOP dictated just that.

Instead, he made his way toward the helm, one hand on the bulkhead for support. Isaac followed behind, probably ready to catch him should he fall.

He did, but it was into the pilot's chair when he got to it. He'd made more graceful descents, but he couldn't find it in him to care. It felt too good to sit. Lying down would have felt even better, but for now this would have to do. To make sure he'd stay upright in the seat, he raked the straps across his chest and fastened them— *better*—before surveying the console.

The Rhenish shipbuilders used different specs than some, but he hadn't yet met a ship he couldn't pilot. This pod was no exception. Some of the buttons and levers were in unusual places, but it wasn't something he couldn't handle once he'd had the chance to familiarize himself with it. And they had nothing else to do for the next three hours.

He could jettison now, he supposed, while most of the Rhenian crew was asleep, and take his chances on the pod's fuel supply being enough to get them to Marica. The fuel gauge showed a full tank, so it ought to be enough. But to be honest, punching through the atmosphere would be much easier if they were part of the bigger shuttle, and besides, he'd prefer not to pilot anything for any longer than he had to. Two to three hours in heavy air would be more than enough; add another four or five in zero-gee, and he wasn't sure he'd have the strength left to land the pod once they reached the ground.

"Problem?" Isaac said.

"No." Quinn shook his head. "Systems are a bit different than

I'm used to. I haven't had the chance to pilot anything Rhenish before. But a pod's a pod. We'll be fine."

"If they don't fry us," Isaac said.

Well, yes. If the shuttle's lasers didn't fry them.

"This thing have any weapons?"

Quinn checked the panels. "Looks like a single gun on either side. Strap in and have a look." He nodded to the chair next to him.

They worked in silence for a while, familiarizing themselves with the pod's systems. After that, there was nothing to do but wait. Quinn dozed, still held upright in his chair by the straps crisscrossing his chest, while Isaac prowled the tiny confines of the shuttle, from the second nav chair to the airlock to the rear—four steps away— and back. Eventually he sat down and tried to rest, too, the plasma rifle cradled in his arms.

The first vibrations brought them both upright. Initially, it was hard to know exactly what was causing the motion, with no visual and no systems up. They couldn't fire up the console without alerting the guards, so for the moment, they were working blind.

"Laser fire?" Isaac suggested, his voice low and gravelly from sleep.

"Could be. But I think it's just hitting Marica's atmosphere."

"Already?" Isaac rubbed his eyes.

"What d'you mean, already? This has been the fucking longest day of my life. If we've finally hit the bands, then hallelujah."

And it seemed as if they had. The vibrations intensified, and soon it sounded as if large rocks were hitting the outside of the pod.

"Strap in," Quinn ordered, searching the dash for the lever that would disengage the docking clamps. "Once we're through the bands, we'll have to jettison."

"Yessir," Isaac pulled the straps across his chest and secured them.

"It'll be a while yet. But I want you ready. We're gonna drop outta here like a bomb and let gravity take us, and if you're not strapped in, it could get ugly."

"Yessir," Isaac said again. After a second he slanted a look at Quinn and grinned. "It's good to be back, ain't it?"

Yes, it was. Even with the threat of being blown out of the sky once they dropped, this beat being at the mercy of someone else. He'd rather go out in a blaze of glory in a bid for freedom than waste away in a cell on Marica-3.

"Damn straight." He grinned back and set about waiting.

• • •

The vibrations woke Elsa from dead sleep, rattling her teeth and practically throwing her out of her bunk and onto the floor. It took a disoriented second or two before she remembered where she was and what was happening. Not an earthquake. She was on the shuttle bound for Calvados. She had left the prison and everything she'd trusted and thought she knew behind to get Quinn and his crew to freedom.

The vibrations intensified, and she realized what they had to be. They were passing out of zero-gravity space and going through into the atmosphere of Marica. They'd be on the ground in two to three hours at the military spaceport in Calvados.

And as soon as they were into heavy air, Quinn would jettison the pod.

She scrambled out of bed and into a dressing gown, the only thing on her mind to get to the bridge before the pod dropped. She'd promised Holden she'd do everything she could to stop the crew from firing on the pod, and being there in nothing but a dressing gown would surely not hurt.

Because crazy as it had sounded at the time, Quinn had been right. As long as she stayed on the bridge, the crew had been loath to leave. Even the mechanic—the monkey, she corrected herself—a Rhenian guard almost as small and spare as Toby, had stuck around, looking at her, talking and flirting, until the various little malfunctions Toby and Holden created had demanded his attention elsewhere. But he'd always come back to stare at her some more.

It had been hard, spending all day away from Quinn. Now that she had him, and he was alive and almost well, she just wanted to spend all her time with him, making sure that he was breathing and not suffering. But he'd been right: keeping the guards occupied—or preoccupied—had been something she could do, something that would help, and she had to do it.

She lashed the belt tightly around the gown and slipped out into the hallway outside the cabins as what sounded like large hail began to spatter the outside of the shuttle's hull. Her knock on Holden's and Toby's door was answered by Toby, already up and dressed in the Rhenish uniform. He may not have been to sleep at all. Over his shoulder, she could see Holden, seated at the comconsole, tapping on the keys while lines of text and schematics flashed by on the screen.

"I want to go to the bridge," she told them both in Rhenish.

Toby blushed, probably at the sight of her in her gown. It wasn't very revealing—opaque and covering her from neck to floor—but it was the most feminine piece of clothing she owned.

"One minute," Holden answered over his shoulder, "and I'll go with you. C'mere, Toby." The two of them lapsed into Standard, which Elsa could understand well enough under normal circumstances. At the moment she had a hard time following the conversation, both because of her own jittery nerves and the noise from the hull, and because the discussion was largely technical. Something to do with the pod and the docking clamps and dropping away first. Toby understood, anyway.

After a minute or two, Holden got up and Toby took his place at the comconsole. Holden watched for a moment, then gave Toby a clap on the shoulder. "We'll be on the bridge if you need us."

Toby nodded. "Be careful."

"Always." Holden turned to Elsa and grinned. "Ready?"

"Whenever you are, Thorsten."

"Right," Holden said in Rhenish and offered her his arm. "Did the rattling wake you?" They keyed the door shut behind Toby, who sat hunched over the comconsole, and headed up the hallway toward the bridge.

Elsa nodded. "I want to be there. Just in case." There was no need to spell out in case of what.

"Of course." His reply was courteous, solicitous, proper—for a Rhenian guard escorting Doctor Sterling's favorite assistant—but the look in his eyes betrayed his own need to be on the bridge, too. Just in case.

She used her access code to key open the door and stepped across the threshold, pulling the skirts of her gown around her legs. Only to stop when confronted with three startled faces.

"Oh." It took her a moment to find her smile. What were they all doing up so early—or so late? Last time she'd been on the bridge, the first pilot and monkey had been in bed. She'd assumed they'd stay there for a few hours yet, until the shuttle got closer to Marica. She'd thought she and Holden would have only the second pilot to contend with. "Hello. You're all here."

"Doctor." The first pilot nodded. The monkey stared. The

second pilot kept his attention on the shuttle's instrument panel.

"The rattling woke me," Elsa said, doing her best to sway her hips seductively as she moved toward them. *Get their attention. Keep their attention.* "What happened? Are we under attack?"

"No, ma'am." The first pilot shook his head and managed to keep a straight face in spite of the idiocy of the question. There was nothing outside the view screen except the blue-green-brown orb that was Marica. From up here, she could see mountain ranges and deserts, huge green swathes of forests and blue oceans.

"What's that…rattling?"

"We're passing through into Marica's atmosphere," the first pilot said. He and the monkey exchanged a glance.

"Oh." Elsa bit her lip. "So there's nothing wrong?" She did her very best to appear helpless and ladylike. It was difficult, after spending so many years suppressing everything soft and feminine about herself.

"No, ma'am." The first pilot turned back to the instrument panel. "It'll get worse, though, before it gets better. You should consider going back to your cabin and strapping in."

"Can I just strap in here?" She looked around. "I'd like the company."

The first pilot and monkey exchanged another glance. The second pilot was still stubbornly focused on the task at hand. "Of course, Doctor," the first pilot said. "Sit anywhere you'd like."

"Thank you." She headed for two seats out of the way, yet close to the view screen, with Holden—Thorsten—trailing behind. They sat and strapped themselves in, and Elsa clutched the arms of her seat and peered out. There was nothing there. The shuttle jittered and jerked as if pummeled by rocks and stones, the hull banging and cracking on impact, but the view screen showed nothing but clear air.

"It's a bit like thunder," Holden told her in his flawless Rhenish. "Hot air and cold air making sound when they meet. Only it's the shuttle going from no air to heavy air, with the same result."

She nodded. She knew the concept, but that didn't make her feel any better about the sensations. Nor did it help with the mingled anticipation and dread at what she knew was coming. Quinn was below, in one of the pods. As soon as the rattling and shaking stopped, he'd disengage the docking clamps and drop off. And she had no idea what would happen then. Was he strong enough to maneuver the pod? Would the crew engage the lasers and fire? Would they hit him?

And there was nothing she could do to change the outcome either way. Just sit here and wait.

Slowly the rattling and shaking decreased. The second pilot shook out his tense shoulders and looked up at the view screen. The first pilot and monkey exchanged another glance. So did Holden and Elsa.

A minute passed. Then another.

"Portside pod's loose!" the first pilot exclaimed.

Elsa froze. Here it was. Time.

The mechanic jumped up from his seat and ran toward the door. She could hear the hissing of the door seals, but she didn't look in that direction. The second pilot, still at the helm, banked the shuttle to the right, and through the view screen, hurtling toward Marica, she could see the silver pod dropping like a stone.

She crossed her fingers in her lap.

Go. Go.

"Maybe it shook loose in the turbulence," Holden suggested next to her, his voice low and his accent impeccable.

"Arming lasers." The second pilot's voice was calm, his hands steady on the controls.

"No!" She fumbled with her harness, her fingers stiff and uncooperative.

But before she could gain mobility, Holden reached out and stayed her hands. "Elsa."

Elsa looked up into the muzzle of the first pilot's laser pistol.

He smiled. "Please, Doctor Brandeis, stay where you are. You, too, Mister…Conlan, is it?"

"Sinclair," Holden said, his jaw tight. "Captain Conlan's in the pod. Doctor Sterling won't like it if you blow him up."

Elsa shook her head. No, indeed. Although between being blown to pieces and going back to Doctor Sterling's lab, she knew which Quinn would prefer.

That didn't make it any easier to sit here and watch him be killed. Again.

The first pilot snickered. "Nice try. But I happen to know that Captain Conlan is dead and in our cold storage. That means it must be the mercenary in the pod, and nobody cares if we kill him."

"Lasers at fifty percent," the second pilot said calmly from the helm.

Elsa glanced at Holden. He was pale, his jaw clenched.

There was a scuffling at the door. The slide panels hissed open, and the shuttle's mechanic pushed Toby ahead of him across the threshold. Unlike Holden and herself, Toby must have put up a struggle, because his uniform was disheveled, and he had a split lip. The little Rhenian mechanic was grinning in an ugly way as he shoved Toby into a chair and told him to strap in. When Toby wasn't fast enough, the mechanic stood over him and yelled.

"Lasers at eighty percent," the second pilot said.

"Aim."

Elsa glanced out the view screen to where the pod was still visible, like a silver arrow slicing through the air. Toby was supposed to have disabled long-range lasers. Would they be able to hit the pod from here? Or had he been interrupted before he'd had the chance to finish the job?

"Lasers at a hundred percent."

"Fire at will," the first pilot said.

"No!" She jerked against her harness, helpless as the shuttle's portside laser banks spit out streaks of light. They chased the wayward pod through the air. Elsa clutched the arms of her chair, her knuckles white and her eyes staring, as the beams hit the pod. A breathless moment passed, and then there was a flash of light, bright enough to burn her eyes. She closed them automatically, and when she opened them again, the silver pod was gone. All she could see was a cloud of debris, spreading in all directions from where the pod had been a moment before.

"Direct hit," the second pilot said.

Elsa closed her eyes again, this time in an effort to hold back the tears.

CHAPTER TWENTY-EIGHT

The first pilot turned to Elsa with a grin. "Let's you and me take a walk."

A walk?

The second pilot looked at them over his shoulder, his hands still on the instrument panel. "Are you sure that's a good idea?"

"Who's gonna know?" the first pilot said.

"They will." The second pilot glanced at Holden and Toby.

"Nobody'll care what they say. If they survive to tell anyone."

"We'll know."

The first pilot hesitated. "You can have a turn after I'm done."

The mechanic grinned and turned to Elsa, blatantly looking her up and down in a way that made her turn pale.

"She's still a Rhenian," the second pilot said. "We don't misuse our own people."

"She stopped being a Rhenian when she helped these traitors escape. You heard what the major said."

The major? Stephen Lamb? Was that how the crew had known what was going on? Someone on Marica-3—probably Stephen himself—had discovered that Quinn's crew was gone from their cells and had put two and two together and realized she was helping them?

It made sense, she realized with a sinking feeling. She'd reasoned that unless someone specifically went to Holden's, Isaac's, or Toby's cell, they wouldn't know of her substitutions. But she should have anticipated that upon waking, Stephen would feel the need to go visit each man to tell him that Quinn was dead. He'd get off on the psychological torture; she'd seen his enjoyment in telling them that Quinn had been recaptured that night she'd accompanied him to their cells.

Stupid, Elsa.

She was so preoccupied with her thoughts that for a few seconds, she forgot all about the shuttle crew and the first pilot, who wanted her to take a walk with him. To her cabin, no doubt. Or his. Anywhere there was a bed. It wasn't until he waved the laser pistol in her face that she came back to herself. "Let's go."

Holden made an instinctive move forward, checked by the straps across his chest, and the first pilot turned the gun on him.

"Don't shoot!" Elsa unstrapped herself and scrambled to her feet to throw herself in front of Holden. At this point, all she could do was make sure he and Toby had the best chance of survival and escape. And if that meant going along and letting this sorry excuse for a man have his way with her, then she'd do what she had to do. It wasn't like it mattered anymore, what happened to her. She was still numb from watching the shuttle blow up, anyway. She might not even feel it. "It's all right. I'll be fine." She met Holden's eyes for a moment. "Just take care of yourselves."

His lips tightened, but he nodded.

The first pilot grinned and reached for her arm. She twitched away. "I can walk on my own."

"Fine." He waved her toward the door. "We'll be back in ten minutes."

Toby muttered something, and the Rhenian mechanic backhanded him for his trouble, but not before they'd all heard Toby's opinion of the first pilot's prowess—or lack thereof—in bed, if he only planned to take ten minutes.

Elsa keyed the exit code into the keypad with hands that were amazingly steady, everything considered, and waited for the seal doors to hiss open. Once that was done, she stepped across the threshold and into the hallway. The first pilot followed, and the doors closed behind them. She looked him straight in the eye. "Where do you want me to go?"

He hesitated for a second, perhaps surprised at her lack of cowering. Then he waved the pistol. "Guest cabin."

Good. There were things there she could use to incapacitate him, if she could only get to them.

She stopped in front of her own door and keyed it open. He gestured with the pistol. "Go ahead."

Elsa stepped over the threshold and made for the pouch of medical supplies, sitting on the bedside table. The supplies were severely depleted after her hard work on Quinn, but she had a syringe full of spider-scorpion venom, an extra she'd prepared for the getaway, that she hadn't used. One jab of that, and the first pilot would be out cold in two seconds.

But— "Halt!"

She stopped, her hand on the pouch and frustration seething through her. *So close.*

"Turn around."

She took her time, wiggling the seal seam as she did. There was no time to actually grab the syringe, but she might be able to get to it later, if the pouch was open.

"Get undressed."

It was almost funny. Twice, Quinn had given her that same order. The first time she'd misunderstood. Her relief when she'd realized he didn't want her to get naked had been overwhelming.

The second time he'd meant it, and she'd obeyed, under the threat of being shot, just like now. And he'd kept his distance and hadn't touched her, the very opposite of what she'd expected.

This time it was one of her fellow Rhenians holding the pistol and giving the order, and the irony was incredible. When it had been Quinn, she'd have given anything to see a Rhenian guard. Now she was looking at one, and he was the bad guy.

She undid the belt of the robe and let it fall from her shoulders to pool around her feet. Her nightdress was no more revealing than the gown itself had been—opaque and plain, covering her from chest to mid thigh—but the guard swallowed convulsively. When she began to pull the material up and over her head, she could see him flush with what was either excitement or embarrassment.

He was just a boy, really. Nineteen, maybe twenty. And already destroyed by the power given to him and that Rhenish superiority drummed into him—as it had been her—at an early age.

She dropped the gown on the floor and put both hands behind her. It had the dual benefits of pushing her breasts forward as a distraction and allowing her to fumble for the syringe behind her back.

He stared at her, up and down, his eyes wide and the pistol in his hand almost forgotten. It dipped from her chest down to her knees. She could have sprung forward then, and maybe gotten to him before he could get it back up to shoot her—but she hadn't found the syringe yet.

His lips must be dry, because the tip of his tongue came out to moisten them. "Get on the bed."

"You don't have to do this," Elsa said, still fumbling for the syringe. "We can go back out there and you can pretend you did."

He stared at her.

"I'll back you up. They won't have to know that you changed your mind. That you decided you're not actually an animal." *There.* She could feel the shape of the syringe under her fingers.

He laughed at her. "You think I'm afraid? You're nothing but a whore. Less than a whore. A collaborator. A traitor. Filth."

Fine. So reasoning with him wasn't going to work. By now the pistol was back up again, too, and pointing at her. The muzzle was more compelling than the tone of his voice when he gestured with the pistol and said again, "Get on the bed!"

She got on the bed. Flat on her back with the syringe hidden in one hand.

"Arms over your head."

She did as he said, stretching her arms over her head and crossing her wrists, doing her best to cover the hand with the syringe in it with the other, hoping that her nakedness would keep his attention below her neck until it was too late to notice anything going on above.

The narrow cot dipped when he got on beside her. He hesitated for a second before laying the pistol on the bedside table next to the medical pouch. "Don't try anything," he warned. "I can get to it before you can."

Maybe. Maybe not. But she wasn't about to put it to the test. She had no interest in the pistol. Not yet.

When he touched her, the revulsion was such that she almost

threw him off, just because she couldn't stand the feel of his hands on her. But she needed him fully committed, fully focused, his reflexes slow, before she could make her move. So she steeled herself and lay there, her teeth gritted and her muscles jittery, while he stroked her skin. She could see the arousal on his face and hear it in his quickened breathing—he was panting, like an animal in heat—and she could feel it in the unsteadiness of his hands.

Any moment now.

When his hands moved to his zipper, she knew she had him. She also knew there were lines she was unwilling to cross, even if it meant helping Holden and Toby. So she waited until those shaking hands got him in trouble—the zipper got stuck, and he looked down for a second—and then she struck.

The syringe went into his upper arm, and she jabbed at the plunger. But before she could get it all the way in, he wrenched away from her. She had to let go of the syringe, but it stayed in his arm; hopefully it was leaking its insidious spider-venom into his blood stream. And then he grabbed her upper arms, hard—she'd have bruises—and pushed her back down on the bed. "Bitch!" he hissed in her face.

Elsa didn't bother to respond; instead, she saved all her breath for fighting. Twisting away, out of his grasp, she slapped at the syringe again, and this time, managed to push the plunger all the way home. He snarled, trying to catch her free arm, while squeezing her other wrist so hard she could feel the bones grinding together. She'd have bruises on top of the bruises Quinn had given her when he tried to save her from falling in the river.

And then, finally, the venom kicked in, and his grip slackened, and his eyes rolled back in his head, and he collapsed on top of her, his heavy weight pushing her into the mattress.

Elsa scrambled out from under him and stood for a moment beside the bed, shaking violently. Her chest heaved, and her hair straggled down her back, while shudders of mingled fear and adrenaline, revulsion and anger, ran through her body.

Finally she made herself step close enough to pull the syringe out of his arm and put it on the table. She stayed out of reach after that, and kept a close eye on him while she got dressed—in clean underwear, a proper dress, and shoes—but he didn't twitch.

Even so, she put his arms together behind his back and wound the belt of her dressing gown around his wrists a few times. She did her best to tie the ends in a solid knot before grabbing his pistol from the night table.

She unsealed the door and hesitated. What she had to do now was figure out a way to free Holden and Toby. Somehow.

They were pretty much helpless, strapped into their seats on the bridge. The shuttle crew had taken their weapons away. The Rhenian mechanic was loose, walking around, but the second pilot was at the helm, driving the shuttle. When she came in, he would have to take his hands off the instrument panel, reach for his pistol, swivel his chair around to fire at her…and by then, hopefully she would have managed to dispatch the mechanic.

She'd feel a lot better about the odds if she'd had any sort of experience with laser pistols—or any other kinds of pistols, or for that matter any kind of weapon at all—but she was a scientist. A scholar. Target practice hadn't been part of her education. And then there was the slight problem of flying the shuttle if she killed the second pilot. She hadn't had piloting practice, either. And from what she'd understood, none of Quinn's crew, save for Quinn himself— who was dead—knew how to pilot an eighteen-ton shuttle.

The seal doors began to close, and she slid sideways through the opening before they could, into the hallway. Only to find herself brutally spun around and slammed up against the opposite wall. All the air left her lungs, and the pistol fell from her grip at impact.

No sooner had it happened, than the man behind her stepped away. "Sorry, Doc."

She was able to turn around. And immediately had to lean on the wall because her legs threatened to give out. Finding breath to say anything was difficult, too. "Isaac? How…?"

"Wrong pod," Isaac said.

Wrong pod?

She latched onto his jumpsuit, both hands fisting in the material. "Where's Quinn?"

"Still down there," Isaac said with a glance over his shoulder. "He's in no condition to play hero right now."

The relief was such that her breath went again. Quickly followed by worry. "What's wrong with him? Is he hurt?"

"No more than he was earlier," Isaac said. "He's just weak. It's hard for him to get around."

She made a move to go in the direction he'd indicated, and Isaac took hold of her. "Nuh-uh. I'm gonna need some help first. You know how to use that thing?" He glanced at the pistol she'd dropped.

"No," Elsa said and bent to pick it up. "What happened?"

"Not real sure," Isaac said, "but best as I can figure it, Holden or Toby overrode the command Quinn gave the shuttle and locked the docking clamps on us. They jettisoned the other shuttle instead. When we saw it blow, we figured they knew something we didn't, and we'd better figure out what."

"They mentioned Major Lamb," Elsa said. "The crew did. I think he must have figured out what happened on Marica-3. They know you're here." After a second she changed it to, "We're here."

"That's too bad." Although Isaac didn't sound like he cared overmuch. "Tell me what we're looking at."

"Looking at?"

"How many people do I have to kill," Isaac said, "and how quickly, to get us outta this mess?"

Oh. "The first pilot is in my cabin. Unconscious. He tried to... um..." She floundered, not quite sure how much to tell him.

Isaac's eyes flashed. "Tried? Or succeeded?"

"Tried. I knocked him out before he could succeed."

His lips curved. "He tied up?"

When she nodded, he added, "We'll leave him for Quinn. The captain will wanna deal with him personally, no doubt."

No doubt. "Holden and Toby are on the bridge, strapped into their seats. The shuttle's mechanic is keeping an eye on them while the second pilot is at the helm. They're both armed, or so I assume. I know the mechanic is. Holden and Toby are not."

Isaac shook his head. "Damn. That's almost insulting."

Insulting? "How?"

"There's just two of 'em," Isaac said. "It's way too easy."

"I'm glad you think so. In that case, we should probably get going. The sooner we get this over with, the sooner I can get back to Quinn."

"Right," Isaac said. "When we get there, you open the door. I'll take care of the guards."

"Both of them?"

He grinned. "No offense, Doc, but I can probably take 'em both out quicker than you can get the pistol up. Just stay outta my way."

With pleasure.

Nonetheless, her heart was beating so hard when they

approached the door that she had to look down at her chest just to make sure it didn't show outside her clothes.

It was hard to catch her breath, too, and when they stopped in front of the door, she had to stand there for a few seconds, centering herself.

"Gimme the pistol," Isaac said softly.

She glanced at him. "You already have one."

"If I have two, I can shoot two people at the same time."

"You're joking."

"No," Isaac said. "Gimme."

He held out his hand. It was the biggest hand Elsa had ever seen. When she put the pistol into it, his hand dwarfed it.

"Thank you." He twitched it around in a businesslike grip and nodded to her. "Let's get this show on the road. Anytime you're ready."

Elsa took a deep breath, squared her shoulders, and punched in the access code on the keypad.

The double doors slid aside.

Isaac was through the opening before she'd even thought about stepping forward. The pistols spit fire—yes, faster than she could have aimed. The small mechanic crumpled to the floor, a smoking hole in his chest. The second pilot fell forward onto the instrument panel, the back of his head obliterated.

The shuttle took an abrupt nosedive, sending them all stumbling, and overhead, a red light began flashing. Somewhere, an alarm blared shrilly.

"Shit," Isaac said, looking around the bridge.

Elsa did the same, panic lacing her voice. "What's going on?" Nothing like this had happened on her previous two interplanetary trips.

He glanced at her. "Not sure, but it ain't good."

He strode over to the helm and yanked the second pilot off the console by the back of his shirt. The light didn't stop blinking, and the alarm didn't stop shrieking, but the shuttle straightened.

"Shit," Isaac said again and straightened, too. "We need Quinn."

"I'll go." Holden had already unbuckled his harness and was on his feet. Toby was still fumbling with his.

"You okay, little man?" Isaac asked, as Holden loped for the door. He glanced briefly at Elsa on his way past but didn't say anything.

"Fine." Toby's clipped tone didn't invite sympathy, and Isaac didn't offer to help.

"Anything you need from your cabin, Doc?" he asked instead.

"My medical supplies." Elsa rushed through the doors into the hallway. Ahead of her she saw Holden running for the pods.

The first pilot was still out cold on the bed of the guest cabin. She took a few moments to close up the pouch with the medical supplies and stuff it into her bag along with the clothes she'd used onboard—minus the belt on the dressing gown—and seal it. She dragged it back out into the hallway with her just as Holden and Quinn came in the other direction.

"Captain!"

He looked pale as death, and Holden was practically dragging him along, but he managed a weak grin. "Doc."

Elsa dropped the bag where she stood and rushed to support his other side. "Are you all right?"

The answer was obvious, and he didn't bother making it. "Gotta get to the bridge," he said instead.

"Can you fly a shuttle?"

"I can fly anything." He smiled at her. "The *Good Fortune* has the best crew in the universe, Doc. Ain't nothing we can't do."

"Right," Elsa said.

Chapter Twenty-nine

Sitting down in the pilot's chair—after Isaac dragged the dead Rhenian out of it and tossed him in the corner—was the greatest feeling ever. And not just because Quinn needed to sit before his knees gave out, but also because it meant he was finally in charge of his destiny again. His and everyone else's. He could fly them away. Their options were limited, sure, but they had options. Beyond just waiting to see whether they'd die now or die later.

He fumbled the harness across his chest and examined the instrument panel for what was causing the lights to flicker and the alarm to sound.

"Can you turn the damn thing off?" Toby said. "It's giving me a headache."

Quinn glanced up at him. Toby's bottom lip was split, and his cheek was red and puffy. "The bastard who did that dead?"

Toby nodded and indicated the second Rhenian, the one Isaac was currently hauling to join the other in a heap in the corner. The small, limp body looked almost like a rag doll in Isaac's huge hands. Quinn couldn't feel much sympathy for the bastard.

"There's a third," Isaac told him over his shoulder. "He's in the doc's cabin, out cold. She shot him up with something."

"Spider-scorpion venom," Elsa muttered. She stood behind his shoulder, and Quinn turned to glance at her. She avoided his eyes.

He had to force himself to ask the question. "What was he doing in your cabin, Doc?"

She pressed her lips together. Nobody else answered, either.

"You want I should go kill him?" Isaac offered.

It took a second for the wave of red-hot anger to subside enough that Quinn could speak. "No."

"You wanna do it yourself?"

"Not right now. We have bigger problems."

"What's that?"

"Goddamn Rhenians think of everything." He took a breath and glanced up at Elsa. "Sorry."

She shook her head and put a hand on his shoulder. "What's wrong?"

"The seat's wired for life signs. Just like everything else around here. When you shot the bastard—" He glanced at Isaac, since the neat hole in the back of the pilot's head couldn't have been anyone else's doing, "—the goddamn seat registered that the pilot died. That's why the alarm's going off, and the lights are flickering."

"Can't you turn 'em off?" This was from Toby, who seemed to be more bothered by the shrill wailing than the rest of them. His eyes were narrowed as if his head hurt him.

"I can. But again, we have bigger problems."

"What's that?"

"When the autopilot kicked on, it charted a course straight for the military base at Calvados. I can't override it. The shuttle won't respond to other commands. We can't land anywhere else."

There was a pause. "That's not good," Holden said.

No, it wasn't. But that wasn't the worst of it. "The shuttle also sent a distress signal. We'll have company soon. Two BG-7s have gone out from Calvados to provide an escort."

"Escort?" Isaac said. "Or will they fire on us once they're in range?"

"They might. If they think their crew's dead, and they believe I'm dead, and they think they killed you in the pod, they may just decide to make a clean sweep of it. They'd lose an eighteen-ton shuttle, but they may not be thinking too clearly."

Everyone was quiet after that.

"So we're on our way to the military base," Elsa said eventually, "in a shuttle you can't pilot, with laser banks Toby butchered to incapacitate the long-range lasers, and there are two Rhenian fighters coming?"

"That's pretty much the gist of it."

She nodded. And reached for his hand. He took it, because he needed the comfort, too.

"How long do we have?" Isaac asked.

"They're showing up on the long range. Two and a half hours out. At the rate we're going and the rate they're going, that means less than an hour before they can fire on us."

"Shit."

Quite.

"I can fix the lasers," Toby offered, "maybe get us a bit more range."

That would only help if they could maneuver the shuttle. "We're still headed straight for the military base at Calvados. Even if we can get rid of the fighters, we'll end up there."

"So we have to bail," Isaac said.

Quinn nodded. "Pretty much."

"There's still one pod left."

There was. It would be tight quarters for all of them, and the pod would fly like a lead balloon with their combined weights onboard, but it was better than having a military escort to Calvados and being sent back to Marica-3.

"We had to disable it," Holden said, "to stop the two of you from dropping."

"Can you un-disable it?"

Holden and Toby exchanged a glance. "I can try," Toby said, "but what I did was quick and dirty. Dunno if I can fix it. Not this fast."

"Try."

Toby nodded. "I'm on my way."

He headed for the doors with Holden and Isaac behind him. Quinn tugged on Elsa's hand. She came around to perch on his lap, and he wrapped both arms around her. "Did he hurt you?"

They both knew who he was talking about.

She shook her head. "He touched me. I feel dirty. But I stopped him before he could do anything else."

What the bastard had done was more than enough. He'd touched her. He'd made her feel bad. He'd made it necessary for her to defend herself. "I want to kill him."

She snuggled into him. "Don't."

"I won't. He'll die soon enough, anyway."

There was a moment of silence while they just sat and breathed. The feel of her body nestled against his, her arms around his neck and her cheek against his hair, centered him.

"We'll end up back at Marica-3," she asked, "won't we?"

"If we don't get outta here."

"Do you think we will?"

He hesitated. "I think I have the best crew in the universe. And that if anyone can do it, they can."

She nodded.

"But I also think if we don't make it, I'd rather die like this, here, with you," he glanced over his shoulder, "with all of you, than being back on Marica-3."

"I would, too." Her own punishment, after aiding and abetting the enemy, would be at least the equal of anything Quinn had endured. The Rhenians weren't kind to traitors, especially among their own ranks. "I just wish we could have had more time."

He didn't answer. Instead he just tightened his arms around her and watched the console as the outlines of the Rhenian BG-7s came closer.

· · ·

When the screen showed that the fighters were fifteen minutes away, Quinn nudged Elsa off his lap and got to his feet, not without a little difficulty. They didn't speak. There was nothing to say. Toby, Holden, and Isaac were still hard at work, and no one had come to the bridge to announce they were ready to evacuate, so they had to assume the pod was still nonoperational.

Elsa slipped an arm around Quinn's waist and supported him on the way down the hallway. Outside her cabin door, they stopped to pick up the bag she'd dropped. He glanced at the closed door, wondering if killing the guard wouldn't relieve some of his nervous energy. But then he looked at Elsa, who watched him with such love in her eyes—those eyes he'd thought were cold and hard as ice—and he decided she didn't need to see him commit murder. Killing in the heat of the moment was one thing—she'd seen that and forgiven him—but this was something else, something she didn't need to watch him do. So he settled his arm more securely over her shoulders and smiled. "Ready?"

They continued their slow and limping course toward the pod.

The sound of angry voices reached them as soon as they turned into the alcove where the airlock was. Toby and Isaac were standing face to face—or nose to collarbone, since the biggest and the smallest members of his crew were almost a head apart in height—arguing. Toby had color in his cheeks again, and his hands were fisted, while Isaac was scowling. Holden stood off to the side, watching.

When Quinn turned into the alcove, all three of them straightened and turned. He looked from one to the other, and decided against asking what was going on. "Progress report?" he said instead.

Toby shot Isaac a look before saying, "She'll fly. The problem's getting her loose."

"Getting her loose?"

"When the two of you were inside and we were trying to stop you from dropping," Toby explained, "I had to jam the docking clamps. That's why she didn't drop when you gave the command."

Quinn nodded.

"I can't unjam 'em except manually. From the outside."

Isaac shook his head. "Ain't no way I'm leaving you here, little man. There's gotta be another way."

"There isn't."

"Find one," Isaac said flatly.

Quinn looked from one to the other of them. "Whoever undoes the docking clamps can't get into the pod?"

Toby shook his head. "The second I undo the clamps, she'll drop like a stone."

"So we're talking about leaving someone behind?"

They both nodded.

"No," Quinn said. "We didn't go through all this to lose someone now."

"There's no other choice, Captain."

"Find one," Quinn said, echoing Isaac. "If you can't, I'll stay behind." At least that way, he'd have given his crew their best chance at survival.

Toby shook his head. "With all due respect, sir, you have to pilot the pod. We don't know what could happen between here and the dirt, and you're the only one who can get everyone there safely."

Shit.

"I'll stay behind," Elsa said.

He swung on her. "Hell, no!"

She met his eyes, her own that calm, unearthly green. "You did all this for them. They're more important than I am."

"The hell they are!" He shook his head. "I ain't leaving you here, Doc, and that's final."

"None of us are leaving," Isaac said. "Not unless we're all going."

There was silence. Until Quinn broke it, chuckling. "I was just telling the doc how I have the best crew in the universe. Ain't nobody else coulda fucked things up for ourselves so thoroughly."

Isaac and Holden smiled. Toby said defensively, "I was just doing what I had to do, Captain."

"I know, Toby." Quinn touched his shoulder for a moment. "Nobody's blaming you. If you hadn't jammed the clamps, we'd have been dead by now."

There was silence again.

"I'll stay," Isaac said. "You've all been together longer. I woulda died on Sumatra anyway, if it hadn't been for you. Might as well die here as there."

Quinn had his mouth open to answer, but before he could, Toby beat him to it.

"I was the one jammed the clamps. I'm the one should fix 'em. And it's no problem finding another monkey." He flexed his crooked fingers briefly before realizing what he was doing and stuffing both hands in his pockets.

Quinn shook his head. "We're not leaving anybody behind. No matter whether they joined us first or last. And another monkey won't be the same. We're not just crew, Toby. We're family. You know that." He glanced around the circle of faces. "I don't wanna hear nobody else volunteering to stay behind."

Nobody said anything for a moment. Then Holden continued, as if Quinn hadn't spoken.

"I'm the only one of us with half a chance of being able to convince anyone I'm actually Rhenian. If anyone should stay on the shuttle, it should be me. The rest of you would be shot on sight. But if you take the guard in Elsa's cabin with you, and I take his place—"

Quinn fixed him with a glare. "I guess you didn't hear me when I said I don't wanna talk about it anymore."

"I heard," Holden said. "I just chose to ignore you. Every second we stand here arguing, those BG-7s are coming closer. Pretty soon it'll be too late. For all of us."

There was another pause.

"Maybe we can shear the docking clamps," Isaac suggested.

"In a pod?" Quinn shook his head. "I doubt it. She don't have enough power for that."

"Worth a try, ain't it?"

It was. It was certainly better than standing around doing

nothing. At least they'd die still trying to get away.

"Get in," Toby said, nodding to the open hatch. "I'm gonna have one last look at the clamps. See if maybe I can't loosen 'em up just a bit. Make 'em easier to shear."

He turned to the front of the small craft.

"Want help?" Isaac asked.

"No." Toby didn't look over his shoulder as he trotted away. "Get inside. Help the captain get strapped in."

Isaac hesitated, looking from Toby to him.

"I don't need help," Quinn said as he made his slow way toward the open hatch. Picking up his feet was a lot harder than it ought to be, even with Elsa's help, but when he stumbled, Isaac was right there to catch him. When they reached the pilot's chair, he sank down with a grateful grunt and looked around. It looked just as it had thirty minutes ago, when Holden had come and retrieved him.

"You can pilot this, can't you?" Elsa sounded worried, and he glanced up at her.

"Sure, Doc. She'll fly like a lead-lined bullet, but I can steer her."

She nodded, her teeth worrying her bottom lip. Quinn reached out and captured her hand. "Relax, sweetheart. We've been through too much to fail now."

She squared her shoulders and managed a smile. "Of course."

Outside, there was a sharp snick, and the pod jiggled a bit and tilted sideways. Elsa jumped and looked around. "What was that?"

"Toby's jiggling the clamps," Quinn said. "Good. Just wait; he'll do the other one in a second."

There was another sharp snick outside. The pod jerked again, and Holden stumbled. So did Isaac, even as he fisted a huge hand in the back of Holden's uniform and yanked him out of the opening and into the pod. "Damn him, he—"

They slid backward, more than just an inch this time. Straight back, away from the docking bay, away from the interior bulkhead. There was nothing to do but watch in horror as the pod picked up speed, and then they reached the back of the docking bay. They tipped backward into the bright sunshine and heavy air of Marica's atmosphere—Elsa screamed and Holden swore breathlessly as the wind whipped violently through the interior of the pod while Isaac struggled to close the hatch. Gravity pushed Quinn's back against the pilot's seat and flung Elsa across his lap, and the last thing he saw out the view screen was Toby, clinging to the bulkhead with one hand and lifting the other. Whether it was a salute or a wave good-bye, Quinn couldn't tell. And then Toby was gone, and all he could see out the view screen was the pale blue of the Marican sky and the shuttle, becoming smaller and smaller as they plummeted like a rock toward Marica's Southern Ocean.

ACKNOWLEDGEMENTS

No book comes into being on its own, but this one may have had more than its fair share of supporters.

Great big hugs to the following, who had a hand in shaping this story and in bringing Quinn to life:

Fellow author Wilfred Bereswill, for challenging me to write a 200-word piece of flash fiction back in February of 2010. See, Will, I told you I couldn't write anything short!

And on that same note, thanks to the Working Stiffs for hosting our Flash Fiction Smackdown that month and for the feedback I got on Quinn's teaser.

Awesome instructor (and writer) Heather Graham and the other participants in the Writing Suspense online workshop in August 2010. Your feedback, enthusiasm, and encouragement meant the world to me.

The always wonderful Misa Ramirez, for being awesome in general—I'm so happy we're friends, chica!—and in this case, particularly, for asking me to send her the work-in-progress that no one wanted but that I was so excited about. Without you, Quinn and his story would never have made it out of my head and onto the printed page.

Heather Howland and Liz Pelletier, fabulous Entangled Publishing editors, for liking Quinn and for being willing to take a chance on a cozy mystery writer who'd never written anything resembling romance, let alone science fiction, before. I'm SO happy to have landed with you!

Heather Riccio, Dianemarie Collins, and the rest of the Entangled marketing team, without whom this book would be nowhere. That's you, too, Misa—again.

Another shout-out to Heather Howland, for the gorgeous cover this time, and to the entire Entangled Publishing staff, just for being you, and the most awesome and happening publisher in the business right now!

Friends, beta readers, and critique partners Jamie Livingston-Dierks, Addie J. King, D.B. Sieders, and Kourtney Heinz, for reading Quinn's story and for telling me it's the best book I've ever written. I don't know if you're right, but I hope so, and that everyone agrees with you!

Last but certainly not least, my family. My husband and my two boys, who know the real me and love me, anyway. Without you, I wouldn't be able to do what I do, and I'll be always grateful to you for letting me fly!